Thief

"I've read and loved many of Linda Windsor's novels, but *Thief* runs away with the prize as my absolute favorite! The conflicts are real, the characters more so, with larger-than-life Caden O'Byrne fighting body and soul to win a spirited woman worthy of his warrior's heart. Stirring romance, high adventure, and genuine faith all beat like a drum from first page to last. Once you start reading, *Thief* is sure to steal your every waking hour!"

Liz Curtis Higgs, best-selling author
of *Here Burns My Candle*

"A beautiful thief who steals so that she can rescue enslaved children, a warrior who courts death to escape the horrors of his past, a romance forged in exotic and tumultuous sixth-century Scotland— Linda Windsor's *Thief* captured my imagination. With its amazing historical details, great spiritual truths, and richly layered love story, *Thief* stole my heart."

Sue Harrison, national speaker and author of the
international best-seller *Mother Earth Father Sky*

"What a wonderful story! Linda Windsor blends unforgettable characters, heart-pounding drama, and intriguing facts about sixth-century Scotland to create another keeper. I highly recommend *Thief* to anyone searching for a story of love, faith, and second chances."

Amanda Cabot, author of *Tomorrow's Garden*

"If you are up for a Scottish adventure in the time and land of King Arthur, this book is for you! The colorful characters are full of faults, but they learn that God is a Father of forgiveness. There is never a dull moment as Caden and Sorcha fight for their lives on every page."

Rhonda Larson, book review for
Affaire de Coeur magazine

"From heart-wrenching to heartwarming, *Thief* is a nonstop adventure that will capture you until the last page. And long after you've closed the book, you'll find that Windsor's characters are unforgettable."

Michelle Griep, reviewer for Novel Reviews
and author of *Undercurrent* and *Gallimore*

"Linda Windsor's *Thief* is riveting! Don't miss this compelling harmony of courage, spirit, and legend."

Deb Stover, award-winning author

"*Thief* catapulted me into the sixth century with adventure, intrigue, and realistic characters. I had no desire to leave until I consumed the last delicious morsel. Stunning and unforgettable!"

Miralee Ferrell, speaker and author of
Love Finds You in Tombstone, Arizona

"A beautifully written redemption story, *Thief* encompasses the faith journey of two strong-willed individuals who are both self-sufficient and determined to survive. After being betrayed by people bent on their destruction and sentenced to punishment despite their innocence, Caden and Sorcha learn to trust God for the future and are rewarded with something they never thought they would experience again … hope. Linda Windsor has crafted an intriguing and spiritually satisfying novel that will keep readers hooked on the Brides of Alba series and longing for more."

Michelle Sutton, author of over a
dozen inspirational novels

"Sorcha knows how to sing to the crowd, and so does Linda Windsor. With deft skill, Linda unfolds a tale of life and death in an unforgettable bygone world. Bright melodies of friendship, forgiveness, and second chances rise above darker tones of betrayal, revenge, and hopelessness in a masterful composition. Don't miss Linda Windsor's *Thief!*"

Janalyn Voigt, literary judge, social marketing
mentor, and author of *DawnSinger*

"Linda Windsor pens another amazing novel. Her storytelling skills effortlessly take you back in time. Enjoy!"

Lindi Peterson, author of *Her Best Catch*

"The time of King Arthur comes alive again in *Thief*. Through her characters, Windsor demonstrates that personal salvation through Christ is a choice available to everyone. *Thief* is not a novel written for ladies only. It's full of enough swordplay, intrigue, and action to please readers of both genders. Windsor's artful use of believable dialogue, combined with her ability to draw compelling word pictures of the scenes, make *Thief* a fast-paced and pleasant read."

Lee De Bevoise, award-winning former newspaper and magazine editor and author of the *Book Talk* column at www.knowaboutjesus.net

"Linda Windsor swept me away in *Thief,* captivating me with her unpredictable and vibrant characters, and the historical, clan-divided Scottish landscape, heavy with spiritual and magical elements, enchanted me, keeping me reading until the end. I'm eager to read the next book in the series."

Elizabeth Goddard, author of *The Camera Never Lies* and *Freezing Point*

"Linda Windsor's *Thief* is another painstakingly researched, beautifully written, and imaginative tale of love and adventure and transforming faith in sixth-century Scotland. I'm eager to read the next book in the series."

DeAnna Julie Dodson, author of *In Honor Bound*

THE BRIDES OF ALBA

THIEF

LINDA WINDSOR

David C Cook®
transforming lives together

THIEF
Published by David C Cook
4050 Lee Vance View
Colorado Springs, CO 80918 U.S.A.

David C Cook Distribution Canada
55 Woodslee Avenue, Paris, Ontario, Canada N3L 3E5

David C Cook U.K., Kingsway Communications
Eastbourne, East Sussex BN23 6NT, England

David C Cook and the graphic circle C logo
are registered trademarks of Cook Communications Ministries.

The website addresses recommended throughout this book are offered as a
resource to you. These websites are not intended in any way to be or imply an
endorsement on the part of David C Cook, nor do we vouch for their content.

This story is a work of fiction. All characters and events are the product of the author's
imagination. Any resemblance to any person, living or dead, is coincidental.

Scripture quotations are taken from the King James
Version of the Bible. (Public Domain.)

LCCN 2011923884
ISBN 978-1-4347-6477-5
eISBN 978-0-7814-0686-4

© 2011 Linda Windsor
Published in association with the literary agency of Alive Communications,
Inc., 7680 Goddard St., Suite 200, Colorado Springs, CO 80920

The Team: Don Pape, Ramona Tucker, Amy Kiechlin,
Sarah Schultz, Caitlyn York, Karen Athen
Cover Design: DogEared Design, Kirk DouPonce
Cover Photo: Shutterstock 1671724, royalty free; 123RF 5457426, royalty free.
iStockphoto 9276724, royalty free.

Printed in the United States of America
First Edition 2011

1 2 3 4 5 6 7 8 9 10

032911

To my mom and children,
for their continued support and sacrifices to allow
me time to research and write this novel.

My son Jeff's by-the-Good-Book faith helped keep me grounded,
while my daughter, Kelly, challenged me to find ways to *fish* for men
who discount Scripture from the other side of the boat.

To David C Cook,
for all their efforts to make this project the best it can be.

And finally, to my Heavenly Father,
the Great Creator who continues to show me how to fish in places I
never would have looked. Thank You, Jesus, for Your love and grace.

Dear Reader,

In *Healer,* I mentioned how a magazine article explaining what happened to the Davidic line after the nation of Israel scattered (1 and 2 Kings) started me on a research journey that resulted in this Brides of Alba series. With Book One introducing the O'Byrne clan, Book Two, *Thief,* carries on with Caden's story. It isn't easy to take the villain from one novel and make him hero material in the next, but, with God's grace, anything is possible. Like our own faith journeys, early on or way down the road, it's a bumpy ride, especially when God forgives but we won't let the past go.

I found a delightful old Scottish proverb that became Caden's theme: *"Love of our neighbor is the only door out of the dungeon of self."* And how true this is. When we stop focusing on ourselves and think about others, reaching out to them, our own troubles seem to fade. I know this helps me when I start sinking into chemical depression, though sometimes I have to force myself out of my cave when I don't feel like it. The reward is relief from my own troubles and the joy of helping someone else.

Like *Healer, Thief* is also set in the late sixth-century Scotland of Arthur, prince of Dalraida, the only historically documented Arthur. Most scholarly sources point to Arthur, Merlin, and even Guinevere/

Gwenhyfar as titles, so it's easy to see why the Age of Arthur lasted over one hundred years. The Dark Ages become even darker when you consider that there was no standard for dating and even the records that exist are written in at least four different languages. Neither names, dates, place names, nor translations are completely reliable. So I quote eighth-century historian Nennius: "I have made a heap of all I could find."

In *Healer* and *Thief,* we see how the Grail Church sought to preserve the royal bloodline of David and that of the apostolic priestly line from the first-century family and friends of Jesus. (See *Arthurian Characters* on p. 337 and *The Grail Palace* on p. 341.) Nora Lorre Goodrich, in several of her authoritative books on Arthur and company, suggests this was done by arranging marriages of both lines into the royal families of the British Isles. The offspring born of both lines were raised and trained by the church to become kings, queens, warriors, and priests.

The arranged marriage of Princess Eavlyn, my heroine's benefactress and mentor, to the historical Saxon Prince Hering of Northumbria exemplifies this. Eavlyn's goal is to build a church in Northumbria as its princess and future queen. Many Saxons were converted in this way—by the Christian queens who married pagan Saxon kings and built churches where the people might hear God's Word. Such marriages (*peaceweaving*) also brokered peace between the two enemy peoples. The early church was very involved in this type of matchmaking and diplomacy.

Again, *nature magic,* or protoscience and dark magic, both involving the supernatural aid of angels and the Holy Spirit or demons, clash. I read and reread Scripture as I worked on this project and endeavored to show how nature magic was used by Christian and nonbelieving druids, with their fruit—good or evil—separating the two. Bear in mind that *druid* in that time was a word for any professional—doctors, judges, poets, teachers, and protoscientists, as well as priests. *Druid* meant "teacher, rabbi, magi, or master," not the dark, hooded stereotype assumed by many today.

In *Thief,* I address astrology as used according to Scripture. It is not forbidden to look for signs in the sky, but it is forbidden to worship the creations instead of the Creator. God's kings and prophets have said the heavens declare God's glory. In *Thief,* the princess states that God has been teaching/giving mankind signs in the heavens since He hung the first clock and calendar by setting the planets and moon into motion in Genesis to keep time and mark seasons. God further ordained Jesus as His Son by the star of Bethlehem on the day of Christ's birth, and He mourned His death on the day of the crucifixion with darkness. These astrological events were key in most of the druids' accepting Christ. They believed man *might* make up Scripture, but only the Creator God could write such messages across the sky, messages that were recorded and passed down in histories of believers and nonbelievers across the world at that time by the druids/magi. The website www.BethehemStar.com details how this history is combined with NASA technology to validate Scripture.

The heavens guide us but do not dictate to us. Astronomy is the science; astrology is probability and statistics based on historically observed and recorded data. Think mathematics, a great tool deserving of study and use, but nothing worthy of worship. Only God is a certainty and beyond the realm of man's measure. Many call Him the Great Mathematician. Think of all the knowledge man has gained, the mathematical advances learned, and mysteries unfolded from watching the stars.

I have to thank God up front that we all don't have to be mathematicians or scientists to get into heaven. To me and those like me, He gave parables.

> *And he said, Unto you it is given to know the mysteries of the kingdom of God: but to others in parables; that seeing they might not see, and hearing they might not understand. (Luke 8:10)*

Thank You, Lord, for parables.

> *Beloved, believe not every spirit, but try the spirits whether they are of God: because many false prophets are gone out into the world. Hereby know ye the Spirit of God: Every spirit that confesseth that Jesus Christ is come in the flesh is of God: And every spirit that confesseth not that Jesus Christ is come in the flesh is not of God: and this is that spirit of antichrist, whereof ye have heard that it should come; and even now already is it in the world. (1 John 4:1–3)*

Here is truth, plain and simple. God gives us wonderful gifts and revelations. But how we use them—for good or for evil—determines what is of God and what is not. The fruit will tell in abundance.

> *I am the vine, ye are the branches: He that abideth in me, and I in him, the same bringeth forth much fruit: for without me ye can do nothing. (John 15:5)*

As I was writing this today, I'd just read Matthew 10 in my morning devotional study, and I think it is no accident. In verses 1–5, Christ equips the disciples with power over disease and demons. *But* He goes on to tell them not to use these gifts to amass fortune and recognition for themselves. They are instructed to go in poverty and depend on the generosity of those they help for their basic needs. Instead of glory and praise, they are to expect hostility sometimes.

The druids who earnestly sought truth, light, and the way gave up their high positions of power and prestige to become Christian priests of little material means, like Christ. The healer Brenna received such hostility from believers, even though she accepted no glory or payment for her gift. The princess in *Thief,* when criticized by believers and nonbelievers, states clearly that only God is certain, but heavenly signs can point to a *probable* outcome, as they do with weather.

Now, please, I am not advocating everyone take up astrology. I am stating that there is a purpose for it, that God speaks through the heavens, and that we should be reluctant to judge those who do study the heavens for signs from God. We may have more in common with them than we think. Frankly, God is enough for me … although I do check the Weather Channel quite often.

I mentioned in my last book how my daughter had been stalked and assaulted in college, blamed and turned against God, and became involved in Wicca, or white witchcraft. It was through research of the Dark Ages that I learned by God's grace to witness to her effectively when she would not hear anything from the Word. I continue to include this type of faith-affirming information in *Thief.*

Everyone knows the story of the disciples' fishing all night to no avail. Then Jesus told them to try the other side of the vessel. They did and netted a boatload. My child would not listen to Scripture, but, Celtophile that she was and is, she was all ears about the history and oral traditions of that era and culture that evolved into many of today's New Age beliefs. These historical and oral traditions underscored or clarified what Scripture revealed and separated the wheat from the chaff.

The results of my *fishing* for my daughter were not as instant as that of the disciples. It took a journey of many years before she was ready to jump in the boat. But the net had been cast and repeatedly *mended* each time I found something new to share—some common ground to draw her to Christ. Both mother and daughter have emerged stronger from that storm—stronger in faith, friendship, and love. We still love the Celtic music, history, and lore of our heritage but know now what vital part God played in it. I share this story because maybe someone out there needs to know how to approach a beloved nonbeliever who will not hear Scripture or traditional witness but must be reached from the other side of the boat.

This is my passion. To reach out and enable others to reach out effectively to those who are swimming on the other side of the boat from the written Word with a net that will bring them to Christ, the Living Word.

In His love,

Linda Windsor

CRARACTER LiST

O'BYRNE Clan of Glenarden
(colors are red, black, and silver/gray)

Aeda—Tarlach's late royal Pictish wife; mother to Ronan, Caden, and Alyn

Alyn—Tarlach and Aeda's third son

Brenna—Ronan's wife, lady of Glenarden; a gifted healer, formerly of the Gowrys subclan

Caden—Tarlach and Aeda's second son

Conall—Brenna and Ronan's four-year-old son

Daniel of Gowrys—friend and schoolmate of Alyn's and cousin of Brenna

Delg—Caden's prized sword, meaning "thorn"

Egan O'Toole—Glenarden's champion

Forstan—Caden's horse, meaning "courage"

Hretha—Caden's shield with an image of Saxon goddess Hretha of March on it, taken from a battle with the Saxons

Kella O'Toole—Egan's daughter; foster sister to Ronan, Caden, and Alyn

Rhianon—Caden's wife from Gwynedd of N. Wales; daughter of Idwal and Enda; mistress of Tunwulf in Din Guardi

Ronan—Tarlach and Aeda's eldest son, heir

Tarlach—Caden's late father and former clan chief/king also known as "the Glenarden"; of royal Irish descent (Davidic bloodline)

DIN GUARDI, Ancient Bamburgh, Northumbria

Aella—Hussa's present queen

Aelwyn—Sorcha's late adopted mother; tavern owner and singer/scop; former gleeman with her best friend, Gemma

Aethelfrid—Frisian trader of textiles

Aethelfrith—Hussa's Saxon nephew and prince of rival Bernicia; cousin to Hering; eventually overtook the Northumbrian throne after Hussa's death, exiling Hering

Aine—three-year-old Cymri girl rescued by Sorcha; younger sibling of Ian

Athelstan—moneylender; brother-in-law of Giswald, the sheriff

Blaise of Dunfeld—lesser Lothian king of large estate on the Northumbrian border; father of Eavlyn

Burlwick—Hering's province/kingdom in Northumbria on Lothian's border

Cynric of Elford—an ealdorman and thane of Hussa; betrothed to Sorcha; former sword-friend of Wulfram

Eadric—Sorcha's maternal Saxon-Cymri cousin (by her adopted parents); bard

Eavlyn—Blaise of Dunfeld's daughter; a princess betrothed to Hering of Northumbria as a peaceweaver, sealing a peace pact between Lothian and Northumbria; astrologer tutored at the Grail Castle

Ebba—Hussa's late wife and mother of Hering

Ebyn—seven-year-old boy rescued by Sorcha whom she keeps, since his parents sold him

Elfwyn—Sorcha's chestnut mare, golden mane

Gemma—female dwarf, like a second mother to Sorcha; an entertainer and thief who helps Sorcha rescue captive British children from the Saxon slave market

Giswald—sheriff of Din Guardi; brother-in-law of Athelstan, the moneylender

Hering—son of Hussa; Saxon prince of Bernicia; lord of Burlwick on the Lothian border; betrothed to Eavlyn; cousin of Aethelfrith of rival Bernicia

Hussa—ruled as bretwalda or king of Northumbria from 585 to 592; father of Hering; uncle of Aethelfrith

Ian—Cymri boy rescued by Sorcha; older sibling of Aine; older than Ebyn

Mann—tavern keeper in Din Guardi

Mildrith—Hussa's seneschal's wife

Ninian—Eavlyn's teacher at the Grail Castle; Merlin Emrys's
protégé

Rhianon—Tunwulf's mistress (also previously Caden's wife
from Gwynedd of N. Wales; daughter of Idwal and Enda)

Sorcha—abducted Cymri daughter of Fintan and Myrna of
Trebold Law; adopted and raised as a Saxon by Aelwyn and
Wulfram in a Din Guardi tavern; a singer/scop and thief who
uses stolen money to rescue captured British children from the
Saxon slave market

Talorc—slaver

Tilda—neighbor of Sorcha; a weaving woman

Tunwulf—son of Cynric of Elford; renegade warband leader

Utta—tavern maid; friend of Sorcha

Wada—henchman of Athelstan, the moneylender

Wynnie—Cymri girl rescued by Sorcha

Wulfram—Sorcha's late adopted Saxon father; former horse
thane to King Hussa's warband; sword-friend to Cynric; import
business and tavern owner.

KINGDOM OF LOTHIAN

Fintan of Trebold Law—Sorcha's late birth father, who died trying to find her

Malachy of Trebold Law—the aged and reluctant lord of Trebold; prefers to return to his role as a priest in the church; Sorcha's paternal uncle

Modred—king of Lothian; priest of the Celtic Church; Arthur's nephew and son of Morgause and Cennalath of the Orkneys

Myrna of Trebold Law—Sorcha's birth mother; owner of Trebold Tavern and lady of Trebold Law's hillfort

Owain—eel fisherman; scholar; healer; most likely from Ireland

PRIESTS

Father Martin—priest who assists in Caden's healing

PLACES

Trebold Law—Sorcha's former home; a hillfort and land on the Lader, belonging to Lady Myrna and Sorcha

Trebold Tavern—Myrna's tavern

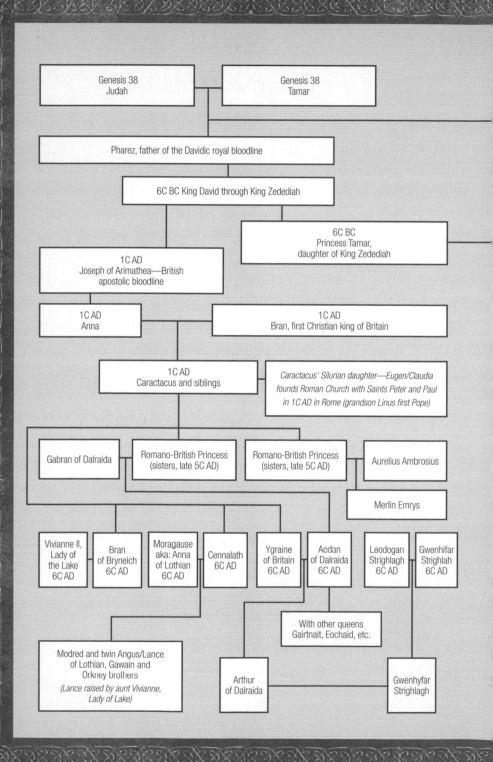

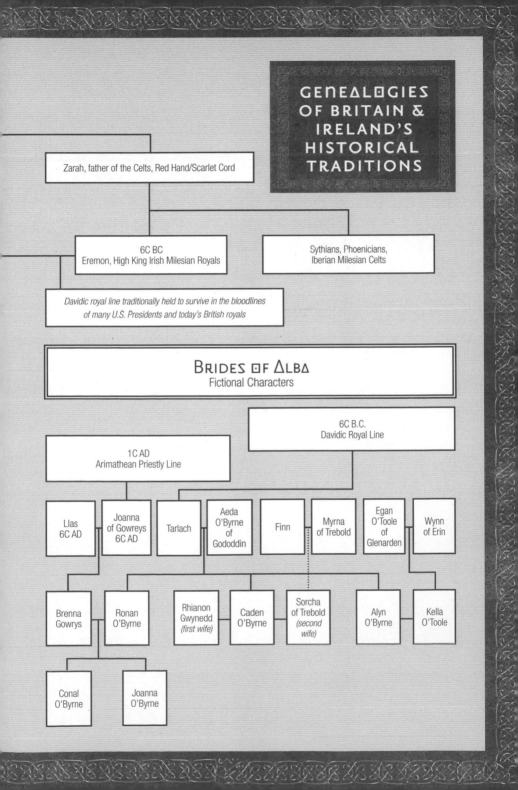

GENEALOGIES OF BRITAIN & IRELAND'S HISTORICAL TRADITIONS

Zarah, father of the Celts, Red Hand/Scarlet Cord

6C BC
Eremon, High King Irish Milesian Royals

Sythians, Phoenicians, Iberian Milesian Celts

Davidic royal line traditionally held to survive in the bloodlines of many U.S. Presidents and today's British royals

BRIDES OF ALBA
Fictional Characters

6C B.C.
Davidic Royal Line

1C AD
Arimathean Priestly Line

Llas
6C AD

Joanna
of Gowreys
6C AD

Tarlach

Aeda
O'Byrne
of
Gododdin

Finn

Myrna
of Trebold

Egan
O'Toole
of
Glenarden

Wynn
of Erin

Brenna
Gowrys

Ronan
O'Byrne

Rhianon
Gwynedd
(first wife)

Caden
O'Byrne

Sorcha
of Trebold
*(second
wife)*

Alyn
O'Byrne

Kella
O'Toole

Conal
O'Byrne

Joanna
O'Byrne

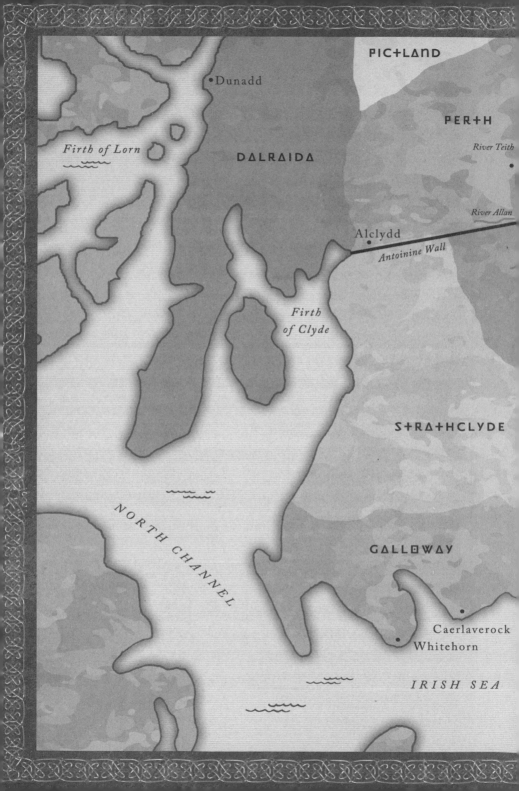

LATE 6TH CENTURY ALBA

Scone
Forteviot
River Tay
FIFE
Glenarden
Strighlagh
X Battle of CAMLAN
King's Knot
River Carron
Din Edyn
Falkirk
Traprain Law
Berwick
Firth of Forth
NORTH SEA
Fort Camlan
LOTHIAN
River Tweed
Lindisfarne
MANAU
Gododdin
Din Guardi
BERNICIA
GWENDOLEU
Hadrian's Wall
Carmelide
Solway Firth
RHEGED
ELMET

PROLOGUE

Kingdom of Lothian
Late sixth century AD

Leaf Fall

It was a good day to die. But then this warrior had lost count of such days, hoping that each one would put an end to his miserable existence … to this exile of body and soul. Beneath him, his horse strained at the reins, eager to join the fray between the Pendragon's forces and the Saxon invaders seeking to win yet one more chunk of the ever-shrinking Bryneich. Once, the Cymri kingdom had swept to the North Sea, but the Sassenach had hacked away its coastal settlements with their axes. Now they wanted more.

Caden O'Byrne held his stallion back, waiting with the other mercenaries for the signal to sweep down the hill and relieve the first line of warriors already engaged. None of them knew him by any other name but Caden. Like everything else that mattered, he'd left his clan name behind. Only shame followed, haunting him night and day.

The clang of blades, the cries of rage and anguish rose in a disso-
nant chorus from the edge of the summer-blanched forest of oak and
alder that had hid the enemy until the last moment. Anxiety weighed
upon the faces of Caden's battle-hardened comrades—at least those
with something or someone to go home to. But there were a few,
like him, who grinned, teeth bared in anticipation of, if not death
and escape from their personal demons, at least a chance to take out
their pent-up need for vengeance on an enemy they could see and lay
hands on … an enemy they could kill.

Down the line, Modred, Arthur's nephew and now regent of
Lothian, sat upon his horse, clad in somber priestly robes, his arm
raised. Priests and druids were untouchable in battle, at least among
the tribes of Britain. That made Modred a bit of a paradox in leading the Lothian warband, though *coward* came to Caden's mind. He
wondered if Modred's following his mother Morgause's calling into
the high Celtic Church made the man fit for the Lothian kingship
he'd assumed from his late father, Cennalath. Or loyal enough to
his uncle Arthur, now engaged in the battle below. After all, it was
Arthur—known as Pendragon to the Welsh, Dux Bellorum to the
British, and High King to the Scottish Dalraida—who was responsible for the Saxon-loving traitor Cennalath's death.

But who was Caden to judge when he was naught but a mercenary bound to the highest bidder? In this case, the priest-king Modred.

Besides, in these times of rivaling British kingdoms, today's
enemy was often tomorrow's bedfellow, especially when the Saxons
entered the scene. It was the Christian High King's mission—and
nightmare—to unite the squabbling Christian and pagan Britons as
one against the wolfish enemy who would devour—

Modred lowered his arm, commanding the signaler to blast his horn. Caden forgot about the questionable loyalty and merit of his employer and gave Forstan a nudge with his knees. The steed, aware of the meaning of the horn's blast, shot forward, shuddering not at the sound of clanging swords and death as some of the other horses did. Like its rider, the costly stallion—worth two years of war prizes—seemed to crave it. Unflinching bravery had earned Forstan his name. Caden's courage stemmed from the will to die.

Joining the roar of the charge, Caden rode straight for the well-executed chaos. That was Arthur's genius, the reason he led Britain's kings, though he had no proper kingdom of his own. It was what the church had trained him to do: lead kings. The Britons had the best ground, the best warriors hewn from experience, and word that the Saxons were on the march along the Lader Water. Some said this good fortune was all due to the image of the Virgin that Arthur wore on his shield, but Caden leaned toward experience and skill over the painted image of a woman.

The name and image of the Saxon pagan goddess Hretha on Caden's own shield had been beaten nearly into oblivion. She certainly hadn't brought glory or victory to the shield's previous owner. Nay, it was skill and passion that won the day. And Caden sported Hretha now, not for the goddess's protection, but for the well-made wicker and leather laminate backing her image.

Caden's blood began to race at battle speed, its cadence matching that of Forstan's muscled flesh hurling downhill toward the fray. Above it flew the banner of Arthur's Red Dragon, the rallying point.

The Saxons also had reinforcements. Caden spied them in the periphery of his vision. Perhaps, just perhaps, the enemy would put up a fight worthy of a warrior's end. The drums thundering in his head drove Caden into the dust cloud enveloping the battlefield. He inhaled it and exhaled fury. A wild-haired Saxon with a deep red scar across his cheek rushed to meet Caden before he could dismount, hurling a lance with all his might. It glanced off the stallion's breastplate.

"Your gods take you if you wound my horse!" Caden slid off Forstan's back and broke into a dead run toward the unfortunate warrior now brandishing an axe. "I was going to dismount to meet you fairly."

Horses were used like chariots before them, to deliver men fresh to the thick of battle and carry the weary off, though Caden had done his fair share of fighting from horseback. But he had no use for cowards who targeted a man's horse.

While Forstan cantered off, trained to await him a distance away, Caden unsheathed Delg, a prize from another battle and more deadly in his skilled hands than the thorn after which he'd named it. The Saxon charged, his axe a deadly blur of continuous motion—down, around, up, around again, ever forward. Caden cut its frenzy short with a hard blow. Hretha's oak and leather took the brunt of the impact and sent the weapon flying.

The Saxon made the mistake of looking after his weapon in disbelief. He still wore that expression when Caden separated the man's head from his body with Delg. Easy. Too easy. Thanks to Egan O'Toole, the O'Byrne champion from another lifetime, Caden had been trained to incorporate skill and instinct into one. Plunging deeper into the thick of dust and battle, Caden faced enemy after enemy after enemy. And with each kill the drums in his head grew louder. His breath became bursts of rage, until he no longer faced men but the demons that deprived him of peace with their ceaseless torture.

Just then one of the Saxon curs approached the back of the Pendragon, whose blue and white tunic had long since been stained with dirt and blood from those who'd fallen victim to Excalibur. Arthur had led his men into the first clash and fought not only his own demons but, it seemed, those of his nephew Modred, watching safely from the heather-dashed knot above them. Caden judged the pace of the yellow-haired warrior running, axe aimed at the Pendragon's back.

So much for the protection from the Virgin on Arthur's shield. Caden hefted Delg like a spear and gave the sword a mighty thrust, closing a distance he could not make in time afoot. True it went, straight into the heathen's abdomen. It stopped the assailant long enough for Caden to set upon him and end his writhing misery.

Arthur spun at the unholy death scream, but instead of a flash of approval or gratitude on his beleaguered face, there was warning. Before Caden could comprehend, a shaft of blinding agony entered his back. He swung about, pulling Delg out of Arthur's attacker and slashing at the other cowardly assailant who had attacked him from behind. The tip of his blade laid open the man's neck.

But Caden kept spinning. Blood splatter, white clouds, blue sky, and dust—always dust—swirled about him. Arthur, his men, the Saxons … all were consumed by it. Thick and gray it was, choking out everything except the pain. Only when it turned to blessed blackness did the pain go away.

One thought drifted up through the abyss, pulling the corners of Caden's mouth into a smile. *It's a good death.*

CHAPTER ONE

Kingdom of Lothian
Late sixth century AD

Leaf Fall

Where was he?

Caden came to himself in the midst of battle, once again. But this time he was surrounded by beings not of This World. The fight was fierce, yet bloodless. Never had he seen the like: spheres of light and darkness clashing like thunder, lightning swallowed by blackness, then blackness split again by light. He watched, mesmerized … until he realized the fight was over him. But Caden wanted nothing to do with either. Give him an end where he'd quickly dissolve into the very dust from which he'd been created, and let him be done with life and its emotions.

Determined to be finished by one warrior or the other, it mattered not whom, Caden threw himself into the fray, but to no avail. He was no more noticed than a bone between two fighting dogs.

At first.

His will to deny life gave the forces of darkness the edge. Those of light stilled, taking on the form of solemn, golden warriors as the opposing orbs began to drag him away, shrieking in victory. And the torture began. Shifting into demonic shapes, they picked at his flesh and ate it before his very eyes. Yet more flesh grew in its place to be ripped from his body again by their gnarled claws. Anguish, raw anguish, again and again.

Curse them all—he'd suffered enough in life. Must he now suffer a lingering death?

As the hideous creatures inhaled, the breath left Caden's body, leaving his throat and tongue parched and burning. It was only then that Caden realized his error. He would not die. This was to be his eternity. The one he'd chosen himself. Panic unlike any he'd ever known clawed at him. He wrenched his gaze from his captors toward the beings of light.

"Call Him. Say His name, and this will end," one said. Which, Caden had no clue, for their mouths did not move.

"In the name of Jesus," said another, "thy spirit be healed, Caden of Glenarden, freed by Him who has fought the battle for you and won."

If this was so, why was he still being torn to shreds by claws of darkness?

Wait.

He knew *that* voice. A priest from the past, pulling him literally from damnation's black grip.

He knew those words. Echoed by his brother's wife as she, too, fought with prayer for Caden.

He knew what *he* had to do … if it wasn't too late.

Caden inhaled deeply, air scorching clear to his lungs, and pleaded with all that was left of him. "Jesus!"

Simultaneously the beings of darkness and light were gone, along with the great in-between. His head grew light, his consciousness drifting with the abandon of a falling leaf until it caught up with his body. The crackling of a rush-stuffed mattress registered as body and spirit melded with a jerk. He heard himself gasp.

"Praise God, you have chosen life." Again that voice.

Caden opened his eyes to see the old priest from Glenarden smiling with a delight that made his time-weathered face look youthful.

"What're you doin' here?" Caden slurred, his tongue thick and dry as his pillow. He looked about to see where *here* was. This Side. A low-beamed ceiling. Clean, fresh linens that smelled of sun's drying.

"Be thankful, Brother," someone said from the other side of Caden's bed. "Father Martin came straightaway with a bag of Brenna's healing balms and teas as soon as Glenarden learned you'd been gravely wounded. And I followed quickly as I could."

Brenna. The comely healer his elder brother, Ronan, had married. Aye, Caden was definitely in This World. And shame's beast waited for him, assailing him once more for having betrayed his own kin under the spell of greed, ambition, and a lust he mistook for love. The golden beauty of his late wife shape-shifted in his mind to the snarling, panic-stricken witch she'd become before leaping to her death.

With an involuntary shudder, Caden sought his younger brother Alyn's blue gaze. Nothing but adoration shone from it. Adoration and something Caden didn't deserve or want. Forgiveness.

"You're s'pposed to be at Llantwit tending your studies."

"Try a sip of this, son," the priest said, offering water.

His thirst overriding his curiosity, Caden tried to rise up on his elbow when the lance he'd forgotten about plunged into his back again. When the white pain dulled just short of unbearable, he allowed Alyn to help him upright for the drink. No wine tasted sweeter or soothed his raw throat and tongue more. He drank every drop. It didn't relieve his pain but cleared his thought and voice.

"Thank you, Brother."

"'Tis Father now," Alyn reminded him. "The bishop finally got him out of our glen."

And here to plague me, Caden mused.

"Or save you."

Caden started at the inner voice. Lady Brenna's herbs, perhaps. Resentment mustered, shoving the voice aside. "She sent her herbs and her priest. I'd venture neither she nor Ronan would bother to see me live or die."

Alyn brandished a half-cocked grin. "You are wrong, Brother. Brenna's time is at hand for their second child, and Ronan would not leave her, much less allow her to make the journey here."

"We were scarce able to stop her," the priest said.

Second child. Another nephew or niece Caden would never see. A part of him mourned that. "How old is the first one now?"

"Conall is four and has Ronan's looks and bold disposition. Though he has his mother's eyes and won't be parted from his wolf-skin blanket."

Alyn didn't have to highlight the irony. The wolf that had died by Caden's hand, protecting Brenna, still protected her offspring. Or its fine white pelt did.

"You should see the wee laddie tugging at it for all he's worth with the half-wolf pup Daniel gave to Brenna. He's O'Byrne stubborn."

Caden almost smiled at Alyn's portrayal of the future laird of Glenarden holding onto his blanket as his father, Ronan, had held onto the fugitive Brenna and the prophecy of the division of the O'Byrne clan for the sake of peace. And that was just what young Conall would inherit as laird of the once-warring clans.

No thanks to Caden. He reined in his memories, desperate to stop them. He was alive. Wallowing in the past only brought misery worse than that in his back. Yet there was a part of him that longed for his home.

"Is the pup white like the wolf?" he asked.

"As snow. Brenna said 'twas a gift from God. Daniel thinks her Faol was a bit of a gallivant about the hills."

"I thought young Gowrys was attending university with you, not in the high hills with his kin."

"He is, but Wales is not far enough away to keep us from visiting home … or to come here."

Here. Caden came back to the present, grounding himself with a glance about the strange room. "Exactly where is *here*," he asked, "and how long have I been here?"

"You are in Trebold Tavern," Father Martin replied. "Arthur insisted you receive the best of care, so he sent for Brenna."

Trebold. Aye, the estate by the crossing of the burn where they last camped before meeting the renegade Sassenach who dared to cross the Tweed.

"Seems someone saved the Pendragon's life," Alyn put in.

Caden remembered. For Arthur's sake and that of Albion, he was grateful to have helped the High King. But as for himself …

"I should have died," he said flatly. *Had the struggle on the Other Side been a dream?*

"For the last fortnight, we thought you would," Alyn replied grimly.

A fortnight. Time aplenty for his younger brother to receive the news at Llantwit and come to his side … and for his elder brother to make it plain that Caden was dead to him. Not that Caden blamed Ronan.

Father Martin interrupted Caden's thoughts. "It seems God has other plans for you. And when you are on your feet again, so does the High King."

"Aye, after we get you home where you can—"

Caden's brow hiked. "Did Arthur forget he exiled me from my home?"

Never again was Caden to set foot in Glenarden or Gododdin. That was why he'd fought with the Lothians, now under the command of Modred.

"Our God is one of second chances," the priest continued with annoying reassurance. "Who is His servant Arthur to be different?"

Caden grunted. "Better you'd let me die."

Yet his heart was no longer behind his words, thank God. In truth, he was grateful to be alive, if his dream had been reality and death was not the end but the beginning of another life.

Thank God? Was that a prayer? Before Caden could ponder the startling thought, a door opened, drawing his attention to the female entering the room with a tray of food.

Her face, a handsome one despite the crinkle of lines bracketing her eyes and smile, lit up upon seeing Caden. "He's awake, praise God!"

With a regal bearing uncommon to a serving wench, she approached to place a wooden trencher laden with joints of roast fowl, cheese, and bread on the bedside table. Caden's stomach rumbled in anticipation, though his mind wasn't as certain. As he labored to decide what appealed to him, she broke off some of the soft inner part of the bread and dropped it into a cup of broth.

"The broth is his, sirs, but the rest is yours. Unless you'd rather eat in the tavern below." She sat on the edge of the bed next to Caden. "I'm Myrna of Trebold Law. Welcome back to This World, Caden of Glenarden."

Caden's appetite withered as Alyn made for the meat like a starved pup, stopping only long enough to cross himself through a hasty prayer of thanksgiving. So she knew of his shame. The old priest, also giving thanks over the food, must have told her.

"Come now, I've let it cool," she cajoled, lifting a spoonful to his thinned lips. "You must regain your strength. A fortnight abed for a healthy man will leave him an invalid, but you have fought fever and death's grasp like none I've seen."

Caden accepted the nourishment. To his surprise, it awakened the need for more. "It's good. Thank you." He winked. A habit when in the company of an attractive woman, though this one was near twice his age.

"You are most welcome, sir, but don't mistake my interest as anything but that of a Christian heart and a mother's hope. For all the years I've seen, I could be your mother."

A maidservant's sass with the eloquence and demeanor of a gentlewoman. "Then time has been kind to you, milady. Beauty demands nothing less than a man's full attention, and yours shines both without and within." If eyes were windows to the soul, Myrna's green ones revealed wisdom, generosity, empathy, and something else … something his sister-in-law Brenna demonstrated in abundance.

Faith.

"Ever the silver-tongued devil, aren't you, Brother?" Alyn mumbled, his mouth full of bread.

Heat rushed to Caden's face. "Never mind the twit, milady. 'Twas a heartfelt compliment with no ulterior motive … save more of that broth."

"Has God gifted all three of your O'Byrne brothers with charm, Father?" Myrna asked Martin.

The priest looked up from a joint of fowl. "They have their moments." He stiffened in dismay, putting down the bone. "Forgive me, Milady Myrna. The sight of such good food has robbed me of my manners." Not willing to take full blame, he shot a reprimanding glance at Alyn, who hopped to attention.

"Yes, right," he said, wiping his hands on his tunic. "This isn't just Myrna; she is the mistress of Trebold *and* this tavern."

Caden recalled an old nobleman, much older than this lady, who offered the hospitality of his keep, such as it was, to the Pendragon. "Lord Malachy is a lucky man."

This time color leapt to Myrna's face. "Nay, sir, Malachy is my brother-in-law. When my husband, Fintan, died, Malachy left the church to help me with Trebold as best he could. But he's more a priest than laird, I fear. Between us, we've managed the land to keep our people fed and pay what we can to King Modred in food rent. Our lot is meager, but enough."

Myrna brushed a lock of fading copper hair off her face as though she might again tuck away the pain grazing it. She helped Caden to more bread and broth before continuing. "Many of our people have fled to Wales or Cumbria with the Saxons savaging our borders. So many fields lay fallow, yet God provided us another boon. Our location at the ford is the perfect place for a hostel."

"And *you* don't fear the Sassenach?" Caden asked.

Myrna shrugged. "God will continue to provide. Whoever rules the land will take their tolls and need food and lodging, though I'd prefer to serve a Briton king," she stipulated.

"*If* you live to pay the tolls and run your hostel," Caden pointed out. Knowing what Saxons did to helpless women, he couldn't imagine Myrna wanting to live when they were done with her.

"If not, then I shall see my Maker and have no worries at all." She twirled the spoon in the broth, at peace with that possibility, judging by the wistful tilt of her lips.

She wouldn't think death so grand if she'd been as close as Caden had been to the Other Side.

"And now God's answered this lonely widow's heart-held prayer by sending you."

Somewhere in the back of Caden's throat, the wet bread lodged. The coughing it triggered drove lance after lance through his wound with each strangle of breath. His head grew light, a lack of consciousness momentarily pulling him up out of his misery. When he came to himself again, he was surrounded by Alyn, Father Martin, and Lady Myrna, who looked on the verge of tears.

"I apologize, milord, if I've upset you," she fretted. "'Twas too soon to heap another burden on you."

"She doesn't want you for a husband, twit." Concern overrode Alyn's stab at levity.

"What then?" Caden managed. Had they left the cursed lance in his back? With every movement his wound felt as though it were still there, being twisted by a vicious hand.

"God sent you to me to find my lost daughter." Myrna fluffed the pillow behind his head. "But for now, you need to rest and regain your strength for your mission. Will you take more broth?"

Caden shook his head. He wanted to know more about this mission. Unfortunately, he was too weary to form the questions in his mind, much less voice them. He closed his eyes like a babe, and the world around him drifted away.

CHAPTER TWO

Across the fells and moorlands to the east of Lothian, the salt scent of the German Sea and the rush of waves upon the Bernician shore were blotted out by the cluster of humanity and goods of Din Guardi's marketplace. Exotic fabrics and spices from the East, tableware from the Mediterranean, the finest wines and oils the continent had to offer—all were on display to tease and tempt the buyer.

Yet where Sorcha, adopted daughter of the late merchant Wulfram, stood, the pungent stench of the slave warehouse surrounded her. A line of British captives, shackled in irons and despair, left the raised dais one by one, sold to work in some thane's hall, barn, or fields. They were able men, not of warrior stature—for those would have died fighting their Saxon captor—but still fit for common labor.

Then came the women, the more comely ones examined with looks and touches that made Sorcha shudder. Her betrothed, despite being twice her age, sometimes looked at her with the same raw hunger.

As her adopted father's best friend, Cynric of Elford had watched Sorcha grow up. She'd seen him as a fatherly figure, but now she was a woman, and he was, for all his kindness and generosity, a man. For a year she'd kept him at bay, asking time to mourn her parents, who perished in a fire that had consumed their home and tavern near their business at a port warehouse.

The image of Wulfram and Aelwyn's smiling faces squeezed at Sorcha's heart. But for a twist in the Wyrds' way, Sorcha might have perished as well. Instead, she and her mother's friend and servant, Gemma, managed to leap from their loft bedchamber to the roof of an adjacent building. Her parents were not so fortunate.

With their home in ashes, Sorcha and Gemma moved to Wulfram's warehouse near the waterfront and, with what assets had not perished in the fire, finished part of it as their new home. Living among the swarms of strangers and seamen who came into the port below Din Guardi's great rock wasn't the safest place for two women to live alone, but then, Sorcha and Gemma were well acquainted with the use of a sword or knife. Not that they'd had to use either. Those who lived and worked in that section looked out for their own....

"Each lot is more sorrowful than the last," Gemma said, pulling Sorcha from the horror of that night. Though she stood on an empty wine cask, the dwarf strained on tiptoe to see over the heads of the crowd.

"Aye," Sorcha agreed. Some would marry and be lifted above their lot as a slave, but 'twas still an indignity to a free soul.

"Better them than me," Gemma observed. She was not without heart but was pragmatic to a fault.

Gemma had been born on the same day as Sorcha's adopted mother, both to a troupe of gleemen or entertainers. Copper-haired

Aelwyn grew into a tall, lithe beauty, while her brown-haired counterpart's growth was stunted by the whim of the Wyrds. Aelwyn's voice and sharp wit earned her a living as a singer to the common folk, while Gemma's unique size, sleight of hand, and light fingers filled the needs song did not.

A wail, followed by a harsh command for silence, drew Sorcha's attention to where a barrel-chested oaf tugged a string of dirty and disheveled children, some in rags, toward the platform.

"Here come the little ones."

Even as Sorcha mouthed the words, she was seized with empathy for the frightened children led like livestock across the slaver's dais. For just a second, she was one of them again, snatched from a loving home by barbarian invaders, monsters with swords who trussed her up and marched her over hill and dale into a foreign land with a language that sounded harsh to ears accustomed to the lilt and flow of her native tongue.

Though only seven when she was taken from Trebold Law, she'd heard stories about the Sassenach barbarians. Would the brigands kill her and eat her? she'd wondered, trembling. Would they sacrifice her to their heathen gods? Where were her parents? Why hadn't they come after her? Or would they never come? Was the blood staining the clothing and blades of her straw-haired captors that of her loved ones?

With each day that passed in the new land, her mother's last words, a promise called out to Sorcha as she was dragged away from her homeland—that God would bring her home again—turned a child's hope into contempt. If her parents' Christian God was so good, was even real, this would not have happened.

Sorcha shook off the flashback. "I count four."

At least she'd been one of the lucky ones. Wulfram and Aelwyn had purchased her and adopted her as the daughter of their hearts. Aelwyn had been barren, and Sorcha might have been her own, given her mane of fiery red hair. But where Aelwyn's eyes were summer blue, Sorcha's were a winter green—the soft color of pine needles, so Wulfram often teased, or a gemstone fire when she was angry.

"Three," Gemma disagreed with a stubbornness twice her size. "We can only afford three."

Scorcha knew her friend was right. Having spent what little coin they had after her parents' deaths on building a room in the warehouse for a home, they'd had to borrow from the moneylender to purchase the spring supplies this year. And the betrothal gift that Cynric had given her had gone toward previous auctions. If she asked for more, the thane might think her dowry—the business—was not worthy of marriage.

"The littlest one won't remember. A child-starved mother will give her all her own mother would, same as Aelwyn did you," Gemma reminded her.

Sorcha couldn't deny that Aelwyn *and* Wulfram loved her with all their hearts. But that didn't erase the memory of Sorcha's birth mother. Myrna's loving face was forever etched on Sorcha's heart.

"So, Sorcha, I see you've come for more children to while away."

Talorc, the Frisian slave trader whose *goods* were on the auction block, ambled over to Sorcha. Giving Gemma a less than dismissive glance, he set himself between the two of them for Sorcha's undivided attention.

Gemma jumped down from the cask before she was knocked over. "Watch yourself, trader, or you might awaken tomorrow as the swine you are."

"Ach, you've no more magic than me." The Frisian scoffed at the threat as Gemma gave his tunic a hard tug of indignation. "Careful, little woman, or I'll sell *you!*"

With a sniff, Gemma hustled to Sorcha's other side, but something told Sorcha it was not because of fear. Gemma was too quick for all that excess flesh and bone to catch her.

"Talorc, I am a person of business like my father before me," Sorcha said. "These children will fetch me a profit as well as you." Sorcha's smile was as empty as her growling stomach. In their haste to make it to the market in time for the auction, she and Gemma had failed to break the fast.

"Exactly what is it you do with the urchins?" the man asked, fingering his necklace of gold coins and buttons, a financial reserve, as well as a boastful sign of his wealth. "I hear you keep them about from time to time, and then they are gone. Does *she* turn them into toads?"

"You said you don't believe in the magic of little people," Sorcha replied.

Although a good many did, something Gemma used to her advantage when it suited her purpose.

Talorc peered around Sorcha. "No, but I do believe someone would pay dearly to have her as a pet."

Sorcha sank her fingers into Gemma's shoulders in time to stay her friend's impulse to respond, although she could well imagine what was going on in Gemma's quick mind. Something about a knife and rendering Talorc so he would never sire children.

"Gemma is a free woman," Sorcha reminded him sweetly.

The sad thing, though, was that what Talorc said was true. The wealthy had kept dwarves as pets since the pharaohs, although most were pampered to the utmost in exchange for their unique presence and entertainment. Sorcha had even heard it said that parents tried to arrest their babes' normal growth with diet and potions, both within the womb and without, to produce the same result.

"As for my business," Sorcha continued, "I and my network of associates find child-starved homes for them inland where they'll be raised as natural-born sons and daughters, not slaves."

It wasn't exactly a lie. Gleemen and bards, or scops as they were called in Bernicia, were welcome anywhere in the isles no matter their nationality, as long as they might sing their stories in multiple languages or simply entertain with their theatrics or acrobatic abilities. A few in Sorcha's close circle had heart enough to help her return these children to their rightful homes. Any rewards were shared, with her portion used to save future captives. Sadly, gratitude was all most broken families could afford.

"The reward must not be much, else you'd rebuild your home." Talorc laughed at her sentimentality, but the humor didn't reach his eyes.

It seemed to amuse her betrothed as well, but Sorcha had been adamant that she'd remain free to help those whose position she'd once been in. Or maybe it was her way of dealing with her grief this past year. A distraction to fill the emptiness of her loss.

"Milady's business is none of yours, Talorc," Gemma reminded him. "Now leave us be so we can attend to it." The dwarf motioned Talorc along, like a queen dismissing a minion.

"Hah," Talorc guffawed. "If only you were big as yer mouth was."

Gemma cocked her head at him. "Big or nay, we're *both* big enough to tell the thane of Elford all about you."

Talorc raised his thick hedge of brow at Sorcha. "So it's true. You're to be a lady of Elford Hall now."

Sorcha nodded. The skim of his jaundiced gaze over her body reminded her all too much that it soon would not be her own. But Elford's wedding gift would go a long way toward her purpose, she reminded herself. And at the rate her mission to help the children had dwindled her resources, she should consider herself honored that her late father's sword-friend would even consider her. After all, she was not truly Saxon.

"No wonder you haven't found another place to live," Talorc remarked. "You'll have the great hall at Elford as your own." He glanced at Gemma. "And a jester besides."

Before Gemma could come back at him, Talorc walked away, chuckling.

"Chuckle away, oaf," the dwarf said under her breath. "I've three Byzantine gold pieces for the insults you've hurled."

Alarm struck down the sense of being soiled by Talorc's presence. The trader's purse hung on the verge of falling by only one of its pull strings. "Gemma! Not here where—"

Sorcha broke off as Gemma raised a finger to her lips. "I only skimmed the top," her companion said with the demeanor of a well-fed cat. "He'll never know when the bag came loose or if he lost anything."

There was no thrill like that of a well-executed theft from someone who deserved it. Sorcha knew that firsthand. But here in the marketplace, where she and Gemma were well known and respected …

Sorcha ushered Gemma closer to the auction block. "Let's just do our bidding and get the urchins home, eh?"

That evening, *four* bedraggled youngsters scrambled for small meat pies that Gemma had purchased for them in the marketplace, since neither Sorcha nor her companion claimed to be decent cooks. The eldest, a lad from a village in the nearby British kingdom of Elmet, gathered up his little sister and offered his pie to her. Sorcha put aside the hearth poker and left the warmth of the now-growing flames to help out.

"You're a good brother, Ian. But I'll help Aine, so you can join the others."

Ian, black-haired as the rest of them, hesitated. Ten years if a day by Sorcha's guess, he was clearly hungry and exhausted. And thanks to Talorc's unwitting contribution, they were able to purchase his sibling.

"I'll get a knife to remove that rope off your wrist now that you're safe in here."

Sorcha hated keeping them on leashes like dogs, but she had seen the fear and panic in their eyes and known that they might bolt away in the marketplace and wind up lost and hungry on the streets, no matter how she reassured them in their native tongue that she was going to see them returned to their families.

"Are you a heathen queen?" the eldest girl asked as Sorcha cut away the binding on Ian's wrist.

"Queens don't live in places like this," Ian told his fellow captive with a degree of authority. The boy looked at the heavy beams overhead, supporting a loft mostly used for storage. Since the fire, Gemma and Sorcha lived and slept in the downstairs quarters, even though the loft was just as toasty with the rising heat from the hearth.

"Ian is quite right," Sorcha replied.

"But you had gold. I saw it," Wynnie protested through a mouthful of food. "Queens have gold."

"Don't speak with your mouth full," Gemma scolded gently, dabbing off the dribble that escaped onto Wynnie's coarse linen shift.

"Aye," Sorcha told the girl, "I had a piece of gold, part of which I've spent to share food and lodging with you this night and every other until you return to your homes."

To her surprise, Ian handed Aine over. Like a living doll with bright blue eyes, the child was so engrossed in the meat pasty, she didn't seem to care that Sorcha was a stranger.

"You won't be going with us?" Ian asked. He selected one of the biggest pies and bit into it eagerly.

"Nay, I have a friend who will take you. He's a bard."

"What is that?" Wynnie stopped eating, alarm and suspicion creeping back onto her round face. Having been reared in a remote farming village, chances were she'd not been to a fair or tavern. Sorcha hadn't at that age.

"A bard is a traveling entertainer who sings at fairs, taverns, or in noble courts," she explained.

"I've seen them," Ian assured the girl smugly. "They also put on marvelous plays, dance, and sometimes juggle and do acrobatic tricks."

"Actually, that kind of entertainer is a gleeman." Sorcha pointed to Gemma. "Gemma and my mother were gleemen … and I sing and play music as one myself, though I've had some bardic training."

A glaze of confusion settled over the older children's faces.

"Unlike gleemen," Sorcha told them, "a bard has to study for years and years to memorize the great songs of his people—"

"And to learn how to compose new ones in a rhyme and meter that will not be lost through the ages," Gemma added as she removed the fourth child's bindings.

"So I've memorized songs, but not as many as a master bard." Though she'd picked her cousin's brain clean. "And I can read and write but am not good enough to write bardic poetry." There just hadn't been enough time with Sorcha's helping her mother and father in their businesses.

"Ach, Ebyn," Gemma tutted, examining where the rope bindings had rubbed the younger boy's wrist raw. "I do not like the looks of this, but I've a salve that will heal it."

"Is it magic?" Aside from his name, these were the first words Sorcha had heard Ebyn utter.

"I'm no fairy, lad, just a wee woman who didn't eat what my mother told me to when I was your age." Gemma tossed up her hands. "Now look at me. Too old to be a child"—her dramatic twirl made her skirts flare—"and too small to be a woman." Catching her skirts, she floated down into a graceful bow.

Ebyn smiled for the first time, perhaps since he'd been captured. Like Wynnie, he was seven, the same age as Sorcha when she'd been plucked from the love of her family and brought into this foreign place. At last he was relaxing.

But a sharp knock on the door sent the boy scrambling beneath the food board with Wynnie not far behind. Ian grew still and pale. Sorcha handed his little sister off to him and went to the entrance.

"Get on with you," she shouted through the heavy plank door. "'Tis too late for business at this hour, and you'll wake the babes."

The mention of sleeping children usually sent drunken patrons or seamen who stumbled home to the wrong door from waterfront taverns on their way.

From the other side came a rich baritone Sorcha knew only too well: "My heart is sore, for I've been long from the bower of my fire-haired lady...."

With a laugh, Sorcha unbolted the door and flung it open. Leaning against the frame, grasping a harp in a bag tucked under his arm and brandishing an incorrigible grin, stood her cousin Eadric. A raven-haired rogue, the illegitimate son of an Elmet chieftain and Aelwyn's sister, Eadric had a voice and a charm that left maidens' hearts broken and twined with longing in his wake.

"Eadric!" Of Elmet, or Cumbria, perhaps Powys or Glamorgan. His home was where his harp was. So tonight ...

"You can come out from under the table, Wynnie, and meet your first bard. Children," Sorcha announced, "may I present Eadric ... of Bernicia."

CHAPTER THREE

Leaf Fall took hold with the first frosts searing the foliage from green to shades of red, gold, and brown. Today the air was crisp enough to make a cloak welcome to some, but a nuisance to Caden as he looked over the fields from the dun at the top of Trebold Law. He'd lost most of September abed. To rebuild his strength, he'd insisted on helping around the tavern and making the climb daily to visit Malachy, Lady Myrna's brother-by-law.

Alyn had set off for Glenarden to visit their elder brother and his wife before returning to Llanwit to resume his studies, and Father Martin, too, had taken his leave. But not without one last sermon.

"Ours is a Lord of second chances, Caden. Make good use of this one," the priest told Caden before taking off in a northerly direction along the old Roman road toward Din Edyn.

Never specific, Caden had grumbled to himself. But Martin read his mind like a tavern sign. "There's an old proverb you'd do well to ponder, son. *Love of our neighbor is the only door out of the dungeon of self.*'"

Caden loved his neighbor … as long as said neighbor left him be. Yet his life was a dungeon, a chamber of endless torture, in spite of Trebold's gracious treatment. Myrna had nothing but the highest regard for him. Her brother-in-law, Malachy, picked up where Martin had left off in fishing for Caden's soul during their games of draughts and even suggested that Trebold Law might be Caden's if he could charm the long-lost Sorcha.

A decaying hillfort with half its surrounding fields lying fallow, Caden thought as he surveyed the land below. The old Caden would have leapt at the chance to have an adoring people and land of his own. The people of Trebold Law thought he was a hero, the warrior who saved the High King. But a man who'd nearly murdered his family for power wasn't worthy of even this ramshackle place where the earthen works and the remains of a stockade were so overgrown, it was hard to tell where one ended and nature took over.

Nay. The sooner Caden fetched Sorcha home, if the lady was to be found and fetched at all, the sooner he could return to the battlefront, where the enemy was clearly defined and deadly enough to suit him.

A horn's blast pulled Caden from his dour speculation to the north road from Din Edyn converging at the ford that was the tavern Trebold Law's only hope for survival. As if in answer to his heart's plea, the double eagles of Lothian fluttered in the wind above a large procession.

"What is it?" Above Caden, Malachy ventured out of the patched hall, his cloak whirling about his scrawny frame in the fall breeze.

"King Modred's company approaches," Caden replied.

Malachy grasped at his chest in dismay. "The shame of it that we've no laird to properly greet him. I've failed my brother's wife miserably."

Caden grinned, familiar with the old man's cunning. "I'll help Lady Myrna entertain the king at the tavern," he promised. Given his way, Malachy would hasten back to his church and hand Trebold over to Caden with or without Sorcha. And in truth, it felt good to Caden to have such a fatherly figure hold him in high esteem, even if that esteem was foundless.

"You know how much we need you, son," Malachy told him. "And we're grateful God has sent you to us."

Son. The word twined around Caden's heart, so tempting to accept. But he couldn't. Not now. Not ever.

By nightfall, the downstairs of the tavern had been converted into Modred's hall, with the king seated at the center of a food board that had been set up along the left side of the central hearth. The room was filled with the delicious aromas of roasting beef and venison. To Caden's surprise, he was seated at the king's board with Princess Eavlyn of Dunfeld to his right and a now-composed Malachy on his left. The irony was not lost on Caden. He'd used to be pleased as a hornet in honeyed mead to dine in the company of royalty; yet now he'd rather be fetching wood for Myrna's cook fire or lurking in the shadows of the buttresses supporting the high timber walls.

"But you saved my uncle's life," Modred reminded Caden when he demurred at the invitation to join the king's guests.

Caden was starting to regret that. Or at least the attention it garnered.

And now he was expected to accompany the royal wedding party to Din Guardi. It was an excellent excuse to have free access to the town in the atmosphere of truce and pick up the search for Sorcha of Trebold where her true father had left off so many years ago. According

to Myrna, Sorcha's father, Fintan, died of a fever from a trip to the coast
in search of the child. He thought he'd seen her on the waterfront, but
she disappeared in the throngs. He'd asked at every cottar's house and
business stall about his missing red-haired daughter, but the moment
he mentioned her name, no one knew anything. Worse, the poor man
was set upon by brigands and left for dead. Fintan made it home to his
wife, but only just, before the fever took him.

"More mead, milady?" Myrna asked the princess.

"Thank you," Princess Eavlyn replied, folding delicate, gold-
ringed hands in her lap.

His dinner companion was comely enough, with unremarkable
brown hair and eyes. She ate like a bird and had little to say to anyone, save pleasantries.

Modred had changed tactics from battle to peaceweaving since
Caden had last seen him. The poor lassie had been promised to a
heathen prince, one of Hussa's many sons. In theory, Prince Hering
of Burlwick would rein in the Saxon raiding parties on Modred's
side of the Tweed in exchange for marriage to a Lothian princess
descended from Petros, the brother of Joseph of Arimathea. Hence
the Celtic Church would have planted the seed of victory for Christ
and the apostolic bloodline in heathen Bernicia's ruling family.

"I'm sorry Father Martin was unable to join us," Malachy told
Princess Eavlyn. "I've missed conversing with my fellow priests,
though young Caden has been delightful company and a challenge
at draughts these last weeks."

"Father Martin is already at Din Guardi, working with the Saxon
witans on the nature of the ceremony," Eavlyn replied. "Their word
for marriage is *wedd,* which means a gamble or wager."

Caden nearly snorted his beer through his nose. "Aye," he managed, "I can see that."

Ignoring his outburst, Eavlyn continued. "The witans will make their sacrifices to their gods, and Father Martin will bless the wedding in Christ's name before the eyes of God."

"You are a courageous woman, Eavlyn, to willingly go into that den of heathens," Malachy observed.

"If we do not go to them with Christ, who will?" she asked simply.

It was no secret that a majority of the British church balked at the idea of taking the Word to the barbarians who'd pillaged their churches, murdered their priests, and savaged their women. They'd not forgotten how Ida had killed a weaponless priest for praying for a Briton victory. The heathen considered such an act of war, holding not even the knowledge of druid or priest sacred.

"I understand you've studied under the Lady Vivianne on the Holy Isle," Malachy said, turning the subject.

At the mention of the Holy Isle, Eavlyn's dull demeanor came to life. "Mostly the Lady Ninian, Father Malachy."

Malachy had mustered himself together enough to make the trek downhill with the help of a servant. Instead of wearing his royal but worn tunic and braes, or trousers, the elder had donned priestly robes of undyed linen and wool, nicely embroidered with golden thread about the neck, cuffs, and hem by the women at the monastic settlement of his former home. Balding negated the need to shave his forehead in the druidic tonsure of the Celtic Church.

"Then you've had the pleasure of meeting her teacher," he said.

Passion kindled in Eavlyn's fawn-brown gaze. "And conversing about God's great creation, especially the heavens."

"How fares Merlin Emrys?" Malachy inquired.

Eavlyn's smile faltered. "His health limits his travel … but he is thankful that it has given him longed-for time with his studies," she recovered brightly.

"I envy him." Malachy sent a meaningful glance Caden's way before returning to his conversation with the lady. "So you are learned in astronomy."

"My teachers say I have a gift for it." Genuine modesty brought color to Eavlyn's pale complexion, unlike the rouging on her attendants.

Caden stiffened, wary. He knew astrology was like his sister-in-law Brenna's nature magic, a science and studied as such by priests and druids alike. There were signs in the heavens that measured time, predicted weather, and guided farmers and seamen alike in making their livings. But it also led to soothsaying, something not approved of by the church, at least as his pious mother, Aeda, had warned him. Fortune-telling was more foolrede than blasphemy in Caden's mind. Foolishness.

"Did you see your future marriage in the stars?" he asked.

Eavlyn smiled, tolerant of the skepticism in Caden's voice. "Nay, sir, my future is not in the stars, but in God's hands. But the heavens suggest probability, based on observation from the time when God set the stars on their courses, that it could be a good one."

"So the Sassenach aren't so different. This wedding *is* a wager," Caden reasoned. "A probability."

Aye, she was a druidess, one of God's, but still able to confound a man with fancy words and theories of no use on the battlefield. Give Caden weather signs and eyewitness reports on the enemy's position and strength. *Those* were worth pondering.

"*Only* our Creator God and His Word are certain," she clarified emphatically. "As such, while it appears from the long-established meanings of the heavenly signs that this marriage will work, it is not certain. For that, I place my life and future in God's hands."

Evidently eavesdropping on the conversation, Modred turned from her father, Blaise, to the lady. The candlelight danced off the coronet sparkling on his onyx-black hair, not yet cut in the tonsure of the Celtic Church he also served. Still another contradiction in the myriad of his character.

"Milady, such matters are for scholars and lost, I fear, on some of our most valiant warriors. Even our Pendragon," he added, as Caden bristled at the insult.

Modred's sting was smooth as silk, for it put Caden in good company and rang of some truth. Arthur was educated as a warrior king, accomplished in the art of war with the devotion of his sword-brothers. For other matters, like diplomacy, he leaned on Emrys.

"'Tis no secret my uncle's tutelage on the Holy Isle was short-lived, compared to that of my mother and her sisters," Modred explained. "He is more like his father, Aedan—better suited to bashing heads than to the exchange of ideas."

Yet Modred pondered his lofty ideas while his uncle risked life and limb to bash Saxon heads south of the Tweed in his stead. Caden had little use for his slippery liege and his half-truths, but serving Lothian put Caden closer to the Saxons and risk, the only thing he lived for.

"That is why every king needs a merlin to balance action with wisdom, that the people may be best led," Eavlyn said, her words worthy of a queen. "Those who embody both are rare indeed."

"Indeed we are." Modred raised his goblet, Romanware gilt studded with garnets. One of his attendants had unpacked it earlier from a box that contained the king's personal tableware. Suddenly the Lothian lord burst into laughter, as though the comment had been a jest.

Caden pretended to sip from his leather drinking mug. He was on Modred's pay as a mercenary, but he didn't have to drink with him. Lothian was high enough to drink to himself.

Malachy wasn't fooled either. "Ah, but you must remember, young king, that Merlin Emrys has never stopped Arthur's education of mind and spirit. Our Pendragon has become kingly in both since his callow days in Aedan's court."

"Come now, Father," Modred drawled, annoyance darkening his gaze until the black center nearly consumed its dark brown rim. "We all know that with Emrys retired to his observatory in the west, Arthur becomes more devoted to Rome than to the British church. He wears the Virgin's image on his shield. He only flies the Red Dragon for fear of losing the non-Christian kings in our Cymri alliance."

"Roman or Briton, we are one in Christ," Malachy insisted.

"If Rome has its way, we will not only lose the Grail customs of Arimathea but our freedom of faith and the pursuit of learning. Only priests and nuns may study creation and the mystic healing arts … the very arts passed down from the magi and Hebrew priests. Christ taught them to the apostles." Modred slammed his fist on the table. "That is why Arthur *must* come to his senses and distance himself from Rome's influence. Faith, since he returned from the Holy Land, he has not been the same."

Was it possible that it was not greed and revenge against Arthur for the death of his father alone that motivated Modred, but his position in the Celtic Church of Britain against the Roman doctrine his uncle supported?

Though what difference it made whether Britons observed Easter at the Passover instead of the new date set by Rome, or considered Saturday as its Sabbath instead of Rome's Sunday, eluded Caden. But then he wasn't exactly religious and didn't intend to be.

Malachy struggled for a response, a sign to Caden that there was some merit in Modred's words. "We live in a dark time," the old priest said at last. "A time where such knowledge in the wrong hands is abused."

"Knowledge has been abused since time began, by both men of God and nonbelievers. But it has been used for good by both as well," Modred argued. "We have learned from each other, coexisted in peace here in Albion. Rome would deny the free choice God gave us."

His late wife's image came to Caden's mind, as angelic outside as she was evil within. Knowledge had certainly fallen into the wrong hands with Rhianon and that conniving nurse of hers.

Modred's hands tightened about the stem of his goblet till Caden expected it to snap. "The time will grow darker, Father, if we allow Rome to dictate to us, as the Pharisees did the Jews. Is such control not what Christ rebelled against?"

"He also said, *'Give not that which is holy unto the dogs, neither cast ye your pearls before swine, lest they trample them under their feet, and turn again and rend you,'*" Malachy quoted.

"Matthew 7:6," Modred acknowledged. "But Rome considers anyone who is not of the church swine. Why, Princess Eavlyn is no nun, yet she is gifted, educated on the Holy Isle. Is *she* swine?"

Caden rubbed his temple where his brain clenched in effort to follow the conversation. The only headaches he was accustomed to came from a hard blow in battle or too much ale in celebrating a victory, but never words.

"I am a woman of God, milord," Eavlyn objected. "That I serve Him as Esther did, an enemy king's wife, does not change the fact that I serve Him and His children."

"And have you not learned from good, yet nonbelieving druids as well as godly ones?" Modred asked. "It is the loss of *their* knowledge I fear. We have much to learn from each other in a kingdom where we can exist together as neighbors."

"Gentlemen, I can see no resolution to the dilemma of the church this night," Eavlyn interjected, her hands held up in surrender, "but you are welcome to seek it without me." She rose from the bench, giving Modred a slight bow. "Tomorrow's journey will come early. If it please milord, I will retire with my maid now."

"I pray my fervor has not offended you, Princess Eavlyn," the king apologized. "I have nothing but respect for your service to God and our kingdom."

Plain Eavlyn grew radiant before Caden's eyes. "Oh nay, my liege. It has been most invigorating." Her face fell. "And vexing."

"And I plead old age, milord, and a long uphill walk to ask your leave," Malachy said after the lady retired from the board.

"I'll walk you back to Trebold Law," Caden offered, glad for a chance to be free of Modred and the conversation.

The scrape of hearth benches being moved to the side so that the entourage might bed down around the fire for the night followed Caden and his elderly companion out into the cool night air.

"All of Albion is in trouble," Malachy said halfway up the hill. "We are surrounded by the enemy, but we will not despair." His feeble clap on the back turned into a fatherly embrace. One Caden accepted out of respect. Maybe something more. "With God on our side, son, we have nothing to fear. Believe it."

"Aye, Father," Caden replied. "I believe it."

He'd seen God heal his father's bitter madness and protect his brother Ronan and Glenarden from overwhelming odds. Caden just didn't know if God was on *his* side.

CHAPTER FOUR

Eadric would take only three of the children on the dale ponies he'd acquired over the roll board. Sorcha wrapped her cloak tight about her shoulders in the cool morning air and stared, hopeless, at the shore where cottars wrestled their cobles, or small fishing boats, off the sand to try their fishing nets in the overcast sea beyond. The familiar wash of the water on the sands, the salty essence of the air normally embraced and invigorated Sorcha, but not today.

Not when she had to choose one child to remain behind.

Yet her cousin was not being hard-hearted. Just practical. Three youngsters day in and out on a pony across wetland, hill, and dale, accompanying a man who'd never had bairns of his own? What had she been thinking?

She hadn't. Impulse was a weakness. Now, not only did she have to choose a child to remain behind, but she had to explain it to her betrothed, who'd already agreed to Gemma's coming with Sorcha.

"I promise I'll return for the fourth child in the spring," Eadric assured her. "Even if I have to travel alone with the wee one."

Just till spring. That's what she'd tell Cynric. For now, she had
to face four very excited children and tell them one had to remain
behind. And it wouldn't be the siblings.

Upon entering the house, Sorcha avoided Wynnie's excited gaze
as she rushed for Eadric in one of the new cloaks Gemma had made
the children. Wynnie was very helpful around the house, a natural
with a needle.

No longer wary of Eadric, the little girl grabbed the bard in a
fierce hug. "I can't wait to leave. Will we be home in time for the
harvest celebration?" she asked, breathless. "I love the dancing and
all the food."

Sorcha groaned inside.

"You'll be home much sooner than that," Eadric promised.
"Three days on my ponies, if the weather holds."

"Ponies!" Aine squealed, proudly mimicking a whinny.

"What if it storms?" Ian held Aine a little closer, concern grazing
his young face.

"I have many friends to offer us shelter along the way for a song
and news of the land," Eadric assured him.

"Bards are welcome wherever they go," Gemma informed the
lad.

Ian was clearly impressed. "Maybe I should be a bard instead of
a cooper, like my da. I could see the whole world." Although he'd
thought Din Guardi was all there was to it beyond his home when
he first arrived.

"You don't choose to be a bard, Ian. You're chosen to be one by
another bard who thinks you've potential," Eadric explained. "Then
it takes twenty years of studying with the masters."

Ian grew aghast. "I'd never live that long!"

Sorcha couldn't help but join the others in laughter, but there was no joy in her heart.

And Gemma could see it, plain as the nose on her face. "What's wrong, lassie?"

All eyes shifted to Sorcha, the atmosphere sobering. "Eadric can only take three children with him," she announced. "One must stay with us until spring."

Wynnie caught her breath, her gaze searching Sorcha's with reluctance, as though she feared to see her name there. Making his thoughts on the matter clear, Ian pulled little Aine so close that she wailed in protest.

But from the fire where he'd retreated after breakfast, Ebyn jumped to his feet. "Me," he exclaimed with more fervor than Sorcha had ever seen in the child. "I'll stay."

Eadric clapped Sorcha on the back. "Problem solved. Now the rest of you gather your things. We've a long day ahead of us."

"Don't you want to go home, Ebyn?" Sorcha asked quietly while the others scrambled under Eadric's authority to get ready. That the child would offer to stay was an idea that never occurred to Sorcha.

Shrinking back into withdrawal, Ebyn shook his head, staring into the fire. "I like it here."

Except that *here* wasn't going to be *here* for long. Sorcha was to marry soon.

She hugged him. "I'm glad you do … but I'm sure in the spring your parents will be even gladder to see you when Eadric takes you home."

Again, Ebyn shook his head. Silhouetted against the firelight, his chin trembled. A single tear left a glittering trail in its wake. "They'll just sell me again."

⊕

The Crowing Rooster near the market at the mouth of the Oose was packed with patrons. Traveling merchants and seamen who chose to winter over in Din Guardi mingled with the influx of peoples here for the royal wedding under the low-beamed ceiling separating the tavern from the keeper's living quarters upstairs. While Sorcha tuned her harp, her thoughts centered on the little boy who'd told her so much in those few heart-wrenching words. *They'll just sell me again.*

No wonder he'd said so little about his home life when the other children shared theirs. At least Sorcha had been abducted, even though her parents hadn't come after her. His parents couldn't afford to keep him, the youngest of seven children, and Talorc had promised he'd find a good home for the boy. *At the slave market,* Sorcha fumed. *Curse the man!* Now she wished Gemma had taken his entire purse.

But she was grateful that the rest of their precious gaggle was on their way to their homes, where they'd be welcomed and loved. For tonight, Gemma had talked one of the women from weavers' row into allowing Ebyn to spend the night. They both needed to be at the tavern, where drink was as plentiful as the coins in the purses of the patrons.

Eadric and his company had no sooner vanished into the early morning mists than a knock came on Sorcha's door. She'd thought perhaps the bard or one of the children had forgotten something, but when she opened it, there stood Wada, a round giant of a man with missing teeth and fetid breath, who worked for the moneylender Athelstan.

At first, Sorcha's heart lodged in her throat. Had she lost track of time? The money she owed Wada's employer wasn't due until Freya's day. She had at least another day to try to make up what she'd spent on the children. She had enough to repay Athelstan for what she'd borrowed last spring but was short on the toll.

Sorcha had no doubt that Athelstan would exact his tribute for the service in some despicable way. A broken arm or smashed knee was his usual punishment. Thankfully, Sorcha had gotten by with a grudging promise that Wada would return the next evening for the full amount. The gods only knew what might befall them if she didn't have it.

She and Gemma *had* to work this crowd tonight. The more the men drank, the more generous they became, especially to a comely wench with a pleasant voice. And men did consider Sorcha comely and talented with harp and song. She was her mother's daughter. Though sometimes it won her unsolicited attention. That's where her skill with the dining dagger at her waist proved helpful, for she was Wulfram's daughter as well.

Harp tucked under her arm, Sorcha made her way to the corner where a small raised gallery had been built for the entertainers. All around her, the royal wedding of Hussa's son, Hering of Burlwick, to the Briton princess Eavlyn of Dunfeld, dominated conversations. The princess's entourage had arrived that afternoon with trumpet blasts loud enough to wake the dead.

Even now a cluster of the Lothians, clad in their multicolored cloaks, sat in a corner of the room, while the room buzzed with speculation.

"I hear this Lothian princess is descended from a sacred Briton lineage through her father and Pictish royals by her mother."

"Prince Hering is no fool. Lothian Picts inherit rule from their mama's side of the family. If Mama has no son—"

"Some say she has knowledge only our witans are privy to. She reads the stars."

So did Sorcha. But only for signs of the weather. There were some who saw even more. The idea of watching the heavens night after night and charting what one saw sounded boring to her notion. Her element was the tavern joys of happy hearts, the latest news, and stirring song.

"With Hussa's many enemies, this princess may prove an asset worth having."

"A man must conquer territory with whatever sword is best suited, eh?"

Men. Sorcha bit her tongue at the crude innuendo. In truth, she felt a kindred spirit with this princess, each of them having to marry without love. That the Wyrds played them as pieces on a board of political and social survival vexed Sorcha sorely. As for the influence of the ancient Saxon gods and goddesses, she gave up on them when their images burned along with her parents, who'd sacrificed far more to the idols than they'd received in return.

"Hering has already given his betrothed a hundred twenty hides of land in Burlwick as the bride gift at the betrothal."

Cynric had offered Sorcha ten hides of land when the betrothal was negotiated, enough to support herself and that many families, should the marriage not work out to both their satisfaction. She was to receive that many more if she bore him a child. 'Twas more than enough to support her and Gemma *and* continue helping captured children.

A sudden rush of cool air stirred the smoke from the central hearth and drew Sorcha's attention to the entrance, where a giant of a man with wild flaxen hair strode in ... alone. The moment he ordered beer from Utta, Sorcha knew he was another Briton, a warrior by his strapping build. And handsome enough, in a wild way. His face was rough-shaven and his clothes worn, yet of quality. But what caught Sorcha's eye most was the fat purse from which he paid Utta for his beer.

Instead of joining his countrymen, he settled on a bench near the wall and cast his quicksilver gaze about, like a hawk searching for an unsuspecting mouse. To her surprise, Sorcha seemed to be his prey. But instead of appearing threatening, like Wada's snaggle-toothed smile earlier that day, the smile he sent her way stirred her blood from the inside out till she surely glowed like a torch.

He raised his drink to her as she began to play the harp, a tune her fingers knew well without the aid of thought. But the words, ah, they were a lost clash of attraction versus warning behind the coy smile she tossed him. Was his purse worth the risk?

Ebyn's pitiful reply played through her mind. *They'll just sell me again.*

Aye, Sorcha decided. This would be the last time. Soon she'd be a lady and never have to steal again. With that, she began to sing.

CHAPTER FIVE

So *this* was Sorcha. Caden could see the resemblance to Myrna the moment he laid eyes on her. Her hair was touched with fire, yet unblemished by the snow of her mother's age. It almost looked hot to the touch. Hot as the fierce blush that colored her creamy complexion and deepened the green of her gaze. This fair minstrel had to be the one he sought. How many Sorchas could there be in Din Guardi of that description?

The port reeve had not steered him wrong, although the man was reluctant to give up any information until a gold coin warmed his hand. Even then, Caden had to convince him that he had a small inheritance for Sorcha from a relative in Aberwick, a lady Caden had worked for.

"Our Sorcha an heiress," the reeve exclaimed. "The Wyrds must be makin' up for the way they've treated her of late."

Caden learned, while treating the man to a drink near a warm tavern fire, how she'd lost her parents in a fire a little over a year ago, well-respected folk who adopted the seven-year-old captive. That her father's sword-friend and gesith, or companion to Hussa himself, had offered to marry her.

"Though the ol' thane'll have his hands full, mind ye," the reeve said. "That one has a mind of her own. A bit queer, if ye ask me. Most maids her age are wedded, bedded, and raisin' their own children by now, not buyin' 'em at the slave market. Says she an' that dwarf of hers finds good homes for them."

So Sorcha had her mother Myrna's good heart. Caden tucked that and all he'd learned away in his memory. His red-blooded reaction to her smile was harder to cast aside. But it had been the same the first time he'd seen Rhianon. And since being freed of his late wife, he'd run from any woman who affected him so, making him vulnerable to her manipulation.

Unbidden, the last time Caden saw Rhianon came to his mind: her clothes stained with the blood of the men she'd murdered, her hair wild and matted with brush from hiding in the woods. Hissing and snarling at the priest who approached her, she'd turned and leapt over a crag, taking their unborn child with her into the depths of the river below. Caden had lost a part of him that day that he still mourned, but his grief was for the innocent babe, not his late wife. Caden shuddered. He'd rather face a battle-crazed Saxon or Orkney Pict any day.

A dwarfish woman nudged him with a wooden cup, startling Caden from the nightmarish memory. "If you liked the song, a copper for milady's cup will bring on another."

"Aye, I did," Caden said, fishing a copper from his purse, "though my understanding of Saxon is limited."

Truth was, he'd rather sit with his countrymen on yon side of the hearth, where he'd understand all being said. Here, it was more difficult, although camping and fighting side by side with Saxon warriors for hire had taught him enough to gather the gist of conversation.

"Milady sings in Cumbric as well." The little woman shoved the cup at him again. "Have you a request?"

Caden parted with another copper. "Any song in Cumbric will do." And then he added a silver coin. "And I would like to speak to the lady when she is finished this night." What was it the reeve called the dwarf? "Gemma."

Gemma's dark eyes narrowed. "You have the advantage of me, sir, for I do not know your name."

"Caden." A man without a true home, Caden hesitated. "Of Lothian." For now.

"Well, Caden of Lothian, milady does not meet men after her work here is done. She and I go straight home as decent women do."

Caden nearly laughed. For someone so small, Gemma's indignation was big ... and sharp enough to whittle a man's esteem down to her size. "I assure you, Gemma, my intentions are completely honorable."

One of the dwarf's eyebrows arched with skepticism.

"I'm come to deliver an inheritance to the lady."

In essence it was so. Trebold would be hers—if this impending marriage did not stand in the way.

Gemma's other brow hiked. "You might as well go on and practice your lies on someone else. Milady has no other family than myself."

Caden pulled the strings to his purse closed and let it fall into his lap. The hard jingle of coin was not lost on Gemma. "There is more coin ... just to talk. That is all I ask."

"Good," the dwarf replied. "Because that is all you will receive."

Caden watched as the little woman wove her way through the crowd to where the lovely minstrel finished another melody for a group of foreign merchants nearby. It was a hearty song that they sang with her about a cuckolded husband, if he heard right. One tossed a silver ring into her cup, and no wonder. The lady had a gift.

Still laughing at something one of the men said, Sorcha lent an ear to Gemma. The joviality on her face remained, but her startled gaze shot Caden's way. His news had unnerved her, even frightened her, if he was any judge of women. Then something caused her green gaze to snap, sparks lashing out at him.

Caden hid his surprise behind a sip from his mug. By any standard, this was a strange reaction to learning one was about to receive an inheritance. That he'd found Sorcha's whereabouts on his first day in Din Guardi almost convinced him that maybe God was helping out a bit, opening a door for this second chance the priest spoke of. Though the bribe and mentioning the lady had an inheritance coming to her certainly didn't hurt … until now.

Sorcha struck up a familiar tune, all the while glaring his way. It was in Cumbric, earning a cheer from the Cymris' far side of the room. She sang of a handsome swain and master of lies, who left a trail of broken hearts in his wake … until he met a maid who was his match and left him broken and alone.

Whatever Gemma had told her, it had not set well with the lassie.

Caden would never understand women. He'd have wagered Sorcha might leap at the chance for an inheritance, if it meant not having to marry an old codger as a brood sow.

By his father's bones, Father Martin's proverbial door of service to mankind that led out of the dungeon of one's self became more cumbersome by the hour.

Sorcha didn't know who the lion-maned stranger was, except that he was no friend of hers. An inheritance indeed. If her birth parents thought anything of her, they'd have come for her, not waited till they'd gone earthways to reach out to her. And sending a pouch of coins! As if that could take away the fears she'd lived out until she realized that Wulfram's and Aelwyn's harsh-sounding words were meant to comfort her. That they meant to love her and nurture her as their own.

Like as not, this Caden had already helped himself to what there was of the money. That is, what he didn't toss to the serving wench Utta for her more than willing service. But then, Utta was one of those women born flirting. And with some customers, she deserved every copper her winks and smiles earned.

Sorcha winced as she plucked the wrong chord to the ballad she sang and forced her attention back to her work. Not that anyone seemed to notice. Not even the stranger, who rarely took his gaze away from her. And that distracted her all the more. Leers, she could ignore, but this scrutiny probed as though he were trying to see who she really was behind the facade of song and a comely face. And no one, save Gemma, saw that Sorcha.

When the tavern keeper at length rang the bell mounted by the door to signal the end of drink service, some of the patrons had already cleared benches to make their beds on the floor. The wealthy merchants had departed for a hostel or one of the haws some maintained year-round. But the Cymri stranger had not moved from his bench, except long enough to relieve himself outside.

Sorcha put her harp in her bag and slung it over her shoulder. It had been a decent night's revenue, she thought, taking up the heavy cup Gemma had passed about. But it was filled with coppers mostly, not nearly enough to pay Wada tomorrow … which meant she wouldn't have the satisfaction of throwing the bag of money that Gemma had told her of back in the stranger's face. She'd have to take it and be thankful, at least to the Wyrds. It was times like this when her upcoming marriage promised more relief than concern.

"You've the voice of a siren, Milady Sorcha."

Sorcha gasped at the nearness of the stranger, for she'd only lost track of him in the time it took to pick up her cloak.

"And you've the footfall of a ghost," she shot back. Already she could feel her skin warming, when such an approach should make the blood rushing it flee. "And a smart man, as I recall, should run fast as he can from the sirens I've heard about."

"Hah, a sharp wit and tongue to match."

The stinging compliment disconcerted Sorcha all the more. "I've no mind to speak long, so say what you must."

A momentary scowl grazed his face, but he kept his voice cordial. "Fine then. Your mother, your birth mother, nursed me to health from a near fatal wound. I promised to—"

Her birth mother … alive? Sorcha wrestled between disbelief and shock. After so long? It had been a contrary solace to think that her parents had never searched for her because they couldn't … because they were dead.

Why now?

Surely it was a lie.

But how could he know she was adopted?

"I ... I'm sorry." Sorcha shook the seesaw of her debate to catch up. "You promised to *what?*"

"I promised her I'd come to Din Guardi and search for you."

"Come to buy me back with *that,* I suppose?" Sorcha eyed the plump purse tied to the man's belt.

That would more than pay off the moneylender.

Instinctively, the man's hand went to it. "Nay, lassie. This is mine. 'Tis land your mathair offers ... and her love."

Bitterness smacked down Sorcha's rise of hope. "Her love," she scoffed. "'Tis too late for that. I had a good mother *and* father, parents who would have hunted for me to the ends of the earth if I'd been taken from them. But *nay.*" She silently cursed her stinging eyes. "My blood folk left me to the whim of the fates, and thankfully the Wyrds were kinder than they. Wulfram and Aelwyn are the parents who filled a child's broken heart with love, not this woman who sends you so late with an offer of land. I've no more need for it than for her."

"The land can save you from marrying an old man and submitting that lovely body of yours to him."

So that silver gaze had been feasting on more than Sorcha's inner self. Which, by Freya's curse, seemed to ignite on its own at the thought that this Caden knew so much about her.

"Cynric offers me land and wealth, as well as his love," she replied. "Old he may be, but he is kind and gentle, a sword-friend of my departed father who has known me all my years here." She lifted her chin at the man in defiance of the plaintive gaze. As if he needed her to say yes to going with him. Sure, such need reached out and touched her, making her shiver with uncertainty. "So you can see, sir—"

"Caden," he reminded her.

"You can well see, *Caden,* I've no need for anything you have to offer, so step aside." And why should it matter so much to him whether she went or stayed?

"You heard her. Off with you, now." Gemma, who'd been helping Utta make beds on the floor about the hearth, tugged on the stranger's tunic as though to pull him away.

Caden gave the little woman a cursory glance. "I will, *mite*, when I've finished with the lady."

Gemma marched off, mumbling under her breath as if to make the man think she might be conjuring some sort of spell, but his chuckle belayed any concern he might have. Yet, when he turned back to Sorcha, his purse was no longer at his side.

Oh, Gemma, not this one! Every alarm in Sorcha's body told her this Caden was not one to be trifled with.

"There's nothing left to say, sir," Sorcha declared. Maybe if she could get Gemma alone, they could figure a way to return it. "Tell her to keep her land."

But the man moved to block her path down from the raised gallery. "I have lots more to say, milady. I've not come all this way to leave unheard. Have you Sassenach no sense of hospitality?"

"Sorcha, we'd best be goin' home soon," Utta called to her as she drew on her shawl, making ready to leave. "Mind if I walk with ye?"

"We'll talk a bit more, thank you, miss," the stranger told her.

Polite, but bullheaded.

"That would be lovely, Utta. I was just saying good night to this fine gentleman," Sorcha replied to the coded question. It was a signal among the tavern staff for discerning when a patron caused, or looked as if he were about to cause, trouble.

The unsuspecting Caden was about to take a trip to the land of temporary darkness and painful awakening. Mann, the tavern keeper, waited just around the partial wall on which Sorcha had hung her cloak—with a club that had sent many an unruly patron on such a journey.

"Leave me be now, sir," she warned him, her voice loud enough to garner the attention of the people trying to settle on the floor. "I'll have none of your nonsense."

Sorcha made to push past him, but Caden grabbed her arm.

"Let me go," she demanded, "*then* I'll talk."

But as she pulled away, he mistook her action as intent to escape. His fingers tightened like iron tongs, making her wince in pain. Yet there was a plea in his words. "It wasn't like you thought, lassie."

What? Sorcha looked past him, widening her gaze as if to shout "No!" at the tavern keeper before he carried out his intent or gave himself away.

"Your father died," Caden continued, "trying to find—"

But it was too late. Down came the club. The tall stranger crumbled to his knees, his face a mirror of surprise, and sprawled forward on the gallery step. Sorcha jumped back with a gasp.

Across the room, some of the Cymri guests who'd witnessed the attack started to their feet, but Mann held up his hand. "I've no quarrel with you, sirs. This 'un was in his cups and manhandlin' the lady," Mann explained hastily. "I doubt yer countrymen take that sort o' thing any more kindly than mine."

The two men hesitated, uncertain, glancing from Sorcha to the unconscious Caden … and to a few of the Saxon patrons who were also stirring, ready to defend Mann and the ladies.

"But I'd forego yer lodgin' coin, if one of ye'd help me settle him amongst ye, till he comes around."

Money talked to Cymri and Saxon alike. They came forward, eager to help.

Fingers shaking, Sorcha pinned her cloak, her mind racing as to how to get the man's money back to him without being seen.

"Go home, lassies," Mann told her and Gemma, who stood ready by the door. "I'll tend to this 'un as always. No doubt he'll think better of botherin' women, come tomorrow."

"We'll see you tomorrow's eve, Mann," Gemma said, stepping outside and leaving Sorcha little choice but to follow. The scrape of the stranger's boots on the floor as his countrymen dragged him across the room echoed in Sorcha's ears as she hastened after Gemma and closed the door behind her.

"Would you'd left Caden's purse on his belt," she told Gemma as they departed from the flickering light of the lantern beside the entrance. "I was trying to think of a way to give it back."

Gemma stopped midstride. "'Twas *yours*. He said as much. Your inheritance."

"My inheritance was land, Gemma."

"If there is one," Gemma countered. "He fancied you, and that is certain."

Yet his appraisal had been different from others who simply sought a wench to warm their night. Gathering her cloak closer, Sorcha hurried even more toward the alley. Gemma practically had to run to keep up.

"And you can't pay Wada with *land* tomorrow, unless it is here in Bernicia with a clear title from its lord," Gemma argued. "Slow down!"

Sorcha had to force herself to obey. She wanted to put as much distance between her and the stranger as possible. "He'll know we took the money."

"No one saw a thing, him included."

Which of course was true. Gemma was good at her craft.

"And even his own kind saw he gave you trouble. 'Twas more than reason enough for Mann to do what he did. That Caden of Lothian is a giant."

Sorcha could imagine just how large he must have appeared to Gemma. She rounded the corner of the street and stepped into an alley leading straight to the beach. Without the sun to warm it, the cold blown inland from the water made Sorcha shiver to the bone.

"I hope the children are sleeping in some hall this night," she thought aloud as they rushed through the alley to Water Street. Was it only that morning they'd left?

"Eadric will find them shelter," Gemma replied with absolute certainty. "When there's no chieftain, there's always a farmhouse to welcome a bard. And the babes have warm cloaks."

"Aye."

Ahead was the door to their home. After checking both ways to see if any mischief makers were about to give two lone women trouble, they hurried across Water Street and into the welcome haven.

"I hope little Ebyn was no trouble this night," Gemma remarked, heading straight for the banked fire in the hearth to add more turf. "He was fascinated by the weaver's loom."

Sorcha hardly heard her. What was it Caden had last said? The words hadn't quite registered at the moment.

It wasn't like you thought, lassie. Your father died trying to find—

To find what? Her? By Freya's mercy, had she been wrong all along?

Sorcha's mind spun along with her emotions but refused to settle on any conclusion. Except that Sorcha had not seen the last of Caden of Lothian. She was no soothsayer, but that much she knew.

CHAPTER SIX

The throbbing lump on the back of his head forced Caden to use every bit of his self-control not to take the tavern keeper's club to the man himself. But for the witness of Caden's fellow Cymri that Mann had misunderstood Caden's intentions toward the lady, he would have.

Although, Caden berated himself, a seasoned warrior with keen senses should have known someone was behind him. But by the time he realized the alarm widening Sorcha's incredibly green eyes was not because *of* him, but because of what was about to happen *to* him, it was too late.

And no one could account for how he'd lost his purse. He'd been unconscious, so it could have been any one of them. Perhaps the tavern master, who generously waived the fee for spending the night on his floor, although Mann had seemed genuinely distressed that he'd had to knock Caden senseless. He'd even had the woman Utta tend the swelling with a cloth wet with cold water.

The barmaid's compassion seemed real, and the willow-bark tea helped ease the throbbing in his head, although there was a lump on the back of his head the size of a goose egg. But his pride stung most at falling for one of the oldest tricks in time, his instincts dulled by a pretty face. That weakness had led to his first fall, and, by all that was holy, it was not going to ruin his second chance.

The wind off the German Sea swept in at dawn but gentled by mid-morning. Inside their home, Sorcha and Gemma counted out their earnings from the night before while Ebyn targeted the hearth with a string slingshot and dried peas, courtesy of Gemma.

"We have *more* than we need," Sorcha declared, stopping her companion from taking another coin from the leather purse lifted from the Cymri stranger. She'd measured their gold and now the silver on her scale until it came to the exact amount due Athelstan. And half the Cymri's purse remained.

Gemma grinned, hefting the purse in her hand. "We can put *this* toward spring stock."

"My *husband* will purchase spring stock. My dowry will be the goodwill of my vendors and patrons."

And Athelstan would never be part of her life again.

"You want to return it." Gemma's words held no question, just surprise.

"What if we claimed we found it outside the tavern, as if it had fallen from his belt while he relieved himself?"

"Half of it?" The skeptical arch of Gemma's brow hit its mark.

Sorcha heaved a sigh. "You're right."

But what if the stranger spoke the truth about her mother's wanting her? She'd spent the night tossing and turning, the part of her that missed Aelwyn urging her to find out more and the wounded child within telling her to forget about her birth mother. *If* she existed.

Yet someplace in Sorcha's soul, she believed it was true. But why hadn't her birth parents tried to find her before now? Some of the children captured with her had been ransomed, but not her. Resentment sank in its teeth.

"Your grief haunts you, child, as it still does me from time to time," Gemma said, placing a gentle hand over Sorcha's. "Aelwyn has only been gone a bit over a year now." Her dark eyes glazed over. "At least—"

A sharp knock on the door jolted them both. Ebyn scurried under the table as Sorcha rose to see who it was. If it was Wada, he was early. The clink of coin behind her told her Gemma gathered the moneylender's due and, Sorcha was certain, hid the stranger's purse, lest Wada help himself to that as well. His employer's status as a relative of the sheriff made the thug a bold one.

Sorcha unbolted the door and opened it. "I wasn't expecting you till eve—"

It wasn't Wada, but this visitor wasn't much better.

"Hello, Tunwulf. Milady," she added, upon noting her betrothed's only son had brought along his female companion. Mistress, so it was said.

"Good day, *Mother*," the young man mocked. He put his hand to his mouth. "But wait—I am premature, aren't I?" Tunwulf, a few years Sorcha's senior, made it no secret that he resented his father's notion to marry her. Should she give Cynric a child, he would have to share his inheritance of Elford.

His humor was made worse because Sorcha had refused Tunwulf first. She'd held off his clumsy advances with Wulfram's sword.

"Will you invite us in?" the lady demanded haughtily.

"Of course." Sorcha would wager what fortune she had that Tunwulf hadn't shared that tidbit of information with his consort. For all his noble upbringing and education, the man was no more than a renegade with allegiance to none but himself, his purse, and his appetites.

Sorcha backed away to let them enter. Beyond, a servant struggled with a trunk from a two-wheeled cart to which their riding horses were tied. "Are you in Din Guardi for the royal wedding?" she asked.

The last she'd heard from Cynric, Tunwulf had been leading a band of miscreants to wherever they might find plunder beyond Bernicia's border. It not only made relations with Mercia and their British neighbors more tenuous than they already were, but it was an embarrassment to Cynric that his allegiance to Hussa meant nothing to Tunwulf. It was the father who fought at the king's side, while the son served himself.

"Tunwulf wasn't going to attend, but I persuaded him. After all, Hering might well be the next king," the lady said.

What *was* her name? All Sorcha could recall was that she was a Briton, an outcast from her home for practicing witchcraft by all accounts. Not all Britons were Christian, but those who were could be a hysterical lot. Not that Sorcha believed in magic. Magic was no more than illusion performed by a master gleeman. Manipulation, not otherworldly spells, was the art of women like this one.

"Wise advice, Lady Rhianon," Gemma said. "Will you have some tea?"

"Yes, do sit down," Sorcha murmured.

Leave it to Gemma. Sorcha's companion forgot nothing, including the obligation of hospitality.

Where *were* her wits? Sorcha fretted. She hadn't had a clear thought since last night.

At that moment, Ebyn shot out from under the table. Lady Rhianon shrieked as if she'd seen a rat. Tunwulf swore at the boy, who promptly, rather than effectively, hid behind Gemma.

"Ebyn is a lad we took in. He's very skittish," the little woman explained, undaunted. "An orphan." She motioned toward the bench at the crude board. "Do sit while I make the tea."

"Is he *another* of your rescues?" Tunwulf asked. "You know all of Din Guardi thinks you lost your mind when you lost your parents, the way you've been purchasing Cymri brats."

"*I* was once one of those Cymri brats," Sorcha reminded him. "But how I spend my money is no one's concern but my own. Your father and I agreed on that before the contract of our betrothal was made."

"Were you my betrothed, that would not happen."

Tunwulf's estimation of himself was more than she could tolerate.

"That, sir, is why I did not accept *your* offer," Sorcha threw back at him.

Given the sharp slant of Rhianon's blue gaze toward her companion, Sorcha would have won her bet. Tunwulf *had* been keeping his secrets.

The man laughed as the noose of his deception tightened about his neck. "Silly woman, that was a *test* ... to see if you fancied Father for his kindness, as you profess, or his wealth, which I will eventually inherit."

Well played. Though if the woman believed him, Sorcha had sorely overestimated her.

"All except the property he has gifted to me," Sorcha reminded Tunwulf. "And should the Wyrds bless us with a son, well—"

She didn't have to finish. A shade of furious red betrayed Tunwulf's true feelings.

Fearing her own discomfort at begetting a child with a man twice her age might betray her, Sorcha turned abruptly to fetch four wooden cups from the cupboard containing her and Gemma's food stores and limited tableware. Flat bread served mostly for plates when there was meat to be had. The cups doubled as bowls or porringers.

"Given Father's age and health, that's not a likely event," Tunwulf pointed out. Though the clench of his fist revealed he wasn't as certain or pleased as he made out.

"Actually," Lady Rhianon began as she drew off a pair of kid gloves as rich as the vibrant royal cloak she wore, "*you* are going to the royal wedding. Thane Cynric asked Tunwulf and I to deliver something you might wear, since most of your belongings were lost last year. Not that a tavern singer would likely know what is appropriate for such an occasion."

And a slut would? Sorcha bit her tongue. "That is very kind of Elford's lord ... and you. But—"

A knock, followed by the servant's "The trunk, milord," sounded from the other side of the door.

Sorcha swung about to answer it. "But I've work to do at the tavern," she said over her shoulder. "I am no man's wife yet." Still, her heart was atwitter at the idea of a new dress—

"But you may be singing, Sorcha," Tunwulf called after her, "at the royal court of Din Guardi."

"What?"

"What?" Gemma echoed Sorcha with equal astonishment, stopping midstride toward the table with her steaming pitcher of tea.

Sorcha turned to question Tunwulf, but he motioned toward the door and rose to take the trunk from the servant.

"It was Rhianon's idea," Tunwulf told her as she lifted the latch and pulled the door open.

Without so much as a thank-you to the poor man, the younger Elford took the small trunk from him and dismissed him.

"Will you come in and warm yourself by the fire?" Sorcha asked the servant.

The servant shifted his gaze beyond Sorcha to Tunwulf. Whatever he saw made him shake his head. "Nay, milady. I've got to get back to me pony. 'E don't like bein' left alone, ye know." He pointed toward the sun, now high overhead. "'Tis a fine enough day for this time o' year."

"Wait." Sorcha picked up one of the cups Gemma had poured and returned to the door, where she handed it to the meanly attired cart driver. "Sip on this."

"*Rescuing* children." Tunwulf glanced toward the corner, where Ebyn sat quiet and wide-eyed. "*Serving* servants." He snorted. "If you are going to do honor to our house, you must learn to act the lady and"—he put an arm around his companion—"my Rhianon is going to teach you."

"My father was a *king* in Gwynedd," Rhianon replied.

Sorcha longed to ask her, why then did a princess consort with the likes of Tunwulf? "I have never been in a royal court," she admitted instead.

Rhianon left her tea to open the chest. "Come, see what I've chosen for you. The dresses belonged to Tunwulf's late mother, but I'm sure your dwarf can alter them to fit you."

"Gemma is not mine," Sorcha corrected. "She is a free woman and dear friend."

Rhianon's mouth drew into a rosy *O* of dismay. "I'm so sorry, Gemma. I'd just assumed—"

"You're not the first, milady." Gemma had clearly not made up her mind on Rhianon either. Elsewise, one could mince an onion with the edge of her words. "And I *am* handy with a needle." Curiosity spurred her closer as Rhianon lifted the lid.

To Sorcha's astonishment, the late lady of Elford had excellent taste. No dowdy colors here. There were two overdresses with gusseted skirts for fullness—one of the softest moss-green wool, its long sleeves and hem bedecked with a darker contrasting shade, and another of fine russet trimmed in a tablet band of russet and black chevrons. To complement them was a stiff brocade robe, in shades of bronze that fell to the knee with dark fur trim. And there were the most delicate of linen undershifts with embroidery such as Sorcha had never seen. And ribbons and veils and strings of glass beads and pearls—

"I assured Lord Elford that you will be the most beautiful woman there." Rhianon held up the green dress to Sorcha, her blue gaze dancing with the delight of a sister.

Perhaps Sorcha had misjudged her. From Gemma's approving smile, Sorcha knew that Rhianon had chosen well for her. Sorcha had sold the makings for such finery through her father's business but had never worn anything like this.

"And these are my mother's also." Tunwulf reached into the bottom of the trunk and withdrew a fabric-covered chest with three drawers.

The first drawer contained a necklace from the Far North made of three golden strands of amber with ear cuffs from which dangled three strands no more than the length of a finger joint. The second contained a gold torc with one end spiraling into a Cymri medallion with a large emerald from the East at its center. And in the third drawer were brooches, both gold and silver, some jeweled or inlaid with colored glass, all exquisitely formed by both Cymri and Saxon jewel smiths.

"'Tis a king's ransom," Sorcha gasped, unable to believe what Tunwulf displayed on the tabletop. "You must take these back." If word got out that she and Gemma housed such a fortune, every thief on the waterfront would be after them. "It isn't safe to keep them here."

"But they're yours," Tunwulf protested halfheartedly. Surely it vexed him to see Cynric so generous with what he considered his. "Father insists."

"And if you want her to wear them at the wedding, then you'll take the jewels now," Gemma explained. "Unless you'd invite our misfortune."

After a moment of silence, Rhianon placed a beringed hand on Tunwulf's thick bicep. "Perhaps the women are right, dearest. The docks are full of unsavory sorts. I can't understand why your father has allowed his bride-to-be to remain in such a place, singing in taverns to survive."

"Because I asked for a year to grieve my parents and pick up the pieces of my life," Sorcha said in Cynric's defense. "Lord Elford is a kindhearted man." More than she could say of his son, who profited from slaves taken during his renegade raids into Cymri territory … after the women had been brutalized and the children half-starved.

Tunwulf spoke up. "And now it's time you acted like a woman betrothed to the ealdorman of the king. Father expects you to move to the royal keep from hence until your wedding."

"Since you speak Cumbric so well," Rhianon injected, "*I* suggested he ask the prince to appoint you as an attendant to Princess Eavlyn."

The clothing was wonderful. The jewels beyond anything Sorcha ever imagined wearing. But it would take more than the contents of that trunk to prepare Sorcha for royal court, much less attending a princess. Unless attending meant entertaining her or showing her how to thimblerig. Sorcha grew clammy beneath the weight of her shift and plain woolen dress.

And what would become of Ebyn and Gemma? The laddie needed someone to care for him. Just the thought of leaving her cozy, if humble, abode without Gemma and Ebyn made Sorcha feel as if her great plan for the future was closing in on her as fast as a Leaf Fall fog.

"I need to sit," Sorcha said, dropping onto the other bench.

"When?" Gemma asked. She came up behind Sorcha and rested comforting hands on her shoulders. "When is all this to happen?"

"Why, as soon as possible," Rhianon replied. "The princess is already at Din Guardi."

"Fortunately you are close to my mother's size, so your" —Tunwulf shifted his words before insulting Gemma again— "*companion* should be able to have your clothes ready by the morrow."

"*Tomorrow!*" The blood drained from Sorcha's face and straight out her toes.

"And I shall be with you," Rhianon reassured Sorcha. "You needn't worry about the princess. I can instruct you how to act and help you dress, since Gemma won't be allowed in the royal bowers."

Much as Sorcha wanted to take comfort in that, she couldn't. The same inner warning that troubled her last night about the stranger was ringing again. But this time her circumstances had gone from bad to worse. Whatever would she do without Gemma?

CHAPTER SEVEN

Caden had finagled the location of Sorcha's home out of the port reeve and hastened toward it as soon as his wits were about him. An attendant waiting with a cart and two horses in front of the warehouse told Caden that Sorcha had visitors. Patience not being one of his virtues, Caden paced in the alley until he heard the door open, followed by voices.

Curiosity drew him to the corner in time to see a well-dressed man and a woman emerge, leaving Sorcha standing at the door pale as ash, as though she might be sick at any moment. The gentleman placed a box in the cart and then helped his lady companion atop a fine bay. He must have said something humorous, for the lady threw back her head and laughed, her velvet hood slipping off.

The haunting familiarity of the laugh, followed by the sight of an upswept mass of golden hair and a face Caden could never forget drove him flat against the wattle-and-daub wall of the building as though belly-punched by a battering ram. Now it was he who felt sick. But for the wall's support, he might have slumped into the mud. By all that was unholy, he had seen a ghost. The ghost of his late wife, his curse and downfall.

"Rhianon." Just the whisper of her name formed a cold knot of dread in his chest, squeezing the very breath out of him.

But how? She'd leapt off a cliff to her death. Dozens had seen it.

Caden remained in place until he heard the horses' hoofbeats and creak of the cart wheels retreating toward the stockade fortress that towered over the sandy beachhead. When he peered round the corner again, the street in front of Sorcha's establishment was empty, save for a fishmonger pushing a cart of special orders for the taverns and houses in the finer section of the village. Tuesday—also known as Tewsday—was the Din Guardi market day, but fresh seafood sold any day of the week.

He watched the retreating figures growing smaller along the causeway leading to the royal seat atop the rock. Perhaps he'd been mistaken. He hadn't gotten a head-on look at her face, but that laugh and profile he knew by heart. Perhaps the woman had simply borne an uncanny resemblance to his late wife. And Rhianon couldn't have a twin. If so, neither her mother nor the secondborn would have survived, for it was commonly thought that the secondborn was spawn of the Devil. Both mother, for consorting with a demon, and her child would have been put to death.

Faith, he needed a drink. More than one. But Caden had put drunkenness behind with Rhianon and his past. Like a pretty face, it made him vulnerable. Besides, he had no coin to pay for it, even if he *were* of a mind to go back to his old ways.

Instead he walked past the warehouses along Water Street toward the strand of sand spreading north of the towering Din Guardi stronghold. Caden passed small craft, turned bottom up just beyond the reach of the tide line. Some children dug with sticks in the sand for mussels, while younger ones chased seabirds from their feast among the slippery green algae left behind by the ebbing tide. No doubt the children belonged to the fishermen who lived in the mean, isolated cottages along the barren strip.

Caden wasn't sure how long he'd walked before his breath returned to some semblance of normal. As he propped himself against one of the cobles, he allowed the combined sounds of laughter and gulls and the sun dancing off the waves to work like a balm to his rattled nerves. If God were anywhere, He was in these things.

"The heavens declare the glory of God; and the firmament sheweth His handywork," a voice boomed behind Caden, almost as if the Almighty had read his thoughts.

Except that Caden knew that particular voice well. He pivoted away from the sea to see Father Martin standing behind him.

"Martin." It wasn't much of a greeting, but the priest's uncanny timing left Caden a bit disconcerted.

"Psalm 19:1," Martin informed him with an enthusiasm that ordinarily would have annoyed Caden. Strangely, he was intrigued.

"And the firmament is shouting glory to God this day, is it not?" the priest asked.

"You grow more like Emrys by the day," Caden grumbled. Merlin Emrys was another one known for coming and going like a spirit.

"I will take that as a compliment. Although the heavens and firmament were speaking to you, holding you enrapt from what I saw. What was God saying to you?"

"God said nothing. We aren't on speaking terms."

Peace.

There it was. Exactly what Caden was seeking … and hadn't found. Until now.

"God reaches out to us in many ways, through nature as well as people," Martin advised him. "Sooo"—he dragged the word out—"many ways."

Was it possible God had been speaking to *him,* who begrudged admitting that the Creator was real? Caden believed in some higher power. God, Jesus, Spirit—it was confusing. All Caden knew was that calling out for Jesus had saved him from a fate worse than most could imagine. He shivered involuntarily.

"I find God most in nature." The priest inhaled the salty air until Caden thought his chest might burst … although Father Martin always looked as if he would burst. Indeed, the priest's face glowed. Martin preempted Caden's question. "You want to know why I am so filled with joy, no?"

"You are brighter than usual," Caden admitted.

"I am," Martin agreed, "and for good reason." He turned Caden toward the north shoreline and pointed farther down the coast toward a rise of land and rock in the water. "I am a hermit by nature. So I walked to that island this morning to escape the press of this heathen place. To pray for their souls."

"Have you been endowed with the gift to walk on water like your Christ?" Caden drawled, for as far as he knew, an island was surrounded by water.

Martin ignored his skepticism. "God parts the sea with the tide twice a day to reveal a causeway of sand to the Isle of Medcaut. 'Twas *that* I crossed. Sure, my feet sank in it, but not enough to dissuade me. It was as if I was being called there. Have you ever felt drawn to isolation with nature?"

That he and a priest had anything in common left Caden even more dumbfounded. "Aye. I'm here, aren't I?" For the first time, Caden noticed that Martin was barefoot; his boots were tied to his waist. "You crazy priest, you'll catch your death of cold." Caden pointed to the seagulls running from the incoming tide and then after it. "Not even God's creatures want to wade in that icy water."

Martin chuckled. "My feet are not cold, son. My joy is such that it warms me head to toe." As if to verify his words, the old man lifted his foot for Caden. "Go on, see for yourself."

Caden seized the man's foot and then his arm to keep him from falling backward into the sand. "Father, have you indulged in too much monks' mead?" He'd never seen the man so giddy. Although his feet *were* as warm as Caden's booted ones.

"I have partaken of the Living Water, my son."

Caden groaned. Holy talk.

"While I prayed on the island for Princess Eavlyn and for God's Saxon children, He showed me a vision." Martin's gaze took on a faraway look, as if this vision were still there in a realm invisible to Caden. "I saw a monastery, there on the very ground on which I knelt. It started as a circle of stones with hundreds of eider ducks nestled among them. And it grew and grew, an Iona for the Sassenach."

Martin continued to stare through pools of emotion at the marvel with such fervor that Caden's scorn died on his lips. Whether he hallucinated or nay, this holy man truly grieved for the lost souls of a people who had murdered his own in Christ and pillaged what he held sacred.

Something within Caden crumbled at the realization. Martin didn't act holier than Caden. He *was* holier. To pray for an enemy—

"I may not live to see it, but God has shown me that these children will not be lost," Father Martin said, coming back into the focus of This World. "Nor will you be lost, Caden of Glenarden."

At the mention of his former home, Caden hastened to repair the defense that separated heart from spirit. "God may forgive me, but Glenarden will never."

Ronan had said as much when Caden last saw his eldest brother.

"God is not finished with Ronan either, Caden. We are *all* unfinished works being sculpted by His hands."

Caden wanted to rebel, to resist that infectious warmth he'd seen in Father Martin. *God wouldn't dirty His hands on the likes of me.*

"Father, I saw Rhianon today." Caden couldn't believe the words that came out of his mouth of their own accord. Something more powerful than his cynicism was at work. "She's alive."

Astonishment claimed Martin's face. "Are you certain?"

"No—" But Caden was. At least part of him was. He knew the woman he loved. *Once* loved. "Yes, I'm fairly sure."

"Where did you see her?"

"At Sorcha's home."

Martin leaned against the overturned boat, more thoughtful than alarmed. "So you found Myrna's daughter as well."

"Aye. And she wants no part of her inheritance or her mother. But 'tis Rhianon that troubles me." Caden helped Martin unfasten his boots from his belt.

"You still love her?" Martin asked, pulling stockings out of them.

"Nay, never again," Caden averred. "She's a witch ... a demoness ... a—"

"You've ample grounds for a marriage annulment."

Marriage! Caden grew cold all over. He hadn't thought about being still wed to the woman.

Martin pulled on one stocking and hastily donned a boot over it, as though the mention of Rhianon had chilled him.

"Father, I—"

What exactly did Caden want to say? Just her image caused his chest to knot. And the nausea ... it all came back to him. Feeling as if he were being turned inside out by some hideous force he had no power to fight. Watching from somewhere outside his body as he did horrid things and not being able to stop himself.

And if Rhianon had survived death, then she was even stronger. Panic knocked Caden to his knees, cold perspiration soaking him from the inside out. "Father ..." His voice cracked. "Can she do it again?"

Caden couldn't help himself. The warrior sobbed like a terrified babe and clung to the priest so hard he feared he might break the man. "I cannot f-fight what I cannot see! I would face an armed Pict or Sassenach with my bare hands, but this ..." He caught his breath. "Father, how can I stop her demons from taking me again?"

Father Martin stroked Caden's hair. "My son," he said gently, bracketing Caden's face and raising it to his. "A demon cannot occupy a place where Christ dwells."

How Caden wanted to believe that. "What must I do?"

"'Tis already done. You have called to the Christ to save you in your darkest hour—"

Caden shuddered at the memory. It had been nightmarish, yet so real.

"—and thereby acknowledged Him as your Savior."

And the nightmare had ended. At least the spiritual one. His dreams had haunted him since.

"But I am not worthy. Not fit to kiss *your* feet, much less call on Jesus."

"Yet He saved your life when you should have died … *twice.*"

At Ronan's sword point and again at the Saxon's.

"Son, Jesus has been with you all along," Martin told him.

"How?" Caden hadn't realized he'd voiced his question until the priest replied.

"You are a changed man since that day you cried out for His mercy, Caden of Glenarden. Even though bent on your own destruction, you are still changed."

No more drunkenness. No womanizing. But that was from fear.

"I have seen it," Martin continued. "Your fear of weakness has been gradually leading you toward faith. To total acceptance of Christ's saving grace. What you must learn is that in that very weakness you yourself admit, Christ becomes stronger *in* you. He enables you to do great things in His name."

The path to Sorcha had certainly been smoothed—if Caden didn't count the lump on his head or the fact she was betrothed to one of Hussa's companions. And there was that voice, so faint, yet entrenched in his mind. Had Caden been conversing, even arguing with God instead of himself?

"I need proof," he said. "I'm not a spiritual man. Give me something I can see or feel. A cross."

Martin gave him a benevolent smile, the kind a father gives a thickheaded son. But at this point, Caden didn't care. He wanted to understand what was happening to him. To get back in control.

"Fine clothes do not make a king," Martin told him. "Likewise, wearing a cross has no power. It's just a symbol that professes faith, that Christ lives within. The power comes from belief."

"Is there nothing then?"

"Yes, and it will come from within you. Like love, you cannot see it, but you will feel it and know it is there. And you will see its results, its fruits," Martin explained. "They may not be instant, but they will come, one change, one conflict at a time. Where you fell short of God's grace yesterday, you will succeed tomorrow. Pottery is not formed at once, but requires constant shaping, reshaping, hardening, glazing, baking. Our spirits are clay in the Master Potter's hands."

Just as Caden was about to protest that he wasn't a blasted piece of stoneware, something Caden's mother said came to mind. Adam had been made from clay. And man did grow bigger and bigger, from infancy to adulthood.

"So the spirit grows and matures," Caden concluded.

"So it is," Martin replied. He placed his hand on Caden's forehead. "Peace be with you, Caden of Glenarden."

Peace. Yes, that is what Caden wanted more than anything. A peace that would not leave him, as that garnered from nature's surroundings did, when he was in the presence of his fellow man.

"What is it you seek from God, Caden?"

Herthfire! And just as he began to grasp the priest's words. Was there a right or wrong answer?

"Peace—what else?"

"Everlasting life with your Father in Heaven?" Martin prompted.

Instead of nothingness? Or worse, the demons of his dreams? Caden supposed that would lead to peace.

"Yes, that will do." To Caden's astonishment, something deep within kindled. Something he had not known for a long time. Hope? Nay, more than that. More than even peace.

"I've longed for a *father*," he managed past a blade of emotion thick as a plowshare.

"I know, son."

Though the words came from Martin's lips, Caden heard them from the voice within. More of the hard wall about his heart fell away.

"And our Heavenly Father is love, *unconditional* love. No matter how much we fail Him, all He asks of us is that we try again. He even picks us up to help with a second chance."

As his maithar had when he'd fallen as a child, Caden recalled. Not Tarlach, though. The only way to get his father's attention was to invoke his wrath. The hurt was unbearable, even now twenty-odd years later. And there was no holding it back. It bled from his soul, racking his body, wringing his eyes until Caden wondered where the water came from.

"If, then, you wish to inherit everlasting life with the loving Father on High, keep the commandments: *'Love the Lord thy God with all thy heart, and with all thy soul, and with all thy strength, and with all thy mind; and thy neighbor as thyself.'*"

"I will." At least Caden intended to try.

"With God's help," Martin added.

"Aye, I will, with God's help." Caden frowned. "Though calling Him God makes Him sound so far away."

"Jesus called Him *Abba* … which is much like our da," Martin clarified. "Something tells me God won't mind if you do as well."

Abba. It felt right.

Father Martin spit on his thumb and made the sign of the cross on Caden's forehead. "Receive then, this sign of the cross on your brow and on your heart. Trust with your whole being in the Word, and lead a life that will make you fit to be a dwelling place for the Holy Spirit."

Abba. The earlier quickening in Caden began to warm, igniting an otherworldly flame that crept slowly to the furthest reaches of his body.

"Pray with me, child of the Living God," Martin said. "Lord, if it pleases You, hear our prayer …"

"Lord, if it pleases You, hear our prayer …"

"By Your supreme power, protect Your chosen son Caden, now marked with the sign of our Savior's holy cross …"

"By Your supreme power, protect me, now marked by the Savior's holy cross, Father …" Caden's clasped hands seemed welded by the heat that flowed through them.

"Let *me* treasure this first sharing of Your sovereign glory …" Martin coached.

Was *that* what it was? Caden wondered, echoing Martin's words. For no longer did he feel the cold, damp sand beneath his knees or the sea breeze lifting away his cloak to penetrate his clothing. This … this *glory* would not allow it.

"Help me to keep Your commandments that I might attain the glory of Heaven to which those born anew are destined, through Christ our Lord. Amen."

As Caden repeated the plea, he began to understand the glow he'd seen earlier on Father Martin's face. Like that of a man standing too close to a blazing hearth fire, yet this fire came from within. Caden started to rise with it, but Martin was not finished.

Holding up a finger to stay him, the priest walked to where the water lapped upon the beach. On gathering a palmful, he returned to Caden.

"Almighty and everlasting God, Father of our Lord Jesus Christ, look with favor on Your son Caden, whom it pleases You to call to this first step in the faith. With this water, wash him of all inward blindness."

The tiny bit of seawater Martin poured on Caden's head penetrated his thick hair. It was a small amount, yet it washed over his spirit like a soaking rain.

"Sever all snares of Satan that have heretofore trapped him. Open wide for him, Lord, the door to Your Fatherly love."

Fatherly love. The words knocked Caden from his knees, prostrating him on the damp sand. The control he'd sought was gone. In his mind's eye a small boy escaped from his earthly body to take off across the beach, dancing joyfully out of control with upstretched arms toward Heaven where his Abba watched.

"May the seal of Your wisdom so penetrate him as to cast out all tainted and wicked inclinations, and let in the fragrance of Your lofty teaching, that he shall serve You gladly in Your church and grow daily more perfect, through Christ our Lord. Amen."

But Caden the man could not move. A floating sensation precluded the need, as if Abba was gathering him up in His arms. And from deep inside Caden's very soul—aye, at last he'd found it beneath the refuse of pain and rejection that had buried it for so long—he shouted, "Amen!" It was no more than a whisper to his ears, but in his mind his Abba heard it. And He smiled at His adopted son.

CHAPTER EIGHT

Sorcha agreed to take Ebyn down to the beach after midday. The laying breeze and bright afternoon sun made even the cool October day seem warmer. Gemma decided to join them, bringing along her hornpipe.

"What more can we ask for?" her friend had demanded when Sorcha initially balked at the idea of leaving the haven of her home so soon. "A beautiful day *and* a fine man to practice your dancing with."

Her dancing. One thing more for Sorcha to worry about. Aye, she'd been taught basic manners, but she was a singer and musician. She played *for* the dancers. Yet, as a thane's betrothed, she would be expected to be one.

"You simply play the tune with your feet as fingers upon the ground, which is your instrument," Gemma instructed from her perch on a log washed ashore long ago, judging by its salt-dried finish.

"Milady, will you dance?" Ebyn, solemn and gallant in his role, bowed as Gemma had taught him. Despite her apprehension, a smile tugged at Sorcha's lips as she responded in kind.

"Now you, Sorcha, tap the sand with your feet. No, no," Gemma cried out as Ebyn started one way and Sorcha the other. "I should imagine Thane Cynric would have you dance near him. *Together*. Hold hands, perhaps … not too close. And not as if you fear catching the pox," she added when they pulled back at arm's length. "We are frolicking together to my music. And make eye contact with your partner. Smile."

And so it went. Walking, skipping, turning, weaving, sometimes hand-holding, but always near. At least until Ebyn's attention was thwarted by some youngsters his own age batting oyster shells with sticks along the water's edge.

For a lad his age, he'd been uncommonly well behaved, given the morning they'd had. But Sorcha had seen the energy he and the other children ran off when she and Gemma had taken them to the beach to get them out of the house during their short stay. *Poor fellow must be about to burst with it,* she thought.

"I've an idea," she said. "Ebyn, why don't you run off with yon lads for a bit, while I practice? When I'm ready for a partner, I'll call you."

The grin he gave made her small consideration well worthwhile. "Aye, thank you, milady."

He was off before Gemma could put in her thoughts. But from the way she followed Ebyn with affection in her gaze, she approved. "'Tis no wonder Tilda offered to keep him again tonight without pay. He's a dear *and,*" she added, "Tilda swears he has potential at the loom."

"I know what you're thinking." Sorcha lifted her unbound hair off her neck to cool herself from the exertion. "But Tilda is old enough to be his grandmother. What would become of the lad, were she to die before he's grown?"

"Aye," Gemma sighed in agreement. "Let's try something slower." Putting the pipe to her lips, she began to play a dignified tune.

Step, two, three. Sway to the music. Step, two, three.

"Skip," Gemma said to the side as Sorcha beat out the time on the sand with the ball of her foot.

Curtsy, two, three. Sorcha stooped low. *Up, two, three—*

And there stood the Cymri stranger, as if conjured by elf magic, offering his hand. "Well done, milady."

Sorcha and the music stopped. Finally, shock freed her tongue. "How did you find me?"

"Well, now, you"—he fingered a lock of her hair—"and your companion don't exactly blend into the crowd. Not that there's much of one."

He only touched her hair, but that and his dazzling smile caused her pulse to trip. Indeed his humor was uncommonly bright, given what had happened to him. Sorcha cut her gaze to Gemma, who seemed as taken aback as she.

"Gemma," he prompted, "if you'll continue, I'll—"

"Now what would a man like you know of dancing in a king's court?" Sorcha challenged.

The sun played on his golden hair, as wavy as the sea and tamed with a band of leather at his neck today. When he slipped his cloak over his head and tossed it near Gemma on the sand, there was a fringe of the same gold showing at his throat in the vee of his tunic.

"I have danced in the courts of most of Arthur's kings," he informed her.

True, Caden spoke and acted more refined than most of the men who frequented the tavern. He even looked different from when she'd last seen him, though she was hard-pressed to say what was different.

"So you're a prince, then?" Gemma spoke up.

Wistfulness graced the gaze he turned to her. "I *was*, milady, but today I'm a soldier. Nothing more."

A prince? Now *that* intrigued Sorcha all the more.

"Courtly dance is nothing more than moving to the music as nature bids in a closer space than the outdoors. In it, man and woman are companions, one mirroring the other," he declared, before she could frame her curiosity into a question. "Lady Sorcha," he said, taking Sorcha's hand.

"I'm not a thane's wife yet," she reminded him, although she allowed him to position her opposite him. He certainly exuded more charm than last night.

But charm could cloak wolf as well as lamb.

"The tune you were playing is perfect, Gemma. A fling is more suited to the freedom of meadow than the confines of a hall."

Sorcha wasn't certain exactly how Gemma would take to his compliment. She looked at Caden as though she were reading one of their song sheets, looking past the words to what lay behind them.

"Why?" she asked bluntly. "Why are you so interested in teaching Sorcha to dance?"

Caden gave a short laugh. "Milady, it is a lovely day beside the sea, and Sorcha is a lovely woman. Is it so odd that a man should want to while away the afternoon in her company, when yon Din Guardi fortress is so thick with people a man must walk sidewise through them?"

Lighthearted. Maybe that was it. Like Ebyn kicking away at an oyster shell on the beach, laughing at this fine dose of life.

Caden's lips twisted wryly. "And I've no coin to pay for drink and conversation at a friendly tavern. Seems I was robbed last night while unconscious from our *misunderstanding*."

Had his eyes narrowed at Gemma, or was guilt causing Sorcha to imagine it? Though if Caden did suspect them of the theft, his beguiling act was worthy of a master gleeman.

As Gemma put her pipe to her lips, Caden turned back to Sorcha. "Your blush shames the fairest rose, milady," he said, smiling as he bowed low.

"A sunny day adds color to every woman's complexion," Sorcha managed during her curtsy. Though guilt probably had its hand in the mix as well. When she straightened, Caden's hand was outstretched to meet her own.

"Dance is much like courtship," he told her, smoothly leading her through half skips. "The touch"—his fingers closed on hers—"is as close as the lovers dare to get, for others are watching."

Whether it was the word *lovers* or the touch that made her trip and kick sand over his feet, Sorcha couldn't say. He caught her waist, steadying her, guiding her into a spin that went straight to her brain. "But their hearts are already entwining, beating drum to drum in a melody of love."

Her blood hammered through her fingertips in answer to his. Pinpricks of awareness spread from the contact like nothing she'd felt before. She couldn't stop it, save to break away and run.

"And sway, milady," he told her, letting go just when Sorcha thought she could bear it no more.

As Sorcha swished her skirts to the right and left, he clapped hands. And then one hand hovered at her waist—not touching, though she could feel its heat as they circled in opposite directions. And then she was his mirror again, standing side by side, connected only by their thrumming fingertips.

"Undoubtedly, your betrothed will continue to offer compliments. You are light as a fairy on your feet...."

He hadn't noticed the sand on his boots.

"*Ma chroi*, you have put the twinkle in the eye of every man here this night," Caden continued. "Any man with red blood in his veins."

Ma chroi ... my heart.

"Now twirl," he said, lifting one of her hands over her head as she spun like a puppet on unseen strings from his fingertips.

"And ..." He backed away to face her. "Mirror, milady."

Sorcha mimicked him, dancing one hand on hip, the other in the air. Then his lower hand slipped to her waist and hers flew to his of its own accord. Lean muscle, devoid of excess flesh, awaited it. Indeed she could feel the battle-toughened sinew working in sync with its counterparts beneath his woolen tunic. Around and around they skipped.

"Alas, this is as close as you and your betrothed will come to the joys of your bower, but your pulse will quicken just the same. And the soft pine green in your gaze will deepen as it does now to the bright gloss of the holly."

If Sorcha's gaze had changed color, it was not the only one. What manner of magic was this, that the cool polish of silver gray could shimmer so bright as to draw her like a moth to its flame?

"And," he said, backing away and breaking the contact that had shaken every sense she had to full wakefulness and more, "we bow."

Sorcha curtsyed low and slow, giving herself time to catch her breath.

Gemma put down her pipe and clapped. "Well done, well done."

Sorcha could not believe her ears. Had Gemma been enchanted as well?

"Well done, yourself, Gemma," Caden replied. "You should share the gallery with Sorcha at the tavern."

"I do at times," the little woman replied, "though more are willing to toss a coin in a cup taken to them, than in one that stays in one place. But you two—" She clasped her hands in delight. "You dance as if you were one, instead of flailing all about the place like chickens with their heads cut off. It is almost poetry to watch."

"Caden led me well," Sorcha said. She pulled her cloak, fastened by a brass brooch at her neck, more tightly around her, as though she'd taken a sudden chill. She had. The distance between them robbed her of her partner's warmth. "If Elford dances as well, I shall have no worries."

"I had hoped, milady, to speak with you once more about your betrothal and my proposal. *Then*," he emphasized, stopping Sorcha's objection with a finger to her lips. Surely elfin magic forced her attention to his mouth, tempting her with more than words. "I will trouble you with it no more."

"Then let's hear it." Gemma patted the log next to her for Sorcha to sit. "'Tis the least we can do for your generous help."

Sorcha didn't believe in magic, but she took a seat, obedient.

"Apparently," Caden began, "your birth father did try to find you. He bribed a slave trader to ask about and discovered that a red-haired girl your age at the time had been adopted by a Din Guardi family. And then your father went straight to Din Guardi, just this time of year, and asked around, but no one would tell him anything more. He even thought he saw you once in the marketplace, but you were gone before he could catch you."

Plausible, Sorcha thought. Her family and friends were a tightly knit group and not likely to tell a stranger anything about their own.

"Then he fell afoul of the likes who robbed me last night. But *they* left him to die on this very beach."

Sorcha could almost see her father, distant and faded in her mind's eyes. But his image kept merging with Wulfram's until she wasn't certain which she mourned. "He died *here?"* she whispered.

"Nay," Caden answered. "He managed to make it back home to Trebold, where the chill from being abandoned for dead on a wet beach took him." Caden dropped to his haunches, the thick muscle causing the woolen weave of his breeches to pull taut across fine thighs. "But even through her grief and hardship over the years, your mother never gave up hope of finding you. And that is why I am here," Caden concluded matter-of-factly. "I'm the first to agree to come look for you. I was obliged to do so for her kindness."

"I am certain the lady did face grief and hardship, losing a child and a husband as she did," Gemma empathized. "What was her name?"

Myrna.

"Myrna." Caden echoed Sorcha's thought aloud to Gemma. The name gently cradled Sorcha's heart. "A fine, honest woman who makes a living running a hostel at the river crossing. She provided for Arthur and his companions on this Leaf Fall's campaign."

"I wouldn't say such things too loudly, were I you," Sorcha warned him. "The king lost some of his good thanes on the borders."

"I will take that advice to heart, milady. And now …" He rose, a golden giant against a blue sky. "I'd best be making my way to the fortress. I've made good my promise to Myrna. The rest"—he offered a hand each to Gemma and Sorcha to help them to their feet—"is up to you. Good day, ladies."

With that and a short bow, the Cymri sauntered down the beach toward Ebyn and the boys. Language never posing much of a barrier for children—the friends were now batting seashells into the sea. Her mind awash with questions tossed by her unsettled heart, Sorcha watched Caden borrow one of their sticks to try his hand at the game. Once struck, his shell soared over the surf and landed far beyond. In an instant, he was a master, showing the other lads how to hit the shells just so.

Just as he'd taken over Sorcha's dance. They'd danced as one, Gemma said.

"He's a strange one," Gemma remarked at Sorcha's side. "I can't make him out."

"Aye."

"But something tells me we haven't seen the last of him."

"Is that good or bad?" Sorcha wondered aloud.

"I haven't made up my mind yet."

"Do you regret stealing his purse?"

Gemma looked at Sorcha as if she'd grown a third eye in the center of her brow. "Of course not! I did what I had to do. And speaking of which—" She glanced at the sun dipping toward the Cheviot Hills to the southwest. "We'd best get home. We've got the boy to feed and need to leave early to meet Wada at the tavern."

Wada. Sorcha hesitated, stunned. Stunned that she'd forgotten about the moneylender's man. Stunned that she'd even forgotten her anxiety over going to Hussa's keep. Instead of fretting, she'd danced *as one* with a total stranger. And she had warmed not only to the man, but also to his mission.

"You go on ahead," Gemma told her. "I'll fetch the lad and catch up."

Sorcha nodded without so much as a look toward her friend. She knew Gemma sensed her inner turbulence.

It was too much to take in all at once. One foot went before the other as though they marched to someone else's command. Yet with each step, the resentment Sorcha had built toward her parents faded like footprints in the sand. The very sand where her father had nearly died, trying to find her.

And to this day her mother still tried.

CHAPTER NINE

Sorcha stared into the pot of peas she stirred, trying to sort her thoughts. But if anything, they swirled like the thick soup in the pot. She'd buried her parents in her seven-year-old mind. It had been the only reason she could think of for their not coming for her. That had given Sorcha a certain peace, a freedom to love her kind, adoptive parents.

Just the thought of her father lying cold and wounded on that beach, the image of Myrna sacrificing to hold on to his land for Sorcha's sake …

Sorcha stood and squeezed her head between her palms as if that might stop the jumble of thought and emotion waging war in her head. She'd cried herself numb, hardly remembering Gemma's catching up with her in the alley.

"I imagine Ebyn will be here soon," the dwarf said from where she had taken one of the new dresses to examine it in the waning light from the window. "I guess we should count on feeding Caden as well before heading to the tavern."

When Ebyn had begged to stay on the beach with the other boys, Caden had offered to see Ebyn home before dark.

"Do you think you're up to the tavern?" Motherly concern infected Gemma's voice.

"Of course." She wasn't, but Sorcha was committed to entertain, and she kept her commitments.

Including the one to Elford?

"You know, this shouldn't take much work at all," Gemma said, turning the dress to see its back. "This lacing takes care of the ample girth, though you're taller than Elford's late wife. I'll need you to try it on, to see if I need to add some to the hem."

"I suppose I could visit my mother as Lady Elford," Sorcha thought aloud.

Of course she meant to keep her commitment to Cynric. To even think otherwise was an affront to her honor and his.

"When her land is in Saxon hands, aye." Gemma rarely approached a hard truth with gloved words. "Good-natured as Cynric is, I don't see him approving of a trip into Lothian, unless it's a raid."

Gemma was right. Sorcha wasn't thinking clearly. "That's more Tunwulf's bent."

The villain had more lives than a cat, if all the raids he boasted of were true. Cynric's having no real sway with his son should alone be enough to make Sorcha reconsider marriage to his father.

Sorcha tamped down the rebellious thought. She would not shame her father's friend and her father's name in the court.

A knock on the door preempted the rest of her internal debate. Sure, it was Ebyn and Caden, who had dropped this awful dilemma in her lap. "You get the door, Gemma," Sorcha suggested. "I'll dip up our supper."

Gemma tossed the dress over her shoulder as she walked to the door and opened it. "Wada!"

Sorcha nearly dropped the bowl in her hand at Gemma's exclamation. Wada was supposed to come to the tavern *tonight*. Her nerves plucked mightily by yet another surprise, Sorcha hurried to where they'd stored the payment they'd barely put together.

"I should make you wait to be paid as agreed upon, but since you're here—"

"Well, what is this?" Wada fingered the rich silk of Sorcha's new dress.

Gemma clutched it all the more tightly. "It's a dress. Have you taken an interest in dressing like a woman?"

Sorcha tossed the bag of coin and valuables at him. "It's here— all of what I borrowed *and* the toll."

"Ye must have had good *collection* last night," he derided, "seein' how you was so short this time yesterday. Whose purse did you lift?"

Sorcha inserted herself between Gemma and Wada. "The prince's wedding put the patrons in a generous humor. You have your money, now off with you. I must get ready to go to the tavern soon."

Wada stared greedily at the garment. "I might be tempted to leave sooner if I had somethin' to make it worth me while. *I've* no use for such a fine dress, but I know a wench who'd warm me many a night for such as that 'un."

"Then buy one from your extorted profit, but you'll not have this one." And even if Sorcha did give it up, no wench would see it unless she paid the oaf a sum only a noblewoman could afford. Nay, Sorcha would not line his ratty pockets with gold.

She stepped to the side, as though to lean wearily on the door-jamb. Just inside it hung Wulfram's short sword, hidden beneath her hanging cloak. "*This* one is a gift from Thane Elford for his bride-to-be. He'd not take kindly to anyone taking it from me."

Wada's weasel-like gaze shifted from Sorcha to the dress. "Now, Sorcha ..." he said, bullying her backward until his bulk filled the entrance. He reached for her cheek as though to caress it, but instead he clamped her face between his thumb and fingers, digging them into the knot of her jaw muscles.

The pain hurled Sorcha back to another time. A slaver twisted her face one way, then the other. Just a child, she couldn't back away from him. His arm was like a bar of steel crushing her toward him. She couldn't flee....

"I'm sure ye can come up with some story—"

Her fingers locked on the hilt of the sword.

"—as to how it was lost, to please his lordship," Wada cajoled.

But this time she could fight. The old fear curdling in her throat gave way to a roaring rage. Sorcha pricked Wada's thick neck with the point of her father's blade before the bully even reacted to her outburst.

"'Tis not his lordship you need fear," she growled between clenched teeth, "you foul-minded son of a slop bucket."

"You crazy wench, I'll have ye arrested—"

Wada backed out of the house and into the street, Sorcha ushering him with her blade.

This time of day, laborers and fishermen found their way home along Water Street. Sorcha made certain they all heard her. "Touch me again, Wada," she shouted, "and you'll find yourself food for the fish."

"Ye've drawn blood!" In his haste to escape the press of the sword, one foot tangled with the other. Wada flailed backward, landing like a sack of grain flat on his back.

Sorcha pressed the sword against the fleshy part of the chest just below the heart. "I've a witness to what you've just tried with me"— let the folk think what they would—"and *more* now," she bellowed for their sake. "People who have no love of you, you thieving bully."

His face beetled a mix of anger and humiliation, Wada flung a curse at her and lowered his voice for her ears only. "Ye've not seen the last o' me, wench. Yer father learned the hard way about pushin' Wada about."

The hard way. A vision of fire devouring the only home she knew flashed in Sorcha's brain. "*You!*"

Sorcha had never dealt more than a scratch to dissuade any who threatened her or Gemma. But at that moment, she could already savor the plunge of her father's sword through the heart of his murderer. All she had to do was lean into it. Just lean …

Her hesitation was a mistake.

Wada hurled himself to the side, knocking the sword away with his arm before she could put her weight behind it. As it thudded to the ground, both she and Wada scrambled to retrieve it—

When a heavy, booted foot pinned it to the dirt.

"I've heard and seen enough to put a rope around your neck, villain." Caden of Lothian stood upon it, so not even Wada could wrench the weapon free.

"Stay out o' this, Cymri," Wada snarled. "You don't know *what* you heard."

"Ah, but I do," Caden said. "I heard you threaten to burn this

young lady's home to the ground, the same as you did to her parents'
… with them in it."

"I could have killed him." Hoarse fury lodged in Sorcha's
throat.

"Not in front of a street full of witnesses," Caden reminded her
lowly.

It was true. A dozen or so people drew closer, once they saw the
big blond stranger was in control of the situation.

"I'll not forget this, missy." Wada struggled to his feet and
knocked the dirt off his clothing with his big hands.

"Neither will I," Sorcha promised. Never while she drew breath.
She'd always wondered, suspected. Wada's presence often left her
parents' faces marked with concern and anger. Then came the fire—

Caden drew her from the suffocating vision. "In the meanwhile,
sir, you'd best hope a fire doesn't start in this warehouse, for three of
us heard your threat, and every man and woman here will now know
the source."

"Arson is a hangin' offense," a woman cried out.

The ruckus had brought Tilda out of her house, armed with a
broom and mad as a hornet.

"Arson ain't got nothin' to do with this," Wada averred. "I said
yer father learned his lesson the hard way *'cause 'e got in debt over
'is head*," he mocked, smug with his quick answer. "I don't know
nothin' about no fire."

But he did. Sorcha knew exactly what he'd meant.

Caden stood on her sword, but the dagger she kept lashed to her
thigh could be just as deadly. Although the witnesses who held her
back from a murderous offense would serve her purpose just as well.

"Take up your money bag and bear witness before all standing here that my debt to Athelstan is paid in full, including the toll," she demanded.

Wada reached down and hefted the bag in his hand. "Feels about right."

"Count it, Wada!" Her voice wavered along the line she walked between rage and nervous collapse. "Gemma, fetch our scale please. He'll count it now in front of witnesses."

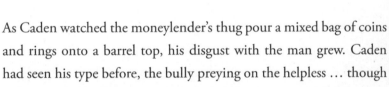

As Caden watched the moneylender's thug pour a mixed bag of coins and rings onto a barrel top, his disgust with the man grew. Caden had seen his type before, the bully preying on the helpless … though Sorcha had proven she was not as helpless as one would think. She'd even drawn a trickle of blood.

Impressed, he reached down and picked up the weapon. It was well balanced. Too short to Caden's notion of a sword, and too long to count as a knife, but deadly either way.

And it was clear Wada knew just how close he'd come to journeying to the Other Side. He was so rattled that the simple task of separating the gold from the silver and copper to weigh on the small scale Gemma had placed on a nearby barrel top proved cumbersome for his shaking hands.

"I'll be needin' a knife." Wada lifted a string of mixed precious metal coins and medallions held together by a thin leather thong.

Recognition punched Caden in the stomach. He'd won that money over the throwboard from a spice merchant in Din Edyn—one of those men who didn't trust a purse for their treasure but wore it around their neck. Outrage charged in like a bull, trampling Caden's incredulity. He'd throttle the wench—nay, *both* of them!

Instead he slapped the flat of the sword down on the barrelhead, stopping Wada from reaching for the dagger tucked in his boot. "Use this."

Wada cut the thong easily on the sharp blade. As the coins slid off, clinking into a pile, Caden shot a festering gaze at Sorcha. Too caught up in her own emotions, she didn't notice. But her dwarf companion did. And the look Gemma returned was a silent plea.

A plea! By all that was holy, Caden had been robbed by two wenches. Not even two full-grown ones. Worse, Sorcha had set him up so that the others in the tavern had thought he had made ungentlemanly advances toward her, earning him a knot on the back of the head as well. Her timing had been perfect. But then the singer, dancer, swordsman, and thief was a consummate actress as well.

Hadn't she frolicked on the beach as if learning a simple dance was her greatest worry … without so much as a pang of guilt? And he'd thought it was *his* charm breaking through her stiff resistance to her mother's wishes. The same charm he intended to use to find out more about Rhianon.

You've met your match.

The dawning staggered Caden for a moment. Until the dwarf woman clasped her hands, reaching for him with desperate dark eyes. As if the pagan mite even knew there was a God.

The last of the coins separated, Wada piled the copper on the scale and announced the weight, standing back for the man closest to him to verify. While Sorcha returned it to the pouch, the observer verified the weighing of the silver and the small bit of gold as well.

"It's all there," Sorcha announced for all to hear. "*Twice* what we borrowed to purchase a season's goods and make a home for ourselves after my family's tavern house *mysteriously*"—the word dripped with sarcasm—"burned to the ground. But then Athelstan is as much a thief as a moneylender, and Wada is worse."

"Watch what ye say, missy," Wada warned her. "Them what sows the wind will reap the whirlwind." He snatched the purse from her and tied the drawstring into a knot. "But yer debt's paid and we're done, fair and clear afore all present."

At the consensus of nods, the villain straightened, thrusting out more belly than chest. "Then good day to ye … and," he added, bowing to Sorcha, "*especially* to you, missy."

Sorcha's hand fisted the material of her skirt, answering with a glare that should have turned the man to ashes. Caden would bet the contents of Wada's bag that there was a dagger strapped to a slim, milky-white thigh beneath the common wool bunched in her fingers. And the strange thing was, though part of him was inclined to wring her lovely neck, another part admired her for her spirit.

Well, let her brandish hidden steel or try to work her wiles on him. No matter. Caden was all the wiser … *now*.

"He knows," Gemma whispered to Sorcha as she led the way into the house after the crowd dispersed.

Sorcha gave her friend a quizzical look. "Who knows what?"

While watching Wada measure out his payment, her head had begun to ache, as if all the blood in her body hammered at her brain. Sheer will alone kept her knees from buckling.

Caden slammed the door behind him, causing her to jump. "I know," he thundered, "that it was *you* two who stole my purse last night, that's who and what."

His gaze was as cold as the steel of the blade he still held in his hand.

While Sorcha could try to deny the fierce accusation there, that would require wit, the last of which had withered away under this verbal assault. She'd been plagued by pain such as this only once before. After the fire. It lasted a week with its peaks and valleys, laying her low in a dark room where she lost what little she ate before it nourished her.

Summoning every ounce of her strength, Sorcha marched over to the cupboard and opened a red-ware jar where Gemma had hidden Caden's purse. She took it out and tossed it at him.

"There's half of it. 'Tis all we have." She was spent, emotionally and physically. "We'll try to pay you back before you leave Din Guardi."

"By stealing another man's purse?" Caden sneered.

"Only if song doesn't provide enough. And if that will not do," she said, her candor bare of any emotion that might cause her head to crack like a jarred egg, "then take off my head with my sword and put me out of my misery."

"It's come again?" Alarmed, Gemma hustled to her side.

Blinking affirmation more than nodding, she gave in to Gemma's press to sit at the table.

"Is this another game of yours?" Caden's challenge rumbled from her pain-dazed head to her churning belly and back with each foot-fall he made toward the table.

"A basin, Gemma," Sorcha beseeched. The room started to swirl, drawing her toward the beams overhead. She wasn't going to be sick after all. She was going to be swept up in the whirlwind she'd sown.

At least it was a whirlwind without pain.

CHAPTER TEN

Sorcha rolled from the bench to the floor at Caden's feet like a crumpled doll. So fast, he hadn't time to register what was happening. He knelt beside her and touched her neck, where a pulse fluttered to his relief. Though she was pale as ash and cold and clammy to the touch.

"Help me get her to bed," Gemma snapped, as if this were somehow his fault.

But Caden obeyed. He gathered the unconscious woman up in his arms and struggled to his feet. Rhianon had been light as a feather, as though she had the hollow bone structure of a bird. But this one was as solid as she was tall. With a grunt, Caden straightened and adjusted his grip. A soft moan came from her pale lips.

Mumbling an apology for jostling her so, he carried Sorcha to a cot nestled against the wall next to a narrow ladder leading to a loft.

"I give you my word, I will explain what I can as soon as I give her something for her head," Gemma called to him from the cupboard, where she searched through an assortment of jars and bags. "I hope I still have some of the powder the healing woman made."

Could that be Rhianon? Witches *sometimes* healed, he argued against the part of him that scoffed at the very idea of Rhianon doing something good.

"Does this healing woman have a name?"

"Does it really matter?" Gemma shot him an exasperated glance.

Yes, it did, but Caden held his peace. Actually, he was stunned. With all that had happened this day, Caden had nearly forgotten Rhianon. After fighting the memories that haunted him night and day for the last four years, he'd been free ... for a while. Still, he determined he'd hear more of what Rhianon was about and if—*how*—Sorcha fit into her plans.

"She suffers like this often?" he asked, focusing on the latter.

"Only once before. For better than a week after her parents died, it wouldn't let up," Gemma replied. "Ach, here it is. I'm thinking Wada brought this malady back."

Uncertain what else to do, Caden unfolded a blanket from the foot of the bed and spread it over the sleeping beauty. Even though deathly pale, that was how Sorcha looked at the moment. Lovely, fragile ... and innocent.

Deceptive even now.

"Athelstan doubled the toll we owed when we didn't have enough to pay him a month ago," Gemma told him as she mixed the powder into a tea. "We'd hoped to make enough last night to pay it off—"

A timid knock on the door cut her off.

"Ebyn!" Caden had forgotten the lad. When they'd heard the confrontation between Wada and Sorcha, Caden had ordered Ebyn to stay put beside the warehouse in case things turned violent. Caden hurried to the door and opened it to see the boy shivering in the shadows cast by the setting sun.

"Come in, laddie, come in."

Ebyn was more concerned about Sorcha than warming himself by the fire. Caden assured him that Wada wouldn't be bothering them anymore and set about fixing some hot tea for the laddie while Gemma tried to get Sorcha to drink the medicinal concoction.

While Ebyn eagerly sipped his honey-laden brew, he plagued Caden with questions about the oysters, the creatures that had lived in the shells on the beach. Caden answered as best he could, but his attention was fixed on Sorcha. She took the medicine but kept her eyes closed, as if even the dim light in the room seemed to plague her. She looked dreadful now that she'd regained consciousness. Misery creased her brow.

"*I'll* take the harp and pipe to the tavern tonight," Gemma told her gently when Sorcha had drained the cup. "You stay here and let Ebyn take care of you."

Sorcha cast a half-lidded look in Caden's direction.

"If he was going to kill us, he'd have done so by now," Gemma assured her.

"Though I would have some answers," Caden injected. "When you're up to it." He stretched his long legs beneath the board. "I'm in no hurry to leave till I get them."

Gemma gathered up Sorcha's harp bag and her pipe and carried them over to the table, placing them there before settling opposite Caden on a bench smoothed by use.

"I've not much time, but you've shown yourself to be a fair man, Caden of Lothian. You well deserve a few answers." She folded her small arms in front of her with a look direct as a spear thrust. By the way she shifted her tongue from one cheek to the other, she took measure of him and the words she was about to speak.

"Taking your purse was as unfair as anything I've ever done," she said at last. "But as you have seen, we were desperate. And when I took it, I thought that the money you sported in front of me *was* this inheritance you spoke of."

The memory of the woman's greedy gaze lighting upon his purse came to Caden's mind. Were he not so distracted by Sorcha, he would have been more cautious.

"'Twasn't till later that I learned otherwise, and by then, you were out cold as fish. So it was, in essence," she reasoned, "a great misunderstanding all the way about."

"I think *misunderstanding* is a poor word for it, milady."

Gemma glanced to the bed where Sorcha either slept or listened to every word. "Be that as it may," she said, rising, "I must go, if we have a chance of making it up to you. I won't earn as much as Sorcha, but some is better than nothing. All I'm asking is that you let her rest. The medicine should make her sleep."

So first he made tea for a child, and now he was a nursemaid. Some plan God had for him, he thought, recalling Father Martin's promise of plans for him to prosper.

"I'll do it," he agreed slowly, "but I'm not going anywhere."

Staying here in Ebyn's company by a warm hearth wouldn't be so bad. It was still quieter than up in the town proper. Too many tensions betwixt Saxon and Lothian and among the Saxons themselves.

"I give you my word," Caden promised Gemma, who checked Sorcha once again before leaving, "I'll not bother the lassie. Monster that I am, I can see plain that she's sick."

The dwarf's no-nonsense demeanor softened. "And no wonder, after what she's faced this day. Barely scraping enough together to keep Wada at bay … threatened by her future son-in-law and his trollop …"

Ah hah! The man who was with Rhianon. A trollop, eh?

"… finding she has to take up residence in the royal court on the morrow, and crowning it all, finally finding out what really happened to her parents."

A tell in Gemma's voice pulled Caden back from her opinion of Rhianon. "*You* knew, didn't you? About what happened to her folks?"

"I knew a storm took two of Wulfram's ships, so he had to borrow from Athelstan to cover the loss," she told him. "When time to pay came, Wulfram was short. But the moneylender tried his underhanded ways with the wrong man. Wulfram threatened to go to the king himself if Athelstan doubled the toll like he did to us." She snorted in disdain. "The slippery eel didn't realize he'd crossed someone with Hussa's ear."

"Why didn't Wulfram ask the king for help in the first place?" Caden asked.

"Pride. We Saxons are a stubborn lot." Gemma heaved a sigh and took up her instruments of trade. "And now I must be off. Send the boy if you need me."

"I will." Caden shot Ebyn a wink.

"And Caden," Gemma said, poised in the open door.

"Aye?" he replied.

"You're no monster." She paused a moment in thought. "I've yet to make out just what you are. But I will," she promised. With that she was gone.

Caden might have taken the compliment at face value, though with Gemma it was hard to tell what was tucked in and around it. But her regard came second to the bits of information she'd given him.

After he'd fed Ebyn and tired the boy out playing a peg game, Caden sent the lad up to the loft to bed and settled on a bench, his back to the wall. Of all the kingdoms in Albion, how was it that he wound up in the same one as Rhianon? He wondered about the child she'd carried. Was it lost, or was it calling a Saxon *Father*? The only thing that Caden knew for certain was that as long as his not-so-*late* wife breathed, there would be trouble.

Glancing down, Caden found he'd clasped his hands until they were bloodless. One word filled Caden's mind. *Abba*.

"Papa!"

Sorcha's gasp brought Caden to his feet and into the present. On the cot, she tossed her head from side to side, as though wrestling with the horror she watched behind closed eyelids.

Caden sat on the edge of the cot and shook her gently. "'Tis a dream, lassie, a nightmare." He could well imagine what he drew her from. A tavern consumed in fire. Perhaps the cries of her adoptive parents burning alive. He shook her again, glad to spare her. Wishing he'd had someone to draw him out of his night terrors. "Wake up. There's no fire. You're safe in your own bed."

When that didn't work, Caden gathered Sorcha into his arms. "Wake up, lassie. Wake up. I'll not stop shaking you till you look at me."

Suddenly Sorcha opened her eyes, wide and glazed with panic. As they came to focus on Caden's face, the shock faded, washed away by a swelling tide. She blinked, her dark lashes dipping into it, fanning tears down her pale cheeks. Not knowing quite what to do, Caden pulled her face against him so that his tunic absorbed them.

"I h … hurt."

The sob shook Caden as well. He knew the hurt and the fear that made her tremble so.

Ever so gently he stroked the wild tendrils of copper curls away from her face, over the contour of her head, and down to the nape of her neck. Again. And again. As though to coax the pain splitting her forehead into furrows away. With each stroke, he could feel the tension coiled in her body release notch by notch.

Until he thought she slept again. Ever so gently, he lowered her head back and eased his hand from between Sorcha and the pillow. Turning her head slightly, she found it with her cheek and brushed against it.

"Such tender hands," she sighed through parted lips that held Caden's gaze glued.

Until her words registered. *Tender* hands? The irony shoved Caden to his feet. His hands were weapons, stained with the blood of his enemies. He stared at the calluses worn by his spear, sword, and Forstan's reins. *Tender* was the last word Caden would use to describe them. Yet even as he scoffed, Sorcha's sentiment wormed its way into the heart so newly laid bare that very day upon the beach.

As though it belonged.

CHAPTER ELEVEN

"Peas don't work as good as oyster shells," Ebyn complained the following morning as the bean he'd slung into the hearth with the larger sling Caden had made him on the beach bounced back into the room. "Guess I'll have to use the little one Gemma gave me."

"And pick up the peas where you missed," Gemma reminded him from near the window where she worked on one of Sorcha's new dresses in the sunlight filtering through the pale hide covering.

"Aye, there's a limit to the peas we allow for such practice," Sorcha chimed in. She stirred the bitter medicinal tea on the table in front of her, working up the will to drink it.

Ebyn had worked his way into everyone's heart, including that of the man sitting across the table from her. The lad was eager to please and so afraid of more rejection. It was horrid enough feeling abandoned by her parents as a child captive, but at least hers hadn't sold her like livestock.

"Aye, now that's better," Caden approved as Ebyn fitted a pea into the little patch sling Gemma had fashioned for him. It had been only right that Gemma offered the Cymri lodging after he'd remained with Sorcha and Ebyn, rather than turn him out into the night. "Always choose your stone to match your sling, laddie. You wouldn't heave a boulder with an eye patch, would you?"

While the menfolk were gathering fuel for the fire earlier, Gemma had told Sorcha how, upon arriving home from the tavern last night, she had found Caden sleeping on the floor beside Sorcha's cot, his big hand covering hers. Of course, he awoke with a start as Gemma bolted the door behind her. A bit sheepish, he'd mumbled something about Sorcha having nightmares and wondering if she needed another cup of the medicinal tea.

But Sorcha had slept through the night without further incident and awakened with the dawn to find Gemma on her own cot on the opposite wall, Ebyn in the loft space they'd made for him, and Caden wrapped in his cloak by the hearth.

And now the Cymri let his breakfast of gruel and honey cake settle before he set off for Din Guardi. Though he seemed in no hurry to go.

Suddenly Caden's study of Ebyn's target practice turned toward her, catching Sorcha in her own contemplation. He pointed to her cup. "Best finish that, lest your head renew its anguish."

The worst of it was over, the healing woman be thanked, but a soreness lingered. That and a bit of a daze. Instead of fighting him, Sorcha took another tiny sip of the bitter medicinal tea. It was a weaker brew, just in case the terrible anguish flared up again. At least Sorcha had all day to gather her wits for her last night at the tavern. Tomorrow, she, too, would be in Din Guardi … in the princess's service.

"You are a curious man, Caden of Lothian," she thought aloud. A quickening in his gaze triggered wariness in Sorcha. Had he lied about his homeland?

"And how's that, milady?"

She let the doubt go. With his fair hair and rugged, square-jawed features, Caden reminded her a bit of her father Wulfram. A man's man, built for war and the hunt, yet possessed of a gentleness he reserved for those closest to him.

"You have all the appearance of a hardened warrior, the light-footedness of a dancer, the charm of a prince, the patience of a father with the lad …" Sorcha remembered the way he'd stroked her head and cradled her until the horrors of the past had gone away. "And the gentle hand of a nurse." She boldly searched his gaze. "What other secrets do you hide, I wonder?"

The man's relaxed warmth disappeared as though an iron visor had fallen over it.

"I'm a sinner, a selfish oaf, far from prince *or* father material," he replied stonily. "I am no more than a messenger from your mother to you. If you wish to return to Trebold, I will take you there. Beyond that, you need know nothing more of me, milady."

The reply smacked of rebuke, but Sorcha didn't feel like taking issue with it.

"It's too late for me to go home now," she replied wearily. "Bernicia *is* the only home I know. More important, I've given my oath." The path of least resistance held more sway at the moment.

"If your Cynric is as kind and understanding as you say, he'd understand," Caden countered.

"But the insult and shame to my father's dearest friend would still stand. Battles are fought over less. Even we *thieves*"—Sorcha pointed to the purse she'd tossed at him last night, now tied to his belt and heavier with most of Gemma's take from the tavern—"have some sense of honor."

Gemma snickered over her handiwork as Sorcha continued. "And I will see you paid back in full, if you choose to remain in Din Guardi long enough."

For now, the cot beckoned her with the loudest voice. No more medicine for her. Just rest.

"You may deduct a night's lodging and breakfast from that debt," he said, returning to a more amiable disposition. "And if no is your final answer, then I've no more business here except the attendance of my lord Modred and the princess."

Caden rose to his feet and, to Sorcha's astonishment, caught her hand up to his lips. "*Unless* ... " The word stroked her ear like silk. "You have a change of heart before the Lothian party leaves after the wedding. I can only hope."

He was flirting. The man flipped humors as easily as a coin. Worse, an annoying giddiness scrambled the reply on the tip of her tongue, so that she had to concentrate to sort it out.

"For whose sake, I wonder?" she drawled, taking up his game. Not that she was in the least interested in the Cymri. Her place was with her adopted people, helping the children. With Cynric as the Lady Elford. A lady with her own estate and more to come.

Wasn't it? Sorcha groaned at the rearing doubt. Between Caden's game and the medicinal tea, she was thinking in circles.

"For your mother's sake, why else?"

Confound the man. May he trod through every manner of dung between here and Din Guardi's keep!

"Your regard for my *mother* is admirable," she shot back with words stiff as her back. "Perhaps I shall draft a letter before—"

A knock at the door cut Sorcha off. As she made to get up,

Caden motioned for her and Gemma to remain seated. "I'm on my way out. I'll see to it."

Irked beyond her ken, Sorcha followed Caden's long strides toward the entrance. *Better yet, may he fall face-first behind an oxcart,* she thought as he slid back the bolt. *And may the ox have a belly full of green apples.*

Big as the lord of the day, Caden swung open the door. "Good day—"

He broke off his greeting at the sight of the golden-haired woman standing there, garbed in rich clothing and flanked by an equally bedecked man. But then Tunwulf's mistress was a striking woman.

Caden's voice turned as cold as the air that rushed in. "—*milady.*"

Rhianon's scream surely raked the rafters of every building along Water Street and brought Gemma and Ebyn to their feet. Tunwulf swept the hysterical woman off her feet and barreled past Caden and into the house. Rhianon had swooned to a whimpering low, but the moment she saw Caden again, she became undone.

"A ghost," she shrieked. "By all that's sacred, a ghost." Sobbing, Rhianon clutched and burrowed into Tunwulf's cloak. "Make it go away! Make it go away!"

"Come to your senses, woman!" Tunwulf gave her a rough shake. "This man is no more ghost than you or I."

"'Tis true, Rhianon."

Caden's reply drew Sorcha's attention away from the wailing woman. He knew her name?

Caden caught Rhianon's face, forcing her to look at him. "I'm no more spirit than you. The flesh on my fingers is as warm as yours, dearest—"

Rhianon struggled to turn away from him. And no wonder, for this was an entirely different Caden than the charmer who'd opened the door.

"—*wife*," he finished with a venomous sneer.

Wife? The last remnant of the medicine's effect cleared from Sorcha's brain. How dare the villain flirt so with her when he was married, much less wed to the likes of this witch!

"Strange," she scoffed. "I don't recall your mentioning *marriage* in your earlier confession, Caden of Lothian. *If* that is even who you are."

Her instincts had been right. He *had* been lying to her. And just when she had begun to warm to the man, perhaps even his mission.

"Stay clear of this, woman," Caden warned without so much as a glance her way.

Sorcha fixed her hands upon her hips. "Well, that would be hard to do, considering *your* business is in *my* house."

Gemma grasped her arm as though to rein her in. "Easy, lassie, lest you fire up that headache again."

Oh, Sorcha was fired all right.

Tunwulf eased Rhianon onto the bench at the table, but she would not let go of him. "Close the door, little woman," he snapped at Gemma as he tried prying Rhianon's fingers from his shirt. "Easy, darling. I promise, no harm will come to you." He glanced over his shoulder at Sorcha. "Have you *anything* to drink besides tea?"

How dare he address her like a servant in her own house! "Aye," she declared, "and I'd fetch it, if I were asked properly."

For a moment, they locked wills. Tunwulf finally condescended with a nod. "A Flemish red, *if* you would be so kind, milady."

What Sorcha wanted to do was physically toss the lot of them out, but imagining such a pleasing prospect was the only satisfaction she had. Only the finest would do for the not-so-honorable Tunwulf and his *lady,* she grumbled in silence.

Although if ever an occasion called for a strong, full-bodied drink, this was it. Sorcha imported many fine wines for the taverns in Din Guardi. Her father had seen that she had discerning tastes.

"I'll fetch the wine." Gemma stepped between Sorcha and the door leading into the warehouse. "*You* pay attention," she added lowly, ushering the wary Ebyn away with her.

Sorcha moved next to the hearth as though to warm herself and studied the gathering at her board. Rhianon sat across from Caden with her face buried in her arms, trembling like a wet dog on a cold night.

From love or fear?

As for Caden, if that was his name, he had eyes for none but the distressed creature. But such regard, no woman would desire. Especially not a wife. One that had taken up a tryst with another man.

Tunwulf was the only one who remained above the drama. "I remember you now," he announced, draping a possessive arm over Rhianon's shoulders. "The last I saw of you, your brother's blade was pressed to your throat, and he showed little sign of mercy."

In an effort to see everyone's faces, Sorcha took up a towel and bucket of water and carried it to the table to wash the wooden cups she and Caden had used earlier. Neither man paid her any heed, for each now assessed the other like hounds circling a tasty bone. 'Twas tempting to douse them both.

"So you have eyes in the *back*," Caden slapped him with the word, "of your head, eh, Tunwulf?"

Sorcha gasped as one of the copper-banded cups slipped from her hands back into the bucket. So Caden knew Tunwulf as well.

"As I recall, you were running from the fight as fast as your legs could take you," Caden taunted. "I didn't recognize you at first in all that finery."

So they'd fought in some sort of border raid, and Tunwulf left Caden behind to die? The latter didn't surprise Sorcha. Tunwulf thought only of himself.

"I—" Rhianon drew in a shaky breath, raising a red, tear-swollen face to Caden. "I thought you were d-dead."

With a smirk, Caden opened his hands, palms up. "Surprise, *dearest*."

Whatever could the Cymri have been thinking to marry a woman like that? Sorcha could slap him on that one principle alone.

By the time Gemma returned with the wine and it was served, the tension between the two men at the table was strung tight as a bow. If they were to dispense with one another, Sorcha would be all for it. She'd even provide the weapons.

"This is none of our matter," Gemma whispered when Sorcha lingered at the head of the table. "Come help me with my sewing while our guests work out this interesting quagmire among themselves."

Reluctant, Sorcha followed her companion to the window stool, where Ebyn had already retreated.

"So now what?" Tunwulf asked after draining the wine like the oaf that he was. He put the empty cup down like a gauntlet.

Rhianon saw the challenge too. "You ... you do understand, Caden, that I ... we *both*," she emphasized, "thought you dead."

Caden took a deep, labored breath, as if that action alone kept the coiled muscle of his body from exploding in a vengeance-starved rage.

Tunwulf slid his free hand under the table to where there was, no doubt, a dirk hidden in his boot.

"No need for the dagger, sir," Caden told him. "There's really nothing to discuss as far as I'm concerned." As if to demonstrate his peaceful intentions, he placed both hands square on the table. "The past is past."

Victory, the kind Sorcha had seen light a man's eye over the throwboard, flickered in Caden's steely gaze. "She's all yours, if you want her."

Rhianon gasped, bristling like a doused hen. That she said nothing told Sorcha she was torn as to how to respond. Though his indifference was callous, Caden had in essence just set her free.

But why?

Tunwulf was also wary. "What of your marriage?"

"It was a Christian ceremony." Caden shrugged. "What do either of you care about that? Besides, given our lovely lady is known to be a devious witch, as witnessed before a priest, an annulment by the church can easily be had."

Sorcha resisted the urge to spit at any evil that might ride on the tail of such a statement. While she believed only in the Wyrds or fate and used gods to swear by, she did believe in evil. Would she had an iron amulet to touch, lest it somehow infect her. As it was, she hoped touching the poker by the fire with her gaze would suffice.

"How ... *did* you survive?" Rhianon asked.

"I would ask you the same, *milady.*" A mocking tilt grazed Caden's mouth.

"My men found her half drowned on the riverbank," Tunwulf informed him. "Mad out of her mind, she was at first."

Caden leaned forward. "What about the child?"

"What child?" Rhianon froze, a quick pause that implied the wish to retract her impulsive reply.

Caden's expression grew hard as granite.

Sorcha wrung her apron in her hands. Perhaps he'd counted his victory too soon.

"Oh," Rhianon said, as though suddenly pricked by a ghost from the past. Her face fell. "It did not survive the plunge into the river." She leaned forward and placed her small white hand over his. "And what about you?" she prompted softly.

Hair pricked at Sorcha's neck when she detected a scam afoot and, at the moment, it was even dancing. Surely Caden didn't believe that drama of remorse-turned-concern, even if it was skillfully performed.

The wench didn't even remember a child!

"The better man won, in spite of all your schemes, *milady.*"

Better man? Surely not Tunwulf.

"Ronan spared me, and Arthur exiled me from kin and clan lands—" he told her.

Ronan ... his brother.

"—and the peace beyond ken came to be after all."

Peace beyond understanding? Sorcha picked up the end of a twisted length of golden trim that Gemma was sewing over a seam where she'd added to the length of the dress. Whatever was *that* about?

"That accursed *prophecy.*" Rhianon touched one of the many jeweled rings on her finger as though warding off an unseen threat.

A prophecy with a power to make a witch squirm, a battle of brother versus brother, and an adulterous affair. The songstress in Sorcha recognized the makings of a good ballad, though she was more interested in Caden's part in it.

"And I have sought warfare elsewhere," Caden went on, "as a mercenary in Lothian. It suits me better than wedded bliss."

"Hah!" Tunwulf helped himself to another cup of wine. "We're more alike than I thought, friend."

"You can surely see why I was so attracted to Tunwulf, after I thought I'd lost you." Rhianon leaned against her companion's broad shoulders, helpless as a kitten … with very sharp claws.

"You two are the better match to be sure." Caden shoved away from the table to rise, when Tunwulf stopped him.

"But wait. Now that that's settled, I'd know what business you have with my future stepmother?"

Sorcha caught herself midgroan, hoping no one noticed. Tunwulf was as much bane of her present as of her future. He'd use anything Caden told him against her and Cynric.

"I came upon a villain giving these two ladies trouble yesterday," Caden replied smoothly. "He threatened to burn this establishment down over a loan they owed the oaf's employer."

"It was Athelstan's man Wada," Sorcha informed Tunwulf. "He all but admitted in front of Caden and several others that he was responsible for the fire that killed my parents. I intend to tell Cynric about his extortion, but Gemma and I offered Caden a night's lodging to keep watch for us … in case Wada made his threat good to come back," she added for propriety's sake.

"Athelstan the moneylender?" Tunwulf questioned. A sly smile widened his mustache. "I wonder if Father realizes he's marrying for a debt instead of a proper dowry?"

Sorcha's cheeks flamed again. And her neck. Even her chest grew hot. "Your concern for me is overwhelming, sir. As for the loan, it was paid in full before a host of witnesses, so my business and dowry are sound. If you knew anything at all about trade, you'd know loans are part of the business for most of us."

She got up from the bench she shared with Gemma. "And now it's my turn to be asking questions, I think. What is *your* business with us?"

"The princess has requested you attend her immediately," Rhianon informed her. The lady was still wan, but calculation had rekindled in her gaze. "It seems the Saxon servants' mastery of the Cymri tongue is sadly lacking."

Sorcha gasped. "Do you mean she wants me to come *today?*" Her dresses weren't ready. *She* wasn't ready.

"*Us*, darling," Rhianon corrected, as though that should be reassuring. "Between us, we can see the princess properly received by the women in Hussa's court."

"And Father is expected to arrive from Elford this morning," Tunwulf put in. "He will want to see you at the king's reception tonight, of course."

The mention of Cynric's presence was more comforting to Sorcha than Rhianon's assurance. Cynric, Sorcha trusted.

Although Sorcha wondered if she'd lost her ability to read people. She'd begun to trust Caden as well. But his association with Rhianon and Tunwulf and the events they alluded to had unraveled any scrap of goodwill that Sorcha had for him.

"Then I'll make ready," Sorcha decided aloud. Known factors suited her better than the unknown represented by the stranger, whoever he was.

"And a court life is what you really want?" Caden studied her from across the room.

No. Sorcha wanted to be a lady in her own right so that she could help the captive children. This was simply a means to an end. One that would do honor to her parents as well.

"If serving the princess honors my betrothed, then it is what I want."

Sorcha only wished she were as confident as she sounded.

CHAPTER TWELVE

The population of Din Guardi worked like bees in a hive to feed the king's court and guests from Lothian. Above the unwalled town's support system of shops and cottages loomed the wooden fortress itself, enclosed by a palisade. As the cart sent to bring Sorcha to Princess Eavlyn passed through the gate, Sorcha was so taken by the elaborate gilded carvings adorning the posts that she forgot her anxiety. Above, banners fluttered like great winged birds against an azure sky.

The place seemed bigger than when she'd visited with her father. To one side of the massive compound, there were stables, barns, and sunken shelters for harvest storage. On the other were similar structures, the shops and homes of the artisans. But it was the great hall and its surrounding buildings that took Sorcha's breath away.

The rising mass of timber framing was big enough to entertain Hussa's warband and those of his thanes. The bright afternoon sun practiced its alchemy on it, turning its steep straw roof to bright gold. The field where the warriors would hone their skills during the Long Dark was a spread of colorful tents belonging to those guests and servants whom the hall could not accommodate.

"I have to say, your dwarf did a good job of adding length to your dress. The cord looks like it belongs," Rhianon observed from the fur-lined bench next to Sorcha. Rhianon meant it as a compliment and, rather than put off Sorcha's only friend in this strange place, Sorcha let the insult to Gemma go.

But how she missed Gemma already! Her friend had not put down her needle all day. There'd hardly been time to say good-bye as the little woman helped her into the dress and robe. But as Gemma sewed, Sorcha expressed her misgivings, regarding both the plan to marry Cynric and, after learning some of Caden's secrets, accompanying him to Trebold.

Gemma favored neither one option nor the other. "Take your time and think it over and then over again before you make your decision. Consider what would make you most happy and the price you are willing to pay for that happiness. Decide accordingly."

Sorcha drifted off in thought, only to be drawn back by Rhianon's delighted gasp.

"Oh, how lovely!"

The women's compound had come into view. It was separated from the king's hall by a garden spotted with evergreen shrubs and beds filled with late-blooming flowers and herbs. A trellised walk covered in vines connected the queen's hall to that of her husband. Other trellises connected the network of private quarters to the smaller hall. About it all was a wattle fence to keep the wandering livestock out.

"Prince Hering's mother had a fondness for growing things," a rather robust woman announced, stepping out from under the cover of a trellis. "I am Mildrith, the seneschal's wife," she continued in a booming voice. Given her height, half a head above Sorcha's, and her wide-shouldered build, Mildrith had the wherewithal to back it up.

"Queen Ebba had this area laid out in squares separated by these stone-paved walks—" Mildrith opened the gate and led the way into the compound —"as a reminder of her father's vast farmlands along the Rhine. Since she went to Valhalla, our new Queen Aella and the royal ladies have seen it maintained. On warm days, they sit in the sun and sew on yon benches."

She pointed a thick arm to massive tree trunks laid upon the ground, their tops planed smooth. Sorcha took note of the various creatures befitting a meadow that had been carved into their bark exterior—hare, deer, and fox. Four of the seats were situated around a moss-bedecked statue of a woman, a goddess, perhaps, with a lyre tucked in one arm.

"It's quite unlike anything I've ever seen," Sorcha marveled. "How Gemma … my friend," she explained, "would adore such a place!"

"It's very pretty come spring and through summer till late fall," Mildrith said with a smile of approval.

Clearly the royal ladies were not the only ones who took pride in the garden.

Mildrith led them to a small house and pointed to the door. "Your attendant may stay here with the other servants. You will stay in yon princess's bower." She indicated another dwelling next to the queen's hall.

"But this is not acceptable," Rhianon objected. "I must attend Milady Sorcha. She'd be lost without me. I'll have you know I'm soon to be Thane Elford's daughter-by-law."

Sorcha stared at Rhianon in disbelief. Hadn't Tunwulf disparaged marital bliss in their presence just yesterday?

"Then when you are elevated to the rank of lady, perhaps the princess will reconsider," Mildrith replied, unfazed by Rhianon's indignation. "Until then, it's in with the servants you go."

"We'll see about this." Rhianon sniffed. The viperish look she gave Mildrith might have withered the stone goddess, but not the seneschal's wife.

"And now, Milady Sorcha," Mildrith said as Rhianon huffed away after the servants with her trunk, "Princess Eavlyn is most anxious to meet you. It seems someone has been singing your praises in her ear."

"Oh?" Not Cynric. Rhianon said he had arrived only this afternoon from Elford's southern borderland.

"Come along," Mildrith prodded when Sorcha's tumbling thoughts caused her to fall behind. "Just because you're young doesn't mean this damp air won't settle in your joints as well when you lay your head down tonight."

Sorcha sped up, unable to hold her grin back any longer. She liked Mildrith. Thank the Wyrds that Mildrith seemed to like her as well.

CHAPTER THIRTEEN

Mildrith admitted Sorcha to the princess's bower and told her to wait until Eavlyn, who was in the queen's hall, joined her. The building was little more spacious than Sorcha's main room, but divided by screen into what Sorcha assumed was a private sleeping chamber to the rear and a section containing cushioned benches around the central hearth. A shelf beneath a mirror on the wall near its single window held a carved ivory comb and a brush, as well as an oil lamp and vials, perfumes no doubt.

In the corner nearest the door, Sorcha spotted a harp with Celtic knotwork carved into its rich, oiled wood. The edges of the frame were gilded in contrast. Surely such an instrument was fit for a princess.

Unable to resist, Sorcha picked it up and plucked at the gut strings. Whoever played it kept it in good tune. Pleased, she began to play a soft, soothing melody that Eadric had taught her. It was supposed to have eased the pain of the Irish god Dagda's wife during childbirth. Closing her eyes, Sorcha let it work its magic until she no longer played the melody but was a part of it, swaying in time.

It was thus that Princess Eavlyn found her, though how long the lady had stood listening in the door, Sorcha had no idea. Only when her fingers had wound down to the final notes was she aware of her audience.

"Don't stop, please!" the lady implored in the Cumbric of the Britons. In a flow of soft blue woolen skirts lavish with gold embroidery, she took the bench next to Sorcha by the hearth.

But Sorcha was on her feet, embarrassed. "I'm sorry, milady," she responded in the same tongue. "I didn't mean to be presumptuous, but I've never played such a fine instrument as this."

"It's never been played so well," Princess Eavlyn replied sheepishly. "My father had it made for me, but alas, my interest was more in the stars and their secrets than in music." She motioned for Sorcha to sit. "And in truth, the commotion of the men in the hall, boasting about who will take down the biggest prize on tomorrow's hunt, has left me with a slight headache. So you have come to my rescue in more than one way."

A hunt. Now that piqued Sorcha's interest. But her duty was to the princess. "Has your maidservant prepared a medicinal tea for your head?" she asked, adopting Gemma's caring yet authoritative manner.

"She fetches it from the kitchen as we speak."

Eavlyn smiled, her inner beauty lending a glow to what were, at first glimpse, plain features. It was her eyes, Sorcha decided, that caused the glow. Bright as a fawn's on a spring morning. And warm as sunshine.

"Thank you for your concern, Sorcha. May I call you by your given name in the privacy of my chamber?"

Sorcha was taken aback by the woman's humility. Such a vast difference between this princess and Rhianon. "By all means, milady. I was just plagued with the same ache yesterday, so I can surely empathize."

"Just the walk from the hall has helped." The gentle lady clasped her hands in delight. "God has so blessed me! You not only speak my language fluently, but you play the harp like an angel. *And*," she added in a low voice, "I heard you sing like one too."

An angel. A Christian's fairy or elf, or so Sorcha had heard. Regardless, it was intended as a compliment. "Thank you, milady. Although, if you know that, you also know that I am but a lowly scop who sings for a living in a tavern … when I'm not carrying on my father's business."

"Lady Sorcha, I can tell you now that you have more heart and honor than most of the royal ladies with whom I've spent this day," Eavlyn declared. "They cackle like hens in their own tongue about me, and I know enough Anglish to tell my interpreter is not translating all that is said."

"Whyever not?"

"She's a Saxon, herself a slave purchased by my father when I was twelve," Eavlyn explained. "It's natural, I suppose, that her loyalties lie with her own people, no matter how well we've treated her."

Slavery. How Sorcha detested the notion. Yet it was widely practiced, accepted as the norm in all the known world. "Mayhaps your woman hopes to save you from embarrassment or insult."

Eavlyn grew somber. "That may be so," she admitted, "and shame on me for not thinking of that. But I need to know who my enemies are and who are not. I need someone who will tell me all. Surely you know my position is weak in this foreign court."

"And yet, you trust *me?*"

"We have common ancestry in Lothian. More than that in common," Eavlyn added.

Sorcha's wonder continued to climb. "Oh?"

"We're both to be married not for love, but for a larger cause."

Had Caden told the lady about the children? Somehow Sorcha imagined him as a lowly guardsman, not someone with the lady's ear. Though he'd said he was once a prince.

"My hope," Eavlyn continued, "is to bring God's Word to my husband's kingdom, and yours is to save captured children."

So it *was* Caden. Except this lady had naught but admiration in her eye for Sorcha's quest. No disdain or looks of pity.

"I have tried to see as many as I could back to their homes. Sad to say, I couldn't save them all."

"Nor will all listen to God's Word," Eavlyn commiserated. "But for each one who does accept Jesus the Christ as Lord and Savior, all Heaven celebrates."

Christian Valhalla. Somehow Sorcha couldn't imagine the warriors who'd gone on caring whether those left behind joined them or nay. The main objective of a warrior was that those who were left behind remembered the warrior's greatness in song and esteemed his family as well for it.

"The important thing is that we *try*," the lady emphasized. She leaned forward, animated with passion. "*We* have a purpose for our lives, Sorcha, more than filling a lord's cup and warming his bed."

"Aye." Though Sorcha would consider herself blessed not to be reminded of her future in Cynric's bed. "And I am honored to help you in any way I can."

Still, she liked the Princess Eavlyn. Never in her dreams did she think she could have something in common with a woman of Eavlyn's rank, much less a foreigner. Yet here Sorcha was, drawn to want to help and protect her. And made to feel like a sister, rather than a servant. It was almost magical, this common ground they found.

A tap on the door brought Eavlyn to her feet. "That must be Lunid with the tea."

A slender, shy maiden, muffled in a robe the gold of autumn oak leaves, entered the room, carrying a tray with a teapot and three cups. After introductions, Lunid served them, lacing Eavlyn's tea with ground elm bark, and put the teapot over the coals to keep the water warm.

"God has answered our prayers with Sorcha, Lunid," Eavlyn assured the servant, who kept a wary eye on Sorcha.

"But she's still a heathen," the maidservant pointed out.

Sorcha stiffened at the quiet reproof in Lunid's tone.

"Sometimes *we* are as well," Eavlyn said over the cup of steaming tea. "As when we forget the source of our blessings and try to move on without Him. We are all on a spiritual journey, but not always on the same road."

"I've never given much thought to such things," Sorcha admitted. "But I work too hard to offer sacrifices to some god who may or may not exist. Better the food be in the bellies of my family and the children or my coin toward their welfare."

Lunid crossed herself.

Had she sensed evil, Sorcha would have spit like her fellow *heathens.* In this case, all she felt was Lunid's pious disapproval. Perhaps even fear of her. Christians were a superstitious lot.

"Though I do swear to Freya," she added, just to see what Lunid would do.

Another cross.

"Not that I worship the goddess," Sorcha explained. "But 'tis better than swearing on my loved ones' bones when I can find no words to suit my exasperation or anger."

Unlike Lunid, Eavlyn neither shrank from the subject nor acted superior.

"We believe that Christ made the sacrifice of His life for us," Eavlyn told Sorcha, pulling her from her mischief. "That freed us from such burdensome sacrifices."

Sorcha scowled. "Your God sacrificed Himself? What manner of god would do such a thing?"

"One who came to earth in human form so He would know firsthand the trials we face. And He, who was sinless, sacrificed Himself to pay for all our sins."

Stories were filled with gods taking human form to practice their mischief upon the mortals, but this was the first Sorcha had heard of one coming to be sacrificed for mankind's sake. Still—

"Why should we have to sacrifice anything, sinful or not?" she objected. "Fate cast us our lot, no matter how good or bad we are. Life is naught but in the hands of the Wyrds."

"So if we've done something bad, you don't think it affects us and our future?" Eavlyn asked.

"Aye, but we are punished by a blood price. If you commit a crime against another man, you'll have to pay the wergild. That blood price is the consequence. Or death, if the crime is vile enough," Sorcha reasoned aloud. "That has nothing to do with gods."

Eavlyn smiled. "That is mankind's justice. We have similar judicial practices for dealing with breakers of the law on This Side. But God's justice may not be dealt to the offender until after his or her death. Christ's sacrifice or pardon applies on *both* sides of the divide between life and death."

"*If* there is life beyond death," Sorcha countered, wondering just how many times she could force the silly maidservant to cross herself.

Some Saxons believed in Valhalla like their fjord-dwelling neighbors to the north, though it seemed reserved for warriors or people of great accomplishment. Certainly such a place was beyond her means. Others said the deceased was given another life, one better blessed by the Wyrds than the last one. All she knew was that when one was buried, the body stayed in the ground until naught but bones remained … along with whatever material goods that would not perish. Goods that could better have been put to use by the living left behind.

"We believe that upon death, the spirit, not the body, ascends to Heaven, a paradise, if one has accepted Christ as their Savior. If one has not, then their spirit is trapped in hell, a place of the dead where eternal torment awaits. The body itself returns to the earth, for it was but a house for the spirit on This Side."

"But you cannot know this for certain," Sorcha challenged. "No one has returned from the dead."

"Christ did."

"You *say* He did," Sorcha replied.

"There were witnesses who saw Him after His death and burial," Eavlyn assured her. "It is His resurrection that we celebrate every spring."

When Sorcha's skepticism did not waver, the princess tried another approach. "Does not human life mimic all nature with its seasons?"

Leafbud—birth; Sun Season—prime; Leaf Fall—old age; and the Long Dark of death.

"Aye," Sorcha said slowly. "But no one knows where mankind's next Leafbud will be."

"Jesus came back to tell us. It will be in Heaven for those who believe in Him. He told His followers of the many mansions in His Father's Heaven being prepared for them."

"Jesus Christ isn't the Father God?"

"God is three forms in one. The Father, the Son, and the Holy Spirit."

That was it. Sorcha had heard enough to make her head spin.

Apparently sensing that Sorcha had reached the limits of her curiosity, Eavlyn reached across and patted Sorcha's knee. "We'll speak more of this later if you so desire. If the Holy Word is so great that it cannot be fit into one book, how can we possibly absorb it all with our small brain?" She pointed to her head and laughed.

It was a lot to fathom and an interesting story as well. And Eavlyn was adept at telling it.

"You would make a good bard, were you not so curious about the stars," Sorcha complimented her.

"Perhaps because this is more than just a story to me. It is the truth indelibly etched in my heart and soul. I live my life for it, according to it."

Indeed the fire of the lady's belief burned in her gaze.

"And you, Sorcha, follow Jesus' commands, even though you aren't familiar with Him," Eavlyn told her.

"*Milady!*" Lunid would surely wear the front of her overdress threadbare if the conversation continued much longer.

But Sorcha had to know what it was she did that would please this Jesus God. "And how is that, milady?"

"God instructs us to care for the widows and orphans. You care for the helpless," Eavlyn explained, "just as He does, by saving the children orphaned by captivity and returning them to their families. The same love in your heart that presses you toward such a goal is the very love that made Him die for those of us who didn't even know Him."

Sorcha wrapped herself in the thought. Aye, she'd risk her life for the little ones. *Had* already risked her livelihood.

"I see much of Jesus in you, Sorcha," Eavlyn went on. "And I pray that you will see His love in me."

Sorcha saw goodness in her companion. And compassion. And a faith that made her seem stronger than she was at first appearance. And more beautiful.

Yet it was like Valhalla, beyond Sorcha's reach. Somehow she couldn't see such a loving God wanting anything to do with a thief. Truth be told, Sorcha had too much to worry about on This Side to spend much thought on the Other.

The king's hall was as immense inside as out. Rows of great columns elaborately carved with animals of all sorts, as indeed all exposed wood seemed to be, supported the high-pitched roof. Tapestries, banners, and shields adorned the plastered walls, lending color enough for a spring fair. Smoke from the great hearth fire in the center of the building wafted upward toward an opening in the ceiling, while the scent of roasting meats and ales tempted the appetites of the guests. Servants wound in and out of the benches with great trays of meat, puddings, cheeses, and breads for the taking.

At the center of the longest wall, a board had been set up on a raised dais where King Hussa, Prince Hering, and the Lothian royal guests were seated. If the display of gold were any standard to judge by, both Saxon and Briton were equal in their costume and ornament. Crowns, torcs, armbands, and rings reflected torchlight all about them. While maidservants made water and towels available for hand washing, Sorcha waited with Eavlyn and the other noble ladies for Queen Aella's instruction next to barrels of drink stacked near the kitchen's entrance.

"You are to fill Hering's goblet and those of his men from Burlwick as his future princess," Sorcha explained to Eavlyn after the queen finished. Aella and her daughter would serve the king, Modred, and Eavlyn's father, Blaise of Dunfeld. The other ladies in waiting would pour drink for Hussa's thanes. "Our noble ladies only serve the alcohol. And hopefully," Sorcha translated out of earshot of Aella, "you will be a better cupbearer than a weaver."

"She's right," Eavlyn admitted with a grin. The pale veil and coronet she wore over her head and shoulders shimmered in the torchlight. Sorcha's headcover was more like a fishnet of golden thread, allowing her hair, brushed loose over her shoulders, to show beneath. Unaccustomed to wearing a headdress, Sorcha resisted the urge to keep fiddling with it.

"If Hering expects me to clothe him," Eavlyn confided, "he will go naked."

Eavlyn had shared that most of her training had been academic, not domestic.

"Does he know—" Sorcha began.

Eavlyn cut her off. "He is more interested in my knowledge of the stars. *That* was made clear before the arrangement was agreed upon. Though I shall supervise weavers and seamstresses to be certain my husband and his company are properly attired."

"Good thing." Sorcha snickered. "Papa once told me of a widowed thane whose men nearly revolted, insisting he remarry because he *and* they were in rags."

Cynric knew as well that Sorcha, like her mother, was neither weaver nor seamstress. She was a scop and businesswoman. He'd assured her that his seneschal's wife proved most capable in the running of the household at Elford.

So Cynric was only interested in her as a brood sow.

Sorcha pushed the troubling thought aside, but Caden's words took its place.

And life with a man twice your age is what you really want?

She stepped into Eavlyn's shadow, as if to cower from the answer that thundered in her head. No. She'd prefer having wealth enough of her own to continue helping the children. But that was not possible.

Besides, going to Trebold with Caden held no guarantee of happiness either. Her birth mother struggled to make a living, just like Sorcha. Women sacrificed happiness for wealth and security all the time. As Eavlyn said, she had a mission. One worth sacrificing for.

A servant handed the princess a flagon of beer from a dark oak barrel. Sorcha would serve the same to Cynric and the Elford company ... including Tunwulf.

As Sorcha made her way to Cynric's board, he rose from his place of honor near the king's table to greet her with boisterous enthusiasm. "Milady Sorcha, you grow more lovely by the day."

Sorcha put the pitcher on the table, no more than a board and trestles, and allowed him to kiss her hand. He was not uncomely, even with the gray fringing the brown hair at his temples.

"Your gifts would make any woman beautiful. Am I not the luckiest man here tonight?" he boasted above the music of a twosome playing the harp and pipe.

And his face was kindly ... until Sorcha poured his glass full and caught him staring at her bodice.

"If not *the* luckiest," a graying contemporary of Elford agreed, "you're *one* of the luckiest, milord. Seems like only last year she sat upon Wulfram's knee."

Sorcha knew some of the men with her future husband. They'd frequented her father's tavern and considered their former comrade still one of them. "The Wyrds are kind to us both," Sorcha demurred.

It was true. At Cynric's side, she felt safe, protected from the world. But was she prepared to pay the price for such protection?

Once she finished serving, she took her place by Cynric. As a maidservant passed her by with a platter of roast beef, Sorcha took a piece with her dining dagger. The cold peas she'd had at her home no longer kept hunger at bay. The meat was succulent, but she was glad she still had good teeth.

"Would milady have some bread as well?"

It was Rhianon from the yon side of the board. There was a hunger in her and Tunwulf's eyes as well, but it was not for food.

Rhianon pushed an untouched loaf, still warm from the oven, toward her. "I feel as though I've been cast aside like a broken doll," the golden-haired woman complained. "I told Tunwulf that if I'm to sleep with the servants, better I should retire to my own bed in our haws below the rock."

Rhianon had so looked forward to participating in the court that Sorcha felt a pang of pity for her. Had Sorcha been an exiled princess, she, too, would likely crave a chance to regain some of that prestige. "Perhaps I can speak to Her Majesty about moving you to the ladies' quarters," she offered, although everyone knew Rhianon was Tunwulf's mistress *and* rumored to be a witch. Poor Lunid would faint dead away when she found out who, or what, Rhianon was.

"After all, I was the one who suggested to Cynric that you should attend the Princess Eavlyn."

Sorcha doubted the same ladies who belittled Princess Eavlyn would accept Rhianon even *after* she was wed to Cynric's son. Persuasion and wealth was what evened one's lot at Hussa's court. Tunwulf, who spent as freely as he plundered, had neither.

"Not *all* the power is in the king's hall," Rhianon added with a meaningful look. She slipped her arm through Tunwulf's and gave him a smile that kindled fire in his gaze. Elsewhere, too, if Sorcha was any judge.

Rhianon utterly bemused Sorcha. She'd feel foolish melting into a man's side like butter to a scone. Such was her state of nerves that, should Cynric move suddenly, Sorcha feared she'd squeal. The moment his glass was emptied, she set about filling it and left the table to refill the flagon for the others.

On her return, Hussa tapped on the table with the hilt of his dagger. When that couldn't be heard over the revelry, he had an attendant give a short blast on the horn. As silence fell upon the room, he motioned toward the Elford company. "I have heard that Thane Cynric's bride-to-be is gifted in music and song."

Sorcha could feel a multitude of eyes seeking her out. Blood burned a path to her cheeks.

"She sings like a lark, milord," Cynric replied. He ushered Sorcha away from him. "Go on, my love. Sing for the king."

Sing for the king. It was something she'd dreamed of, being a court musician. But singing in one's mind and actually standing before the imposing Hussa of Bernicia were two different things. Sorcha steeled her knees as she walked forward to take the harp Mildrith held out for her. It was Eavlyn's harp, and most likely the princess's request.

"Would the king have a favorite song?" Sorcha asked, marveling that her voice didn't squeak through the anxiety clenching at her throat.

"I leave the choice to you, milady," Hussa replied. Fierce as his reputation in battle was, when the king smiled, his rugged face with its wide mustache was handsome. Not even his robes and finery could hide his warrior's physique. Running into such a man, shield to shield, would be akin to striking a stone wall. Some even claimed he had stone for a heart ... at least toward his enemies.

Sorcha strummed the harp, allowing the vibrations to reach into her soul. Music could be soothing or stirring. She needed the first for herself and the latter for her audience. "Then I choose a story of Sigheld and Aelfhilde … in Cumbric for our guests and then in our tongue."

The murmur of approval rippling through the hall silenced as she stroked the harp.

> "To Avindr, thane of thanes and his great meadhall,
> such that children of men ere had heard and to his
> queen and bed companion, Gillaug, was born a
> princess of beauty great. The hand of their Aelfhilde
> was sought by warriors, their names sung in glory,
> their conquests rivaled by none in Valhalla's halls…."

Sorcha threw herself into the tale. The princess was abducted by an evil giant and held for ransom. She played the weariness of Sigheld and his servant when they at last reached the rope bridge leading to the giant's hall. Then the low thunder of the giant's approach as he met Sigheld and the high-pitched fury of their blades. There was a full stroke, high to low as the bridge collapsed, sending both to their deaths. Stillness turning to dirge, when Sigheld's man returned to Avindr's meadhall.

But as he sang the stirring eulogy for the fearless warrior, into the hall came Sigheld, leading a horse with the beautiful princess on its back. Sigheld had caught himself in the thick of branches growing out of the cliff side and climbed back up to the top, where he found and rescued the princess.

The Cymri listeners came to their feet in wild approval first, having first heard the happy end of the song. But Sorcha's fellow Saxons soon followed. The shouts, clapping, and stomping of feet continued until the rafters shook loose their dust. Sorcha handed over the harp to a beaming Mildrith and approached the king's table, where she curtsyed.

"And so," she shouted, turning with a magnanimous wave of her arms that finally dampened the noise so she could be heard, "I dedicate my story to our own brave warrior prince and the gentle woman he is to marry two days hence."

Again approval shook the hall, this time in honor of the betrothed prince and princess.

Cynric fairly beamed when Sorcha returned to the seat beside him. "You have your mother's gifts, milady." He took her hand to his lips again, caressing it with them.

The musicians had started playing once more. Hering led Eavlyn to the area in front of the dais, a signal for others to join him.

"I would consider it an honor if you would agree to dance for me, milady," Cynric whispered in her ear.

Still flushed from the excitement of performing for the king, Sorcha nodded. "My pleasure, milord."

Try as Sorcha might, it was not as it had been with Caden on the beach. Though she met his eyes, Sorcha danced apart, only touching Cynric's callused fingers when he reached toward her. But when their fingers met, there was no tingle of awareness. Cynric was no Caden.

"I am the envy of every man here tonight, milady," Cynric told her.

Sorcha smiled, but it was Caden's voice from their frolic on the beach that she heard. *Dance is much like courtship … the touch is as close as the lovers dare to get, for others are watching.*

For that very reason, that others were watching, Sorcha didn't flee. Instead, she twirled away from the thane, lest he see the regret knocking at her heart. Or was it panic?

And when she came back to him, Cynric circled her waist with his thick arm. *Their hearts are already entwining, beating drum to drum in a melody of love.*

The beat within Sorcha's chest was anything but. She grew clammy, cold beneath the hungry stare of her husband-to-be.

Alas, this is as close as you and your betrothed will come to the joys of the bower.

And this close, Sorcha thought she'd faint from anxiety. Try as she might, she could not see herself with Cynric as any more than the child she'd once been to him. It had been easy to contemplate wifely duties when he resided miles away in Elford. But here, close enough to touch, to see that he looked at her as a man, not as her father's friend …

Sorcha sought out the princess as she danced with the prince, savoring his every attention as though he was the only other one in the room. Eavlyn was not only intelligent but brave. Braver than Sorcha. But no matter how noble her cause, Sorcha realized at that moment she could not go through with her wedding to Cynric.

The music came to an end. Red-faced and winded, Cynric bowed before Sorcha. "Milady, you are light as an elf upon your feet and twice as lovely."

Sorcha curtsyed. "Milord is kind." Would he be so kind once she told him she couldn't marry him?

CHAPTER FOURTEEN

Tunwulf shot a glance around the room and swore beneath his breath. "The entire kingdom is hers tonight … and my father, dancing like a pet bear to her tune," he grumbled over his empty cup.

"As I would be, given the chance," his royal companion replied. Aethelfrith, prince of neighboring Diera to Bernicia's south, had left his privileged position near the king's dais to meander among guests. "And so would you," he reminded Tunwulf.

Sorcha's popularity annoyed Rhianon as well, but she was better at hiding it. "The scop may boast a golden voice and pretty face, but you know well I can please far more than the ear and eyes."

Dutifully, Rhianon refilled her consort's cup, allowing him and Diera's atheling another feast for the eye in the dip of her bodice. Rhianon hated the way Saxon women were expected to pour drink for their men like serving wenches. It was demeaning.

"Of that I have little doubt," the prince remarked, staring beyond politeness. "I meant no slight to young Elford's lady." But it was lip service only. Aethelfrith had little regard for women beyond satisfying his thirst and hunger within and without the bower.

Rhianon intended to change that. "None taken, milord prince."

Although she had to be careful. Most Saxons did not tolerate witchcraft but, in their ignorance, drowned those accused of it, sometimes after unthinkable abuse. But Rhianon had seen the Dieran prince secretly forming alliances with the intention to seize Bernicia. She could point out each man Aethelfrith had approached.

Their faces had all appeared in her scrying dish. Not even her nurse and teacher of magic had mastered that art. Rhianon could see what was or had been afoot in any place she could visualize in the water of her sacred bowl. Tunwulf cherished such a gift, and so would Aethelfrith, when the time was right to reveal it. They were cut from the same cloth.

With the pitcher empty, Rhianon moved behind Tunwulf. Pressing her bosom into his back, she whispered low for his ear alone, "Let her enjoy her high ride while she can, darling. We both know it won't last long. I promise you."

Just as she expected, Tunwulf's thinned mouth twitched with the promise of a smile. Men were like clay in her hands, so easily controlled. And unlike Caden, who'd had to be misled subtly, this one would jump to any length to get what was rightfully his. Aware that Aethelfrith still watched her, she blew in Tunwulf's ear and stepped away, mischief lighting in her gaze as he groped at her waist. "The pitcher's empty. I'll be back soon, darling."

"Perhaps we might speak in private," she heard Aethelfrith propose to Tunwulf as she walked away.

Good. Her plan was working. A shadowed alliance between Tunwulf and Diera and the open alliance of Cynric to Hussa placed her lover in both camps, no matter which prevailed in the future.

For scrying revealed only what had been or was afoot, not what was to be.

For now, Rhianon needed to deal with the present. She had to be certain of how the beer was dispensed so that everything would go exactly as she planned … although she might have to use Tunwulf to distract Mildrith. The old crow watched over the barrels as if she'd paid for every dram with her own coin. Blending into the shadows close to the walls where bright tapestries had been hung to give this barbarian place some hint of civilization, Rhianon watched the servants filling the pitchers for the queen and her ladies as they were needed. The goddess forbid any splatter on their gowns.

It would take little effort to stand with Sorcha at the wedding feast and—

"What devious thoughts are churning in that pretty head of yours, I wonder?"

Rhianon spun and caught her breath. Oafish boor that Caden O'Byrne had been when he was drunk, he was a handsome rake who could still make her heart beat like a bird's. She'd mourned his loss as a lover, having found no equal. Certainly not the clumsy and brutish Tunwulf. She cocked her head at him, brandishing a coquettish smile.

"What would you say if I told you I was thinking of you?" she replied, teasing the vee of his plain woolen tunic with her finger. He caught her wrist, stopping her cold.

"I'd say you were lying … *as usual*."

How dare he sling such insult after all she'd done for him? "I lied plenty for you, Caden, and you didn't seem bothered by it then."

"You lied plenty *to* me as well … about the babe, for instance."

Rhianon expelled her breath in exasperation. "Well, what was I *supposed* to do? I wanted more than anything to have a baby, and there was that *woman,*" she said, referring to Caden's sister-in-law, Brenna, "pregnant without even trying! I so wanted to give you an heir that I'd convinced myself I was with child. It's not unheard of."

Caden laughed. "I guess lying just comes naturally from those lips."

Undaunted, Rhianon leaned in. "I remember a time when you worshipped these lips." She ran the tip of her tongue between them, moistening them. "And they worshipped you. By the goddess, I have missed you in my bed."

"Indeed." Leaning against a post between the tapestries, Caden studied her mouth, as if a kiss was merely a breath away.

Rhianon held hers. He wanted her. She knew he did. And she wanted him. The memory of his bare, sweat-damp skin shining in the firelight flushed Rhianon with a warmth she'd not known since that night of dark magic in Keena's hut when her nurse had summoned a spirit to help them.

"But I think those lips have been busy enough without me." He straightened and grinned.

Curse the man! She'd forgotten how playful and absolutely infuriating he could be. Rhianon splayed her hand on his chest. "I'm supposed to sleep with the servants in the queen's hall tonight while Elford and Tunwulf return to their haws below the rock."

"A night without a man." Caden tutted. "You *must* be desperate."

"I am." Her shame was black as a Cheviot bog, but Rhianon didn't care. She recalled what her old nurse had put in his drink.

The black magic she'd worked. Rhianon had the same knowledge now.

"But *I'm* not." Caden lifted the cup in his hand, drained it, and handed it to her. "I don't need anymore," he told her, leaving her to discern whether he meant her or the beer.

The nerve of the oaf! Rhianon swelled with fury in his wake, watching as Caden rejoined the Lothian party and spoke to the priest among them. Whatever Caden said made the holy man look her way, hands clasped, with a milksop smile, as though sending her his blessing. With a curse, she pivoted away rather than meet Martin's eye. Of all the priests in Albion chosen to marry Princess Eavlyn to the atheling, it had to be that old hermit from Glenarden! How Rhianon hated him.

Feared him. Hadn't he driven her and her poor nurse over the cliff with his mumblings?

Her emotions fairly seethed until Rhianon realized that her jaw ached from the clench of her teeth. But she was *not* the hysterical young woman the old fool had driven over a cliff with his prayers to his God. Rhianon was wiser now … and stronger.

Hadn't she amazed Tunwulf when she'd *seen* the Mercians mustering against Diera before the news arrived at Din Guardi? If only the dolt had believed her enough to pass his knowledge on to the king, she might be sitting at the royal table with Aethelfrith himself, instead of relegated as a tagalong to Elford.

Though she hadn't seen Caden's survival.

She hadn't *looked*, Rhianon argued against her doubt. She shoved the empty pitcher at the servant working the beer barrel tap. Why would she, when she'd thought him dead?

And the Devil take Caden O'Byrne now … if she didn't find a way to dispose of him first. The thought drew a smile to her lips. Perhaps she should look into her dish.

⊕

The morning came cloaked in gray, but by midday the sun had batted away the cloud cover and dried the lingering dampness. *Saterdaeg*, the seventh day of the week, was the Christian holy day, so Sorcha accompanied Princess Eavlyn to a Sabbath service held in the front corner of the king's meadhall. The men chose to get a good start on their hunt instead of attending. Later, they would join the ladies at the queen's outing, where a repast of food and drink, as well as a bonfire, would await them.

After a fretful night, in which she could find none of the peace or conviction her royal companion seemed to possess, Sorcha tried paying close heed to the Christian service. Yet her mind would not leave its quandary behind. How would she tell Cynric that she no longer wanted to marry him?

There was no peace to be found in the priest's words. But then, if the Christian God was all they believed, He'd know she was a thief and not deserving of such. Sorcha left disheartened and even more bemused by Christians. The notion of eating the flesh and drinking the blood of the God who'd sacrificed Himself for the sins of mankind was as repugnant as the ancient warriors of Mithra drinking bull's blood. At least the Christians substituted bread and wine for their ceremony.

"It's symbolic," Eavlyn explained later that afternoon in a meadow where the noblewomen had gathered to see the queen's prize falcon hunt. "The bread and wine are consumed to help us remember that

Christ's blood was shed and his flesh torn for our sake. To remind us of His sacrificial love, hence nourishing our spirits as our bodies are nourished by the bread and wine."

"Our heroes are satisfied with a glorious song to honor them," Sorcha replied as they meandered along a well-worn path marked with fresh hoofprints where the men had passed that morning.

It led through a wild hedge of hawthorn and gorse lining a streambed to the forest beyond. Father Martin sat close to the shining ribbon of water on one of two large rocks that Sorcha supposed had been put there to mark the crossing. Elsewise they seemed out of place at the meadow's edge.

"Your heroes are mere men whose deeds are oft undone in time," Eavlyn reminded her. "Jesus is the Son of the Living God, and His sacrifice is everlasting. The heroes are gone, but Christ lives on in Heaven, and His Spirit lives in us."

The other ladies in the party seemed perfectly content to linger by the fire's warmth, but with the sun high overhead, it wasn't that cold. Sorcha's new cloak of chevron-woven wool grew too warm, even when she wandered away from the bonfire to avoid the smoke that continued to shift at whim.

"How can He live in us? How do you know His Spirit is there?"

"By how you live, what you say and do," Eavlyn answered. "We are like trees that bear fruit. Good fruit shows the presence of the Holy Spirit. Bad fruit shows its absence."

That Eavlyn believed in this Christ and that Spirit with all her heart was evident in all she said and did. The princess wanted to serve Him, instead of having the gods and goddesses serve her and paying them for their blessings with sacrifices.

Sorcha wondered what kind of fruit she produced.

"You produce good fruit," Eavlyn said, answering the unspoken question. "The way you care for helpless children."

"But I don't have the Spirit in me," Sorcha pointed out.

"No," Eavlyn agreed, "but I believe your heart is a home ready to receive Him."

But the princess didn't know about Sorcha's stealing. Did that count if it was for a good cause? Gemma always said they did what they had to do to survive. It made sense at the time, but now doubt crept into Sorcha's mind. Yet how could Sorcha have helped the children, if she didn't steal? She couldn't have.

"Hello, Father," Eavlyn called out to the priest, drawing him from his contemplation of the wood beyond. "Do you mind if we join you? The smoke is less worrisome here."

"And the view superb as the day," the priest said, rising from his perch.

Sorcha had to agree. The forest's new dress of reds, golds, and browns was brilliant. A trail left by the men's horses where they'd crossed the stream emerged on the other side of the stream and bore into the wood.

A swift movement in the periphery of her vision drew Sorcha's attention from the sun-dappled trees to the priest, who grabbed at his staff to keep it from rolling off the stone where he'd propped it. This close, it was impossible to miss the carvings on it. A man standing on water. Though Sorcha had been absorbed in her own thoughts that morning, she recalled the priest's speaking about a man walking on water before the bizarre ceremony with the bread and wine.

Another just as curious carving was of a giant fish spitting out a man. Or about to swallow him. Sorcha couldn't decide.

"That's Jonah," Martin said, seeing her interest. "He refused to follow God's command to preach to a city of sinners and was swallowed by a whale as he ran away by ship. But during his time in the whale's belly, he prayed for God's forgiveness and promised to go to the sinners, if God would spare him. So God made the fish spit him out."

"Is that how *you* were persuaded to come to us?" Sorcha teased. Harm to a priest was not as taboo among the Saxon as it was among the Cymri. Perhaps this one took the risk because he had the protection of the Lothian princess.

Father Martin boomed with laughter. "Nay, milady, though I will admit, it might take a while in a whale's belly to get *some* British priests to bring the Word of God to the Saxon people."

Sorcha had heard of the riches plundered from British churches and of the slaughter of their men and women. "Yet here you are," she said. "And Princess Eavlyn." She didn't understand Christians but had to admire their courage.

"We come because God is so wonderful to us that we want to share Him with others," the priest told her. "To tell others what He's done for us and how He is always with us."

"And what is that?" Sorcha pointed to three crude crosses carved at the top of the crosier beneath its mounted silver one.

"The middle one is the cross of Christ. The others belonged to two thieves who were crucified with him," Father Martin replied.

The mention of thieves riveted Sorcha to the spot.

"One thief," he continued, "believed Christ was the Son of God and asked to be remembered. The other scoffed at the Savior and made fun of Him."

"But the one who asked to be remembered," Eavlyn added, "was told he would dine with Christ in paradise that very day."

A thief dining with the Christian God in paradise? Wonder rilled over Sorcha, so much so that she had to resist the urge to pull her cloak close about her shoulders. "Just by asking to be remembered, the thief was accepted by your God?"

"God loves all of us, even though we all are sinners who don't deserve that love," Martin answered gently.

A thief.

"They ask, and He forgives them," Eavlyn explained, "bidding them to go forth and sin no more."

"And if they do?" Sorcha asked, skepticism slowing her words.

"If they fall and are truly sorry and willing to try to do as He bids again, He forgives them again."

"How many times?" There had to be a limit to this God's patience.

"If our repentance is true, seventy times seven and more," Eavlyn replied. "God's love of us has no limit. We are His children."

It simply made no sense to Sorcha. "A father who allows his children to do wrong over and over and doesn't discipline them will have hellions for children." *And thieves.*

"Ah—" The priest held up a finger of caution. "We are often disciplined on This Side, not by God, but by man's law. Or by other consequences of our wrongdoing, reaping what we sow," he explained. "Yet when it's time to cross over to the Other Side, God is waiting with His forgiving love."

"In paradise." A thief dining in paradise … with a God. Sorcha couldn't help but warm to the thought that this God might understand her and Gemma's need to steal. Especially if they never stole again, as Sorcha hoped would be the case. "That is quite a tale, Priest," Sorcha murmured. "Quite a tale."

"I believe on penalty of death that it is a truth that leads to eternal life with the Father who loves us," Martin told her, "or eternal torment by the demons who rebelled against His love. In the end, every man and woman must make a choice as to whom they will give their lives."

Just when Sorcha expected, perhaps even wanted, him to expound more—especially about demons and torment—Martin pointed to where the queen stood with her falconer. "It appears Her Majesty's hunt is about to begin."

At the queen's nod, the falconer untied the straps securing the fowl's hood and removed it to reveal the bright eyes and curved beak of a slate-blue peregrine falcon. With a great spread of dark-fringed wings, the graceful hunter fluffed its breast feathers and took flight, to the admiring applause of Aella's companions. Sorcha watched it shoot away so fast that in moments it was but a tiny speck in the heavens.

"Can your God see the falcon?" she asked.

"He sees even the tiny sparrow when it falls," Martin replied. "He not only created man and all of nature, but He watches over them."

Trained to watch the dogs and heed the clicking object its master used for commands, the falcon just as quickly returned, circling overhead with its sharp gaze fixed on the burnished copper-and-white setter now loosed from its leash. The dog raced along the hedge-row on the meadow side of the water, weaving in and out of brush, searching for hidden prey. Grouse, quail, dove, seabirds ... it was a rich hunting ground. A second dog, a brown spaniel, remained with its master. But it watched its partner, its tail wagging with eagerness to join the hunt.

Sorcha's attention was halfhearted as she mulled over what Father Martin had said about his Christian God, who created and watched over all nature. The same nature many worshipped as gods. She settled next to Eavlyn on a sun-warmed stone beside the narrow crossing. *A God who died and then dined with a thief,* she thought. Perhaps He even watched the setter as it stopped poking around the brush and grew stone still.

"Look, he points," Eavlyn said in a hushed voice.

The master of the hounds gave a signal and unleashed the brown spaniel. It raced toward the spot to flush out the bird. As the dog plunged into the thicket, a startled grouse gave up its cover and flapped desperately for the sky. The ladies, now being served wine, bread, and cheese about the fire, erupted with applause and cries of delight.

The hawk moved like lightning, straight for the hapless bird. Sorcha almost felt sorry for it. Still, she could hardly tear her gaze away as the birds collided in a flurry of feathers. The hawk lifted its prey, soaring in triumph to applause and cheers of the company. The falconer allowed it its glory for a few passes before clicking the command for it to return with the catch.

And God saw it all. The very notion was somehow comforting ... providing one wasn't the grouse, of course. How could there be such an all-knowing, all-loving God as that? Like as not, her new Christian friends had been filling her head with stories. Sorcha believed that Martin and Eavlyn believed, but Sorcha needed more than stories. The other gods had marvelous stories too, and she'd seen no proof of their existence, either.

"Look," Father Martin said, diverting their attention to the forest. "I think I hear the hunting party, the hounds at its head."

The blast of a horn sounded above the distant clamor of the dogs, men, and horses tearing through trees and brush.

"The men return!" one of the queen's ladies exclaimed, distracting the others from the hawk, now delivering its still-quivering prey to the falconer and his men.

Flashes of the men's clothing appeared in and among the distant trees, but their shouts disintegrated beyond Sorcha's understanding. Either the hunters were most anxious for the food and drink awaiting them, or the thrashing of limbs and stampede of hooves meant the hunt was coming to them.

Father Martin grabbed Sorcha's arm and pulled her up. "Get the princess to safety!"

The reason for his urgency was clear now. Another prey ripped through the dense undergrowth, beating a path where there was none. Except that it wasn't a quivering grouse or even a terrified deer. A giant of a boar tore through the underbrush and headed straight for the narrow passage crossing the stream. Blood sprayed from its huge nostrils and throat, from which broken remnants of spears dangled. Its huge black eyes rolled wild in every direction. So fearsome was the sight that Sorcha froze, unable to move.

But at the outburst of screams and the chaos ensuing behind them, she thawed. Grabbing Eavlyn, she pushed the still-struck princess toward cover around the boulder, but Eavlyn tripped over the hem of her skirts.

Sorcha tried to catch her, but in her effort was pulled down across the woman. Time slowed. Enough for Sorcha to reason that the beast might gore her, but the princess might be safe.

Beyond them, the queen's guardsmen, white-faced, raced for the weapons they'd left with the horses. A babe who'd discovered his first legs could have moved faster. There was no way the men could retrieve their spears and stop the beast from plowing straight into her and the princess in its death rage.

"God before me!"

Sorcha looked over her shoulder to see the source of the thunderous summons. Father Martin waded into the knee-deep water, planting himself squarely in the beast's path, his staff of carved stories extended like a spear. Perhaps if it had a blade instead of an ornate cross, the holy man stood a chance.

"God beside me!" he shouted as the beast broke free of the wood, speeding all the faster for him. As though he were the source of its pain.

Sorcha heard herself scream, long and dragged out by the same sluggish passage of time that suspended the beast's great lunge. Its tusks were aimed at the priest with only the staff bridging the two. She closed her eyes and buried her face in the princess's shoulder, bracing for their turn. But a loud rip of cloth bade her look in spite of herself. Instead of boring into Martin, the beast careened off the priest as though he were a stalwart oak....

And rolled to a stop within a finger's length of her and Eavlyn. The tusk that had run through the holy man's robe still bore a remnant of it. Yet Martin himself somehow still stood, unmoved. And, unlike Sorcha and Eavlyn, unbloodied by the fountain that sprayed with the animal's dying spasms.

With one great shudder, the boar heaved a last breath, the hot stench assailing Sorcha's nostrils, making her gag.

"Blessed God in Heaven," Eavlyn whispered as Sorcha struggled away. The princess pulled herself to her knees. Hands clasped, she rocked to and fro, repeating the words again and again.

"'Tis dead, milady," Sorcha assured her from the much-needed support of the rock at her back. Yet in her mind's eye, she could still see the beast charging into the priest. Could hear an ear-splitting crack, as though it had struck the crosier and snapped it in its lunge for the priest. Yet the staff that Martin held frozen in front of him was as untouched as he was. Only Martin's lips moved in fervent prayer.

Two guards reached the princess, pulling her to her feet.

"Are you harmed, milady?" one asked.

She and Sorcha were both covered with the beast's gore.

"Did you see him?" Eavlyn asked.

"Aye, milady. Your priest is either a brave man or a fool," the other remarked.

"Either way, he's the luckiest man I've ever seen," said the first.

"Nay," Eavlyn snapped, impatient. "I meant the warrior who appeared from nowhere and jumped in front of Father Martin. He grabbed the boar by the tusks and threw it to the side, breaking its neck."

Reluctant, Sorcha translated, for she'd not seen anyone but the priest.

"I saw this brave Saxon lady throw herself over you to protect you, but no warrior," the guard replied.

She'd fallen, but Sorcha was in too much shock to set the man right. Though she would have done her best to protect Eavlyn.

Only when touched by the other guardsmen did Father Martin seem to shake off his paralysis. When he did, the poor man dropped to his knees and gathered his staff to him. With his other hand, he crossed himself.

"God be thanked!" he said again and again.

Meanwhile one of the guards who'd come to Eavlyn's aid lifted the head of the dead beast by the tusks. Disbelief claimed his blunt-featured face as he turned to his companion. "What the lady said is true. The priest broke its neck with his bare hands."

Except that Martin hadn't done a thing. Sorcha had seen that much, even if she hadn't seen Eavlyn's warrior. He'd just stood there holding out his staff.

"'Twas a miracle." Eavlyn beamed at Sorcha. "A miracle."

The same wonder infected Sorcha, though she wasn't certain what she'd seen—or not seen. Without doubt something truly amazing had happened. She supposed *miracle* was as good a word as any for it.

CHAPTER FIFTEEN

Weddings were much ado about nothing as far as Caden was concerned, especially if they were held inside a smoke-filled hall. But the morning had come cloaked in clouds that appeared thick with rain, so Caden was all but pressed by the privileged inside guests against one of the gilded carved columns supporting the high roof. A decorative garland of fresh greenery pricked his tunic while he waited with the rest for the arrival of the bridal party, but he'd have to elbow the man next to him to scratch.

Already Prince Hering and the Bernician and Lothian nobles had taken their places at the head of the hall, each contingent boasting its holy man. A richly robed Saxon witan hovered by a makeshift altar brought in for a sacrifice so that Woden might bless the marriage. Akin to Cymri druids, who were doctors, judges, teachers, and more, this witan was a priest. Next to him stood his Christian counterpart in plain undyed wool, belted by a worn and knotted prayer rope. Draped around Father Martin's neck was a narrow scarf of scarlet, adorned with a golden embroidered cross and tassel. Caden had never seen the former hermit wear such trappings before.

Though Martin needed no such finery to impress the heathens. No one in Din Guardi doubted the priest's supernatural favor after yesterday's hunt. No witness told the same story as to what exactly happened, but all agreed it was a miracle that neither the priest nor the two ladies were hurt. Having been with the hunters, all Caden witnessed were the two bloodied, visibly shaken women.

Though that wasn't the first close call with death that day. The prince himself had had a near miss with the boar. Hering had stalked the boar into a thicket and cast the first spear. It hit its mark, but the wild animal charged him. His cousin was supposed to assist the prince, help with the kill if needed, but for some reason, Aethelfrith danced around the then wrestling prince and beast instead of going in for the killing blow. It was only when Hussa lunged in and sank his spear into the animal's throat that Aethelfrith threw his weapon. With a third spear lodged in its neck, the beast wrested free of the three of them and bolted off.

A round of cheering from the outside guests for whom there was no room in the hall signaled the approach of the ladies from the women's quarters. That sent a ripple of excitement over the more privileged clustered inside—and sweating like hard-ridden horses, if Caden was any example.

Such revelry, and for what? An arranged marriage that, if God smiled upon the couple, *might* turn to love. His mother and father's had not. Or a love match that would turn to hate, as Caden's had. The festivities would drag on and on, especially a royal affair like Hering and Eavlyn's. With Sorcha having made her choice to marry Elford, there was little to keep Caden around, were he not part of the Lothian entourage. As such, he was required to wait for at least another two days of revelry after the couple had shared their bower joys for the first time.

Caden snorted. As if the coupling of royal enemies could bring peace. From what he'd seen of Hussa's court the last few days, the king had his hands full watching his back against his brothers and their kin. And Caden knew from his own past actions how low one brother would stoop to usurp another's rights.

"But that was in the past."

Caden perked up, listening, wondering if that voice had been his wishful thinking or from the God he'd committed to serve. How drunk he'd been with joy and thanksgiving that afternoon on the beach, yet now he grumbled as if he were the one having to marry. Why God had smoothed his way to Sorcha and run him smack into a stone wall vexed him.

Unless his task wasn't finished.

A blast from the herald's horns pulled Caden away from his indecision and called everyone's attention to the hall's main entrance. A small golden-haired girl, clad in white linen and wearing a crown of flowers, backed into the room. Her task was to mark the bride's path with dried rose petals. Following her came the maid Lunid, bearing a fine sword, its hilt inlaid with jewels and gilt.

Admiration rippled through the throng.

"Made in Caron," came a wisp of admiration from nearby.

"Maybe magic, like Arthur's sword."

The swordsmiths at Caron's ironworks were unequalled, and this sword was polished to a mirror sheen. But Caden doubted the Lady of the Lake would share the secret of Excalibur's making for a Saxon's use. Some said it contained a metal from a fallen star that gave the weapon a finish that wouldn't tarnish or rust and a strength that could cut through its iron counterparts. Only the Grail keepers knew its secret.

The horns faded. Harpists and pipers struck up a gentler music the moment Eavlyn entered and proceeded toward her waiting groom. Her dress was the color of sun-bleached clouds, flecked with bits of gold sewn into the fabric. With each movement, it made her tall, slight body shimmer in the light. From her shoulders fell a blue silk robe that seemed to float endlessly behind her.

Graceful and stately as Gwenhyfar, Caden observed. Blaise of Dunfeld had every right to swell with pride, while Modred smiled like the cat that ate—

Caden's breath caught.

Carrying the hem of the long robe was Sorcha. If Eavlyn was the purity of gold and snow, Sorcha was fire, like her namesake. Her knee-length robe of bronze brocade caught and threw back the reflection of the torch flames mounted high on the hall pillars. She walked like a queen, with naught but a golden band to tame that glorious mane of red hair.

"Never would I allow a woman in my wedding party who was prettier than I," a female exclaimed from somewhere beyond them.

The remark had merit. No longer pale from shock as she'd been when the hunting party caught up with the boar, Sorcha outshone the bride and stirred the blood of any man with eyes, if Caden was an example. He'd wanted to speak to her yesterday, but Hering and Elford spirited her and the princess off to Din Guardi.

Curiosity drew Caden's gaze to the Elford party. On sighting Cynric, Caden's stomach curled. The man clearly seduced Sorcha in his mind. Caden swore beneath his breath. He needed air. Lots of it. And maybe some beer to make Cynric's expression go away. Except that leaving now was almost impossible, so thick was the throng. Would that he'd left yesterday … the wedding be hanged.

Sorcha fought a gag reflex as the witan slit the throat of a bleating goat at the altar. Its blood spattered his robe and drained into a ceremonial bowl as Sorcha's drained from her face. After yesterday, she'd seen enough blood for a lifetime. And from the pallor of Eavlyn's face, so had the princess. Sorcha tore her attention from the grisly sight of the still-twitching animal. Between that and the heat of the crowd surrounding her, she felt faint.

Or maybe it was due to the fact that she'd spent yet another night trying to muster the courage and words to tell Elford she could not marry him. Eavlyn and Sorcha retired early from last night's feast without censure, given their harrowing experience yesterday. Lunid informed them that it was rumored Father Martin had used magic to turn the boar, but Sorcha was more intrigued by the tall, golden warrior Eavlyn swore had killed the beast with his bare hands.

Sorcha wondered if Eavlyn had seen God Himself.

Lunid, of course, crossed herself. "No one has seen God except Moses!" That launched a story of how the Christian God had allowed His people to become slaves because of bad choices they'd made. Sorcha thought a father who'd do that wasn't much better than Ebyn's folks and said so. The last count Sorcha had, Lunid had crossed herself over fifty-six times.

A growing murmur of awe and approval drew Sorcha to the present, where the gifts between the father of the bride and the groom were exchanged. Never had she seen the like of chests filled with torques of gold and silver, Roman hand mirrors, flasks of Roman glass, piles of jewels, necklaces, brooches, ewers, pins, and clasps.

Sorcha fingered one of the three strands of amber resting against her neck. She'd have to give her jewels back, of course. And the dresses, no matter how she reveled in the feel of the fine linen against her skin and the elegant flow of the russet wool about her form. This was as close to being a noblewoman as she would ever get.

Yet, for all the riches, reality struck when the bride's father handed over her shoe to Hering, who tapped her gently on the head, passing full authority over Eavlyn from father to husband. The princess's life was no longer her own, even if she would live in the lap of luxury. The elegant slipper would later be placed at the head of the nuptial bed as a symbol of Hering's authority. Not a partnership, as Sorcha's parents had shared.

Sorcha wiped a trickle of sweat from her temple. If the ceremony did not end soon, she'd swoon or be sick from this smother of people. Hering exchanged the keys to his household, establishing Eavlyn as its lady, for the magnificent sword that showed she recognized him as her lord and protector.

Then the Christian priest wrapped their hands in his mantel and prompted them with vows made till death took them. Mercifully, he was not as long-winded as he'd been yesterday at the service. His prayer for the union to bring about peace between the two kingdoms, to demonstrate all things were possible with the living God, brought an end to the ceremony.

"And now by the power of the Holy Spirit," Martin announced with his boar-stopping voice, "I give you Prince Hering and Princess Eavlyn of Bernicia, now husband and wife before God and all witnesses."

Thunderous huzzahs filled the room. Guests closed in to congratulate the couple, but Sorcha left Lunid to tend to Eavlyn's robe and made her way with as much haste as she could against the converging tide toward the nearest door … that leading to the kitchens. The moment fresh air filled her lungs, her dizziness subsided. Would that she could keep on going through Din Guardi's gate and down the causeway to her home and Gemma.

But that was not an option. She had a duty to serve the Elford party, though it would be some time before guests settled enough to pass around the drink. She also had to face Cynric. She was not the courageous woman Eavlyn was. She was not willing to sacrifice like the princess and her God. Sorcha wasn't worthy to carry the hem of Eavlyn's robe or bend the ear of her God with her quandary.

Though if You are listening, Cymri God …

"Milady Sorcha, are you ill?"

Sorcha winced at the sound of Cynric's voice. *Nay, I'm just a coward who goes back on her word.*

She gave up the support of the plaster wall at her back to see her father's longtime friend exiting the hall in concern.

"I am, sir," she replied. "Ill with dread for what I must tell you."

Garbed in a splendid black tunic trimmed in silver thread and with gold adorning his neck and every finger, Cynric approached her and put his thick hands on her shoulders. "Am I so fearsome that my bride-to-be grows distraught at the notion of speaking to me?" he asked gently.

Sorcha met his gaze through a glaze of emotion. His expression was as kind as his voice, magnifying her guilt. "I cannot marry you, milord."

There. It was out.

"But I will give you the deed to my father's business and warehouse, just as I vowed," she blurted out. "I owe you as much. And, of course, I'll return your gifts."

"My little Sorcha." Cynric pulled her to him in a bear of a hug. "You've never been as good a thief or vixen as your mother and Gemma. You possess Aelwyn's fire and gift of music and song, aye, but your heart is too big, and your father's honesty runs too deep."

Uncertain what to say, Sorcha held her tongue and backed away as the thane let her go.

"Which is why I ask you now," Cynric continued. "What has changed your mind?"

"I've found my birth mother." That was when this tortuous indecision started. The night Caden of Lothian walked into the tavern. "Or, rather, she found me."

Cynric's brow shot up. "Your birth mother here? In Din Guardi? Is she with the Lothian company?"

Sorcha shook her head. "Nay, milord. She sent a Cymri warrior to bring me home to Trebold."

"Trebold. And where is this Trebold?"

"Somewhere in Lothian. I … I don't remember much about it." She moved farther from the door as a contingent of servants paraded past with large tortoise shells piled high with breads. "But if my mother needs me, how can I refuse her? Especially since I missed her so much when I was first taken in by Wulfram and Aelwyn. 'Tis something I must do."

Cynric pulled thoughtfully on the tip of a bush of mustache. "Then do it, child," he said with a nod. "Go to her and bring her back to Elford. I will see her well cared for."

Sorcha muffled her groan of despair. *How—*

"I've waited all these years for you to grow up," he went on. "I can wait a few more months. Your mother will be there to see us wed."

Freya's mercy! "You don't understand, milord. My mother wishes me to help her run her estate. How could I be your wife and live in Lothian? We've only just arranged a peace between us."

Please don't make me say it. Don't make me hurt you.

"This Cymri warrior she sent for you. Would he be that young bear of a man with wild yellow hair who kept you company a few nights ago?"

A plague on Tunwulf's loose tongue!

"The same who frolicked on the beach with you as well?"

Sorcha's mouth grew slack with shock. "You've had me watched, milord?" Blood flushed warm to the surface of her skin, partly from embarrassment and partly from indignation. "I'll have you know that Caden was every bit a gentleman, who remained one night with the boy and me when I was ill, because we'd been threatened by the moneylender's churl." She crossed her arms, building more of a huff. "And Wada as much as told me that I would suffer the same fate as my parents for crossing him. Better I'd run him through with my father's sword and been done with—"

Cynric pressed a finger to her lips. For the first time Sorcha saw something dangerous flicker in his gaze. "This man Wada admitted to being responsible for the fire?"

She nodded. "I'd have run him through, but Caden stopped me and ran him off."

"He was right to do so," Cynric told her. "'Tis *I* who will deal with him … and this Caden," he added in a voice like a low thunder in the distance.

A shaft of fear pierced Sorcha's anger. "But … but Caden protected me."

"And well he should," Cynric replied. The corner of his mouth tugged, but Sorcha didn't know if it was from anger or humor. "He fancies you."

"Milord!" And curse the heat scorching its way to her face. But the idea was absurd.

"The man cannot take his eyes off you … that is, when he's not watching me," Cynric added wryly. "You are a beautiful young woman. That is why I've had someone keep an eye on you when I've had to be at Elford. For your protection."

The flap of emotion beating blood through Sorcha's veins settled like a sail robbed of wind.

"And that"—his expression grew grim—"is why I will send an escort with you to Trebold. I trust no man with you."

Did her ears betray her? "I have your leave to go?" she asked. "To possibly not return?"

"Sorcha, Sorcha." With a heart-heavy sigh, Cynric put his arm about her shoulders, so much as her father used to do. "I gave my word to your father that I would put your happiness above all else.

That I would spoil you as he and Aelwyn did. If this is the direction your wild heart desires to go, Sorcha, then so be it."

At that moment the gray cloud cover overhead parted, allowing a shaft of the day's first sunlight. It beat down upon them, warming Sorcha's face as Cynric's declaration warmed her heart.

"I did not know such kindness and understanding existed." She meant every word. She'd fretted so much, all for naught. "I thought you would be angry—"

"I am disappointed. I would not be human if I were not," he added with a humorless laugh. "I had hoped that I could make you happy, give you whatever you wanted, but I am not angry, Sorcha." He leaned over and kissed her hair. "But I *will* speak to that Cymri."

"He is an honorable man."

Was it possible? Just like that, Cynric would let her go and endure the humiliation of having their betrothal dissolved?

All things are possible with the living God. The priest's words from the ceremony gave Sorcha pause.

Nay, she told herself. *'Twas coincidence.* She hadn't even asked the Christian God for help. Not in so many words.

"Are you feeling ill again?" Cynric turned her toward him, snatching her from her introspection.

"Nay, milord." She glanced upward at the widening shaft of sun. She'd heard the Christian God lived there. "I'm feeling grateful that my father chose such a kind and understanding man to watch over me."

"It seems as though the sun has decided to grace the prince's wedding day after all." Cynric offered her his arm. "Shall we return to the hall, milady?"

"Aye," Sorcha replied, linking her arm with his. "And I'll be honored to fetch a pitcher of Din Guardi's finest beer for you and your men."

"Just be happy, Sorcha." Elford patted her arm. "Be happy, and I will have kept my blood oath to the man who saved my life and became my dearest friend."

As they went inside, Sorcha cast one last glance overhead. It was as if this God—or the Wyrds—had written hope with a golden pen across the sky … and on her heart.

CHAPTER SIXTEEN

"There you are," Rhianon exclaimed as Sorcha made her way to where the royal women filled flagons of drink for their men and guests. "The princess asked for you before she carried her first wine to her husband."

If Rhianon sought to make Sorcha feel guilty, she succeeded. Sorcha really liked Eavlyn and would do nothing to upset the princess. Which was why she'd made a hasty retreat after the ceremony rather than become ill and distract from the joy of the occasion.

"I needed fresh air. Perhaps now that the sun is coming out, some of the guests will go outside, and it won't be so close in here."

"Just take this—" Rhianon handed her a pitcher of hand-painted Romanware filled with beer—"and serve your lord. He'll be anxious, wondering where his bride-to-be has disappeared to."

Sorcha laughed. She could hardly recall the last time she had. It felt wonderful. "Milord was with me," she told her companion.

With that, Sorcha danced away, leaving Rhianon to speculate. At least it felt like dancing ... until Sorcha nearly collided with Mildrith, who entered the alcove where the kegs of wine and beer were stored. Sorcha nearly sloshed some of the beer on the crisp white apron the steward's wife always wore.

"Oh, s-sorry, Mildrith!" Sorcha stammered. "I didn't see you coming."

Mildrith gave her a rare grin. "I am usually hard to miss seeing, milady."

Sorcha brandished a wide smile at her.

"You look happy," the big woman observed.

"Oh, I am, Mildrith. It's a glorious day for our prince and his lady."

With a slight dip of respect, Sorcha turned and headed through the clusters of celebrating guests toward Cynric and his contingent. To her delight, Tunwulf's dour face was not among them. The day improved by the moment, she thought, approaching Cynric.

"Your beer, milord," she announced, drawing his attention from a conversation with a companion.

Cynric held out his mug. It was rounded at the bottom so that he could not set it down—a means of measuring the amount one drank, since it could not be refilled by a prankster bent on his intoxication without his knowledge.

"Thank you, lovely Sorcha," Cynric said when the mug was filled to the brim. "I hope you will join us soon."

"To be sure, milord. And you are most welcome." With a slight curtsy, she turned to serve the others—

And ran smack into Tunwulf. To her dismay, the pitcher flew from her hands and crashed to the floor, spilling its contents.

"Oh, I didn't see you behind me," she gasped as Tunwulf backed off, brushing spilt beer off his tunic. "I am sorry, milord."

"No harm done." He kicked the remains of the broken pitcher under the table. "Just fetch us another, wen—" He broke off with a sharp glance at Cynric. "Milady," he amended. "Sorry, Father, I still have trouble separating the tavern wench from future stepmother."

"My betrothed has never been, nor will ever be, a tavern wench," Cynric snapped. "She is a gifted singer and musician, a prize for any man she chooses."

If looks could wound, the one Tunwulf gave his father was fatal.

"I'll be back with more drink," Sorcha promised. Hopefully in one of the unbreakable bronze pitchers.

Not even a run-in with Tunwulf could spoil her joy. And she wanted to share it—with Caden, if she could find him. Thankfully, the Cymri guests were easily spotted, due to Father Martin's crosier rising above them. Sorcha wove through the throng, giving broad smiles in answer to the compliments she received from men and women alike. It was unlikely they'd be as open to her once it was made known that she would not become Lady Elford.

But *she* was going to meet her mother. Myrna. No matter how Sorcha tried to picture her, Myrna's face blended in with that of Aelwyn. And just think. In time, Sorcha would be tavern mistress and own her own land. *In time.* She was in no hurry.

"Caden!" Sorcha waved, wading past two Saxon men engaged in a contest to see who might empty his mug first to where the tall fair-haired stranger stood. He and his priest didn't seem to share the amusement of the Saxons surrounding them.

"You disapprove, sir?" Sorcha asked, casting a glance at the merrymakers.

"It's not for me to judge," Caden replied. "I've drunk more than my share of the heath fruit."

"It does seem that your people have an exceeding fondness for drinking until totally inebriated," Father Martin put in. "Which I would think could be dangerous."

"Hadn't you best be serving your lord?" Caden looked meaningfully at Sorcha's empty hands.

"Aye, but he will not be my lord. That's why I sought you out." Sorcha seized the Cymri's hands in her own in her excitement. "I've decided to return with you to Trebold and my mother!"

The food, including roasted boar, was plentiful so that by the time most of it had been consumed, the guests were ready to move about more freely. By then, with the clearing of the clouds, a bonfire had been lit outside the hall, and the musicians led the guests to it. A board and benches were set up for the newlyweds and the royal contingent, while guests brought out even more into the pleasantly cool night air.

In far better humor and more comfortable than he'd been inside, Caden looked up as drummers struck up a primal rhythm that dampened the cacophony of so many conversations. Hering, Aethelfrith, and two other young Saxon men entered the cleared area by the fire, stripped to the waist but for a leather vest and wearing a ceremonial headdress—a stag's head. Each carried a spear and leapt about the high-reaching fire as if on the hunt. Each footfall, each jump and turn, each thrust of the spear melded with drumbeat.

It held Caden's attention for a while, but he was more interested in watching Sorcha when he could spot her in this throng. Maybe what Father Martin had said about God's smoothing the way for Caden, having a plan … maybe there was something to it after all. All he knew was that her news had made him as light as Sorcha's step.

The tempo changed, drawing his gaze to where the dancers had made a full circle about the fire. No longer hunters, they turned warriors and paired off in combat, still to the beat of the music. The grace of combat to music fascinated the onlookers, Caden included, though fighting like that on a battlefield would get them all killed before the first sword ring stopped.

He wasn't sure how a winner was determined, but soon there was only the atheling prince and his cousin pitted against each other and, suddenly, the notion of a show was over. Sweat beaded their wiry, muscled torsos and foreheads as the two faced off. One would think Aethelfrith would yield to his cousin in honor of the wedding, but the Dieran princeling showed no sign of easing into submission.

The staccato beat of the drums, the smoke curling upward from a spark-spitting fire brought out the beast in the men, who were well matched. Aethelfrith made a lunge at his cousin, who sidestepped the blade, but not before it sliced the flesh of Hering's rib cage. With a howl, Hering spun about quick as lightning and took out Aethelfrith's feet. It was over when he pressed his spear to his cousin's throat, but the angry flickering in their gazes spoke of the clash being far from done.

Hering danced away after a breath's pause, his spear raised in triumph. Eavlyn flew to her husband's side to a chorus of "Huzzahs" and cheers and applied one of the linen towels used for hand washing to the cut.

"Hussa and Hering had better keep an eye on that young stag," Father Martin said under his breath, startling Caden from his observation.

"'Tis naught but a scratch," the triumphant prince shouted to his adoring audience. "An accident."

His sidewise look at where Aethelfrith blended into the crowd said otherwise.

"My caution to you all," Hering continued. "Dance with our ladies, not weapons."

That said, the harpists and pipers struck up a lively tune. Gathering Eavlyn's hands into his, the prince began to skip in circles, as if just gazing into his bride's eyes rejuvenated him.

For Eavlyn's sake, and for that of peace, Caden hoped the marriage would serve the purpose of the Grail Church. That Eavlyn could build a church on the land gifted to her by her husband. As long as Hussa was king, it stood a chance. But many Saxons felt this wedding was a coward's way of conquering the land and—

A bloodcurdling scream ripped through the gaiety about the fire, loud enough to silence the musicians and, with that, slow the frolic. Caden looked in its direction and spied a cluster of people gathered near Hussa and his guests. Caden supposed that someone had passed out, either from illness or drink. Curious, he followed Father Martin through the crowd.

"Give way," the priest shouted. "Give way. I am a man of medicine *and* a man of God. Give way."

It seemed an eternity to cross such a short span of space, but when they did, Caden saw the source of the commotion. Cynric of

Elford lay on the ground, his head cradled in Sorcha's lap. One was as pale as the other. Hussa knelt by his loyal thane's side, Tunwulf opposite him.

"Father Martin, can you help him?" Sorcha cried out upon seeing the priest. "We danced, and he suddenly fell ill and dropped to the ground, clutching his stomach. Please!"

Tunwulf gave way for the priest and Hussa for another of the white-robed witans, one whom Caden assumed knew medicine. Not that it took a scholar to see Cynric was clearly at death's door. Yet the man rallied with remarkable strength, seizing the witan's robe as Martin prayed.

"I … I am murdered," Cynric said in a loud voice.

Shock rippled in waves away from the fallen man.

"Nay, milord," Sorcha cried. "Don't say such a thing." Panicked, she looked at Martin. "Touch him with your staff. Call on your God."

Martin placed a comforting hand on her shoulders. "I *am* calling on Him, milady."

"My king …" Cynric gasped as a spasm seized his abdomen.

Hussa moved in closer. "Aye, my loyal friend."

"See … see that my intended bride keeps her betrothal gifts … all of them."

"Nay—"

The Bernician king cut Sorcha off. "I will."

"My horse thane Octa is worthy of Elford," the dying man declared, loud enough for those close by to hear.

"That does it!" Tunwulf dragged Martin away. "Look at him. He's clearly out of his mind. I am his *son.*"

Hussa met Tunwulf's outrage with a hard, level look. "I believe your father is as sane as myself, but," he added diplomatically, "I will consider you *both*."

"My lord, you must save your strength," Sorcha insisted. She wiped her own tears from Cynric's ashen face, shaking her head as though she could not accept the reality before her. "Let the doctors tend you."

"If I don't know what poison he has been given, how can I counter it?" the witan complained.

"Protect—" Another spasm cut off Cynric, drawing up his legs.

"Hush, sweet lord," Sorcha cooed. "You're sore sick—"

The seizure let him go … and with a half-groan, half-sigh, the thane let go of life itself.

Suddenly Tunwulf pointed an accusing finger at Sorcha. "Tell us. Tell us what poison you used, wench, for I have seen none serve my father but you this night."

"Milord …" Sorcha shook Cynric as though to wake him. Tunwulf might have been speaking in another tongue for all the attention she gave him. "Do something!" she pleaded to the priests. "Please. Either of you."

"Ask any of our men," Tunwulf charged the onlookers. "Have you seen any serve my father, save this red-haired vixen?"

"What reason would Sorcha have to poison Cynric?"

Caden didn't realize he'd shouted the challenge until Tunwulf turned his belligerent gaze on him.

Rancor saturated the man's ready reply. "Because Sorcha plans to run away with you, Caden of Lothian!"

CHAPTER SEVENTEEN

"Is this true, milady?" Hussa towered over Sorcha, looking every bit the imposing figure the title *bretwalda* entailed. While the king's voice was gentle, his gaze had turned to stone.

Sorcha held Cynric's head tenderly against her, trying to register all that had been said. What was wrong with these people? Couldn't they see Cynric needed immediate attention?

Because Sorcha plans to run away with you, Caden of Lothian!

Shock at Tunwulf's accusation knocked Sorcha's thoughts one way, anger another.

"Nay, milord." Surely Hussa did not believe Tunwulf's lies. Tunwulf, whose support was always conspicuously absent. "'Tis nothing like that villain says. Caden of Lothian came on my birth mother's behalf to reunite us. I plan to return to Lothian with him and *with*," she said more loudly, "Cynric's blessing. But this is no time for such talk. We need to tend your friend. He'll tell you himself when he's come around."

"Milady Sorcha," the king replied grimly, "Cynric is gone."

It couldn't be. "He's only lost consciousness!" Determined to prove the king wrong, Sorcha bent over, placing her ear to Elford's nose and mouth. No trace of breath.

"A mirror," she shouted in desperation. "We need a mirror." Oft times, when breath could not be felt, it might be seen.

Hussa reached down and took her by the shoulders. "Let the witans see to his body."

Body. The finality of the word slammed Sorcha again. Tears spilling, she eased Cynric's head to the ground before allowing the king to help her rise. "This can't be. It just can't be." Her words tumbled out in a rush, aimed at no one. "We only just spoke of dissolving our betrothal. Cynric gave me his blessing to go to my mother. He said he wanted me to be happy … that he promised my father to take care of me and …"

"Did you serve Cynric his drink, Sorcha?" the king interrupted.

"Yes. I was late because he and I had been talking and—"

Rhianon!

Sorcha glanced around the gathered crowd but saw no sign of Tunwulf's companion. Sorcha pointed an accusing finger at Tunwulf. "'Twas *his* strumpet who handed me a pitcher filled with beer. The very pitcher I took to Cynric."

"But Rhianon had already served me from that same flagon, and I am not sick," Tunwulf pointed out. "Though I would have been, had I allowed you to fill my cup after you'd filled my father's." He looked to where the Elford party stood looking on in a mix of disbelief and grief. "So would you all, had I not bumped into her, accidentally breaking the pitcher with the poison."

"Where is this broken vessel now?" one of the white-robed witans asked above the whispers riffling through the crowd.

"I kicked the pieces beneath the board," Tunwulf answered. "It should still be there. Perhaps you can find the nature of her poison from it."

"If there's poisoning afoot here, I will swear on my life that your Rhianon is the culprit," a voice boomed from behind Hussa.

Attention shifted to where Caden stepped out of the crowd. "Milord," he said to Hussa, "Rhianon was … *is* my wife. And it was with poison that she sought to murder my father."

"The testimony of her scorned lover." Tunwulf sneered. "Why should we listen to you? Were you not behind that scheme?"

Caden cast his gaze down, and Sorcha's heart sank. She knew how to read a crowd, and what she saw on the sea of faces surrounding them was rampant suspicion, even accusation.

"Milord," Father Martin spoke up. "I can personally testify that what Sorcha said about her mother sending Caden in search of her long-lost daughter to be true. And I can also swear that Rhianon, Caden's wife, conspired to murder both his father and brother."

Tunwulf laughed. "At his demand. She told me how he bullied her to help him become chief of Glenarden. The very land from which you are exiled, I believe."

Caden shook his head. "Nay, not at my demand. But I am ashamed to say that I went along with her idea and deserve my exile."

Sorcha swayed unsteadily. His words, humble as they were, only made things worse.

"Enough!" Hussa held up his hand to silence Caden and to Tunwulf. "Enough accusations and speculation. I will have my sheriff look into this matter."

"Milord, Caden speaks the truth," Father Martin declared. "His wife is a witch. I have seen her work her magic—"

"What magic, Priest?" the doctor among the witans asked in contempt. "You Christians accuse most of what we do as magic."

Father Martin shook his head. "Sir, you are mistaken. I respect your knowledge of nature and the elements—"

"Did you see this woman poison your man's father?" the witan inquired.

"Nay," Martin acknowledged, "but her teacher practiced dark magic with demons, and I did myself help free this man of one—"

"Her *teacher*," Tunwulf pointed out, "not Rhianon."

"I said enough!"

Hussa gave a sign to one of his heralds, who promptly silenced the growing murmur of the crowd with a horn's blast so loud that Sorcha started.

"Milords and ladies," the Bernician king announced, "today is my son's wedding. We will celebrate. And on the morrow, we will ferret out the murderer of my brother-in-arms. That I promise as—"

"Milords! Help us, milords!"

Hussa breathed an oath of exasperation as yet another commotion erupted, this time bursting from the hall with Mildrith at its head. The big woman's face was flushed, and her buxom chest heaved from haste.

"We need a doctor," she cried in a voice loud as the herald's horn. "The woman Rhianon—" Mildrith wrung her apron, affording a darting glance at her husband, Hussa's seneschal. "I fear she's dying … poisoned by the look of it."

Sorcha grabbed at her sinking heart as Hussa whirled to face her, bitter accusation hurling at her from his countenance. And who could blame him? She had no answer for Cynric's death, much less Rhianon's misfortune.

"Guards, put this lady *and* Caden of Lothian in irons," he ordered, not taking his fierce gaze from her face.

"Careful, lord king," King Modred advised lowly. "He is one of my finest captains, and she is favored by your new daughter-by-law."

"Both he and the lady will be treated well," the bretwalda assured the Lothian king in the same tone. "But to ensure that he and the lady do not flee before we find out what mischief is afoot, it will be my guardhouse."

"But we are innocent, milord!" Sorcha protested as two guards seized her by the arms.

Ignoring her outburst, Hussa glanced after the contingent of witans who rushed into the hall and motioned his seneschal. "Wilfrid, have the witans see to the situation inside," he ordered. "And you, sir, will fetch my gift stool and treasure chest. We need a distraction to restore the humor to this festivity. I have guests to entertain, and I *will* see my son to his nuptial bed this night."

Caden didn't know what to think. Rhianon was poisoned, hovering between life and death, according to the servant who'd brought him the evening meal. The witans were with her. Seated on the floor, his back to the rough timber wall, Caden contemplated the wood-hinged door, but his thoughts tumbled. Rhianon's was a seemly fate, if she'd accidentally fallen victim to her own scheme.

His fists clenched. So help him, if Caden found out that she *was* at the bottom of this travesty, he'd send her to the Other Side himself. He conjured the feel of his hands closing about her slender neck, the satisfaction of giving her a taste of her own vileness. His anger and frustration fed the notion like fuel to a fire….

But it wasn't enough. Something within him checked. Not reason, to be sure, for Caden had every reason to want Rhianon dead. It was something else. The same something that enabled him to hold his peace upon realizing Sorcha and Gemma had stolen his purse. The old Caden would have exposed them for what they were and taken delight in exacting the revenge.

Had he gone soft, or was this some sort of newfound goodness?

"Grace received demands grace to be given."

Gone soft of heart *and* hearing voices in his head.

Caden ran his fingers through his hair. If this was God working on his spirit, why was he in chains?

"Why?" he whispered softly. "Abba, I don't understand. I was doing Your will. Or trying—"

Voices sounded outside. The outer door opened, and a moment later the bolt to Caden's cell slid loudly from its keeper. Father Martin entered, carrying a lamp. Behind him in the narrow hallway stood Princess Eavlyn with another.

"This is no way to celebrate your wedding, milady," Caden said to her.

"Hering granted me a short leave to see to Sorcha," she replied, "and to give her this." She held up a leather bag containing a harp by its shape. "I think Hering believes you to be innocent, although I must say, the circumstances are against you."

"Tunwulf has spun a convincing tale around them," Father Martin chimed in dryly.

"I promise to do everything in my power to prove your innocence. Sorcha's as well." Eavlyn left the entrance to Caden's cell and turned to Sorcha's. Another bolt slid from its keeper, and the hinges creaked open.

Caden hadn't heard a peep from his fellow prisoner since she'd been locked up. When they were escorted to the guardhouse, she'd walked as though her spirit had been driven from her body by shock. Her replies to his inquiries through the wall between their chambers were no more than a single syllable.

"Did you see Rhianon?" Caden asked Father Martin.

"Only from a distance. She wouldn't have me near her. But she'll live, according to the doctor."

"Then Satan got a reprieve." Caden gave a wry laugh. "He can rule in peace for a while longer."

"The unsaved dead sleep, son," Martin reminded him. Still, the priest smiled at Caden's suggestion. "Only the saved live on with our Lord before His return."

Sleep. That was what Caden had once hoped for. Eternal sleep. No more trials, no more guilt. The guilt was the worst part of his punishment. He'd never been able to escape its weight, not even in Lothian among mercenaries with pasts just as dark as his own. Although admitting his part in the scheme to murder his father and brother and seize Glenarden for his own hadn't been as heavy to admit as before.

Jesus carried it now. The answer came before Caden could form the question. Christ had taken his burden the moment Caden called out His name on the beach just days ago. The memory of that childlike lightheartedness eased some of the tightness in his chest.

"I sent a messenger to Gemma to let her know what happened," Martin informed him, "and to assure her that the princess and I will do everything we can to prove your innocence." The priest lowered his voice. "Including having Tunwulf watched."

"He's a sharp one, that," Caden admitted. "I wouldn't be surprised if Rhianon wasn't outmatched by him. What if he poisoned her with her own brew to make Sorcha look guilty?"

Martin shook his head. "If Tunwulf had poisoned her, be certain, Rhianon would expose him. Were I a wagering man, I'd say Rhianon's misfortune was an accident."

"The stars do not favor him." Eavlyn was back. "I have mapped out the stars, seeking signs for both him and for Aethelfrith as my husband's enemies," she explained.

"How is Sorcha?" Caden asked.

"In shock. Hopefully, the harp will pleasantly distract her. And I'm going to send my maid Lunid with her things that she might make herself more comfortable." Eavlyn grimaced, noting the chains on Caden's hands and feet. "At least she was spared those."

"The stars," Caden prompted. "They spell ill for Tunwulf and Aethelfrith?"

"Ill for Tunwulf. But that doesn't mean his plans will go awry with certainty. Only that nature is not with him. As it plagues the farmer who plows in a downpour." A frown creased her smooth brow. "That uncertainty is why I pray that either I or the stars are wrong regarding possible good fortune for my husband's enemy."

Aethelfrith. Just the thought of his name pricked the hair on the nape of Caden's neck. The Dieran prince was a bad seed, if ever there was one.

"God alone is certain," Eavlyn averred. "He controls the heavens and the earth … and the prayers of the righteous availeth much." A smile settled softly on her lips. "So it is with faith that I go to my husband now for whatever future lies ahead. We are in God's hands, for ill or good."

God's hands. Locked in this place and chained like a villain was hardly what Caden imagined being in God's hands felt like. Nature must be against him and Sorcha as well. Tunwulf's bad nature.

"I don't understand all this talk of stars and nature," Caden grumbled, "but I do understand the workings of a scoundrel. Better I could get my hands about his neck or face him squarely, sword to sword. That is more to my liking."

"But it may not be to God's," Martin reminded him. He clapped Caden on the shoulders. "Have faith, Caden. 'Tis stronger than a sword … or poison. You've seen as much with your own eyes at Glenarden."

Glenarden. Aye, Caden had seen it. Poison that didn't work. Though his father's recovery alone could have been luck. But one after another of his and Rhianon's attempts to seize Glenarden for their own had failed. Neither magic, nor demon, nor sheer numbers had prevailed against the simple faith of his brother's wife. The healer Brenna.

He met Father Martin's earnest gaze with his own. "Then help me pray for such faith, Father, for all reason works sorely against it."

CHAPTER EIGHTEEN

"Caden of Lothian and Sorcha of Din Guardi, you both are charged with the murder of Thane Cynric of Elford and the attempted murder of the woman Rhianon," Din Guardi's sheriff charged, his voice booming in Hussa's hall.

Sorcha didn't want to be here. Even her spare and cold cell would be better, thanks to Lunid's visit during the long night. In addition to clean bed linens, the maid had even brought a kettle of tea, a calming one … and shared it with Sorcha. Before she left, Lunid even offered to pray.

"You might be a pagan," she said, "but the Lord has seen you have a good heart. It is never too late to turn to Him."

So Sorcha had tried praying after Lunid left but found her words were not nearly as eloquent and worthy as those she'd heard in her short exposure to Christians. Instead, her mind was consumed with her defense. She re-created the day just passed in meticulous order, especially recalling how Rhianon had been present, the draft of beer already drawn. How Tunwulf had knocked it from her hand—

"What have you to say for yourselves?" the sheriff asked, once more calling her attention to him and the proceedings.

Back to the hearing that would determine her fate.

"The charges are false against us both," Caden declared before Sorcha could find her voice.

The sight of Tunwulf standing next to the potbellied official with her belongings at his feet robbed her of it. They were hers, bequeathed by his father's dying breath.

"Milady?" the sheriff demanded of her.

Anger breathed into her, stiffening her spine. "As false as Tunwulf's heart, my lord sheriff."

"We are here to determine whose heart is false and whose is not," the sheriff replied, as though haughtiness added to his short stature. "But first ..." He stooped, picking up the upholstered chest containing the jewels Cynric had given her. "Are the contents of this chest not yours?"

"They are, sir," Sorcha addressed the king. "You heard my lord Cynric declare it so with his dying breath."

"And it has been under your lock and key in the Princess Eavlyn's bower?"

"Aye ..." Wariness slowed Sorcha's reply. "I keep the key in my pocket." She fished in the folds of her gown and found it. But as she withdrew it, she could see plainly that the lock had been broken. "I see you no longer need it, sir."

"Milord King," the sheriff said, turning to face Hussa, "I personally broke the lock this morning while searching through the lady's things and found this." He opened the lid and withdrew a pouch. "Your own doctors confirm the contents as the same poison that killed your hearth friend Cynric and nearly killed the woman Rhianon of Gwynedd."

"Nay!" Sorcha staggered back. "Never have I seen that pouch before." Was it possible the sheriff himself conspired against her?

"Then how, milady, did it find its way into your locked chest?"

"Locks can be opened without a key, milords."

Sorcha would know that voice anywhere. Pure joy flooded through her as she turned to see Gemma standing at the fore of the crowd.

"Milord, this woman's statement has no bearing on this. She's naught but a gleeman."

If anything, Gemma stood taller before the sheriff's disdain. "My word may not count as much as the sheriff's, but I will open any lock you provide with naught but this cloak pin to lend them the weight of the truth."

"We are seeking the truth, are we not?" King Modred asked Hussa. The Cymri lord's presence placed all the more pressure on the bretwalda to see a just decision made.

Hussa nodded. "Show us, little woman."

The guard stood aside to let Gemma beyond the bounds of the onlookers. Her cloak pin brandished, she promptly opened one of the shackles on Caden's ankles. Straightening in triumph to the astonished gasp of the onlookers, the dwarf addressed the king with a great show of humility.

"My father was a locksmith, your majesty," she announced, head bowed.

"It seems it is possible that someone might have put the poison in Sorcha's chest to make her, and hence me," Caden added, "appear guilty of a crime we did not commit."

Hope surging, Sorcha chimed with a hearty "Yes."

"But how many are the children of locksmiths?" Tunwulf pointed out. "It is possible, but not *probable*."

"To what purpose would I murder my father's dearest friend and my benefactor?" Sorcha cried out. "He had agreed to my returning to my homeland and mother. I had his blessing."

"Perhaps it was this will, leaving all his wealth to you." Tunwulf drew a document from the leather pouch slung over his shoulder and presented it to the sheriff.

Blood plunged from Sorcha's face. "I … I had no idea such a will existed."

For every argument Sorcha put forth for her innocence, Tunwulf and the sheriff managed to take it and twist it toward her guilt. And Caden's. Father Martin's testimony against Rhianon put Caden in a guilty light. Caden's greed led him once to murder, so why not twice to become lord of Trebold? Sorcha's accusations against Rhianon handing her the filled pitcher and Tunwulf's breaking it before anyone else could be served was counted as coincidence. Why would the murderer poison herself?

Even the charge that Tunwulf coveted his father's estate slid off the villain like rain on a steep roof. "I need not remind my lord bretwalda that the ultimate decision as to who becomes the protector of your border lies solely with you, not my father's wishes," Tunwulf replied smoothly. "I know that I have to prove myself worthy of that consideration."

There was only Sorcha's and Caden's denials against a preponderance of unfavorable circumstances. As the noon hour approached, Hussa was clearly reluctant to make a judgment. The Lothian king's influence was all that stood between Sorcha and

Caden and a hangman's noose, for the witan judges favored her guilt.

"Lord bretwalda, in such a case as this, where clarity of guilt is not forthcoming," an elder judge by the name of Elread spoke up, "I see no alternative but to resort to trial by ordeal."

Ordeal. The word curdled in Sorcha's stomach. No one survived that, regardless of its nature.

Caden rallied at her side. "Aye, I'll fight any man among you to prove our innocence."

The witan cast a disparaging glance at the Cymri. "*Ordeal*, not combat."

"Boiling oil will show if the woman tells the truth or lies," a fellow judge agreed. "If she heals well, she is innocent. If not, they both die."

Oil. Not burning in fire, nor drowning in water, but boiling oil to fry the arm of the poor soul forced to fetch a ring from the bottom of the cauldron.

The appeal of the solution to his quandary settled on Hussa's face.

"It is barbaric. No one survives such burns, even if they retrieve the ring," Father Martin objected. "Infection is certain. Your doctors know this."

"So you say your God can't save her if she is innocent?" Tunwulf taunted.

His smug satisfaction sparked a fury within Sorcha as intense as the one that had killed her parents. Before the guard beside her knew what she was about, she had the dirk from his boot in her hand.

Nothing mattered now. If she were sentenced to death for murder, best make it worth the cost. Hanging for a murder she committed was better than the tortuous sentence for one she'd not. She snapped her wrist to fling the weapon, but a jerk of her dress just as it left her hand sent it flying off course, away from Tunwulf's heart and grazing his arm.

"No!" With an oath, she spun to see Caden holding a bunch of her skirt in his manacled hands. "What have you done?"

"Spared you from blood on your hands."

"You fool!" With all her might Sorcha punched his face, taking out her hopelessness on him. The blow staggered him, but the one that struck her from behind exploded in a flash of light and pain worse than that reported from her fist. Thankfully, darkness consumed it all. Pain, anger, and utter despair.

CHAPTER NINETEEN

Sorcha's head hurt like thunder. She'd come to her senses back in the guardhouse with Gemma tending her. But Sorcha would drink nothing to soothe her aching head. She wanted it clear for tonight. While the wedding celebration approached its third day, she would escape. Caden as well, if he had an inkling of sense when the time came. But Sorcha would not be a victim.

"Hussa wants to preserve the peace bound by my wedding," Eavlyn had told her earlier that afternoon.

But the Bernician ruler also had to placate his witans and those who distrusted Eavlyn's peaceweaving. So no matter how much the priest and Princess Eavlyn prayed over her and assured her that the Lothians would see her spared, Sorcha preferred Gemma's escape plan. Better to die trying to get away than wait submissively on chance to save her from placing her arm in the burning oil for a crime she did not commit.

For now, Sorcha kept her secret to herself, lest someone overhear her sharing it with the man in the cell next to her. It was all arranged. The tavern keeper Mann and serving girl would help. Utta would pose as kitchen help to bring the night guards some beer while the feasting and revelry continued in the hall. Beer laced with mandrake, just enough to make them sleep. Once they were in a dreamworld, the maid would set Caden and Sorcha free and give them what money Mann and Gemma had scrounged together for travel.

Meanwhile Gemma would perform at the tavern to avoid being associated with the escape or giving them away. Certainly two traveling alone would not draw as much attention as two with a dwarf and child in their company. Gemma and Ebyn would catch up with them in Lothian, beyond Hussa's reach, if Princess Eavlyn's peaceweaving held. If not—

Then God help them. If He listened to such as her.

The hours stretched interminably toward the midnight change of the guard. The priest and Lunid came to visit, to pray, and to commiserate. Sorcha joined them, wanting their faith that God was in control. Yet she couldn't help but take more comfort in knowing escape was at hand, rather than resting on their prayers and promises to keep searching for the real culprit behind Cynric's death and change the nature of the ordeal to one of combat. As for who murdered Elford's lord, the answer was as plain as Hussa's beard. It was Tunwulf and Rhianon. But there was no proof.

"We must take care not to upset the fragile peace between Bernicia and Lothian," Father Martin had reiterated as he prepared to leave. "But so must the Bernicians."

"Can your God spare me from the boiling oil … protect my arm so that it won't burn?" Sorcha asked. She hoped against hope that He could.

But Lunid's answer did not reassure her. "God's ways are not ours."

What did *that* mean?

Sorcha only knew what it didn't mean. Escape. How foolish she'd been to even entertain the idea that the Christian God could do any more than the pagan ones.

Except for the incident with the boar. That still played across her mind.

Her mind seesawed from groping faith to heart-seizing doubt until the guard finally changed at midnight. Sorcha strained to listen for Utta's approach above the excited beat of her heart. She paced back and forth till she wore a path in the rushes covering the earthen floor, stirring the scent of old urine in the dampness of the night. At the slightest hint of sound, she stopped and listened.

"Trouble sleeping?" came Caden's husky voice from the other side of the wall. He'd snored on and off since supper had been brought in as though he had not a care in the world.

"Only a fool wouldn't," she shot back. "But then, it's not your arm to be fried tomorrow, is it?"

"Martin will find a way out of this for you. He and Modred both press for a trial of combat by working on the bretwalda's warrior pride. Hussa understands might more than spirits."

"And you will fight?" Sorcha pushed down a second guess at her own plan. But while Caden had the look of an able warrior, her escape plan was more certain. "And you believe God will save us?"

"I've seen His miracles firsthand."

But Sorcha recognized his hesitation for what it was. "And you *believe?*"

"I'm trying hard to, woman!" he snapped, impatient. "I *know* what faith can do. It broke the chains from Paul's hands and feet, opened his cell door."

Sorcha pressed against the bulkhead separating them. This language she understood. "Who's Paul? What had he done?"

But before Caden could answer, Utta's voice sounded from outside.

"Well now, what 'ave we here?" she cooed, although her tone resembled more that of a crow than a dove. Fortunately, with Utta's buxom curves, men didn't seem to mind. Sorcha could almost see her friend sidling up to one of the guards.

"Paul is an apostle," Caden began.

"Shush!" Sorcha rolled her eyes. All the day and half the night had passed, and *now* the man wanted to talk.

"Two men left to duty while the rest revel the night away," Utta continued with the same coquettishness that earned her a good night's wage beyond Mann's meager pay.

One of the guards said something, and the barmaid let loose a raucous laugh. "Maybe," she replied, "after ye have a sip o' the beer the 'ousethane's wife sent ye lads."

"What makes that old bull so kindly?" one of the men queried.

Mildrith oversaw the dispensing of her lord's drink as if it were her own, but Utta couldn't know that.

"In 'er cups, why else, luv?"

Quick-witted and saucy, Utta was. Sorcha hoped the silence meant that the men were drinking.

"Oh, bother," the tavern maid exclaimed in alarm. "Someone's comin'!"

Sorcha's breath caught. No, not now.

"'urry 'n' finish it up, lads, a'fore we're all in trouble."

After another pause, the clang of tin cups being gathered signaled they'd been emptied.

"Hide round the back," one of the guards instructed. Punishment was severe for drinking on duty.

"Something's amiss," Caden observed under his breath from the other side of the wall. "Who'd visit at this—"

"Aye, now hold your tongue!" Sorcha leaned against the cool plaster. A midnight visitor was definitely not part of her plan. What if Utta were scared away? Worse yet, what if she were caught? Although Utta was resourceful. She might play tipsy, finagle her way out of it, but—

What if the guards fell asleep during this nocturnal visit?

Alarm pelted Sorcha from all sides.

"Open the door. We're here to see the prisoners."

Tunwulf! Sorcha groaned. Not him. Not now.

"Expecting company?" Caden whispered.

"Aye, but not him," Sorcha complained aloud.

The outer door creaked open. "This way, milord and lady," a guard instructed.

Lady? Had Rhianon recovered?

Light from a lantern entered the darkness of the narrow hall. The guard hung it on an iron hook for the visitors.

Caden gave a low laugh. "You look well for someone who lingers at death's door, Rhianon."

"I thank the goddesses my stomach rebelled at the poison, ridding me of it," the woman answered. "Though I am still weakened."

"What mischief are you about now?" Caden asked.

"Regret should spill from those lips, Caden, not mockery. I came to say good-bye, for fortune has turned against you." Her voice dropped, suggestive. "After all, you were my husband."

Sorcha pressed her ear to the small opening that allowed the guard to look through the door into the cell as the guard let Rhianon into Caden's chamber. But when another light swung her way, Sorcha backed to the far wall. Whatever Tunwulf was here for, it did not bode well for her or her plan.

When her cell door swung open, Tunwulf filled its frame, the upholstered box that had contained his mother's jewels and the incriminating evidence against Sorcha in his hands. Brandishing a sardonic grin, he held it up.

"I brought you your inheritance, milady."

Anger fired Sorcha's pulse. Oh, for a handy dagger! She'd yet to forgive Caden for ruining her aim. "'Tis a late hour to mock me, sir."

"Something told me you might have trouble sleeping."

"You changed your tunic," she noted. "I hope I drew blood."

Tunwulf chuckled. "I have always admired your fire, Sorcha. So I thought, as a token of our friendship—" he closed the short distance between them—"I'd let you spend your last hours with your *inheritance*." He leaned in, adding in a low voice, "But I am here to make you one last offer to save your beautiful skin."

Sorcha lifted a brow in disbelief as Tunwulf put down the chest at her feet. What *was* he up to?

"The jewels are yours ..." he went on, picking up volume, his mockery returning for the sake of any listeners, "until death do you part."

Sorcha struck him. At least she intended to. But before she could lay a hand on him, Tunwulf caught her wrist and pinned it to the plaster until the rough surface bit into her skin.

"Listen, little fool, and listen carefully," he whispered, urgent. "Marry me, and I will see that you are freed. Even the Cymri."

The stench of his breath mingled with beer forced her face away from his. "What is in this for you?" For there had to be an advantage, one Sorcha couldn't see. Tunwulf offered nothing without motive.

"Besides *this* …" He groped with his free hand where no man had before … at least not since she'd been a child captive. "Father awarded you two estates as betrothal gifts."

But she was no longer a frightened child. Seizing anger over the rise of nauseating panic, Sorcha wedged her hand after his. Finding his little finger, she bent it back with all her might.

"Vixen!" Tunwulf shoved her against the wall with his body, pinning both hands above her head with his.

"I'd sooner die than marry you!"

"You will … and horribly … unless you agree."

"Why?"

"If my wife owns a portion of Elford, it's only right that Hussa—"

"Award you the rest," she finished.

A movement beyond Tunwulf's shoulder caught Sorcha's eye. Perfect. She dared not focus on the woman standing frozen in the doorway, lest she give Rhianon's presence away.

Instead, Sorcha moistened her lips as though preparing them for a kiss. It riveted her assailant's attention. Tunwulf forced himself against her all the more.

"You are not only the most desirable woman I've ever met, but you're smart. You know I've always fancied you—"

Sorcha turned slightly, dodging his descending lips. "Your mistress murders your father and, *you,*" she emphasized as they grazed her ear, "poison your mistress—"

"Rhianon poisoned herself to take suspicion away from her."

The witch! That never occurred to Sorcha in her wildest imaginings. "And yet you would repay her by making me your *wife?*"

Tunwulf shrugged. "I'll keep her as mistress." He half chuckled against Sorcha's neck. "You shouldn't object to that."

"Nay, sir, but *I,*" Rhianon grated out, "do!" She flung herself across the cell as if her outrage had given her wings.

Tunwulf pulled Sorcha to the side with him so that the blade Rhianon thrust at his neck snagged just the sleeve of his tunic and skidded down the wall. Sorcha tripped over the jewel box, knocking it over, and scrambled away. Rhianon lunged after Tunwulf like a fury. There was no sign of the weakness she should have had as a result of the poisoning. Instead, she slashed and shrieked loud enough to bring the entire kingdom down upon them.

This time the warrior was ready. He caught her wrists and spun her around so that she was back to him. "Let go the knife, Rhianon," he demanded, trying to shake the dining dagger from her grasp.

"I'll kill you before I let someone else become Lady Elford!" Rhianon kicked back at him, her heel catching his kneecap.

Tunwulf erupted with a string of curses such as Sorcha had never heard as Rhianon broke her knife hand free and stabbed frantically at his thigh. Again he caught her wrist, but not before she'd drawn blood.

"You *promised* me. You *promised* me," Rhianon seethed through clenched teeth.

"That you would be richly rewarded," Tunwulf replied. For all his strength, it was all he could do to restrain her.

Sorcha backed along the wall, away from the unfurling nightmare, and reached for the harp Eavlyn had sent. It was her only hope. That and the effects of the mandrake on the guards, who'd yet to show their faces.

She swung the instrument, still in its bag, hard against the back of Tunwulf's head. Time froze the pair in midstruggle … for so long that Sorcha drew the harp back again for a second blow. But before she could let go, both Tunwulf *and* Rhianon pitched forward onto the earthen floor. Realizing that she still had to deal with Rhianon, Sorcha shouldered the bag, keeping it ready.

At first, the fair-haired woman remained motionless, face to the floor. But when Sorcha reached for her, she rolled to her side with a moan.

"H … help me. He'll kill us both." She dabbed at where blood trickled from her nose and tried to get up.

Now Sorcha saw the dark circles and wan cheeks beneath the woman's terrified gaze, marks of the poison's effect. With the fuel of her rage knocked out of her, she'd weakened. At last, Rhianon held out her arm for help.

Sorcha hauled her to her feet. But what would she do with the wench now? Certainly not take her with her.

"You … you saved my life," Rhianon said, breathless.

"*Our* lives." Sorcha steeled herself against a rise of pity. Witch or nay, Tunwulf had sorely used her.

"No," Rhianon stiffened. "*Mine!*" With a snarl, she drove the dagger that had been hidden in the fold of her cloak at Sorcha's abdomen.

Instinct kicking in, Sorcha pivoted away from the coming blade and shifted the harp into place to receive the blow. The blade glanced off the hard wood frame beneath the thick leather, giving Sorcha time to put a distance between them. With a frustrated shriek, Rhianon tightened bloody fingers around the dagger's hilt, though whether it was her blood or Tunwulf's was hard to say.

Sorcha hefted the instrument as a shield between them. The witch was mad. Her nose bled freely down the front of her dress, and her full lips curled in an animal-like snarl.

As Rhianon and Sorcha circled each other, the frantic rattling of chains told Sorcha that Utta was freeing Caden, according to plan. All Sorcha had to do was hold Rhianon off—

Rhianon charged again, grabbing for the harp with one hand and swinging the knife with the other. But Sorcha dodged her, spinning full circle and bringing the harp soundly against the back of her opponent's head.

It landed with a terrible crunch of flesh and bone. Rhianon bent over double but didn't fall. It was as though she fought against unconsciousness, slashing blindly. One step … two—

Sorcha sprang out of her way.

Three steps the witch staggered before she went down.

"Sorcha!"

Utta rushed into the room, but Sorcha's eyes were fixed on the wound pouring dark lifeblood from the back of Rhianon's fair head onto the rush-covered floor.

Until Caden knelt beside his fallen wife and blocked the view. He rolled Rhianon over and, with a grunt of surprise, backed away, straightening.

"She fell on her knife."

"I tried to help her and she …" Disbelief, outrage, and the blood rush of battle all razed Sorcha's words. "She tried to kill me! Those two were made for each other."

Caden cast a look of pity at the broken and bleeding remnant of his wife. "She got what she deserved."

Utta tugged on Sorcha's arm. "We haveta hurry. Night is wastin', and you need a head start."

Sorcha looked up to see that the wench had donned a horsehair wig black as pitch to disguise herself. "Aye," Sorcha agreed. Their plan had worked so far, in spite of Tunwulf and his witch. The longer they delayed—

"What's going on here?" Caden turned, his face furrowed, as though still trying to wrap his mind around what had just happened.

"The guards are drugged for only so long." Utta tugged a purse from the depths of her bodice and handed it to Sorcha. "Now 'ere's the money for you two to escape to Lothian."

Caden grabbed Sorcha's arm roughly as she tied the moneybag to her belt. "When were you planning to tell me about this great escape?"

"Would you have had me shout it to you through the wall for all to hear?" she snapped.

"But Martin and Modred worked on our behalf. Now look at this mess."

Mess! As if she'd planned on a midnight visit from the two people responsible for all this, much less contemplated killing one of them. "You ungrateful dullard!" Sorcha raised her chin inches from his, as though daring him to cross her further. "Would that work be before or after *my* arm was fried in oil?"

Utta wedged herself between them. "See now. More'n yer lives are at risk," she reminded them, "so ye'd best be goin'. I'm beggin' ye."

"Great—" Caden swallowed the epithet on the tip of his tongue. He seized Tunwulf by the feet. "I'll put this one in irons. It'll hold him for a while."

"He deserves to die." Sorcha kicked at Tunwulf's ribs. "*She* took poison for him, and he had the nerve to ask me to marry him!" A high pitch penetrated her words. "And *that* after making me face a pot of burning oil."

Now she'd begun to shake. Of all things, of all times, now was no time to lose her nerve. She needed to hold on to what men called *battle frenzy.* Just a little longer.

"If you want him dead, do it yourself." Caden jerked his head toward Rhianon. "There's a knife."

Sorcha's stomach turned at what, only moments before, she could have done without thinking. Hadn't she crushed the woman's skull in? Yet Sorcha reeled away, mustering all her will to push down nausea as Caden tugged Tunwulf into the hallway.

"Chains and a gag will keep him and the guards till morning," Caden called back. "Dead or alive, half of Bernicia will be after us come daybreak ... at least to the river Tweed."

Sorcha leaned against the wall. She'd just fought for her very life and as much as killed a woman, though none would believe it was self-defense. There was no turning back now. Losing her nerve was not an option. Her gaze fell upon the chest of jewels as she straightened.

Her inheritance. The jewels would fit in her harp case. While what was done couldn't be undone, the gem-studded gold would go a long way in a new life. If anyone deserved them, Sorcha certainly did after what Tunwulf had put her through. She huffed, working up her rage. Anything to banish weakness and doubt.

Would there was more she could take from the villain. Something that would wound his pride to its black core.

The image of Cynric's ruby-studded dragon ring came to her mind. Elford's symbol of power and prestige.

Calculation pulled at her lips.

Perfect.

CHAPTER TWENTY

Caden couldn't help his annoyance. Martin had been certain his and Modred's diplomatic pressure for trial by combat would be granted. It was the best hope. That, and Caden's sword arm.

But there was no explaining this mess. No bringing Rhianon back to life. Funny, how someone so evil could look so angelic in death. Even now, after all she'd done, he felt nothing but pity. This time she'd met her match in Tunwulf. More so.

"We'll head inland to the Berwick road till daybreak. Then we'll have to stay off it, for that's where the Bernicians will catch up with us. Unless you've got horses," Caden said as Utta reentered the cell. It was too risky to try to fetch Forstan from the royal stables.

"No horses," Utta apologized. "But I got a cousin married to a cottar who lives at the ford of Hahl Burn. He says if ye follow the burn to its head, 'twill take ye through the moors, if ye always bear to the north. Thing is, ye'll need a boat. An' there's not enough coin in the purse for that."

She glanced to where Tunwulf wore naught but a scrap of blanket and his gold torque. "But *that* will buy the man more boats than he can use."

"*That* won't draw much attention to us." Caden snorted. Though the Bernicians wouldn't expect them to go through the moors. Tunwulf would head straight for the old Roman road leading to Berwick. "I suppose seeing how it's the villain's plan that got us here," he reasoned aloud, "his gold will get us what we need."

Caden hoped God would see it that way. He'd done a lot of things in his time. Sinful things. But stealing was not one of them. For the first time in his life, he had a Father who accepted him. He struggled to the best of his understanding to keep it that way, praying as he dragged the unconscious guards in from outside.

Abba, stay with us. I'm counting this as a sign of what You want us to do. By all rights, this crazy plan shouldn't have worked. Wouldn't have until Tunwulf and Rhianon turned on each other.

A flashback, that of Rhianon's nurse and mentor turning on her, came to his mind. Aye, that was God's handiwork. Evil turning on itself. Still …

Let us be in Your hand, not Sorcha's. She's decent enough, though mighty light-fingered.…

And a fine figure of a woman, even dressed in men's clothing, he finished, as Sorcha walked into the cell. She'd never pass for a man, but by his racing blood, she made a man's clothes look good.

Abba! Caden wasn't certain what else to say, only that he'd need his Father's help to make it right in Heaven's eye.

"Good thing we have more than one set of chains." Her wits more assembled than Caden's, Sorcha motioned to Utta to help her drag one of the guards to a pair of shackles bolted to the wall. "Though we'll need something to gag them." She straightened. Her gaze fell on Tunwulf's blanket and darted away, as if his hairy navel had winked at her.

Caden suppressed a grin. "We can tear strips off your shift," he suggested, pulling the last guard to another set of chains hung on the wall.

Sorcha looked at Caden as if he'd just proposed they go back to their cells. "Or *your* shirt."

"You're not *wearing* the shift," he pointed out.

"But I will, if we get out of this alive." A smile quivered on her lips. "Truth is, I've never had one so fine."

Women. Their necks weren't out of the noose yet, and she was hoarding a wardrobe. Caden looked at the taut leather bag in which she'd stowed her things. "I'll not be carrying that for you. The lighter we travel, the better."

"I've done without a man's muscle this long." There went that stubborn jut of her chin. "I can go a bit longer."

Utta stepped in. "I'll cut strips from the witch's shift before we're all set to swing from a rope."

She drew out her dining dagger and disappeared into the hall. In no time, she returned with the linen, and the men were properly gagged.

Moments later, Caden stepped out into the night air, wearing a guard's tunic, cloak, and weapons. At this late hour, it was eerily quiet within Din Guardi's stockade. A thick mist separated the heavens from the earth, the moon behind it giving their surroundings a ghostly appearance.

Now all they had to do was get through the gate. He hoped the women had thought of that.

They had, and Caden didn't like the plan either, but what other option was there?

Sorcha played the part of a young man caught by his wife, the shorter Utta, with another woman. The tavern maid flailed the life out of Sorcha with a switch, all the while tugging her home toward the village below.

"I'll not stand ye spendin' another hour here with all yer fancy friends while I carry yer own wee babe in my belly," Utta wailed. "Yer comin' 'ome if I have to drag ye all the way."

Such was their commotion that guards along the ramparts watched as well. Caden easily blended into the shadows and escaped into the night beyond without so much as a stray hound's bark to call attention to him.

The thick fog hid him a distance away where, instead of going ahead of them as Sorcha suggested, he waited, hand on sword, in case there was trouble.

"Don't be runnin' away from me, you cheatin' son of a slop bucket!" Utta shrieked close by. "The gods strike ye down if ye ever set foot inside them gates again. An' if they don't, I will." She wailed again at a pitch a professional keener would envy. "'Ow could ye?"

"Run, man, while ye can!" one of the guards shouted.

Sorcha streaked by, her bag clutched to her chest. Utta followed, calling upon a considerable vocabulary of obscenities that left the soldiers behind her laughing and jeering.

It would have been amusing, were their lives not at stake. Tension flowed out with Caden's held breath.

"Thank You, Abba," he breathed softly. So far, so blessed.

Freedom. Sorcha savored it as she and Utta made their way in silence down the causeway of cobbled stone and sand. Salt-laden air filled her nostrils along with the faint scent of fishnets and crafts that rose from the beach below. Even the stench of rotting fish guts wafting from where catch after catch had been cleaned was welcome. Anything but the smell of death left behind in her cell.

She *was* a murderer. 'Twas self-defense, but Rhianon was dead. Life in Din Guardi was just as dead for Sorcha now. She tried to force the image of Rhianon, the knife protruding from her body, out of her mind.

"More'n me's gonna miss ye, Sorcha," Utta sniffed, unwittingly helping her. The maid used a short laugh to hide her emotion. "But I'll wager that big Cymri'll take yer mind off'n us, soon enough."

"Caden?" The toe of Tunwulf's boots caught on one of the uneven paving stones of the causeway, nearly tripping Sorcha. "I hardly think I'm in Caden's good grace now, even if we saved his manly hide."

"That ain't what Gemma says," Utta said in a singsong voice. "Said you two danced like swans bound to mate for life."

"Gemma wasn't closed up in a—"

A strained grunt followed by a loud splash cut Sorcha off. They were closer to the beach than she'd realized.

"What was that?" Utta stopped in her tracks.

"Someone's over there." Sorcha pointed to a tiny golden haze in the mist a short distance away. A lantern, perhaps.

They'd made better time than she'd thought. She could hear the soft wash of waves upon the beach to their left, but little else.

The vision of a body being dumped came to Sorcha's mind. It was not unheard of to find some poor soul who'd been robbed and beaten, drowned upon the beach when day broke.

Sorcha reached for the guard's dirk that she'd stowed in the laces of the oversized boots. "Keep moving," she whispered, touching Utta's arm with the other hand.

She steered Utta away from the light toward a small stone dock where shallow-drafted boats might unload their cargo directly onto land. Then they headed toward Water Street, the last row of buildings before the waterfront. With any luck, they'd heard whoever lurked in the dark before he'd heard them.

Taking painstaking steps to avoid noise or tripping over any debris or discarded pieces of crating, Sorcha listened for footfalls. Suddenly Utta shrieked against a muffling hand, driving a stake of alarm through Sorcha's chest. Something large and furry brushed against Sorcha's leg and scurried over her feet.

"Just a cat," she told Utta, choosing to believe that was all. She shouldn't have insisted on separating from Caden and his going to the warehouse ahead of them. They'd not met a soul on the causeway to question them, although Sorcha and Utta's distraction had allowed Caden to slip out unnoticed and without curious inquiry. Forcing air into her lungs, as if gathering courage, Sorcha moved forward again, her gaze fixed on the far glow of a cresset kept burning at night by the dockyard.

Suddenly the sand crunched against rock beneath heavy feet, and a giant shadow materialized out of the mist, blocking Sorcha's view of the firelight. The night went black as death itself.

"By the gods' breath!" Utta clutched at her heart.

"Well now, what would you two be lookin' at, out as ye are at this hour?" The question was more an accusation, that of a murderer wanting to know what they'd seen.

Dread climbed Sorcha's spine. "We'd be looking to find our way home." She tightened her grasp on the knife. If they needed defending, it would be up to her. Caden was likely warming his hands over the fire in the hearth at home by now.

"An' a bloomin' cat scared the life outta us," Utta chimed in, her voice still shrill from it.

All Sorcha had to do was step forward and drive the blade in beneath his rib cage and upward toward his heart. That's what Wulfram had taught her. The oaf would never see it coming.

"Utta?" The man leaned down, staring closer in disbelief.

Sorcha held back.

"I thought you was workin' at the tavern," he said.

Wait, she knew that voice. The name of its owner caused her heart to leap into her throat.

Wada!

chapter twenty-one

"Utta, run!"

Sorcha let the leather sack, useless as a weapon now that the harp was gone, slide from her shoulder and thrust her pilfered knife upward. But something struck her wrist. Something wooden that surely broke the bones. She cried out in anguish, blinded by the pain. Even if she still clutched the knife—and she couldn't tell—it was useless. Nausea squirmed in her belly, while her senses groped upward, clawing for the numbness of unconsciousness. But the Wyrds were not finished with her.

Nor was Wada. He clamped an iron fist about her arm, pulling her upright. Sorcha saw the club in his free hand coming down again. She threw herself against her assailant, making it hard for his swing to impact ... much. It glanced off her back, but nothing broke.

"I been waitin' for this a long time," Wada swore, trying to shake her free.

Sorcha had to think fast, or she'd be the next person he dumped into the water. With a groan, she let her body go limp, as though she'd fainted. Wada cursed as her dead weight pulled her free of his grasp.

It gave the villain pause. Pause enough to think beyond club-bing. A warm, helpless woman was more than Wada could resist. He seized her wrist—thankfully the uninjured one—and started to drag her away from the glow of the distant cresset and toward the beach. Sorcha used the delay to gather her wits. She'd lost her bag and her only other weapon. She couldn't even put up a fight with one wrist shooting bolts of pain straight to her brain.

Heavenly Father, save me!

Wada dragged her onto the sand, which was cold but softer than the cobbled dockyard. "'Twill take more than a prayer, ye feisty little slut."

A prayer? With nowhere else to turn, Sorcha had instinctively mimicked Princess Eavlyn's pleas for her life. What had the thief said when he was about to die? Because Sorcha knew she was.

Remember me.

That was it. She mouthed a prayer. *Heavenly Father, remember me, a sorrowful thief. Remember me....*

The words surged like a prow through waves of her agony. Sorcha clenched her fist, the injured one, with new resolve. It hurt and was slippery with blood, but it worked.

Suddenly Wada let her go. And no wonder, for he'd dragged her into the pitch of the night. Sorcha could imagine him tearing at the laces of his trews and seized the opportunity to thrust herself away. His heavy foot came down hard on her abdomen. Breath rushed out of her lungs, nearly taking consciousness with it. If he leaned any harder, he'd crush her ribs. If he hadn't already.

Still she eased up her knee, envisioning exactly where to kick. And kick she did. As hard as she could.

Wada shrieked, dropping to one knee—off balance enough that Sorcha's second kick sent him reeling and moaning on his side in the sand. She scrambled away from him, but her limbs moved as though leaden. As she dug in the damp sand to rise, Wada grabbed the hem of Tunwulf's oversized tunic. With a vicious yank, he pulled her to him.

"I'm goin'"—he drew in a pained and ragged breath—"to kill you."

The garment held her enough for Wada to get one giant hand on Sorcha's neck. And then the other.

"An' then I'll have ye" —he pulled in another breath—"'fore the warmth flees that luvly body o' yours." The biting crush of his fingers cut off her air.

Her outcry bottled inside her chest. As she tried to pry his hands away, the sounds around her—the whisper of the waves, her assailant growling like a beast that had tasted blood, the kick of her feet in the soft sand—all started to mingle into a giant hush.

Except for Wada's taunt. "An' not a soul'll care."

Remember me. Sorcha clung to those two words.

Until two more exploded out of nowhere. "*I* care."

Caden's image floated into Sorcha's mind. Bone cracked like thunder in her ear. Hers? Wada jerked violently behind her. The strength in his hands faded until they fell away from her neck.

Sorcha gasped, again and again, gulping volumes of sweet air. The heat and stench of Wada's body drifted away from her. She tried gathering her scattered senses. Through the mist she made out a large figure dragging him toward the water. Caden. It had been his voice, hadn't it? The one that said, "I care"?

Relief ricocheted through her as the two figures blended into the night. She heard a splash followed by Caden's voice. "You'll never harm another soul, you blackguard."

The words gave her peace. Peace enough to realize she was still alive and so were Caden and Utta. Her feet moved, her legs worked. And so did her hands, though it hurt when she pushed herself up. Alive.

The Christian God remembered her?

Caden interrupted her thoughts. "Are you hurt?"

Or was it Caden?

"N-no," she rasped. Alarm edged in. What if she couldn't sing? Her voice was her survival. That, and her inheritance.

"My bag!" Sorcha lunged away from Caden on spindly legs and would have sprawled on the sand but for his quick reaction. The same hands that had just snapped Wada's neck caught her and drew her to him. Just as strong, but gentle. "My bag," she repeated, as he cradled her in his arms. "I need to find my bag."

"You're welcome, *milady*." His sarcasm smacked her.

"Oh, I ... of *course*, I thank you. You saved my life." But she had to find her inheritance before someone else stumbled upon it. More than four-legged vermin lurked the docks. "Will you help me find my bag? Everything I own is in it."

Sorcha heard rather than saw Caden's resignation. "Be quick, else they'll follow us by the trail of corpses in our wake."

It was visible once they reached the cobbled surface of the dock. Despite the thick mist, she could make out the dark lump containing her valuables in the distant glow of the cresset. Sorcha gathered it to her chest.

Thank You, Heavenly Father ... if it was You who saved me.

The stars might have favored them, but the clouds didn't. Their dark cover burst as Caden and Sorcha left the warehouse. What the downpour didn't soak through the oilcloth that Sorcha had found for them, the long walk through standing water to the riverside did. Between the high tide and the rain, even the elevated path was flooded.

Caden didn't even bother to remove his boots when he shoved the small flat-bottomed boat they'd bought with a chunk of Tunwulf's torque into the water and hopped aboard. Soaked couldn't get any wetter. Nor could the boat's owner have grinned any wider when he'd been paid enough to buy a new craft to replace the dilapidated one he'd sold them.

Sorcha sat huddled in the bow beneath a tarp and shivered visibly in the dim glow of an oil lantern hung on the bow. She'd been uncommonly quiet since the attack on the beach, which was far better than hysterical. Caden was accustomed to Rhianon's more dramatic nature.

Rhianon. Caden dug into the water with the oars. He couldn't seem to accept that his wife was finally gone. Not after she'd survived her first dance with death. Nor could he imagine why her end wasn't more satisfying for him. When all was said and done, she'd been no more than a pitiful thing whose own work had been turned against her. The betrayer betrayed.

Sorcha stirred at the other end of the coble and started to set a second pair of oars into the coble's oarlocks.

"I can do this," Caden called to her. "You should look after your wrist."

Once they'd reached the warehouse, he'd wrapped it as best he could. It didn't seem broken, but the skin had split on the bone, and it was swollen and badly bruised.

"I'm freezing, sitting still," Sorcha called back.

"Aye, but using one oar will have us going in circles." He heard her laugh and drank it in like medicine. His heart had yet to recover from hearing the skirmish and being unable to locate them in the dense mist. If ever God had a plan for someone, it was Sorcha. Had Caden not found them when he did—

His fists tightened about the oar handles as though to squeeze out the dampness in the wood. Snapping Wada's neck was too good for him. A bull of a man taking a belaying pin to a woman. It turned Caden's stomach. Especially when that woman was a tall redhead with a voice like an angel and a heart as wild and unpredictable as a gypsy.

When she'd told him that she was returning to Trebold, Caden could have clicked his heels. And when she'd been accused, he could not stand by mute, not knowing Rhianon as he did—even if speaking implicated him. Caden had been ready to put his life on the line for Sorcha's.

He didn't agree with all her ways, but being with Sorcha made him feel alive. Whole again. Even in this mess. She and her family gave him something worth fighting for.

Love of our neighbor is the only door out of the dungeon of self.

Something told Caden this wasn't exactly what Father Martin meant when he quoted the old proverb. When was it? Weeks ago?

Caden dug the oars into the water again. "Well, I'm out, Father." He grinned, squinting to make out the spear length of dimly lit water where marsh grass encroached on either side of them, blocking the view of what lay around the bend. "And running blind for my life *and* my neighbor's. The rest," he added softly, "is up to You, Modred, and Martin."

Half of Bernicia would be on their trail by morning. Hopefully, diplomacy would hold the other half back.

CHAPTER TWENTY-TWO

The rain was the forerunner of a bitter wind. Not a night to be out, and certainly not one to weather in a boat. Especially a leaky one. Whether Utta's cousin knew of the leak or not didn't matter now. Caden was too far into the water-lashed moorland to turn back when he realized that Sorcha bailed out more than rainwater. And to beach the boat in the rushes and try to find sound land afoot in the dark was just as dangerous. Quicksand riddled the moors, so that only those familiar with them might pass through safely. Still, Caden kept the craft close to the bank, searching for a solid place with his paddle, only to find it met with muck ready to suck them in.

"I guess the stars aren't with us after all," Sorcha yelled above wind that made it too dangerous to hoist the sail, even if either of them could spare the time between bailing and rowing.

"Aye, even *they* stayed in tonight," he shouted back.

Despite her injured wrist, she'd bailed water tirelessly for who knew how many hours, while the wind blew more than its share of water back in. Now and then, she'd start a banter or sing, as if to boost her spirit. The harder the wind blew, the more spirited she became. With Sorcha at his side, Caden almost felt as if they could beat the weather.

"Do you think the Christian God is with us?" The question was a sharp shift from songs of sea voyages and fickle stars.

Caden didn't know what to answer. He hadn't known God long enough to be sure. He hoped so. Thought so. "We're still breathing, aren't we?"

"Were you praying earlier?"

Irritation brushed Caden. He struggled enough talking to God without an audience. "Aye."

"What did you pray for?"

"Now what do you think?" Caden dipped the paddle in again, and it sunk easily beneath the pressure he applied. If he had to, Caden would beach the boat on the rushed heathland and stay there until daylight.

"Do you think He heard you above the wind?"

"How about you pray as well, just to be sure?" Anything to stop the questions. They made him uncomfortable, and God knew, he was uncomfortable enough, cold and soaked to the skin as he was.

"Do you believe in angels?"

"Never met one. Now pray ... by yourself," Caden added gruffly. "And bail."

"I'm bailin' all this pail will hold," Sorcha shot back. "And if you were much of a Christian, you'd care about my soul, now that we're about to drown."

"We're not going to drown. Stop talking nonsense."

"Aye, we are," she said. "Every time I move my foot, more water comes in."

Caden was tempted to tell her not to move her foot, but something about her grim demeanor drew his attention to the bottom of the craft. Not that he could see a thing, save a small ball of lantern light swinging wildly over Sorcha's head. "Tell me."

"My foot's near through a rotten spot in the bottom of the boat." She forced a laugh. "I'm wishing I'd never given the cottar an ounce of gold."

Adrenalin shot through Caden. Or perhaps it was fear. Regardless, he crawled forward and ripped off the canvas tarp, which the wind had rendered as useless in keeping Sorcha dry.

"Listen to me now, Sorcha of Din Guardi. We are not going to die. I believe in God, and I believe in angels." To his astonishment his mind and heart joined forces to put fervor in his statement. "Now you must believe in me when I say that I will do everything I can to see you safely home to Trebold. God didn't get us this far to let us drown."

The water was high enough to cover most of Caden's calf as he wadded the tarp into a tight ball.

"On the count of three, I want you to pull your foot from the crack and back away," he shouted at her. "I'm going to plug the hole enough with the tarp to get us into the shallows. We'll be safe there until morning when we can see what we're up against." Caden tried to read her face, but with her back to the light, it was impossible.

"Now then, on the count of three," he said, ready with the makeshift plug. Not that he had any idea the shape or size of the rotted spot. He'd have to seal it by feel.

"One …" *Abba preserve us.*

"Two …" Sorcha grabbed her stuck boot with both hands.

"Three!"

The boot would not come loose.

Caden tried helping her pry it out, but it was wedged firmly. "Can you take it off?"

"Wait."

Before Caden could stop her, Sorcha rose unsteadily, leaning on his shoulder, and used her other foot on the low seat as purchase. With a jerk, her foot came out, followed by a fountain of seawater. Caden threw himself into plugging it with all his might. His feverish fingers worked blindly around the length and width of the opening. More and more rotted wood gave way. He tucked more of the tarp in until, finally, it was plugged. At least as far as he could tell. As he squinted at the dark bottom of the craft, he suddenly realized a faint glaze of light from the bow lantern that hadn't been there before. Sorcha no longer blocked it. His blood turned as cold as the water sloshing about in the boat.

"Sorcha!"

"Here!" she gasped, somewhere on the riverside to his left.

Caden thought he saw a reflection of a white hand in the watery veil between the bow light and darkness. He reached for it and caught something.

'Twas her cloak, nothing more.

Slinging it aside, he dug into the water again and again found a fistful of material. Unlike the cloak, there was substance to it. Struggling substance.

Sorcha surfaced, gasping and sputtering.

Blessed be!

Her arm had pulled out of the sleeve in Caden's hand, but there was still enough of the woman in the garment to haul toward the vessel. He brought her in carefully, for the water level inside the boat had grown deep enough to make it unstable. But just as she reached for the side of the boat, she began to thrash about.

"My inheritance!" she screamed. "'Twas on my shoulder."

The little fool thrust away from the vessel hard enough to tip him over. "Easy, lassie. We'll look for it once you're in—"

Suddenly the water gave up the tunic, but Sorcha was not in it. Caden lunged to catch her by the hair, the shirt, whatever he could seize. Water started over the side, leaving him no choice but to sit upright and start bailing.

"Get back here, ye eel-slippery madwoman," he bellowed. He had to save the vessel. It was their only hope in the marsh.

"Not without"—Sorcha's voice babbled downstream—"my fortune."

The river current wasn't quite as strong winding through the heathland as through Glenarden's steep banks. But bail or go after her? Indecision skewered his thoughts till only one remained.

Abba help me.

Caden threw down the pail and began to tug his heavy boots off. A lighter boat would give him more time to bail … time to find Sorcha before her love of money—

"Got it!" a triumphant, if breathless voice hailed from downstream.

Caden eased the craft around to cast what light he had in her direction. His heart beat against his breastbone like a smith's hammer. She swam toward him against the current as if it hardly existed, the leather pouch strap looped over her head.

If they lived through this, he'd kill her. Fear locked with relief in his throat. Caden started bailing again. Until the water that had seeped in through the bottom was cleared, the boat wouldn't hold even Sorcha's light weight.

The boat tipped precariously as she grabbed its side.

"Stay put!" Caden barked. "I've water to bail out before you dare come back—"

"What?" Astonishment formed on her face.

"The boat's full of water, you dimwit! And I don't swim like a stinkin' otter!"

She burst out laughing. As if that were the funniest thing she'd ever heard.

"Funny, is it?" Maybe she was in shock again … though he preferred the silent response.

Sorcha shook her head, seized by another fit of giggles.

Caden fancied hauling her in by that long slender neck of hers for the fright she'd given him. "Just pray that tarp'll hold when your weight's back in here," he grumbled.

"Ah, Caden," she gasped, unhitching the leather bag from about her neck and tossing it into the boat with a splash. She looked as if she might say more but hadn't the wind for it. Instead, she stood up and shoved the boat away from her.

It hit ground.

Caden swiveled in disbelief toward what was a narrow strip of sand edged by marsh grass.

"We're on land, lovely man," Sorcha crowed as triumphantly as if she'd put them there. "Well, are you going to sit there and gawk or help me push the boat up, so we can empty it?"

Gawk, was it? Faith, he'd thought he'd lost her, and now she taunted him. Caden swung about, about to spit fire, but it died dead as yesterday's embers on the tip of his tongue.

Sorcha stood waist-deep in the lantern light, bright-eyed as a sea imp, the soaked linen of Tunwulf's shirt clinging to every curve God gave her. No otter, but a siren.

Now he gawked.

Until she hoisted hands to her hips, breaking the spell. "Well?"

Caden hefted one leg over the side, then the other. His feet found the bottom, soft but sound. The icy water swirled around his thighs, but, God help him, he wasn't cold enough to stop the fire spreading within. Faith, 'twould be a longish night.

They managed to pull the coble up on the ledge of sand and mud. The rain eased to a drizzle, as though the worst of the storm had passed, but everything they possessed was soaked, as was the spongy turf beyond the waterline. After unfastening the faithful lantern from the bow, Caden made out gale-bent thorn a distance inland. But whatever lay beyond that was shrouded in pitch darkness.

Certainly no light flickered from a cottar's window with the promise of dry warmth. But they were alive, and Sorcha had her inheritance.

When she had fallen over the side, it had come off as she struggled with Tunwulf's oversized cloak. She couldn't bear the thought of it's sinking to the bottom of the burn like some pagan's offering to the gods. But she'd lunged in the direction of the current. Two groping strokes and she'd found it. Sorcha shuddered and climbed to her feet.

"Looks like we've no choice but to bed here till morning," Caden announced. "But we'll have no fire. Bracken's too wet to light."

"If your God didn't get us this far to let us drown, He'll not let us freeze."

She turned the bench planks in the coble sidewise to cover the hole where her foot had slipped through a loose bottom board. If she hadn't shifted when she did, her foot might not have found the leak until it was too late. What if they'd been farther away from the bank, in deeper water?

"We'll wring out our cloaks and huddle," she said, refusing to dwell on what might have been. "Many's the cold night Gemma and I kept warm with blankets and body heat."

When Caden didn't answer, she turned to see him staring at her. No, 'twas at her harp bag hanging on the lantern post.

"Then fetch out whatever you've got in that pouch that'll serve for bedding and wring it dry as you can."

The coble was wide enough for the two of them … just. Sorcha settled in on the hard bottom, cushioned only by the finery she'd worn just hours ago. The jewels were still tied in a gossamer headdress in the bottom of the bag, along with a mantle of gold and copper-like thread, neither the worse for water or wear. It was more than could be said for the rest of the clothing. Thinking to use the bag as a pillow, Sorcha placed it at her head while Caden secured the tarp over them to keep out as much of the light drizzle as possible.

To her surprise he removed the bag and thrust it between their bellies, where the craft was wider. "That was my pillow," she protested.

Caden chuckled and slipped his thick arm beneath her neck until her head rested in the curve of his shoulder. "This will do for your pillow, milady. There's no room for both, and I can't very well toss my shoulder elsewhere now, can I?"

"This is better," she replied after a moment of adjusting. "At least it's warmer and not nearly as lumpy." A shiver rippled through her. "I hadn't noticed the cold as much till now."

To her delight Caden cradled her closer. "Fighting for one's life tends to overcome the senses till the battle's done."

"Then—" she stammered as his warmth seeped through the initial cool of his wrung-dry tunic and her chest molded against his harder one—"then you must still be fighting." Though Aelwyn once confided that men never seemed to chill like women, which made them the perfect hand- and foot-warmers.

"Sleep," he told her, his breath hot against the top of her rain-plastered hair. "I'll keep you warm as I can."

It wasn't long before their combined body heat warmed the damp cloaks that insulated them against the frosty fall air outside the covered craft. Not overly so, for to move away from Caden was to invite the cold. Not that Sorcha wanted to. For the first time in a long time, she felt safe and protected. Like a child in her father's arms, but different. In Wulfram's embrace, she drifted off to sleep with her heart beating a sweet lullaby. Here it played a more primal tune, as if answering the call of the faint rhythm in the chest beneath her head. Regardless, it seemed right. Enough that even it could not hold exhaustion at bay any longer.

CHAPTER TWENTY-THREE

Sunlight struck Caden's face like a sword's blow, startling him into battle-readiness as the tarp overhead was abruptly tugged away. At the appearance of a man's head silhouetted against a brilliant sky, Caden's hand was already closed about the hilt of the sword hidden under the pile of cloaks.

"What do you want?" he demanded, coming up so sudden that the man backed away. Robbed of his arm for a pillow, Sorcha's head struck the bottom boards.

"Hey!" she protested.

But Caden's eye was on the stranger.

"Nothing, sir," the man averred, calm despite fierce blue eyes fixed on the glint of Caden's blade emerging from the bedding. "I swear it."

A fisherman by the look of his patched tunic and cowled cloak. A big one at that. At least Caden's height.

"I came to check my traps, saw the boat, and decided to have a look, that's all," he said in flawless Cymric. "'Twas a terrible storm last night to weather."

The boat wobbled as Caden came to his feet. Sorcha moaned, covering her eyes with her arm. "S'cold!"

Indeed frost made the scrub of the heathland spread beyond them glitter like a fairy world. Caden took in the angle of the sun. They'd slept past daybreak, but not by much. "Is the fishing that good in Saxon waters that a Cymri should ply them?"

"Eels fetch a fine price … and Saxons like them as well as Cymri."

"If you say so." Caden couldn't detect an accent in the man's speech to suggest his origins. But his build was more that of a warrior than a waterman, and his hair, tied at his neck with a leather cord, was so gold it was almost white. Like a Saxon. "So where are the eels?"

"I saw the boat before collecting them."

Caden stepped out onto the spongy bank. "Go on then. *Collect.*"

Sorcha dragged herself up, pulling the cloaks around her as the waterman strode past the beached coble, giving her a nod.

"Who's he?" she asked sleepily. Her copper hair was matted by the dried salt water around her face, which was flushed pink. Uncommonly so.

Caden scowled. She'd been restless during the night, shivering. But he'd attributed it to their circumstances. He called after the fisherman as he waded into the marsh grass beyond where they'd landed. "Have you a name, eel catcher?"

"Owain."

"And where are you from, Owain?" Aside from the knife at his waist, Owain had no other weapons on him.

"Hahlton, upwater."

Caden reached down to help Sorcha to her feet, but she screamed and fell back into the boat. Owain turned and bolted back to the boat, but Caden stopped him with a raised sword.

"My wrist." Tears sprang to Sorcha's eyes. She curled into a possessive ball over it.

"Sorry, milady," Caden averred. He should have taken more care, but a nursemaid he wasn't. Not when a man Owain's size posed possible threat. Caden jerked the sword toward the sun-grazed water. "The traps, *Owain*."

Owain hesitated. "The lady looks ill. I've a cottage up on yon hill with a warm fire and liniments."

"Have you the means to patch this boat?" Caden asked. A quick scan of the hill showed an affirming trail of gray smoke climbing toward the sky.

"Better," Owain replied. "I've a sound curragh."

An Irish boat, light and sound, as the man said. Caden's mind raced. Only a fool—or a villain with an accomplice hid along the way—would announce such a prize in view of their circumstances.

"A warm f-fire," Sorcha sighed through chattering teeth. "I'm so cold and wet, sure I'll never dry again."

Wary, Caden alternated his gaze between a worn narrow path leading toward the higher land and Owain, as he waded into the marsh grass upriver where poles had been set. Had Caden and Sorcha progressed any farther last night, they'd have become entangled in the underwater traps.

Seizing a line hidden by the water and grass, Owain pulled until a tapered wicker trap the length of his long legs came out of the water. In it was a fine catch of common eels, big ones.

"The adults are on their way downriver to spawn in the ocean," Owain called over his shoulder as yet another emerged. It wasn't as full as the first. "Satisfied, soldier?"

So he wasn't the only one sizing up the other. Caden nodded.

"I've more traps to check, but I'm thinking the lady would rather go straightaway to the fire." Owain glanced at Sorcha for affirmation and smiled.

Concern or something else? It made Caden uncomfortable, whatever it was.

Sorcha used her good hand to shove herself to her feet and swayed so that Caden hastened to steady her with his free hand. The overbright green of her pleading gaze tore the indecision from his mind. As long as he had a sword and a knife, the odds were with him.

"Aye, we'll stay," he conceded. "But just till we dry out and fix the boat."

Owain's shack was that of a fisherman. His wicker-and-hide curragh—big enough to carry four men and, unlike the coble, light enough to carry overland—lay upside down at the back. Draped on the sides of the shelter were fishing nets, well mended. The inside was tended well too. On the entrance wall was a partially woven fish trap, numerous hooks, and fish spears. The stranger put on a kettle for tea, found dry clothing for each of them from a chest beneath a tidy cot—his brother's, he claimed—and left them to make themselves at home while he checked his other traps.

By the time Caden had hung his and Sorcha's clothing outside on poles used to mend nets, Sorcha had already succumbed to the comfort of the bed next to the hearth where a peat fire glowed. The oatcakes Owain had put out by the fire for them lay untouched.

"I need to see to your wrist, milady."

Sorcha groaned and burrowed deeper in the pallet of moss and bracken topping the bed, but he managed to coax the injured hand out. His first look belly-punched him. The wrist was fevered and swollen near twice its usual size. Spreading from the broken skin was an inflamed area that raged from the color of raw liver to a flaming pink fringe. Caden said nothing, but he'd seen flesh like it before, wounded flesh that had turned to poison itself. Not many survived such a wound.

"What happened?" Owain's voice behind him gave Caden a start.

The man moved like a spirit. Caden hadn't even heard the door of the shack creak to admit him. "Finished already, are you?"

"I was attacked with a belaying pin," Sorcha said flatly, not bothering to open her eyes. "Caden saved me."

"Humph," Owain grunted. "Another reason I like living alone. There is no low mankind will not sink to."

"You seem well spoken for a common fisherman," Caden observed.

"I'm not common." The man gave him a mysterious smile, then turned away. "And it's your good fortune that I'm not." He opened a crudely made cupboard to reveal a selection of jars filled with dried herbs, powdered substances, and flagons containing various liquids.

"You're an apothecary?" Caden asked in surprise.

"A scholar educated in many things."

"From Ireland then?"

"My boat is," he evaded smoothly. "Ah, there we are."

Owain took out a pottery jar containing what looked to be salt. Another contained a black powder like Caden's sister-in-law had used to treat his father's poisoning in what seemed another lifetime. Caden watched carefully as the *scholar* sprinkled some of the two on a bandage and poured water from a vial over it to make a paste.

The scent of the *water* whetted Caden's memory. "Aqua vitae?" he asked. "Won't it burn?" The first and last time he'd ever tasted the vile Scandinavian liquor, it had burned from his lips till it hit the bottom of his belly. The Northman who'd shared it with him had called him a baby and offered to buy him milk instead. Caden offered him a split lip.

"It's diluted with distilled water." To the poultice Owain added a clear gel that had no particular odor. "And this will soothe it."

"What is it?" Caden asked.

"A plant derivative."

"And that?" Caden wrinkled his nose as Owain opened a last jar, which emitted a foul odor akin to a rotten egg.

"Something to fight infection." Owain mashed it into the paste with a pestle, before nodding in satisfaction over his effort.

"Fight foul with foul, eh," Caden observed, uncertain.

"If you don't mind, sir, lift her arm so that I can wrap this about the wrist."

Since his knowledge of battlefield medicine—cauterize or pack with mud—hardly compared to what Owain had just put together, Caden yielded. This was out of his hands. But then his entire world had spun out of his hands since he took on this mission to bring Sorcha home to her mother.

Sorcha's eyelids fluttered open as Owain gently wrapped the poultice around her wrist and forearm. "What a pretty man you are," she murmured.

Caden's jaw clenched. As men went, the fisherman, or whatever he was, did have a comely face with smooth, fair skin like Caden's brother Alyn—not a scar or pock mark on it. Owain had been spared a hard life … unlike the life of a fisherman who weathered the elements. So who was he, really?

"I'm going to make you some tea," Owain told Sorcha. "It's important that you drink it all, no matter how it smells or tastes."

"Honey will help." Fatigue slurred Sorcha's words, but she answered the smile he gave her with childlike trust in her pale green gaze. Pale, not the untamed green of the woods that spoke to Caden's own wild nature, he noticed, before she closed her eyes and meekly submitted to the stranger's ministrations.

Once Owain tied the last of the knots to hold the bandage in place, Caden eased Sorcha's arm back under the covers. He could almost feel its heat through them.

"How long has she been feverish?" Owain asked.

Caden moved to the place the man abandoned. "You found out when I did. 'Twas only hours ago that she got the wound." He touched her cheek with the back of his hand. Hot.

"And who are you running from?"

Caden glanced over his shoulder sharply. "Who says we are?"

Again the man brandished that annoying, knowing smile of his. "Navigating the river in the pitch dark during a storm says so. Unless you're both fools," he added. "And I see no sign that you are."

Caden thought before replying. To date, Owain had been truthful with them. But finding such a man here in the middle of the moor did not make sense. He hid something, despite the open hospitality and care he extended them.

Just as Caden decided on a convincing story—that he was escorting the lady to her mother, who desperately needed her—Sorcha replied.

"We're running from a powerful and vindictive man who wants to kill me for refusing to marry him."

Caden winced. He'd thought she'd drifted off to sleep.

"The lady chose to go to her mother's aid instead of marriage," Caden improvised. "The man's a villain with no allegiance to anyone, including the bretwalda, and didn't take her decision well." Waking wearing nothing but chains wouldn't improve Tunwulf's humor either.

"I see." Accepting Caden's elaboration without further question, Owain took more of the foul powder and made tea in a cup with hot water from the kettle. "Then the more of this concoction we can get into her, my friend," he said, reaching for a jar of what turned out to be honey, "the quicker you can be on your way."

Caden latched on those last words, the same as he clung to a trust that this man was indeed as learned as he appeared. Desperation gave him little choice. "How soon?"

"Likely three days. Then I'll take you upriver as far as Hahlton."

In three days Tunwulf, maybe Hussa himself, would be at Trebold, waiting for them. But Sorcha couldn't travel like this.

"From there," Owain continued, "it's no more than a day's travel afoot to the Tweed."

Caden locked gazes with the man. "Who said we were bound for the Tweed?"

"'Tis the fastest way out of Saxon-held land without crossing the forested hills or using the main roads north. How does roasted eel sound for supper?"

An answer for every question. "Three days?" Caden repeated. Because the healing Owain promised and what Caden had seen in the past did not agree.

"Christ rose in three days," Owain reminded him. "She has only an infected arm."

So, Owain was a Christian. Stranger still. British clergy, as a rule, would rather burn themselves than reach out to the hordes who plundered their churches and massacred their brothers and sisters in unspeakable ways. That would make him Irish, whether he had the accent or nay.

Caden lifted Sorcha up gently and worked his way under her till he cradled her in his arms. "I pray to God you are right, *scholar*," he said. "Now hand me that tea."

CHAPTER TWENTY-FOUR

The sickness reeled Sorcha in and out of awareness like a fish in a fever-tossed sea. Sometimes the water was cold, icy cold. Other times it burned the very strength from her body until her brain felt as though it fried and withered in her head. Oh, how it ached. Often more than her arm, which was tender even to the weight of the blankets. Only in sleep was there relief. And nothing put her to sleep like Owain's voice.

"You must be a bard or an angel," she told him during a lull in the agony.

"Neither, milady." He sat on a bench near the hearth with a smile that, like his touch, was warm and gentle as sunshine.

"Something tells me you'd be exceptional at whatever you choose to do," Sorcha observed.

"Well, *I* never heard of bard, or angel, or doctor that smelled like fish," Caden griped from the foot of her bed, where he always seemed to be.

Owain laughed. "'Tis the curse of handling them day in and out."

Sorcha didn't notice. 'Twas the foul stench of the medicine Caden coaxed into her each time she awoke that seemed fixed in her nostrils. Owain came and went and changed her bandage, but Caden was always there. He helped her don a clean shirt, keeping his gaze averted, and held her head in his lap, stroking it when the pain was unbearable, until Owain's voice lulled her to sleep.

And then the pain was gone, even when Sorcha sat up to take her supper. And time began again. For three days, she'd been unaware of it.

"I should like to bathe and don a dress," she announced after a delicious meal of bread and potted grouse, compliments of Owain's hunting skills. "If you gentlemen wouldn't mind."

"Why do you need your dress when tomorrow you'll be back in shirt and trews?" Caden complained. "Are you expecting company?"

"I would like to feel human again … like a woman."

"You need no dress for that, milady," Owain said from the board, where he washed the wooden plates they'd used. "At least on our account. But if it's for yours, by all means."

"Well!" Caden shot up from the stool and slapped his thighs. "Had I known a dress would make me feel better, I'd have kept one in my sack for battle wounds." He snatched up a yew pail, his mouth twisted as wryly as his voice. "I'll fetch your water, milady."

A hand bath was a lovely notion, but by the time Sorcha had completed her toilet, she was too exhausted for the evening she'd envisioned of trying her hand at Owain's harp and joining him in song. She hardly heard Owain's flowery praise at her change of clothing or Caden's grudging compliment. Instead, she slept in the rich gown she'd worn at Eavlyn's wedding.

The following morning, Sorcha climbed into Owain's curragh wearing Tunwulf's clean, sun-freshened clothing and feeling sheepish for indulging her feminine whims the night before. There hadn't been enough decent wood to repair the bottom of the coble, so she had to trust Caden and Owain's assurance that Owain's wicker-framed craft was safe enough. Slung over her shoulder were her belongings, including a linen-wrapped jar of the vile medicinal tea Owain insisted she needed to take morning, noon, and night until it was all gone.

Taking extreme care as to the placement of her foot on the stem to stern willow strips, she settled on a bench in the prow. How on earth could tarred cowhide over a wicker frame be seaworthy enough for the river, much less the ocean voyages Owain told her of?

Heavenly Father, You've protected us thus far, and it's from my heart that I ask You to see us safely on to my mother.

Sorcha smiled to herself, somewhat pacified and most pleased with her prayer. Her time with Eavlyn and listening to Owain pray over her arm and his guests and give thanks for his heathland home and all its creatures had not been wasted. Sorcha had a gift for words. And after surviving this long, she'd begun to think the Christian God might actually be listening to her.

"Do you believe in angels, Owain?"

Caden jerked his head about from where he stowed stores for the day's journey upstream. "Don't tell me you've found a leak already, woman."

Laughter bubbled in Sorcha's throat. "I'm just curious. And Owain's a scholar," she reminded him.

"Aye, he probably knows their wingspan," Caden quipped.

"Scripture says they exist, milady. So I have no reason to doubt them." Owain stood back to let Caden take the middle seat.

"Princess Eavlyn saw one."

With that, Sorcha entertained her host as they started upriver, telling him the story of the hunt and the meanings of the carvings on Father Martin's staff. It turned out Owain was something of a biblical scholar as well and embellished the tales even more while he and Caden rowed upstream, the latter thin-lipped and unaccountably sullen.

"But as to the angel the princess saw," Owain observed, "'twas real to her, I'm sure. No one knows why some see God's messengers and others don't."

"So you think it was real," Sorcha pressed. These things intrigued her. Made her wonder.

"It isn't for me to say. I wasn't there."

"I'm thinking there's a bit of eel in you, Owain, the way you slip away from answers," Caden observed.

"Caden, listen to yourself," Sorcha chided. "Good as Owain has been to us, and you pick at him like a cross old crow." She stifled a yawn.

"Don't upset yourself, milady," Owain spoke up. "The man's been worried sick over you these last days and short of rest."

"Speaking of which, you should rest," Caden told her. "Once we land in Hahlton, we'll be on our way hard afoot."

Sorcha's elation from being well and on their way again wavered. They had to move on, she knew, but the least effort wearied her.

"There's a trader there who deals in livestock," Owain told them. "He has a gift with the wild marsh ponies. They're small and wiry, living on the scrub as they do, but tough. If you've coin, you might find one for the lady."

"We've got gold." Sorcha patted her sack, thrilled at the prospect, until she saw Caden's warning glower.

How could the man suspect Owain would do them harm after all he'd done to help them? Still, it was foolish to announce it. She'd been a thief long enough to know that.

"A little," she added, searching Owain's blue eyes for any betrayal of kindling greed. But all she found was a sincerity that rang true to the bone.

Sliding off the bench, she reached under the cover of the prow and took out a blanket Owain had stashed in there. Her injured arm twinged with warning, but she could open and close her fist now that the swelling and infection had eased. This morning the majority of her flesh had returned to pink, except for what looked to be a burn scar right around the broken skin. Drawing the woolen blanket about her shoulders, she nestled into the curve of the side, her harp sack bundled close in her arms.

Owain continued to tell Caden about Gabon, the old livestock trader for whom the young scholar had worked as a lad. He warned of Gabon's keen business sense. "He'll try to sell the half-broke for the same as the others, but he keeps a few older mares for breeding. It'll cost more, but I'd get one of those for the lady."

Truth was, unaccustomed as she was to sitting astride a horse, she still ached from the ride to the hunt. The Cymri were known for their horsemanship, but Saxons usually preferred to hunt and fight afoot. Even the nobility. Her father disdained horsemanship, believing it was more for prestige than practicality on a battlefield. A bigger target to bring down.

Sorcha closed her eyes as the talk of horses eased the tension between the two men. Caden had a warhorse called Forstan. Like those of Arthur's warband—huge, powerful, and not native to the island. He may have ridden it the day of the hunt, but Sorcha had been too distracted to notice. What a tragedy that he'd had to leave his noble Forstan behind.

Because of her. Granted, she hadn't directly caused their predicament, but if he'd not come for her, he'd not be here now. And who knew where she'd be? Dead by now, most likely.

Cracking her eyes open, she watched Caden rowing the vessel, his rugged face animated now as he spoke of Forstan. But she'd seen that same face wracked with worry as he'd held her over the past three days. Owain's music and medicines soothed her pain, but it was Caden who felt it and suffered with her.

Heavenly Father, I thank You for sending Caden for me.

As she prayed, a sweet peace washed over Sorcha, akin to that she found in Caden's embrace, but deeper, cradling heart and soul.

Hahlton was an unwalled keep, no more than a scatter of cottages and shops around a central grazing area, where the moor began to rise toward the western hills. Landing the curragh meant pulling it up on the riverbank and walking up a long muddy path strewn with straw to the reeve's house, the largest of the dwellings and shops. It was there the king's man collected rents in dried fish and corn raised in the squares of fertile fields tended by the farm folk.

"Why didn't you bring your catch of eels?" Sorcha asked Owain as she tried to keep her steps on a wide length of board placed in front of the row of shops. "It looks like it's market day."

If one could call a few dozen men, women, and children gathered round carts in the square a market. Most of them paid more attention to the newcomers than the wares on the two wagons belonging to traveling merchants, one selling textiles, the other kitchenware. Sorcha knew, from her own business, that these were likely the last the village would see of such things until spring.

"My profit lies in Din Guardi, not here," Owain replied. "Hahlton has fishermen enough to feed its bellies." He motioned to a tavern where a group of men stood under a sign that read *The Blue Crow.* "I'll be there catching up with old friends."

"You're not coming with us?" Sorcha protested.

Owain dazzled her with a smile that kindled fire in her cheeks. "Nothing I say will win you favor with Gabon."

"Grinned stupid till you drove him mad, did you?" Caden quipped. But he offered his hand, removing the edge from his accusation. "So where is this Gabon?"

"His place is the one with all the fences." Owain pointed to a cottage that looked more like a barn from which grew wattled enclosures rather than the golden-grain stubble in the other fields. Beyond it, the scrubland gave way to forest that thickened and rose toward the sky.

"So this is good-bye?" Although Sorcha felt better and had medicine in her bag, the thought of losing her capable physician's company pricked her with dread.

"Come to the tavern when your business is done," he told her, "for the best fish cakes you've ever tasted … and a cup of medicinal tea."

"Ugh." She wrinkled her nose and slipped her arm through Caden's. "We'll see you there, then."

"But we need to get away soon as we purchase provisions," Caden reminded her.

As the two of them walked away, she sighed. "I'm going to miss Owain. What a delightful companion. I wonder why one of those young women ogling the bolts of cloth on that wagon hasn't set her mind on getting his attention."

"Maybe they don't like a man prettier than they are," Caden drawled, dour.

"Is that why you don't like him?" Mischief pulled Sorcha's gaze to Caden's. Dare she hope the big lug of a Cymri was jealous? Just a wee bit?

"I don't trust him." Caden screwed up his face, as though searching for the reason. "He's like finding an onion in a fruit pasty," he explained. "The onion has its place, mind you, but not where it is."

"So you're a cook now, as well as soldier and sailor?"

Caden cut her a sharp look and snorted. "I know I don't like onions and berries in the same bite."

Chapter Twenty-five

Owain was not in the tavern. But after the horse trader Gabon vowed he'd never heard of the man, Caden wasn't surprised. In fact no one they spoke to had ever heard of a fisherman who trapped eels downriver between Hahlton and Din Guardi. Caden had Sorcha check her bag as soon as they'd left Gabon's barn, but her *fortune* at least was intact. Their safety was another matter of concern if greed for their capture was an issue. For all Caden knew, Owain was recruiting help to detain them.

Yet the tavern keeper's son, a pock-faced youth with a shaggy mop of brown hair, told them an uncommonly tall blond stranger had come in and ordered a cup of hot water with which he'd prepared a brew for a beautiful copper-haired lady. He paid the lad a silver coin worth ten times the stoneware cup itself to let it cool and to hold it till the lady appeared. The boy, who was born and raised in Hahlton, had never seen Owain before.

Caden left Sorcha to drink her tea while he purchased supplies for the remaining two-day journey. Telling the curious villagers that he was escorting a lady home to her ailing Cymri mother seemed to answer the inevitable questions. Isolated as they were, they were eager to hear any news from strangers passing through. And of course, having come upriver from Din Guardi, Caden was plied with questions regarding the royal wedding, especially from the women. He'd denied having seen anything but the continuous flow of carts laden with supplies headed up the causeway for the royals and their guests.

It was only after Hahlton lay in their wake and the forested green of the Cheviots met the cloudless blue of the sky in the distance, that the tension in Caden's neck and shoulders eased. Still, he continually swept the heathland scrub and lacework of marsh grass and water behind them with eagle eyes.

While Sorcha maintained her role in their semicharade, she would not hear any of Caden's suspicions regarding Owain.

"That is the most ridiculous notion I've ever heard of," she declared from the back of the underfed warhorse that Gabon had sold them for the remainder of Tunwulf's torque. A warhorse! Caden still couldn't believe their luck.

"Big as she is, she's not fit for the plow," the old man had told them. "An' if she's sick, I won't take her back." Gabon couldn't have known just what he had, or he'd have made straightway to Din Guardi to sell the mare for more than all his little marsh ponies were worth, instead of feeding it the heath grasses that sustained his stock until the poor mare's ribs showed.

But very few Saxons fought on horseback. They were swift and deadly enough afoot, although the prestige of owning such a steed in good condition would have guaranteed a fat purse. This animal had surely belonged to a fallen Cymri cavalryman from Arthur's late summer campaign to drive the Saxons back across the Tweed, so it only seemed right that Caden should rescue it, while it rescued them. Elfwyn—the name Sorcha had bestowed upon the chestnut mare—would fill out with the right care. For now, she had a belly full of grain, and Caden walked beside her to preserve her strength to carry two, in case they were given chase.

"You saw my wrist this morning," Sorcha continued to argue, all the while combing out Elfwyn's copper-gold mane with her fingers. "Owain is a physician and a scholar."

That morning, when Owain applied a new poultice, the wrist was still a bit swollen, but the redness was reduced to pink. Whatever was in Sorcha's stinking medicinal tea and the paste he applied in the wrappings was working better than anything Caden had ever seen for such infections.

"Besides, why would Owain offer us such hospitality and care if he hoped to gain from our situation?"

"Greed," Caden told her simply. "We are wanted for the murder of one of the king's most trusted thanes. It doesn't matter that we're innocent."

"I think he left abruptly because he was afraid we'd try to pay him for his trouble. There are good people like that." She lapsed into silence for a moment and stared off at a rise of heathland where scrawny cattle grazed amidst scrub pine and thorn bush. "What if he was also hiding?"

"What?"

"What if he'd done something that forced him into hiding? That would explain a man of his learning living in such isolation. Maybe he accidentally killed someone."

The only cloud in sight on the fair autumn day settled over Sorcha's face. Caden knew she thought of Rhianon.

He snorted in exasperation. "You have an amazing capacity for worrying more about others than about your own hide."

"*My* hide is well protected by your muscle and sword." The smile she gave Caden warmed him straight to the toes ... and elsewhere. "And my dagger, of course," she added impishly.

So help him, Caden could have skipped, her flirtation knocked him so giddy. He forced Delg's blade deeper into its leather scabbard, as though to pin his feet to the ground. "'Twill take more than my muscle and sword, I fear, when we reach Trebold," he said gruffly.

"What do you mean?"

"I mean that Tunwulf will likely be waiting for us." The possibility had plagued Caden for the last few days of delay.

Sorcha paled. "How would he know where we are going?"

"I believe Trebold was mentioned before Hussa in verifying the reason you were going with me back to Lothian."

"But—" Sorcha fell silent again.

Caden was instantly sorry he'd even brought up what might lie ahead. He liked Sorcha when she was playful. Or when she sang. Or even when she was in a temper. There was a time—

When Rhianon had made him feel the same way. As if his heart would take flight and lift him into the heavens with it.

But Caden knew the end to such feelings. Sooner or later one had to come back to earth, sometimes with a terrible crash. He'd barely survived the last one. Had often wished he hadn't. Now he wasn't sure.

Sorcha was no Rhianon by any stretch of the imagination, but she deserved more than a misfit without a home. Myrna and Trebold deserved more, no matter the old chief's ramblings about how Caden might make a fine husband for Sorcha, if he brought her home.

Hope and despair wrestled mightily in his mind. *Why* was he even allowing his mind to wander down that tangled path? Even if God had forgiven him his past, Caden could not forget it. He was born to fight, not love.

"Caden, slow down. You're forcing poor Elfwyn into a trot and rattling every tooth in my head!"

Aye, slow down, he told himself. Though he hadn't been aware that his thoughts had urged him into a run. He couldn't run away from this, but he could make sure Sorcha entertained no nonsense that they were more than escort and lady. He was no more than a protector till she was delivered and safe. He deserved no more, she no less.

By nightfall, they'd reached a ford on the Tweed where a small hostel that had once been a Roman villa served a delicious venison stew. The hostel was run by a Cymri couple who served anyone who could pay. The borderlands between the Saxon-held coast and Lothian's hills were a no-man's-land, where Saxon and Cymri lived to survive any way they could. Under Rome's peace, it had supported villas like the hostel with farms, but now it was a haven for criminals, outcasts of both peoples.

There were only four other guests passing through, two men and a young woman with a child, allowing for ample room under the tiled roof of what had once been a salon. Secondary rooms were built in a square around an overgrown courtyard, its tiles long removed. Chickens occupied the remnants of a long-dry fountain partially covered with wicker-based turf, while the rest of the building served as a stable. Caden opted to sleep in one of the stalls with Elfwyn after the innkeeper's wife put up a screen for the women and child to have their pallets near the fire built in the center of the main room and vented through a hole knocked into the turf-patched roof.

Even a poor warhorse was a tempting treasure, and Caden trusted no one to watch the mare. But Sorcha needed a warm fire and comfortable pallet, for winter's bite came at night, hinting of the harsher weather to come. With plenty of straw heaped in the enclosed stable, Caden would be more than comfortable. As a soldier, he'd slept in far worse conditions. And always with Delg's blade close by.

But not even a prayer to Abba would still the battling thoughts in his mind. If Tunwulf was at Trebold …

"You should have killed Tunwulf when you had the chance," Sorcha fretted the following day as they entered the forested hills to the Tweed's north.

Behind them lay tattered farms and grazing cattle on the rolling grasslands where people struggled to eke out a living between this or that army's locust-like sweep through the river valley, consuming the fruits of their labors. Above them bronze oak and red beech shed their colors, creating a vibrant carpet that winter's breath would soon turn brown.

"I've sent many a man to the Other Side, but never one who couldn't defend himself," Caden retorted. Though part of him agreed with her. He'd just postponed the inevitable, unless he could convince Sorcha to bypass Trebold in the event Tunwulf did await them. If he'd left immediately after being discovered, chances were he'd not have his full warband with him. Caden might challenge him to settle this with his sword, man to man. Even as he thought it, Caden didn't have much hope for an honorable resolution.

"I should have killed him, then," she said wearily.

"You're a thief, not a murderer. And killing an unconscious man would be murder."

"If Tunwulf is in Trebold, we have no choice but to kill him. And if he's harmed my mother—"

"He has no reason to harm her. He only knows Trebold is your home. Hopefully Myrna can keep the fact that she's your mother from him."

"He's wily as a fox."

"That's an insult to a fox."

Despite the gravity of their plight, Sorcha laughed. "Why don't we pray that Tunwulf hasn't come after us?" she said upon sobering. "Or that if he did, he gave up and went home when he saw we weren't there?"

That surprised Caden. "So you're a Christian now?"

"I think so." The way Sorcha answered, Caden wasn't the only one bemused. "I've been talking in my mind to your God. So I must believe in Him," she reasoned. "And Father Martin said He forgave thieves. So that means He forgives me, right? If I *try* not to steal anymore?"

Caden laughed. It was the wrong response, exacting a scowl from her, but he couldn't help himself. What a pair of misfits they were.

"You've asked the wrong person, I fear. I'm barely on speaking terms with God myself," he explained. "I've done a lot of bad things."

"To your family." It wasn't a question. Evidently Sorcha had remembered the confrontation with Rhianon and Tunwulf and pieced his guilt together.

"Yes. That's the worst of it."

"And you're forgiven, right?"

"So Father Martin says." Caden wanted to believe that. "That day we danced on the beach … just before, I found myself crying out to Jesus for help. I was frightened, and, God knows, I needed a father. A real father."

"*You* were frightened?"

"You'd have been unnerved as well if the woman you saw jump over a cliff and thought was dead suddenly appeared as alive and calculating as ever." Caden shuddered. "And I saw her and her demon-calling nurse do things I cannot speak of. Worse, I let them."

The words spilled out of Caden's mouth like a flood tide. There was no stopping them, nor did Sorcha try. She listened. Gently prompted him to continue. Caden bared everything he'd felt the morning he'd discovered Rhianon was alive, from the fear and anguish to the joy and euphoria.

"So that's what happened," Sorcha murmured in wonder when he was spent of story and emotion.

Caden cocked his head up at her, belatedly self-conscious. "What do you mean, lassie?" She looked at him strangely, as though seeing him for the first time. What had he been thinking to open his soul to her, his fears and insecurities? He'd not even done that for Rhianon.

"You were so different that morning from the way you'd been the night before." She shook her head as though searching for the right words. "The night you came to the tavern, you were older than your years, a man hardened by pain and with a mission—one you would accomplish, no matter how." A hint of a smile pulled at her lips. "And yet, even then I knew that I'd not seen the last of you. Not because of what you said, but what you left unsaid."

That was the problem with women. They saw things men didn't even know took place. *If* they took place. "That sounds like bardic nonsense."

"Our eyes touched. They spoke when we dared not. You didn't just want me to return to Trebold with you. You needed me to."

The observation hit its mark, taking Caden unawares. Aye, he'd needed to do something for someone. It was his escape from the prison of his guilt and misery.

"If I was to help your mother, I needed you to come along. I suppose that's true enough," he mumbled. But he'd admit no more. Sorcha had already heard and seen more than he wanted anyone to know.

"If you say so."

"I do." He could see she wasn't convinced.

"And the following day, you acted as if the weight of the world had been lifted off your shoulders. You were almost childlike in your joy ... years younger."

Aye.

"And when we danced, it was as though we were meant to be together."

No. This dreamy nonsense had to stop. "Like I said before, I needed you to come with me for your mother's sake. If the hard approach didn't work, I knew the charm would."

Sorcha's abrupt silence whipped at Caden's conscience. Just as he was about to change his tack, she sighed. "I see."

She didn't. But Caden allowed her to think she did. And it made him miserable, something comforting in its familiarity.

CHAPTER TWENTY-SIX

The shadows of the forest darkened as the long day approached its close. Sorcha had to watch her step as she walked beside Elfwyn on the downhill slope. She liked the animal well enough, but so help her, if Sorcha ever rode again, it would be too soon. Surely her hips were disjointed, held together only by aching muscle. It was small wonder she could walk at all.

"We'll be home soon," she promised, petting the gentle horse and talking to her as she did from time to time. "You said we'd be home about sundown didn't you?" she asked Caden.

"Aye, I've been smelling wood smoke for nigh over the last two miles."

Neither of them had spoken much since Caden had made it plain that the relationship between them wasn't one at all. That they were just traveling companions for as long as it took him to unite her with her mother.

The pigheaded buffoon!

Sorcha knew better, even if he didn't. She trusted her instincts, born of spending hours singing for people from all walks and of all temperaments, reading them like a priest his parchment. She remembered how caring Caden had been when she'd been ill. And jealous of Owain's attentions. So much so that he'd refused to leave her alone in Owain's company.

So she let Caden stew in the guilt-laced juice of his own making, speaking only when she had to for nature's call or a hunger stop along the way. Indeed, his long face almost made her pity him.

How like her father he was. A man with regrets from previous mistakes and full of bluster to hide a heart as big as he was. Cynric once told her that Wulfram had turned from a savage to a gentle bear in Aelwyn's hands. Putting the word *savage* and her father in the same breath was hard to imagine; he loved people so. And Sorcha, of course, was his little girl, no matter that she'd grown into a young woman.

"Watch how a man treats his mother or any children when you decide to chose a mate," Wulfram once advised her.

"And there is the river Lader," Caden announced, drawing her from her nostalgia. He pointed ahead to where the setting sun cast a red glaze on a ribbon of water beyond the thinning brush and thorn.

Beyond the water were more woods like those they'd passed through all day, both uphill and down. Oak, birch, ash, and maple shedding their leafy coats, evergreen interspersed and thicket beneath, all crisscrossed with wildlife paths. It was those running parallel to the road that they'd traveled, keeping to cover.

Sorcha looked hard into the forest beyond. There was no sign of habitation. Just more trees and thorn. "Where is Trebold?"

"Upriver. But we'll cross here and follow the water to the main ford. Just in case we've uninvited guests waiting there," he reminded her.

Sorcha stopped abruptly, folded her hands, and bowed her head as she'd seen Eavlyn do. "Great Heavenly Father, neither one of us are practiced at being Christians. We've much to learn. But from our heart of hearts we ask that You clear the way for us, that we might arrive safe and sound. You've seen us safe thus far, and we count on Your Word that You will never leave nor forsake us. In the name of Jesus who died for us, that we may live, amen."

"Amen," Caden chimed in. For the first time since he'd made a fool of himself that morning, his long features softened. "And well said, milady. You've a way with words."

"Are you certain it's not bardic nonsense?" she shot back.

Instead of answering, Caden took the lead once more, his face impassive as a stone.

Sorcha followed with Elfwyn's rein in hand and a hint of a smile on her lips.

Easy to read as parchment, Caden was.

Caden's decision to cross farther back had been a sound one. Had they not, they'd have run smack into the campfires awaiting them on the yon side as they neared the edge of the woodland, where the tavern sat nestled in the shade of a circle of oaks. While its yard beyond and the meadowland cleared along the river crossing bathed in the light of the waning moon, the firelight's glow filtered eerily from the other side through a low mist where the cold night air hugged the sun-warmed river. The men who moved round the fires looked more like shadow creatures, but Sorcha knew better.

She could catch bits and pieces of their mead-soaked conversation amidst the occasional yap of their dogs begging for food.

Saxons. And if she could make out the banner fluttering near the fire, it would likely have Elford's black wolf's head on it, with its fierce red eyes. The same as that on the ring in her bag. Glancing sidewise at her companion, she shivered within the confines of Tunwulf's *and* her own cloak.

"I suppose God didn't see fit to listen." Disappointment soaked her words as the water had done her boots when she and Caden had ridden Elfwyn across the water a mile or so back.

"He saw fit to keep them on the yon side of the river," Caden noted.

Catching an odd note in his reply, she followed his gaze to where the tavern sat, its hide-covered windows lit with the promise of food and warmth within. There were men standing outside the door, but that wasn't unusual in a tavern setting.

"What's keeping the Saxon over there?" he asked himself aloud. "Unless the tavern is full of Cymri warriors."

"Is that Arthur's banner?" There *was* some sort of flag flying near the inn door, but, oak being the last to let go its bronze leaves, the trees overhead shadowed its markings. Sorcha had heard of Arthur and his mounted cavalry. His name evoked awe, even among the Saxon. He would surely keep Tunwulf at a distance.

But Caden shook his head. "It's not white, but some darker color." He turned to her, grim. "Milady, the safest thing to do is to keep on traveling."

Sorcha groaned aloud. She was tired, hungry, cold, and wet.

"Or wait the night out until we see if there is friend or foe in the tavern," he offered.

And they were so close to her mother. Her home. "I say they are friends to keep the Saxon at bay."

"*Or* Tunwulf has gathered his entire warband and camps on both sides of the river to cover all routes. We were detained three days," Caden pointed out.

Sorcha ignored the possibility. "I prayed," she said simply. "God would not deliver us into Tunwulf's hands. We can sneak around and enter the tavern from the b—"

A dog barked near them, cutting her off. Too near.

Caden swore beneath his breath. "A patrol."

But whose? Sorcha soothed an uneasy Elfwyn by stroking her quivering, warm coat.

The dog roared again, then yelped, as though someone had pulled back on its leash.

"*Gestillan, hund!*" Someone demanded it stop in the Saxon tongue. There was a low exchange of words. Branches snapped with further movement through the trees behind them. Evidently Tunwulf—who else could it be?—had a patrol on *this* side of the river.

Caden nudged Sorcha. "I want you to mount Elfwyn and, when I say so, make straight for the tavern as hard as you can. Get inside at any cost."

Sorcha allowed Caden to lift her onto the mare's back and sought the strap stirrups with her toes. "What are you going to do? We could both ride that short of a distance."

"I'm going to lead the men away from you. Now go!"

Before Sorcha could protest, Caden slapped Elfwyn on the buttock. The mare, already unnerved by the Saxon hound's presence, bolted forward with such force that Sorcha had to hold on to her mane and grasp her with her knees with all her might just to keep from falling off. Low branches whipped at her face as the horse broke into the clearing in a gallop.

Behind her, she heard Caden shout something vulgar in Saxon regarding the legitimate birth of the patrolmen, and the woods erupted. By the time Sorcha gained control of Elfwyn, she was almost to the barns to the left of the tavern. She ventured a look over her shoulder in time to see Caden break free of the trees and unsheath his sword.

The dog reached him first, a massive, muscled, angry hound like the ones the Saxons turned loose on the Cymri foot soldiers in battle. The animal lunged at Caden's throat. Sorcha caught her breath and reined Elfwyn in short of flying into the darkness of the barn. It looked as if the dog might succeed in its vicious attack, but suddenly Caden sidestepped and swung his sword with both fists, pommel first, knocking the dog hard out of its path. It yelped once and crashed to the ground beside the man, where it lay still.

But now the Saxon patrol emerged. Four men circled the lone warrior. And what a magnificent warrior he was, bathed in the light of the waning fall moon. He put her to mind of a caged lion she'd once seen at a fair in Eboracum, no intent to run and every intent to kill. If Sorcha didn't know better, his footwork might have been a dance instead of a wary assessment of who might charge him first.

And if they charged him at once …

There was no need to finish the thought. Sorcha had no intention of letting the worst happen. She'd run enough. She was cold, hungry, wet, and now more angry than frightened.

She roared to the top of her lungs. "Die, you dogs!" And dug into Elfwyn's sides with her heels. Evidently the mare had had enough of retreat as well, for Elfwyn reared to paw at the air, and, with a great thrust of her back legs, the horse leapt into a charge worthy of a bard's praise.

Sorcha could do nothing but hold on for her life.

Straight into the circle of predators she rode, barely missing Caden as she scattered the men. Groping for the reins she'd lost in order to keep her seat, she managed to turn Elfwyn again and aimed the snorting beast at them as they regrouped.

"Get away, woman!" Caden shouted as he attacked one of the men with a vicious sword swing. Iron clanged. Sparks flew.

But Elfwyn was undaunted. It was as though the warrior spirit of the poor bedraggled beast had suddenly been set free. Two of the men knelt and braced long spears against the ground, intent on running the steed through, but the closer her thundering hooves came, the better they thought of it. Both dropped their weapons and ran, but not soon enough. Elfwyn ran one over as if that had been her intent all along. The other retreated into the woods.

Sorcha lunged for the reins again as the mare slowed enough to trot into a turn. It was only then she saw that she and Caden no longer faced four men, but many times that number. They mustered from inside the tavern like angry bees, shields clashing as they formed some sort of line. All except one.

A big hulk of a man with wild yellow hair and an equally wild beard lumbered toward where Caden fought with the last standing attacker. His tunic, half-pulled on in haste, was black with something white hidden in the folds. As he ran, he gained momentum, though he'd still not drawn the sword strapped to his waist.

And if Sorcha had any say, he wouldn't. She nudged Elfwyn forward just as Caden plunged his weapon into the belly of his opponent.

Four down and one giant with an army to go. Sorcha wondered fleetingly as Elfwyn's hooves pounded into the ground if anyone would immortalize this last battle in song....

The giant reached Caden.

And embraced him.

Beyond them, the line his army formed moved toward the river, where a few Saxons from the other side tried to ford it. A shieldwall, it was called. She'd heard her father and Cynric speak often of holding the line, the push and crush of bodies sometimes so tight it was impossible to use their weapons.

God had answered her prayers. He'd sent an army of black-clad warriors to hold Tunwulf across the river. Amazement assembled the pieces slowly in mind.

Too slowly.

Sorcha reined in Elfwyn as Caden and the blond giant turned their faces toward her. Their eyes widened, and, as if in slow motion, they broke apart from each other. But Elfwyn couldn't stop. Not before plowing through them with a smash of muscle against muscle.

Sorcha's shriek caught in her throat. She pulled back on the reins in desperation to get the horse to stop.

Elfwyn did.

Sorcha did not.

CHAPTER TWENTY-SEVEN

"Sorcha!" Though winded from the impact of Elfwyn's charge, Caden scrambled to his feet and half ran, half stumbled to where Sorcha lay still as death. Sure, their entire journey had not been as long as that distance, but as Caden gathered Sorcha in his arms, she groaned, and her eyelids fluttered as though she wasn't certain she wanted to come back to the present just yet.

"You crazy, fire-headed—" A blade stopped the emotion breaking in his throat. That, and a group of men breaking from the trees.

"Easy, laddie. They're ours," Caden's old friend assured him. "So that's the lady of Trebold we've been hearing about." Egan O'Toole knelt on Sorcha's other side and began to check her limbs for broken bones.

Caden tried to unscramble his feelings from his thoughts. Was he hallucinating? What took men from Glenarden to Trebold?

"Not much of a horsewoman, is she, laddie?" Egan observed dryly.

When Sorcha went flying over the mare's neck, Caden had been certain she'd break her own. And that knocked more out of him than ten charging steeds.

"Nay," he replied, "but she sings like a lark and can lift a man's purse and make him thankful for it."

"Does she now?" The warrior snorted in amusement. "I'm thinkin' she's more stunned than hurt. Scoop 'er up, laddie, and let's take her to her mathair. Them Saxons ain't comin' this side o' the water tonight."

Still dazed himself, Caden looked to where the men of Glenarden formed a solid shieldwall at the ford. In the river mist a few shadowy soldiers summoned by the fracas milled about as if to see what had transpired but made no more attempts to cross.

The last Caden had heard, Glenarden was guarding the Pictish border of Manau for Arthur.

"When?" Caden asked in disbelief. "How?"

"Best ask your brother that." Egan nodded to where a tall, lean warrior and a woman, the Lady Myrna, emerged from the tavern door and hurried toward them along with a servant carrying a lighted torch.

His *brother?* Caden recoiled as if Elfwyn had had at him again. He eased Sorcha back to the ground, casting a glance in the direction of the sword the horse had knocked out of his hand. A tide of bitter memories crashed on his shoulders as he slowly, warily struggled upright against it.

It was his eldest brother. His sworn enemy. There was no mistaking that long, purposeful stride or the grim, humorless features of his face. No warmth. The only warmth Ronan had ever shown was for his strange healer wife.

"Sorcha!" Myrna cried out upon seeing her daughter lying on the ground. The woman rushed to Sorcha's side and, kneeling, gathered her up in her arms.

"She's a bit stunned, milady, nothin' broke, I think," Egan assured her. "Why don't you stand back and let me take her inside for you. I'm thinkin' these lads need to talk."

Finally Caden found his voice. "Ronan. You're the last person I expected to see here."

Ronan nailed Caden with his dark gaze. "You always liked a grand entrance, Brother. I see that hasn't changed." He glanced to where Sorcha began to stir as Egan picked her up. A smile cracked the hard veneer of his expression. "It appears you've met your match."

Caden stared at the hand Ronan extended him, still not trusting his senses. "Why?" he asked. "You swore you'd never forgive me. God might, but you would not."

"I haven't yet," Ronan replied candidly, "but I am willing to try."

"Try?" Caden repeated. Even *that* was something, considering he'd led Saxon renegades against his brother in a shameful night attack with the full intent of killing anyone who stood in the way of Caden's seizing Glenarden for himself. Father Martin said he was possessed due to Rhianon's witchery, but Caden had yet to forgive himself for being such a willing pawn in her manipulative hands.

He couldn't bring himself to that any more than he could move from the spot as Egan scooped Sorcha into his arms as if she were a small child.

"Let's get this plucky lassie inside," Egan told Myrna. "Lead the way, milady."

Ronan sidestepped the big Irishman. "Brenna told me I had to come here," he explained to Caden. "I had to leave her and our new daughter because she dreamed that you were in trouble, and it was what God would want one brother to do for another."

"And you came, simple as that?" Caden still wondered if Brenna was some sort of witch, although she did naught but good for even the most insignificant.

Love of our neighbor is the only door out of the dungeon of self. Truth was, she lived that old proverb of Father Martin's. Brenna was the first to say she'd forgiven Caden. But he'd not trusted her or her God at the time.

Ronan glanced across the river, where the Saxon fires burned. "It's the first such dream like this she's had since you betrayed us."

Caden winced inwardly. The remark cut deep into wounds that had never healed. Yet, in spite of his guilt, hope sprang from Ronan's presence and dashed about in Caden's mind as if to stomp out the sparks of his doubt and distrust.

Abba.

"And you came," Caden marveled again. Was it possible to truly leave the past behind?

"You and I will go our separate ways, Brother, but I will have to live with Brenna." His brother's grin suggested it was a fate he would enjoy.

Brenna had changed him … and for the better. And if Ronan could change—

Ronan reached down and picked up Caden's discarded sword, handing it to him. "What say you we go inside where it's warm, and you can tell me what you've done that has set so sore with this Saxon Tunwulf."

Once the Saxons retreated to their side of the river, the captain of the O'Byrne warriors had his men deliver the staggering, brain-dazed dog and the bodies of the men Caden and Elfwyn had slain with a warning that any other Saxon who crossed the Lader would be sent to the Other World with their compliments. With Glenarden's guards doubled and patrolling the riverfront in case Tunwulf decided on an ill-advised attack during the night, the rest of the men returned to the hospitality of Trebold's tavern.

Once he was certain Sorcha had regained her wits, if she had any left after that mad ride on Elfwyn, Caden left mother and daughter to their reunion in the very room where Myrna had nursed him back to his feet and joined the men downstairs.

His belly full and warmed by mead within and the fire without, he listened in awe as he heard how Alyn, on his way back to the university, had told them about Caden's recovery and new mission so Ronan knew straightaway where to find him, even if Brenna hadn't seen that part in her dream. She'd only known in her soul that Caden's life and lives of others were at risk and that Ronan needed to offer Glenarden's aid as a brother and a Christian chief.

It had been a four-day march from Glenarden to Din Edyn and down the Roman road to the south end of the Lader. When the O'Byrnes arrived, nothing seemed amiss. Myrna was pleasantly surprised to meet Caden's brother and had nothing but praises for the warrior who not only saved Arthur in battle but had gone to fetch her long-lost daughter. Ronan had begun to think Brenna's imagination had run wild with her, what with her just having delivered a beautiful baby daughter with her mother's raven hair and lochan blue eyes.

But that afternoon, a party of a dozen Saxons arrived at the crossing on the other side of the Lader, bearing a wolf banner similar to Glenarden's. Except Glenarden's banner had been designed by Brenna in reverse colors, black with a white wolf in memory of her beloved pet. Tunwulf of Elford and two of his men crossed to speak to Ronan and Egan, their shields turned upside down as a sign of peace, and demanded that Caden of Lothian and Sorcha of Din Guardi be turned over to them for the murder of his father and the bretwalda's friend, Thane Cynric of Elford.

When it was clear that Caden and Sorcha were not there, the Saxons agreed to wait on the other side of the river, encouraged by the presence of Glenarden's seasoned warband. There the Saxon numbers increased by the day as more of Tunwulf's band joined him until it matched the size of Glenarden's.

Caden counted backward the five days of their journey since the escape—three at Owain's and two from Hahlton to Trebold. If Tunwulf's vengeful press had cut his journey to even two sun cycles and he'd arrived on the same day as Ronan, then Brenna had known they were in trouble at least two days before even they'd known. More, for it would have taken Ronan time to gather his levy of men and prepare for the journey.

Abba's name echoed again as it had throughout the exchange between him and Ronan; if anything was a miracle, this was. And when Caden recounted his and Sorcha's imprisonment and how Tunwulf and Rhianon had made them out to be the murderers, he found himself giving Abba more and more praise and thanksgiving.

"'Twas all Abba's doing," he declared, wonderstruck. "All of it."

Ronan's dark brow hiked. "So you've found God."

Caden laughed at his brother's shock. "Aye, He was on the beach the morning I thought I'd seen a ghost."

"Rhianon," Ronan said.

"Aye, Rhianon." Color climbed warm to his face. But Caden had admitted too much to stop speaking now. "I feared she still had some power over me," he began. Emotion welled in his throat, but he cleared it with a cough and proceeded to tell Ronan about that morning, when Caden had found the only Father he needed.

Ronan listened, expressionless. Caden didn't blame his reluctance to accept what even he still wrestled with. He wasn't like Sorcha, who embraced the Christian God in an almost childlike fashion because she thought she'd seen a miracle. She liked what she'd heard about Him and was most intrigued with angels. But when she faced her first disappointment, Caden feared her faith would shatter, as his had years ago.

Yet he wanted to believe unconditionally. He truly did. And in spite of the problems they'd encountered, here they were, safe and sound for the moment. But how much was due to their spirit and resourcefulness and how much to God?

"Who created you with that spirit and resourcefulness?"

"What I want to know is how the witch survived that fall." Egan O'Toole spoke up. "Half of us here saw her go over the falls." The men about them nodded, equally intrigued.

Caden explained how Tunwulf had found her wandering out of her mind in the woods when he saw Ronan's gaze sharpen. "Do you mean to say that this Tunwulf is one of the Saxons who attacked us?"

Shame blindsided Caden. "Aye." His past would never be forgotten or forgiven by Ronan or anyone else who knew. He could see it darken the expressions of some of the men who'd survived that night attack.

"Are you sure the witch is dead this time?" Egan asked. He made the sign of the cross.

"Fell on her own knife," Caden assured him. "Sorcha knocked her down with a harp."

"A harp!" Egan guffawed. "Now that's a fight I wish I'd seen."

"She tried to kill me."

Everyone turned to the staircase, where Sorcha descended in the dark russet gown with black chevron trim that she'd worn during the royal wedding. Her hair had been brushed into a shining cloak over her shoulders, catching the light from the becketed torchlights on the support beams and spinning it into silken fire. Caden's mouth slackened. Not even the bruise on her cheek could detract from the beauty that captivated the eyes and tongues of every man in the room.

"I did what I had to do," she added simply, upon reaching the bottom of the steps.

"Gentlemen …" Lady Myrna put her arm around her daughter. Myrna had always been a handsome woman, but the pure joy on her face lent her a radiance and youth that almost rivaled Sorcha's. "I would present my daughter, Lady Sorcha of Trebold, home at last, thanks to Caden of Lothian." Her voice broke as she looked at Caden. "You, sir, have given me a new life worth living."

Love of our neighbor is the only door out of the dungeon of self. The words haunted Caden's mind as his smile did his face.

Ronan stood as the women approached, reminding Caden of his manners. It was just that Sorcha was so breathtaking, she'd robbed him of his wits.

And his heart.

Caden stiffened in rebellion against that thought. There was no way, no possibility—

"Ronan of Glenarden, at your service, milady," his sibling replied, taking Sorcha's hand to his lips with the gallantry their mother had instilled in her sons as princes of Glenarden. "Welcome home."

"Thank you, milord. I would not have taken you and Caden for brothers, but for that same square jaw and dimple in the chin. It's supposed to be a sign of a dominant nature."

"Then we are betrayed by our chins," Ronan countered with a smile full of teeth that put Caden to mind of a mule with the colic.

"And you, Caden, are you well?" She placed a hand on his chest, and his heart lurched as if it had been mule kicked. "I truly didn't mean to run you and your champion down with Elfwyn."

"You can run me down on a crazy warhorse any day, milady." Egan chuckled. "'Twas worth seein' the look on that buck's face"—he pointed to Caden—"if nothin' else."

Both Egan and Ronan made fools of themselves, but Caden was no better. He'd yet to find his tongue. As she'd adapted to the role of warrior queen earlier, Sorcha now played the refined lady to perfection. Who was this woman, really?

"I think you must have knocked his tongue loose, meself," Egan observed wryly.

The taunt broke the spell, and Caden clutched at the anger he'd felt when he'd seen Sorcha and the horse barreling toward them instead of hying to safety as he'd instructed.

"My tongue is just fine, O'Toole. As for *you*, milady," Caden said to Sorcha, "I am glad to see that you've recovered your mind. You could have been killed out there. I told you to make for the tavern. If that Saxon had held his ground—"

"But he didn't."

Abba help him, he could fall into the round pools of green she turned so sweetly upon him.

There came a time in battle when a man had to fight or flee. Caden had nowhere to run. Not that he'd ever chosen that option. "Now you listen well, woman. I didn't risk life and limb to bring you home to your mother with a broken—"

Sorcha stood on tiptoe and kissed Caden into silence. It wasn't a long or passionate affection, but just as effective as a sword slice through his bluster.

"And I thank you, sir, for all the risks you took for my sake." She glanced toward the door facing the river, her face turning grave. "And for those all of you may be taking for our sake."

Leaving Caden standing speechless, Sorcha took a seat on the bench next to him and folded her hands before her. Delicate hands with long fingers that could make a harp or pipe sing. And no doubt any man with blood still warm in his veins.

"So now, gentlemen, what are our options?" she asked.

Myrna took a place at the board as well, allowing her daughter the role she'd held for Sorcha for so long. The woman fairly beamed with pride and joy.

"Tunwulf will not go away without a fight."

Caden swallowed an oath batted forth from the fray in his mind among anger, exasperation, and something he'd not felt in a long time. The urge to take this firebrand in his arms and show her what a real kiss was.

"The man cannot be reasoned with," Sorcha continued.

At least that much they agreed upon.

ChAPTER TWENTY-EiGhT

The night passed without further incident, but no one rested with the threat of imminent attack. Sorcha hadn't had time to meet Malachy, her uncle. The priest-turned-laird had taken it upon himself to gather his levy of local farmers and fishermen to fortify Trebold's dilapidated fort in case the Saxons forded the Lader downstream and tried to outflank the Glenarden troops by seizing the upper ground on its knoll behind the tavern. They were few in number and with little more than the tools of their trade for weapons, so Ronan had sent a small detachment of spearmen to reinforce them. They at least could warn of a rear attack and detain any ambitious Saxons until the warriors could organize a shieldwall around the tavern. Beyond that, no one ventured to plan, for it would be muscle against muscle, will to will.

The rest of the men had worked in the cover of darkness to dig a ditch the full length of the crossing, which they filled with brush and such pitch as the local fishermen kept for repairing their boats. A hastily assembled wicker and stave fence hid the fire pit from Saxon view. It was only natural for Sorcha to help her mother and the women and children of the men in the hillfort, who'd sought the shelter of the tavern. They kept the children in the kitchen and worked to keep the men's cups and bellies full. In between trips to and from the chaotic kitchen, which was attached in the back with a covered archway, they listened to the men make their plans.

It would be a long and drawn-out battle, with Tunwulf swooping in with his men, stinging like bees, and retreating until one of them had expended their weapons or their manpower. There was no hope of support from Arthur via the Angus at Strighlagh, involved in holding the Picts north of the Clyde, or Modred of Lothian, who was bound by politics and surrounded in Bernicia. Glenarden and Trebold stood alone.

"Our best hope is that Tunwulf will grow weary of losing men," Ronan observed. "As for us, we've made the best defenses we can, and thankfully we've plenty of food and water."

When Sorcha wasn't busy with the warriors or the refugees, she and her mother continued their reunion in snatches. She answered Myrna's questions, assuring her mother that she'd had a happy childhood with Wulfram and Aelwyn, that she'd been educated to read and write by her Cymri cousin, and that music was her love.

"That was your father's," Myrna said, pointing out a harp hanging on a peg over the stairwell. It was plain compared to Eavlyn's, engraved with simple spirals. "He made it himself and played it more to soothe his nerves than for entertainment. I know that neither he nor I could be prouder of you than if we'd raised you ourselves."

If there had been any bitterness left in Sorcha's heart, it was no longer there. Her birth parents had done all they could to find her. And her mother's God had watched over Sorcha when they could not. Even when Sorcha hadn't known Him. The fickle Wyrds had naught to do with her life, and God had everything to do with it. The wonder of it was more than she could grasp.

Her spirit shot upward with such joy, only to plummet when she realized that these men, these brave strangers, were about to fight and possibly die because of Tunwulf's ambition. Sorcha could not rest when the men finally retired to grab the last hours of darkness in sleep. Even Myrna collapsed on the bed next to Sorcha after praising God and thanking Him for bringing her daughter home. Her mother's words weren't bard-worthy, but Sorcha couldn't help the tears that trickled down her cheeks, nor withhold her own "Amen" to them.

Home. Sorcha eased out of the bed and walked to the window of the upstairs bedchamber. Tunwulf's fires had dimmed beyond the river fog that separated the enemy from her home. Soon this side would be a battlefield between two fierce armies, putting the lives of her family and the man she loved at risk.

Sorcha had known when she'd first laid eyes on Caden that her life would never be the same. And Myrna had confirmed that love was what had developed in Sorcha's heart for the man. "Why else would a woman put up with a man's clumsy and surly ways?" Myrna had teased when Sorcha confessed that she would readily die for Caden on the one hand and just as fast slap him senseless with the other. "Because we can see the heart that beats beneath his growling, the one that tells her she is everything to him. The heart that makes hers dance."

Sorcha wrapped herself in her arms. There had to be an answer besides warfare. There was no easy victory in store for either side. And there was no plunder worth taking at Trebold. Only the revenge of one crazed man. A shudder ran her through. She'd die first before submitting to Tunwulf.

Forcing back her panic, Sorcha focused on the still encampment beyond the water. The best Tunwulf's men could hope for were more weapons, armor, and some warrior rings.

But what if she made it worth the while of his men to go home? Warriors fought for wealth from plunder or their lord for their service. She knew what made their hearts beat in anticipation and in fear. She was a scop. A bard.

Her gaze traveled to the hook on the door where she'd hung her harp bag. There was a small fortune in jewels in there. Gold as well. And the Elford wolf ring with its ruby eyes. 'Twas all worth more than weapons and warrior rings hammered from the iron of a conquered enemy's spear blade.

The image of her father's harp hanging over the staircase came to her mind, and words began to flow in her heart. Her plight. The enemy's plight. The foolishness of it all.

Oh, Heavenly Father!

Caden stirred from the pallet he'd made of his cloak near the fire. His nostrils filled with the stench of stale mead, wood smoke, and—he opened his eyes—Egan O'Toole's mucked boots. Caden gathered Delg under him and turned over to face the other way. He always slept with his sword, even among comrades. Though Delg was a poor substitute for a certain soft, warm, redheaded thief. Thoughts of the silken brush of her hair beneath his chin made him smile.

Guilt wiped it away. He hadn't exactly been gallant or grateful over her mad rescue. But then, the greater distance he put between them the better. He didn't need the distraction, and she needed no encouragement to think of a future that would not be. They weren't like Brenna and Ronan. Brenna brought out the best in Ronan. Sorcha seemed to bring out the worst in him, mostly by scaring him witless with her impulsive nature and angering him. Jumping out of a boat, charging on a horse she couldn't ride …

"Come rise, ye men of valor, and hear a tale of hope.…"

The strong and beautiful voice brought Caden bolt upright and shook the men around him with invisible hands. Most just lifted their heads, as though not certain if they were dreaming or waking. With a wonderstruck oath, Egan beat Caden to his feet and led the way to the tavern door, which he threw open. It banged against the side of the building, causing the guards on duty, who stared off into the mist from which the voice emanated, to jump.

"'Tis a fairy," one said in awe.

"An angel," said another.

A woman sat on a horse in the middle of the river. Indeed, with the sun's light barely brimming on the horizon and casting a golden glow onto the lingering mist and the bronze robe swathed about her, she did look otherworldly. Especially when her cloak of shining hair caught its fire.

Caden's heart plunged as cold as the fast-running water under Elfwyn's belly as Egan corrected the men.

"I'm thinkin' it's Caden's bard."

"Lady Sorcha," Ronan echoed from behind. "Fetch two horses," he ordered one of his men calmly. "Be quick."

"I'll get her." Caden started away from the tavern, but Ronan caught him. "You take men to the left side of the ditch. I'll take the rest to the other. But hold there, lest we provoke yon spellbound Saxons into an attack."

Spellbound? This was exactly the kind of distraction he'd worried about. Caden buried his panic to assess the situation as a seasoned warrior should.

Saxons stood beyond the thinning mist, still and speechless. But then they weren't as given to the protocol of exchanging eloquent insults before battle as the Cymri. When the Cymri hurled insults, the Saxons simply raised their axes and charged.

But no weapons were raised. Aside from guards, the rest of Tunwulf's men stood as though caught in a dream from which they'd not yet awakened. The mist was a mixed blessing, for while Ronan and Caden's small force made its way unseen around and to the wings of the disguised fire ditch, Caden could not make Tunwulf's tall, arrogant figure out among the wild-haired, fur-clad enemy.

What did Sorcha hope to do? Sing them to sleep?

It was only as her words penetrated Caden's consciousness that he caught on. She told their story. How she and the Saxon renegades came to be here at this moment. She pointed out Tunwulf's treachery against his own father and Rhianon, who had stood loyally by him.

"Such is the fate of those who serve a mad lord such as he."

By Abba's wonders, a few of the men exchanged glances, although Caden couldn't tell if they laughed or took the words to heart. Sung as the song was, filled with soul sent on the wings of music, it was only a truly hard heart that could not be moved by Sorcha's plight. And what deeds she attributed to the Christian God who protected her. He cast a spell upon the guards, caused Caden's chains to fall away, and enabled her to overcome Tunwulf's untoward advances with a hard blow from her harp.

Snickers from the Saxon warband goaded Tunwulf into revealing himself. He stepped forward, swathed in a black cloak that billowed with his movement. No doubt the bones of some of his victims had been sewn to it. Caden had seen such used for intimidation.

"You lie, vixen."

But if Sorcha was shaken by the sight, she never flinched. *"If I lie, villain, then you were overcome by a mere woman with naught but a song and a harp, sir,"* she replied in song with a royal disdain. Like a queen, a fairy queen bathed in sunlight. *"Do you wish to tempt my God again? For I have just begun to tell of the wonders He has worked on our journey, including the one many have already heard about. He protected me from a wild boar's charge at the king's hunt with nothing more than a priest with a story staff that gloried this God."*

Seemingly uncertain, Tunwulf stepped back. Were she not in danger, Caden would have laughed at him. Instead, he watched the Saxons like a hawk. A few fetched weapons and donned armor, for Sorcha had clearly caught them before they had stirred. But most were enchanted by the ethereal vision who had touched hidden places where fear and awe dwelt.

"And, mark my words," she warned them, *"He watches your slightest move as I speak."*

Her threat gave those collecting themselves pause. But if Tunwulf took one more step, Caden was ready to lead a charge at them—afoot, if need be. Delg was already drawn and hidden in his shadow, lest the sun give away its polished, newly sharpened blade.

With flying fingers, Sorcha drummed up the storm in which they'd escaped in a leaking boat that had miraculously run aground on solid beach in the midst of the marsh. 'Twas the home of a golden angel who cared for them three days and then vanished into thin air. His upriver neighbors had never heard of the beautiful, gentle Owain, and only one other had seen him.

"Vanished." She plucked a high chord. *"As though he'd never existed at all."*

Caden almost believed the story himself, the way she spun it. He wanted to.

By the time Sorcha reached Elfwyn's magnificent change, the thin mare had pranced sidewise upriver against the current, almost to where Caden could easily reach Sorcha with the horse that he'd now mounted.

"And how, good men, could I allow the man I love to be cut down by those whose only quarrel with him was conjured by the vengeful heart of a villain?"

Love? Caden struck his chest as if to knock sense into his skipping heart. *Watch the Saxons, not her.*

"Poor nag that Elfwyn was," Sorcha sang, *"God made her into a fierce warhorse who attacked men with her hooves and snorted fire."* As if to prove herself, the mare heaved up on her haunches and snorted fierce as the thunder god's breath.

The Saxons stepped back as a group, Tunwulf included.

For a moment, Caden thought Sorcha and her harp would tumble into the unprotected water, but she somehow managed to hold on, her copper hair flying behind her like a war goddess. How could he not love her?

Caden's fingers tightened on Delg's hilt and pounded love out of his heart, repeating the word *Sais—Saxon—*over and over in his mind, until rage filled it. Rage would keep him alive.

"'Tis true," one of the Saxons averred. The one who'd escaped across the river. "I saw it with me own eyes!"

"Home at last, and now that home is to become a bloody battle-ground," Sorcha sang, her fingers playing a lament sweet enough to make a grown man cry. *"Men on both sides must die, perhaps even the man I love."* She struck the harp so hard that the second mention of *love* had no chance to survive Caden's start.

"And for what? This dog's revenge?" she challenged.

To Caden's horror, she turned Elfwyn and started toward Tunwulf, where the current swept wide downriver toward the Tweed.

"A noble Saxon warrior fights for plunder and land. I know your plight." The harp strings ached for them. *"You were driven from your homeland the same as my father Wulfram … by a rising sea you could not fight. But not to ride for a father-killing whelp whom you know will never receive his father's inheritance. If you do not fight for Hussa, he will not reward you,"* she shouted.

"She lies. She insults you," Tunwulf growled. He started for Sorcha again, but this time two of his men checked him with low words.

Alarm pricked mightily at the back of Caden's neck as they glanced toward the hillfort. So did Caden. As far as he could see, only the Cymri guard moved about, staring downhill at the river.

"But I will," Sorcha continued. *"And my reward will cost no bloodshed."*

What? Caden's jaw slackened in disbelief as Sorcha wrestled her precious leather sack from her saddle. She reached in and withdrew strings of amber that seemed to burst into blaze, once exposed to the rising sun.

"I have jewels and gold. All you have to do is leave this cur and fetch it for yourselves," she sang and upended the bag. Glittering jewels or rings, lashed to chunks of wood, cascaded in a fall of rich splendor into the water beside Elfwyn, where the current swept it in a rush downstream where the river widened. Wide-eyed Saxons raced toward their horses as Tunwulf screamed at them.

"Not now! Only two of you. Not now!"

But it was too late. Half the men were bent on chasing the floating treasure downriver. The other half wavered, hands on their weapons, waiting amidst the confusion for their furious leader to give them orders.

"Take her!" Tunwulf roared.

But Sorcha already raced for Trebold. Caden gigged his borrowed steed's side, leading his men across the ford and putting the snorting beast between Tunwulf and the retreating Elfwyn. He met Tunwulf's blade with a slash of his own. Metal crashed against metal as he bypassed the Saxon leader and turned his steed. He hated fighting on horseback. He could have finished Tunwulf by now.

Three Saxons raced at Caden, axes hefted. He seized his spear and thrust it, striking one through the throat. Another he knocked into the path of his companion with his horse, and slashed at both with Delg. He nicked flesh, though he doubted it was a killing blow.

As he bore down on Tunwulf again, he saw that Sorcha had crossed the ford and stood in her saddle behind the line his men formed. Ronan held the line at the other end, while warriors, torches ready, manned the firewall.

Midway across the water, Tunwulf hesitated chest deep in the rushing water. When Ronan's Cymri did not charge to meet him, he turned back toward an isolated Caden. "Don't let him cross," he shouted to his men.

Saxons swarmed like flies to his horse's flank. Caden considered riding Tunwulf down, but once he and the Saxon clashed, the water would hold them, and Saxons would close on him. Tempting as it was, much as he laughed at death in the past, four words would not allow it. Words that had etched themselves onto his heart in spite of his resistance.

The man I love.

CHAPTER TWENTY-NINE

Caden swerved the horse at the bank and cut a wide path with Delg, forcing his pursuers away. With a loud "Hee-yah," he made for a wing of the fire ditch where his men had formed a shieldwall. Saxons charged into the water, some afoot and others on horseback. But as they straggled out of the water on the other side and hurled themselves at the flimsy rampart of wicker and staves, the Cymri tossed their torches onto the pitch- and brush-filled ditch behind it. A fire shot up along the length of the pitch-dabbed fence, turning it into a wall of fire with sharpened teeth grinning through it. The burst of heat drove the attacking forces back into the water, where Glenarden's archers sent them a shower of arrows.

Smoke spread like a black monster of death that rose from Hades and dispersed to confuse the living. Saxons screamed and cursed, the fit dragging the wounded back to the waterside encampment. Caden's shieldwall opened, allowing him and his horse through. With the slam of wood to wood, it closed behind him, spear points bristling over it.

But the Saxons regrouped beyond the range of the archers and did not charge again. Not that Caden could blame them. Better than half their number was dead or wounded. No Cymri had fallen.

"Caden!" Sorcha ran from Elfwyn toward him, arms outstretched.

He slid off his panting steed. He wanted to strangle her, to shake her until she never thought to help him again. But more than that—

He caught her as she threw herself into his arms and kissed him.

And he kissed her back. With every emotion she'd ever conjured in him. Fear and desire, exasperation and protection, anger and love. All fierce—not one could he separate from the other. He shouldn't, but, Abba help him, there was no stopping this landslide of feelings he'd kept barreled up inside.

"Good thing the Saxons retreated," Ronan shouted dourly, exacting a roar of laughter from the warriors who'd enjoyed their first taste of victory.

Caden finally pulled away and trapped Sorcha's face between his hands. "If you ever decide to help me again *without letting me know*—"

"You wouldn't have allowed it," she replied with an unrepentant smile.

"No, I would not—"

"And I managed to cut the enemy number in half for you." A smug, unrepentant smile.

"I ... you—" As Caden floundered for reprimand, a shout in the distance drew his attention.

A single man raced down from the hillfort waving a ragged banner made of his cloak. "Saxons!" he shouted hoarsely. "At the fort ... they're upon us!"

"My men," Ronan commanded. "Shieldwall to the rear of the tavern."

"Egan," Caden shouted.

He didn't have to spell it out for the burly champion. "Done!" Half of Caden's men followed Egan's lead to the area just vacated by Ronan; the others remained, tightening their defenses.

"The rest of you keep the fires going," Caden shouted as he shoved Sorcha toward the house. "Get inside and stay there. Promise me, or the sight of you in harm's way will cost me my life."

Sorcha nodded. "We'll defend the house."

"Aye." Caden couldn't help but laugh, for her hand went to the hilt of a short sword hung in her belt beneath her robe. And he had no doubt that his firebrand would use it. She'd bested Wada once, but Wada had been armed with only a knife, not with deadly Sais axes. But then, Caden had no intention of letting a Saxon near the house. Alive, anyway.

Caden joined Egan's remaining men. Their force was now dangerously split into two groups, but thanks to Sorcha, the treasure chasers had halved the number of Saxons they fought, whittling them down to a manageable size. He took the position to the right of the shieldwall, the most vulnerable, for there was no shield to guard his sword arm. But it was also Caden's most deadly side.

Ronan had taken a position across the rear of the tavern rather than racing uphill to fight the Saxon attack there. His men would be spent by the time they raced to the rescue of the hillfort, and those in the hillfort would be dead by the time they reached them anyway. Together, the brothers could protect the tavern … for a while.

Caden's men engaged the enemy and held them at the river with such vigor and valor that if Sorcha lived, this battle would live on in song. But they needed more men. Noting that the Saxons had no band of archers like Glenarden, Sorcha asked for volunteers among the women to keep the fire pit burning, thus allowing a few more men to back up the river force. But she kept her word to Caden. She remained in the door of the tavern, while the womenfolk poured out into the yard carrying brooms, pokers, kitchen knives, and cleavers—anything that could be used for a weapon if need be—and began feeding the fire from the stock of wood and brush gathered the night before. So freed, the fire tenders reinforced their comrades.

And so it went, neither side seeming to gain ground, neither side losing it. The Saxons attacked, did their worst, and retreated from the weapons of Caden's warriors, although the show of blood was enough to turn Sorcha's stomach.

"Malachy is holding on the hill," Myrna marveled at Sorcha's side, startling her. "I don't know how, but Ronan's men have seen neither blade nor spear shaft."

Yet the fight seemed so futile. "God knows, I tried so hard to—"

Her mother put a finger to Sorcha's lips. "Never have I seen braver trust in God. But now it is He who must save us … before our men grow too weary to lift a blade."

"Or have none to lift," Sorcha added, speaking of the tossed spears and spent arrows. The arrows found more Saxon shields than men after that first attack.

"Or run out of fuel for the firewall." Myrna crossed herself, for the stores of brush and wood were nearly gone.

A loud ram's horn blasted through the air from the east road beyond the river. Adversaries who were clutched in a battle of push and pull with their shields fell away from each other, looking in the direction of the borderland between Trebold and Bernicia. Try as she might, Sorcha could not see through the smoke.

One of the women near the fire shrieked, "Saxons! An army of them!"

Ice formed in Sorcha's chest. "No." It couldn't be. Not more of them.

Half of Ronan's shield line abandoned its seemingly pointless position at the rear and raced to the river to reinforce Caden and his men. Sorcha shouted for the women to retreat into the house, but aside from a few, most stood their ground.

"If we die, 'twill be with our menfolk," a round, toothless matron with a shaggy mop of hair shouted in defiance as she brandished a cleaver.

"Mathair, see to the children," Sorcha said. She'd been seven the last time she'd seen such carnage, but she remembered. "The Saxons will sell the young as slaves."

She said no more, for Myrna knew all too well the fate of the old and worthless. Had she not been mistaken for dead the day Sorcha was taken, Myrna would have been taken as well. Not so now, when her red hair was threaded with white.

Sorcha drew her short sword and started into the yard to join the other women when Caden's words stopped her.

The sight of you in harm's way will cost me my life.

With a groan of frustration, she turned and rushed upstairs to the bedchamber overlooking the river. She would not put him in harm's way, but the moment he fell—

She clasped her hands to her heart. *Heavenly Father, don't let it happen.*

But if it did, Saxon blood would stain the metal of the short sword she'd taken from one of the sleeping men in the barn that morning when she fetched Elfwyn.

From the upstairs window level, the smoke was not as thick, enabling her to see the enemy dancing and singing in welcome to the army marching under the banner of the white dragon. Tunwulf—the blackguard in his cloak of bones still lived—threw open his arms in welcome as one of the mounted warriors spurred his horse ahead of the others.

Aethelfrith's princely fur-trimmed cloak flew scarlet behind him as he galloped, his polished sword raised and glittering in the morning sun toward his friend. But upon reaching him, the Dieran prince swung his sword downward and away, lopping off Tunwulf's head in the breadth of Sorcha's horror-stricken gasp. A fountain of scarlet sprung in its place, and Sorcha reeled away from the window at the brutal carnage.

"*Murderer!*" The Dieran prince's shout drew her back. Her stomach roiled as she watched Aethelfrith ride in full circle around the fallen leader's astonished men. "For the Lady Sorcha and the king!" he declared, blood-soaked blade raised to the sky.

Sorcha's head grew light, lighter than the gray smoke drifting skyward. This, Sorcha recalled, was why her cousin Eadric insisted a female bard on a battlefield was frowned upon.

For the Lady Sorcha and the king!

The princeling's declaration swirled in and around her brain. Or perhaps it was the relief that lifted her consciousness away. Relief that, somehow, God had exonerated her. Regardless, it was a sweet escape to a bloodless place.

CHAPTER THIRTY

Caden lowered his sword at the first sight of Modred's Lothian banner flying amidst those of Hussa's thanes. It *was* an army of Saxons, but not one intent on attacking Cymri land. Not with the king of that land riding at its fore. Abba be thanked, Father Martin's peaceweaving marriage of Eavlyn and Hering had evidently held. Somehow the truth had come out.

It wasn't until Aethelfrith had called off the Saxon renegades and Glenarden had stood down that a wary truce ensued. While the respective armies took care of the wounded and the dead and reestablished their camps on respective sides of the ford, Myrna summoned all the local help and resources at hand to set a board for the Saxon and Cymri leaders, Father Martin and his old friend Malachy among them. The tavern brimmed with Trebold's grateful people, farmer and fisherman only too eager to see to their rescuers' every need.

Only then did Caden learn how Sorcha and he had been redeemed at Hussa's court.

"'Twas the Lady Rhianon," Father Martin announced, his thin face naught but one big smile that nearly obliterated the signs of his age. Bless the priest, he'd ridden Forstan home to Caden despite his preference for walking and now hobbled about sore, the worse for it.

"But she was dead when we left," Sorcha objected, seeking Caden's hand under the table. "I knocked her away from me with my harp when she tried to kill me." Her voice trembled. "And she fell upon her knife."

Sorcha had been as pale as bleached linen when Caden and Father Martin had found her pulling herself up on the bed in the upstairs chamber. The plucky lassie who'd held off the Saxon hoard, armed with naught but a harp and a song, had swooned at the sight of Tunwulf's brutal death. Upon hearing the priest's message that Gemma and Ebyn were both safe and well and intended to join them as soon as Gemma sold their warehouse and its contents, she brightened, at least in demeanor, and insisted on a grand celebration.

Myrna agreed, although she wouldn't hear of her daughter working with the women. Her mother insisted that, as the new lady of Trebold, Sorcha act the hostess to their guests at the head of the honored table nearest the hearth. Although Caden preferred a seat near a door with his back to a wall, he succumbed to Sorcha's plea to join her.

"Aye," Father Martin replied. "Even Tunwulf raced off, thinking the woman had gone to the Other Side. But Rhianon had a formidable spirit. She refused to die. For three days, she fought with fever in the space between her and the Other World. I tended and prayed over her night and day in the hope that she would confess her sin and accept Christ."

"'Twould take the prayers of Jesus Himself to get the truth out of Rhianon," Caden said wryly.

Martin blessed him with a tolerant smile. "And on the third day, she came to her senses. She said that Tunwulf forced her to poison his father and tried to kill her."

"He promised to make her Lady of Elford," Sorcha amended softly. She recounted for the group how Tunwulf had betrayed Rhianon and how Sorcha had saved her. "And still she survived the knife?" Sorcha finished, incredulous.

"She has more lives than a cat, Father," Caden sneered, "but that doesn't make her truthful." Nor would the Holy Spirit enter where it was not invited. At least that was Caden's rudimentary understanding of such things.

"Not so, I'm afraid. This life was her last," Martin assured Caden.

To Caden's astonishment, Martin's announcement offered little comfort. Was this pity he felt?

"Don't look so crushed, Martin," King Modred spoke up, distracting Caden from his wonder. He picked a piece of meat from his teeth, clearly more concerned with that than Rhianon's soul. But then, of late, Modred found the worship of pagan gods more tolerable than the doctrine that Rome tried to force on its Celtic brethren. The divide would erupt like a festering boil sooner or later, pitting nephew against Arthur.

Not that Modred needed another reason to dislike his uncle. Arthur had killed his rebellious father, Cennalath.

"Lady Sorcha was exonerated, and the renegade raids in Lothian have been stopped," Modred continued, pleased with his efforts. "Although better that young Aethelfrith explain to Hussa why the villain wasn't brought back alive to face Saxon justice."

Even Abba had used toads for His purpose. Look at the Exodus.

"A man who poisons his father deserves no hearing," Aethelfrith retorted. "My uncle will feel the same as I." He gave Modred a haughty smile that sent a chill down Caden's spine. He'd bet his sword arm that Aethelfrith had other motives for silencing Tunwulf so quickly.

Had it not been attached, Caden's jaw would have hit the ground at the sight of Tunwulf's headless body slumped on the ground while the princeling pranced about on his steed. And not only Caden's jaw, but dozens of others.

Princess Eavlyn's prediction came back to Caden. *I have mapped out the stars, seeking signs for both him and for Aethelfrith as my husband's enemies.*

The stars had favored Aethelfrith, but not Tunwulf.

That doesn't mean his plans will go awry with certainty, she'd said of Tunwulf. *Only that nature is not with him.*

To be sure, Aethelfrith's nature certainly wasn't with him.

God alone is certain.

Sorcha's God. *His* God. Abba had delivered them. When she'd sung, Caden had counted her version embellished, at least the part about the chains falling away and Elfwyn's transformation into something the mare had been carefully trained to do. But the rest—

A banging on the table drew attention to where Malachy struggled stiffly to his feet. "Father Martin and I … and, I hear, my niece—," he added, sending Sorcha a beaming look—"have already praised God for His protection and hand in delivering truth and justice. But I, for one, would like to thank Glenarden for sending such fine warriors to our aid." The old priest, who had, according to hearsay, wielded a sword against the Saxons as if new life had been breathed into him, lifted his cup with a trembling hand that needed the reinforcement of its mate.

Ronan gave him an acknowledging nod. "As I told my brother, my wife gave us little choice. Fight here or fight at Glenarden."

The men about them laughed. Anyone who knew Brenna, Caden among them, knew her gentle, forgiving nature. Ronan risked more danger from a newborn lamb.

"And I especially," Malachy continued, "would like to thank the warrior Owain." The priest scanned the room, eyes squinting. "I can't see him, but he must be here among your commanders."

Egan scowled. "I've leaders by the name of Shea, Ferris, Fergal, and Madoc, but no Owain. 'Twas Shea who defended the fort with you, not Owain."

Awkward from the attention, Shea stood up among his comrades.

"But there must be an Owain! A head taller than me, he was, and fair as sunshine. I say none fought the renegades any harder."

Sorcha gasped beside Caden.

"I saw 'im," Shea announced. "He fought next to Father Malachy, but I didn't recognize him. And there was no time to question where he came from. As long as he was drivin' back the Sais, there was na need."

"My angel," Sorcha said under her breath. "I told you he was an angel. Maybe even Eavlyn's."

"Angel, you say?" For all his years, Malachy still had the ears of a fox. "What's this about an angel?"

"I sang about an angel, the fisherman who helped us for the three days I was ill and then vanished," she reminded the men. She held up her wrist, where barely a scar remained of her injury.

"And I've seen lesser wounds take a strong warrior to the Other Side," Caden heard himself saying.

As if he believed her. Or worse, believed Owain just might be what she said. He shook himself and carefully thought back. But no matter how he tried, Caden could not explain Owain the vanishing fisherman or the warrior as anything but God-sent. Too much had blessed them along their flight and during the fight to allow for anything but God's intervention.

Caden rose to his feet. "I never believed in such things as angels. But I'm here to say that if any man can point to any other explanation, I'd like to hear it."

A collective murmur of awe and speculation raised the noise level in the tavern to the overhead beams until Malachy banged his cup on the table again to restore order. Modred's expression was unfathomable, while Martin's was aglow with joy. The toad Aethelfrith smirked at the notion but held his peace rather than insult his hosts.

"And not to be outdone by man or angel," Malachy continued, "I want to thank Caden for bringing my niece home to Trebold." The old man turned a twinkling gaze at Caden. "And I'd like to think he'll stay."

Caden groaned in silence. Why could he not celebrate this one victory and slip away?

"He will if I have any say in the matter," Sorcha declared boldly at his side. "I've need of a husband, and Trebold has need of a lord, sir," she told Caden. "Maithar and I have already discussed it."

Caden stiffened amidst the huzzahs echoing throughout the room. He tried to be kind. "I never said I'd be lingering about after I delivered you, lassie. Not once. My job here is done."

"Is that so?" Sorcha jumped to her feet and away as though he'd slapped her. "And why is that, when you cannot deny that you have feelings for me?" When Caden didn't answer, her hands flew to her hips. Once again she was the fiery queen ready to do battle. "Well? Will you tell me to my face that you do not love me, Caden of Lothian?"

The rush of triumph and relief from the battle that had bolstered a body denied a night's sleep and wearied by battle drained from Caden, crushed by the weight of too many regrets to count.

"Will you?" Sorcha demanded.

Abba help him, despite her show of bravado, her eyes had turned to pools far more capable of wounding him than the sharp tongue she wielded.

"You deserve more than a rough mercenary who lives from battle to battle," he finally replied.

"I deserve the hero who saved Arthur's"—her queenly disdain faltered—"and my life. A man who isn't afraid to die for what is right and good."

"A proven prince of Glenarden," Ronan observed, peering intensely at Caden through the brackets of dark auburn hair that had fallen forward on his face. Caden's wits abandoned him as his brother stood taller than tall and lifted his cup. "To Caden of *Glenarden*," he enunciated in a manner that dared any man to contradict him.

A log fell upon the embers on the hearth, breaking the silence as wryness twisted Ronan's lips. "Let us pray he comes to his senses and says yes before this lady comes to hers."

Huzzahs and guffaws of humor erupted all around them. Egan clapped Caden hard on the back, but Caden hardly felt it. Grace overcame him, numbing him to everything except awareness of his Father and the two through whom grace was offered. The beautiful woman who would have him in spite of his past—and the brother who strode around to the end of the table where he sat, his arms extended. Caden slid from the bench to his knees, emotion ravaging him, tearing at the guilt he'd held to so tightly, even though Abba had forgiven him.

But Caden never expected forgiveness from Ronan, whom he'd wronged so vilely. He bent to kiss his brother's muddied boots, but Ronan caught him and raised him by the shoulders.

"To whom much has been given, much is expected," he said, his fervor glistening in his cinnamon gaze. "This is the least I can do for the God who has blessed me so. I only ask that you pass the grace God gives you along to others."

They were night and day in coloring and temperament, yet as Ronan embraced Caden, they became brothers, not just by blood but in soul. How long they held each other, how many things were spoken spirit to spirit, Caden had no idea. All he knew was that something kindled within, making him as light as the sun's kiss on a spring morning. Something he'd glimpsed that day on the beach but hadn't fully grasped. Something that had kept slipping through his fingers as he tried to shift his focus from his misery to reach out to others. Something called hope.

Suddenly Egan O'Toole wrapped both Caden and Ronan in a bear of an embrace and roared, "Now it's proud I am to see the two of you rascals put aside your differences and all, but I'm thinkin' Caden's time best be spent huggin' this pretty little lady before I steal her away and show her how a real man would respond to her most temptin' proposal."

Sorcha tossed that copper mane of hers over her shoulder, her hand resting on the hilt of the dining dagger at her belt and grinned. "Are you man or mouse, Caden of Glenarden?"

"For sure, you've met your match," Ronan said under his breath.

"Maybe more," Egan chimed in with a clap on Caden's back.

A man, Caden answered in silence as he closed the distance between him and the woman he loved. *A humble, thankful man.* Abba be thanked that this young, incredible, impulsive, kindhearted, lovely, and so-very-talented creature would even look at this grizzled and scarred soldier, much less that she would want to spend the rest of her life with him.

"Princess Eavlyn said the stars on All Saints Day favor a good marriage," Father Martin spoke up.

"Do they now, Father?" Caden's gaze locked with that sparkling green one. "Seems you'll find your answer to that question soon enough then, woman."

The room was in an uproar as Caden took Sorcha in his arms and kissed her, long and soundly. The floor trembled from stomping of feet and tables rattled with the ear-shattering beat of fists and cups on the boards.

And if that kiss took Caden's last breath on This Side, it was worth it. But he breathed another against her ear, his whisper soft. "Abba be thanked for giving me a reason to live." And another as he kissed her forehead. "A reason to hope."

Abba, may I waste not so much as one breath more that is not spent for this woman.

Caden found Sorcha's mouth again with his. "And a reason to love."

epilogue

The dam of life held through the Long Dark but burst forth with the coming of spring, flooding the fields and forests with vibrant shades of green and the bright bursts of blossoms. Hearths that were cleaned and allowed to grow cold received new flame, some from the pagan Beltane fires dedicated to the old gods and others from like fires consecrated in the name of the Christian God, whose Son was resurrected.

Trebold brimmed with life as well. On the hillock, new timber and stone sprang from the old. It fairly crawled with men from Glenarden and Trebold. The Glenarden party had arrived for the Paschal celebration a week earlier and to celebrate the late Leaf Fall wedding that most had not been able to attend. They'd stayed on to help Caden with the new hall.

Thanks to Gemma, who'd arrived just before winter fully set in with Ebyn and a handsome sum of gold from the sale of Sorcha's warehouse and business, they were able to start the renovation of Trebold Law.

Sorcha adjusted the wolfskin blanket beneath six-month-old Joanna and sat her niece up so that the babe could see Ebyn, Gemma, and Glenarden's heir, Conall, playing with a wooden ball that Caden had carved and painted for him. She and Caden had adopted Ebyn as their own, but how she longed to have more children, a baby like Joanna.

"Let us build a place to put them first," Caden had consoled her when her courses had not cooperated. "God will know when the time is right."

Lady Brenna and Lady Myrna came out of the tavern, engaged in what had been since Brenna's arrival an off-and-on-again conversation on the use of herbs and spices in cooking and healing. Running a tavern required knowledge of both, and Sorcha's mother thought the healer of Glenarden had no equal.

"Look, our men approach," Brenna said as Sorcha dabbed a bit of drool from Joanna's rosebud lips.

"Well, we've enough food to fill their bellies," Myrna observed proudly. Her servants had set up benches and boards piled high with fresh breads, boiled roots glazed with fresh butter and herbs, and roasted meats and fowl in the tavern yard. "Even the big one," she said, nodding to Egan.

Sorcha drew herself away from her adoration of the baby girl to see the man of her heart ambling down the hill with his brothers and Egan O'Toole. Caden and Ronan shoved their younger brother, Alyn, from one to the other, their boisterous laughter preceding them.

"Poor Alyn," she said halfheartedly. "They tease him unmercifully." Of course Alyn gave as good as he got. And most times he gave it first.

"I don't think I've ever seen the men so happy." Brenna sighed, her face radiating the same emotion that welled in Sorcha. Love.

Sometimes Sorcha caught herself just staring in wonder at Caden while he slept, thanking God for sending him when she needed him most. God's timing was impeccable, she reminded herself as she nuzzled the angel-soft wisps of Joanna's hair.

Brenna put her hands on her hips, her head cocked in defiance. "Leave the laddie be, you two," she ordered as though her tall but slender frame, clad in shirt, tunic, and trousers, were big as Egan's.

She and Glenarden's champion had gone hunting, accounting for some of the smaller game on Trebold's tables. 'Twas that talent that impressed Sorcha as much as Brenna's healing skills, although it was Brenna's loving nature that instantly won Sorcha over. Never could she have chosen a better sister. But for God's grace, Rhianon might be her relative now.

"He's too full of mischief to be a priest," Caden complained. He landed another cuff on Alyn's head. "Someone has to beat it out of him."

"I've more brain than mischief, which is more than you can say," Alyn shot back. He tried combing his tousled dark hair with his fingers to no avail.

"I'm thinkin' he'd make a fine husband for me daughter."

Alyn gave Egan an appalled look. "'Twould be like marrying my *sister!*"

Egan winked. "But she's not your sister."

Alyn rolled his eyes heavenward. "Those fancy warriors at Gwenhyfar's court turn Kella's head, not a dull priest. We are like night and day. We never did get along."

Something about her younger brother-by-law's words made Sorcha suspect that Alyn protested too much.

But at that moment, little Conall raced up to Sorcha and snatched the wolf pelt out from under his sister so fast, Sorcha nearly lost her grip on the baby girl. "Mine!"

"Conall O'Byrne!" Brenna scolded.

"My goodness, he's strong," Sorcha gasped.

Ronan scooped his son up in his arms. "I thought you said you were a big boy now and that only babies needed blankets."

Conall buried his face against Ronan's shirt. "Mine."

"Someone's coming," one of the men trailing down the hill shouted. He pointed toward the east road leading to the river crossing. "Saxons!"

Sorcha's blood ran cold. But they should be preparing and planting their fields, repairing their homes … the same as Trebold's people.

"Get the women and children inside," Caden shouted over his shoulder as he ran inside. "Ronan—" He tossed a horn hanging by the tavern door to his brother.

"I'll summon the men," Ronan replied.

The men working on the fortress did so with some weapon close by. It was only prudent in a time where the enemy might be a foreigner or one's neighbor.

Sorcha handed off Joanna, who screamed at her father's loud horn blast, to Brenna and raced after Caden for the upstairs view of the river road from the bedchamber window.

"They've women and children with them," Caden announced as she joined him.

Behind the front line was a cart lined with fur in which some ladies traveled. Hardly threatening. There was even a female riding in the lead with the men traveling under a white banner with a stag painted on it.

Sorcha leaned against her husband's strong arm, excited. "It's Princess Eavlyn!" They'd exchanged missives, but she'd not seen Eavlyn since the escape.

Caden opened the window and shouted to Ronan below. "The warriors' shields are upside down! They come in peace."

There was still chaos, but by the time Prince Hering and Princess Eavlyn's company forded the river, it was tempered with wariness, not panic. Eavlyn, who was huge with child, rested on a bench in the shade with some of the women, while Prince Herring spoke to the men gathered round him.

Hussa was dead. Hering had been with Eavlyn in Burlwick when he received the news. But before the prince could hie to Din Guardi, word came that Aethelfrith had summoned a Dieran army and intimidated Hussa's thanes to elect him as the new bretwalda.

"I'd wager my sword arm that Tunwulf knew of Aethelfrith's plan," Caden told the angry prince.

"Nay, my cousin only slays in the name of justice." Hering's acrimony belied the meat of his words. "And the gods." He swept his arm about to encompass his followers. "These men and women have accepted the Christian God."

So Eavlyn's mission to bring Christianity to Bernicia had not been a total failure. Sorcha looked about. There had to be at least twenty families.

"Did Aethelfrith have anything to do with Hussa's death?" Caden asked.

"Father had been ill this winter," Hering replied. "Although I would not put anything past Aethelfrith. Including sending troops to dispose of me, my wife, and family. Which is why we are here, along with others who will not fight for Aethelfrith."

"These men are loyal to us and to Christ. They *will* fight Aethelfrith," Eavlyn spoke up. "But their women and children need a place to stay." She eased to her feet. "I thought of the abandoned homes here at Trebold ... if you would have them."

"Saxons is Saxons," someone from the crowd gathered round them growled. The translator who had been converting their conversation into Saxon grew silent.

Myrna stepped off the stoop of the tavern and surveyed those gathered with a sharp eye. "And people in need are people in need," she reminded them.

The translator started again.

"*Inasmuch as ye did it not to one of the least of these, ye did it not to me....*" Myrna quoted from her one book of Scripture, a worn copy of Matthew that she paid dearly for from the son of a deceased priest. Her mother used that quote often in administering Trebold's affairs.

Sorcha had used her gift to memorize the entire book that winter. "I agree with my mother. We cannot change all of Alba that one man might live in peace beside another, but we can change Trebold."

"And I cannot change all men's hearts, only my own," Caden agreed. "I serve a God of second chances. He gave me a second chance with good men like you and with Sorcha ... with my family."

Some of the onlookers looked away, struck by guilt.

"We need families to work our fields, to help us prosper. To defend our homes. But I will not offer homes and land to these families without the blessing of the majority of Trebold's people."

The translator repeated Caden's words.

"Those who will welcome fellow brothers and sisters in Christ, I ask you to stand with me." Caden walked a distance away and waited.

Myrna and Sorcha joined him. Then Gemma. For a while, it seemed as though all the crowd would do was murmur and argue among themselves. The first to cross to where Caden and Sorcha stood were two wives, herding their children like mother hens. Their men followed. Then more men. More women. Not all came, but more than half the number. And when that became clear, the others moved over as well.

"'Tis done then." Caden beamed. "What say we welcome our new neighbors?" He took the lead, walking up to the biggest of the lot, a great hulk of a man with long straw-colored hair, and offered his hand with a hearty "Welcome, friend," in Saxon.

The two peoples merged, some of Trebold's Britons and Scots mangling their Saxon as badly as the newcomers mangled their Cumbric. But Christian charity overcame the language barrier.

Gemma caught Sorcha's arm as she moved forward to join them. "You have married a good man, sweetling."

Sorcha sought out Caden's blond mane above the heads of most of the others. Or she tried to. It was hard to see through the mist glazing her eyes. "Aye," she whispered softly.

But she held Caden in her heart's eye and always would from This Side to the Other.

God be thanked.

... a little more ...

When a delightful concert comes to an end,

the orchestra might offer an encore.

When a fine meal comes to an end,

it's always nice to savor a bit of dessert.

When a great story comes to an end,

we think you may want to linger.

And so we offer ...

AfterWords—just a little something more after you

have finished a David C Cook novel.

We invite you to stay awhile in the story.

Thanks for reading!

Turn the page for ...

GLOSSARY

Alba—Scotland

Albion—the Isle of Britain

Alcut/Alclyd—Dumbarton on Firth of Clyde

anmchara—soul mate

arthur—title passed down from Stone Age Britain meaning "the bear," or "protector," connected with the constellation of the Big Dipper; equivalent of Dux Bellorum and Pendragon; the given name of Arthur, prince of Dalraida

a stór—darling

behoved—beholdened

braccae—Latin for woolen drawstring trousers or pants, either knee- or ankle-length

bretwalda—leader/king of Saxon warlords or thanes

cariad—dearest

Carmelide—Carlisle

Cennalath—*ken'-nah-lot;* Pictish king of the Orkneys killed by Arthur for treachery

Cumbric—language of western Celtic peoples of Britain, close to today's Welsh

Cymri—brotherhood of Britons and Welsh, united by the common foe of Saxons

druid—an educated professional—doctors, judges, poets, teachers, and protoscientists, as well as priests. *Druid* meant "teacher, rabbi, magi, or master," not the dark, hooded stereotype assumed by many today. Those who were earnest sought light, truth, and the way. Others abused their knowledge, which was power.

Dux Bellorum—Latin for duke of war, high king, Pendragon, or *arthur*

earthways—to death/burial

Eboracum—York

fell—rocky hill

foolrede—foolishness

gleemen—entertainers for the common people akin to circus performers, as well as singers and dancers

Gwenhyfar—*Guinevere;* considered by some scholars to have been a title like *arthur* and *merlin,* as well as a given name. Some scholars believe the Pictish Gwenhyfar was called Anora.

haegtesse—witch

haws—medieval term for a house in a town/burrough that is part of a larger country estate; a house on a small lot in a burrough

hillfort—an enclosed fortress/village on a hill, usually with earthenwork and/or wood stockade about its perimeter

Joseph, the—the high priest of the Grail Palace on the Sacred Isle

Leafbud—spring

Leaf Fall—fall

Long Dark—winter

mathair—mother

merlin—title for the adviser to the king, often a prophet or seer; sometimes druidic Christian as in Merlin Emrys, or not, as Merlin Sylvester

Merlin Emrys (Ambrosius)—the prophet/seer/Celtic Christian priest descended from the Pendragon Ambrosius Aurelius; thought to be Arthur's merlin; suggested to be buried on Bardsley Island

mind—remember or recall

mo chroi—my heart

Pendragon—Cymri (Welsh-Briton) for "head dragon" or high king, dragon being a symbol of knowledge/power; see *arthur, Dux Bellorum*

rath—walled keep and/or village

scop—Saxon bard or entertainer

Strighlagh—*strī´-lăk;* Stirling

Sun Season—summer

thane—a high-ranking chief, noble, or warlord of the Saxon bretwalda/king; the king's sword-friend (comrade in arms) and hearth friend, who usually led his own warband and received his own lands in reward

toll—interest on a loan

tuath—tŭth; kingdom; clan land

wergild—money paid for injustice, or a blood price, akin to the Celtic *eric*

widdershins—counterclockwise

witan—akin to the Celtic *druid:* a Saxon adviser, doctor, judge, historian, genealogist, and magician/wizard/priest or any other educated professional of that era

ARThURiAN ChARACTERS

Most scholars agree that Arthur, Guinevere, and Merlin were titles
shared by various personas throughout the late fifth and sixth centuries. The ones in this book are the late sixth-century characters.
Because of inconsistent dating, multiple persons sharing the same
titles and/or names, and place names as well as texts recorded in at
least six languages, I again quote Nennius: "I've made a heap of all I
could find."

* historically documented individuals

*Arthur—Prince of Dalraida, Dux Bellorum (Latin "Duke of War")
or Pendragon (Welsh)/High King (Scot) of Britain, although he
held no land of his own. He is a king of landed kings, their battle
leader. A Pendragon at this time can have no kingdom of his own to
avoid conflict of interest. Hence, Gwenhyfar is rightful queen of her
lands, Prince Arthur's through marriage. Arthur is the historic son
of Aedan of Dalraida/Scotland, descended from royal Irish of the
Davidic bloodline preserved by the marriage of Zedekiah's daughter
Tamar to the Milesian king of Ireland Eoghan in 587 BC. Ironically
the Milesians are descended from the bloodline of Zarah, the "Red
Hand" twin of Pharez (David and Jesus' ancestor) in the book of
Genesis. Thus the breach of Judah prophesied in Isaiah was mended
by this marriage of very distant cousins, and the line of David continued to rule through the royal Irish after Jerusalem fell.

*Aedan of Dalraida—Arthur's father, Aedan, was Pendragon
of Britain for a short time and prince of Manau Gododdin by his

mother's Pictish blood (just as Arthur was prince of Dalraida because of his marriage to Gwenhyfar). When Aedan's father, the king of Dalraida, died, Aedan became king of the more powerful kingdom, and he abandoned Manau Gododdin. For that abandonment, he is oft referred to as Uther Pendragon, *uther* meaning "the terrible." He sent his son Arthur to take his place as Pendragon and Manau's protector.

Angus—the Lance of Lothian. Although this Dalraida Arthur had no Lancelot as his predecessor did, Angus is the appointed lesser king of Stirlingshire/Strighlagh and protector of his Pictish queen Gwenhyfar and her land. As with his ancestral namesake Lancelot, Angus's land of Berwick in Lothian now belongs to Cennalot, who is ultimately defeated by Arthur. (See *Cennalot* and *Brude.*) Angus is Arthur's head of artillery. It is thought he was raised at the Grail Castle and was about ten or so years younger than his lady Gwenhyfar.

Scholar/researcher Norma Lorre Goodrich suggests he may have been a fraternal twin to Modred or Metcault. That would explain Lance not knowing who he really was until he came of age, as women who bore twins were usually executed. The second child was thought to be spawn of the Devil. Naturally Morgause would have hidden the twins' birth by casting one out, only to have him rescued by her sister, the Lady of the Lake, or Vivianne del Acqs. This scenario happened as well in the lives of many of the saints, such as St. Kentigern. Their mothers were condemned to death for consorting with the Devil and begetting a second child. Yet miraculously, these women lived and the cast-off child became a saint.

*****Brude/Bridei**—see *Cennalot/Cennalath/Lot of Lothian.*

*****Cennalot/Cennalath/Lot of Lothian**—Arthur's uncle by marriage to Morgause. This king of eastern Pictland and the Orkneys was all that stood between Brude reigning over the whole of Pictland. Was it coincidence that Arthur, whose younger brother, Gairtnat, married Brude's daughter and became king of the Picts at Brude's death, decided to take out this Cennalot while Brude looked the other way? Add that to the fact that Cennalot was rubbing elbows with the Saxons and looking greedily at Manau Gododdin, and it was just a matter of time before either Brude or Arthur got rid of him.

*Dupric, bishop of Llandalf—a historical bishop who *may* also be Merlin Emrys per Norma Goodrich.

Gwenhyfar/Guinevere—High Queen of Britain. This particular Gwen's Pictish name is Anora. She is descended from the apostolic line and is a high priestess in the Celtic Church. She is buried in Fife. Her marriage brought under Arthur the lands of Stirlingshire, or Strighlagh. Her offspring are its heirs, as the Pictish rule is inherited from the mother's side. There were two abductions of the Gwenhyfars. In one she was rescued. In the other she *slept*, meaning she died (allegedly from snakebite), precipitating the fairy tale of *Sleeping Beauty*. In both Gwenhyfar's abduction and that of Sleeping Beauty, thorns surrounded the castle, thorns being as common a defense in those days as moats were. Also note the similarities of names, even if the definitions are different—Anora (grace), Aurora (dawn).

*Hering—son of Hussa, prince of Northumbria. Hering did not succeed his father but fled to Aedan's protection in Dalraidan Scotland after his cousin Aethelfrith of Bernicia won the throne and exiled him. Hering later led the Scots against his cousin Aethelfrith.

*Hussa—the king or bretwalda of the Northumbrian Saxons, succeeded by his nephew Aethelfrith instead of his son Hering.

*Merlin Emrys of Powys—a Christian druidic-educated bishop of the Celtic Church, protoscientist, adviser to the king, prophet after the Old Testament prophets, and possibly a Grail King or Joseph. Emrys is of the Irish Davidic and Romano-British bloodlines as son of Ambrosius Aurelius and uncle to Aedan, Arthur's father. Merlin Emrys retired as adviser during Arthur's later reign, perhaps to pursue his beloved science or perhaps as the Grail King. In either case, he would not have condoned Arthur's leaning toward the Roman Church's agenda. Later the Roman Church and Irish Celtic Church priests would convert the Saxons to Christianity, but the British Celtic Church suffered too much at pagan hands to offer the Good News to their pagan invaders. (See *Dupric* and *Ninian*.)

Modred—king of the Orkneys and Lothian, also a high priest or abbot in the Celtic Church; Arthur's nephew and son of late Cennalath and Morgause

*Morcant—king of Bryneich, now mostly occupied on the coast by the Saxons and called Northumbria. The capital was Trapain Law.

Ninian—Merlin's protégé, priestess in the Celtic Church

*Vivianne Del Acqs—sister to Ygerna, Arthur's mother, and Morgause of Lothian. She is known as the Lady of the Lake. Vivianne is a high priestess and tutor at the Grail Castle. It's thought that she raised both Gwenhyfar and Angus/Lance of Lothian, all direct descendants of the Arimathean priestly lines.

*Ygerna—Arthur's mother and a direct descendant of Joseph of Arimathea, was matched as a widow of a British duke and High Queen of the Celtic Church to Aedan of Dalraida by Merlin Emrys to produce an heir with both royal and priestly bloodlines. It is thought her castle was at Caerlaverock.

The Grail Palace

Norma Lorre Goodrich suggests that the Grail Palace was on the Isle of St. Patrick, and recent archaeology has exposed sixth-century ruins of a church/palace there. But what was it, or the Grail itself, exactly? Goodrich uses the vast works of other scholars, adding her expertise in the linguistics field to extract information from Arthurian texts in several languages. Weeding out as much fancy as possible, the Grail Palace was the church or place where the holy treasures of Christianity were kept (not to be confused with the treasures of Solomon's Temple, which Jeremiah and Zedekiah's daughter Tamar allegedly took to Ireland in 587 BC, or the Templars found during the Crusades). The Grail treasures consist of items relating to Jesus: a gold chalice and a silver platter (or silver knives) from the Last Supper, the spear that pierced Christ's side, the sword (or broken sword) that beheaded John the Baptist, gold candelabra with at least ten candles each, and a secret book, or gospel, attributed directly to either Jesus, John the Beloved, Solomon, John the Baptist, or John of the Apocalypse.

Or was this book the genealogies of the bloodlines, whose copies were supposedly destroyed by the Roman Church?

If the house of the Last Supper was that of the wealthy Joseph of Arimathea, is it possible that Jesus used these rich items and that Joseph brought them to Britain in the first century as tradition holds? The high priest of the Grail Castle tradition was called the Joseph. Of all the knights who vied for the Grail or the high priest position as teacher and protector of the bloodlines and treasures, only Percival and Galahad succeeded. Did they take the place of Merlin Emrys, when he passed on?

The purpose of the Grail Palace, beyond holding the treasures, was one of protecting and perpetuating the apostolic and royal bloodlines … hence the first-century Christianity brought to Britain by Christ's family and followers. It was believed that an heir of both lines stood a chance of becoming another messiah-like figure. Such breeding of bloodlines was intended to keep the British church free of Roman corruption and close to its Hebrew origins. Nennius, who was pro-Roman to the core, accused the Celtic Church of *clinging to the shadows of the Jews*—the first-century Jews of Jesus' family and friends.

But by the time the last Arthur fell, the hope of keeping the line of priests and Davidic kings, as had been done in Israel prior to Zedekiah's fall, was lost. With the triumph of the Roman Church authority, political appointment from Rome trumped the inheritance of the priestly and kingly rights divinely appointed in the Old Testament. Celibacy became the order of the day to keep the power and money in Rome.

Goodrich suggests that there were three Grail brotherhoods: Christ and the Twelve Disciples, Joseph of Arimathea and his twelve companions, and Arthur and the Twelve Knights of the Round Table. After Arthur's death, the order of the Grail with its decidedly Jewish roots gave way to Columba at Iona and the Roman Church. The Grail treasure—which had been brought from the Holy Land by Joseph of Arimathea, first to Glastonbury and later, after Saxons came too close for comfort, to the Isle of Patrick off of Man—had to be moved again. Percival and Galahad returned it to the Holy Land.

And it is there, centuries later, that the Knights Templar allegedly entered into the mystery, perhaps with privileged information kept and passed down among the sacred few remnants of the bloodlines that shaped early Christian Scotland, England, and Ireland.

Etienne Gilson said that the Grail veneration started in Jerusalem with Arimathea and Jesus' family and friends and that it stood for grace. God's grace. Christ's grace by sacrifice.

Or is it that only those truly baptized by Pentecostal fire are fit to care for the Grail treasures, just as only the high priest of Aaron was allowed into the Holy of Holies in ancient Israel? And is finding the Grail a metaphor for the Holy Spirit embodied in the apostles, or entering into the presence of God? Lancelot only dreamed of it, while Percival and Galahad actually achieved it as evidenced by the fires on their tunics.

The truth has been veiled by time, muddied or intentionally destroyed by later anti-Semitic factions in the church, and turned into a fantasy by later medieval writers who vilified most of the women, romanticized the men, and changed the now-lost original accounts to suit the tastes of their benefactors. Yet still this quest haunts the imagination and the soul—to be like, and hence in the presence of, Christ.

bibliography

For Readers Who Want More:

There are *over* seventy-five books from which I've garnered information and inspiration for this novel. However, I am listing those of the most influence for the reader who wants to delve into the history and tradition behind this work of fiction.

David F. Carroll makes a case for the historically documented Prince Arthur of Dalraida as *the* Arthur. This documentation is why I chose Arthur's story as the background for this series, while incorporating many of Norma Lorre Goodrich's observations as well. Her scholarly analysis of Arthuriana suggests that there is more than one Arthur, Guinevere, and Merlin. This, and the fact that there was no standard for dating, explains Arthur and company having to have lived for nearly a hundred years, as well as the many dating discrepancies in historical manuscripts. She, among others listed, uses geographical description and her knowledge of linguistics to place Arthur mostly in the lowlands of today's Scotland. Shortly after she suggested the location of Arthur's Grail Palace on an island near Man, the ruins of a Dark Age Christian church were discovered there.

Isabel Elder's *Celt, Druid and Culdee* provides wonderful insight into the origins of the early church in Britain and how the similarities of these three groups made them ready to make Christ their Druid or teacher/master. A must-read to understand the New Age philosophy of today. Andrew Gray's *The Origin and Early History of Christianity in Britain—From Its Dawn to the Death of Augustine* is fascinating and impacts *Thief* as it lends some credence to some of Goodrich's observations on Arthur and the church.

The oral traditions about Joseph of Arimathea and Avalon/ Glastonbury are underscored by ancient place names and Roman, British, Irish, and church histories in books by Gray, Joyce, McNaught, and Taylor. They also provide a compelling case for the British church's establishment in the first century by Jesus' family and apostles. Books regarding the Davidic bloodlines preserved through Irish nobility that married into the major royal houses of western Europe, Britain in particular, include those of Allen, Capt, and Collins.

To separate magic from science from miracle, I found Charles Singer's book one of the best I've read for clarification throughout history. Kieckhefer's is also an excellent historical resource for medieval customs, superstitions, and medicine and their darker side as well.

I do not advocate the practices featured in Buckland's book on witchcraft, although reading it has helped me develop a clearer understanding of where much New Age thought comes from, that I might more effectively witness to the similarities and differences in the future in my case for Christ. After reading the above and more on my magic/miracle/science research, I found the scriptural perspective in Rory Roybal's *Miracles or Magic? Discerning the Works of God in Today's World* reassuring and spiritually grounding. And, of course, enough can't be said of the King James Version Bible referred to throughout *Thief.*

Arthurian Works

Barber, Richard. *The Figure of Arthur*. New York: Dorset Press, 1972.

Blake, Steve and Scott Lloyd. *Pendragon: The Definitive Account of the Origins of Arthur*. Guilford, CT: The Lyons Press, 2002.

Carroll, David F. *Arturius: A Quest for Camelot*. Goxhill, Lincolnshire, UK: D. F. Carroll, 1996.

De Boron, Robert. *Merlin and the Grail: Joseph of Arimathea, Merlin, Perceval*. Translated by Nigel Bryant. Rochester, NY: D. S. Brewer, 2005.

Goodrich, Norma Lorre. *Guinevere*. New York: HarperCollins, 1991.

———. *The Holy Grail*. New York: HarperCollins, 1993.

———. *King Arthur*. New York: Harper and Row, 1986.

———. *Merlin*. New York: Harper and Row, 1988.

Holmes, Michael. *King Arthur: A Military History*. New York: Blandford Press, 1998.

Reno, Frank. *Historic Figures of the Arthurian Era*. Jefferson, NC: McFarland & Company, 2000.

Skene, W. F. *Arthur and the Britons in Wales and Scotland*. Dyfed, UK: Llanerch Enterprises, 1988.

Church History

Allen, J. H. *Judah's Sceptre and Joseph's Birthright*. Merrimac, MA: Destiny Publishers, 1902.

Capt, E. Raymond. *The Traditions of Glastonbury*. Thousand Oaks, CA: Artisan Press, 1983.

———. *Missing Links Discovered in Assyrian Tablets: Study of the Assyrian Tables of Israel*. Thousand Oaks, CA: Artisan Sales, 1983.

Collins, Stephen. *The "Lost" Ten Tribes of Israel ... Found!* Boring, OR: CPA Books, 1995.

Elder, Isabel Hill. *Celt, Druid and Culdee*. London: Covenant Publishing Company, 1973.

Gardner, Laurence. *Bloodline of the Holy Grail: The Hidden Lineage of Jesus Revealed*. New York: Thorsons/Element, 1996. (Used for tracing Jesus' family/apostles, not His alleged direct bloodline.)

Gray, Andrew. *The Origin and Early History of Christianity in Britain—From Its Dawn to the Death of Augustine*. New York: James Pott & Co., 1897.

Joyce, Timothy. *Celtic Christianity: A Sacred Tradition, A Vision of Hope*. New York: Orbis Books, 1998.

Larson, Frank. *The Bethlehem Star*, www.BethlehemStar.com (accessed January 1, 2008).

MacNaught, J. C. *The Celtic Church and the See of Peter.* Oxford: Basil Blackwell, 1927.

Taylor, Gladys. *Our Neglected Heritage: The Early Church.* London: Covenant Publishing Company, 1969.

General History

Adamnan of Iona. *Life of St. Columba.* Translated by Richard Sharpe. New York: Penguin Books, 1995.

Alcock, Leslie. *Arthur's Britain.* New York: Penguin Books, 1971.

————. *Kings and Warriors, Craftsmen and Priests in Northern Britain AD 550–850.* Edinburgh: Society of Antiquaries of Scotland, 2003.

Armit, Ian. *Celtic Scotland.* London: B. T. Batsford, Ltd., 2005.

Ashe, Geoffrey. *A Guidebook to Arthurian Britain.* London: Aquarian Press, 1983.

Ellis, Peter Berresford. *Celt and Saxon: The Struggle for Britain, AD 410–937.* London: Constable, 1993.

Evans, Stephen. *The Lords of Battle.* Rochester, NY: Boydell Press, 1997. (Excellent resource for the life of a warlord and his men.)

Fraser, James. *From Caledonia to Pictland: Scotland to 795.* Edinburgh: Edinburgh University Press, 2009.

after
words

Hartley, Dorothy. *Lost Country Life*. New York: Random House, 1979. (A wonderful look at county life in Britain by the season.)

Hodgkin, R. H. *A History of the Anglo-Saxons*. Vol 1. Oxford: Clarendon Press, 1935.

Hughes, David. *The British Chronicles, Book One*. Westminster, MD: Heritage Books, 2007.

Johnson, Stephen. *Later Roman Britain: Britain before the Conquest*. New York: Charles Scribner & Sons, 1980.

Laing, Lloyd and Jenny. *The Picts and the Scots*. Stroud, UK: Alan Sutton Publishing Ltd., 1993.

Lowe, Chris. *Angels, Fools, and Tyrants—Britons and Anglo-Saxons in Southern Scotland, AD 450–750*. Edinburgh: Canongate Press, 1999. (Excellent illustrations.)

Marsh, Henry. *Dark Age Britain: Some Sources of History*. New York: Dorset Press, 1987.

Martin-Clarke, D. Elizabeth. *Culture in Early Anglo-Saxon England*. Baltimore: Johns Hopkins Press, 1947.

Palgrave, Sir Francis. *History of the Anglo-Saxons*. New York: Dorset Press, 1989.

Snyder, Christopher. *The Britons*. Malden, MA: Blackwell Publishing, 2003.

Smyth, Alfred. *Warlords and Holy Men: Scotland, AD 80–1000*. Edinburgh: Edinburgh University Press, 1989.

Magic, Miracle, and Science of the Dark Ages

Buckland, Raymond. *Scottish Witchcraft: The History and Magick of the Picts*. Woodbury, MN: Llewellyn Publications, 1991.

Kieckhefer, Richard. *Magic in the Middle Ages*. Cambridge, UK: Cambridge University Press, 1989.

Roybal, Rory. *Miracles or Magic? Discerning the Works of God in Today's World*. Longwood, FL: Xulon Press, 2005.

Singer, Charles. *From Magic to Science: Essays on the Scientific Twilight*. New York: Dover Publications, 1958.

SCRIPTURE REFERENCES

Prologue

And he said, Unto you it is given to know the mysteries of the kingdom of God: but to others in parables; that seeing they might not see, and hearing they might not understand.—Luke 8:10

Beloved, believe not every spirit, but try the spirits whether they are of God: because many false prophets are gone out into the world. Hereby know ye the Spirit of God: Every spirit that confesseth that Jesus Christ is come in the flesh is of God: And every spirit that confesseth not that Jesus Christ is come in the flesh is not of God: and this is that spirit of antichrist, whereof ye have heard that it should come; and even now already is it in the world.—1 John 4:1–3

I am the vine, ye are the branches: He that abideth in me, and I in him, the same bringeth forth much fruit: for without me ye can do nothing.—John 15:5

And when he had called unto him his twelve disciples, he gave them power against unclean spirits, to cast them out, and to heal all manner of sickness and all manner of disease. Now the names of the twelve apostles are these; The first, Simon, who is called Peter, and Andrew his brother; James the son of Zebedee, and John his brother; Philip, and Bartholomew; Thomas, and Matthew the publican; James the son of Alphaeus, and Lebbaeus whose surname was Thaddaeus;

Simon the Canaanite, and Judas Iscariot, who also betrayed him. These twelve Jesus sent forth, and commanded them, saying, Go not into the way of the Gentiles, and into any city of the Samaritans enter ye not.—Matthew 10:1–5

Chapter Three

Give not that which is holy unto the dogs, neither cast ye your pearls before swine, lest they trample them under their feet, and turn again and rend you.—Matthew 7:6

Chapter Seven

The heavens declare the glory of God; and the firmament sheweth his handywork.—Psalm 19:1

Love the Lord thy God with all thy heart, and with all thy soul, and with all thy strength, and with all thy mind; and thy neighbor as thyself.—Luke 10:27

Epilogue

Inasmuch as ye did it not to one of the least of these, ye did it not to me.—Matthew 25:45

ABOUT THE AUTHOR

With an estimated million books in print, **Linda Windsor** is an award-winning author of sixteen secular historical and contemporary romances and thirteen romantic comedies and historical fiction for the inspirational market. Her switch to inspirational fiction in 1999 was more like Jonah going to Nineveh than a flash of enlightenment. Linda claims God pushed her, kicking and screaming all the way. In retrospect the author can see how God prepared her for His writing in her early publishing years and then claimed not just her music but also her writing when she was ready. At that point He brushed away all her reservations regarding inspirational fiction, and she took the leap of faith. Linda has never looked back.

While all of Linda's inspirational novels have been recognized with awards and rave reviews in both the ABA and CBA markets, she is most blessed by the 2002 Christy finalist award for *Riona* and the numerous National Readers Choice Awards for Best Inspirational that her historicals and contemporaries have won. *Riona* actually astonished everyone when it won against the worldly competition in the RWA Laurel Wreath's Best Foreign Historical Category.

To Linda's delight, *Maire,* Book One of the Fires of Gleannmara Irish Celtic series, was rereleased by Waterbrook Multnomah Publishers with a gorgeous new warrior-queen cover in 2009. Christy finalist *Riona* and its sequel, *Deirdre,* are now available with print on demand through standard and Internet booksellers.

Another of her novels, *For Pete's Sake,* Book Two in the Piper Cove Chronicles, is the winner of the Golden Quill; finalist in the Gayle Wilson Award of Excellence, Colorado RWA 2009 Award of Excellence, and Holt Medallion Avon Inspire in 2008; and winner of the Best Book of 2008 Award—Inspirational (Long & Short Reviews). It also won the 2009 National Reader's Choice Award—Best Inspirational and Best Book of the Year—Inspirational (*Romance Reviews Today*).

Linda's research for the early Celtic Gleannmara series resulted in a personal mission dear to her heart: to provide Christians with an effective witness to reach their New Age and unbelieving family and friends. Her goal continues with the Brides of Alba series, which reveals early church history, much of which has been lost or neglected due to intentional and/or inadvertent error by its chroniclers. This knowledge of early church history enabled Linda to reach her daughter, who became involved in Wicca after being stalked and assaulted in college and blaming the God of her childhood faith—a witness that continues to others at medieval fair signings or wherever these books take Linda.

Linda is convinced that, had her daughter known the struggle and witness of the early Christians beyond the apostles' time and before Christianity earned a black name during the Crusades and Inquisition, she could not have been swayed. Nor would Linda herself have been lured away from her faith in Christ in college by a liberal agenda.

Linda's testimony that Christ is her Druid (Master/Teacher) opens wary hearts wounded by harsh Christian condemnation.

Admitted Wiccans and pagans have become intrigued by the tidbits of history and tradition pointing to how and why druids accepted Him. She not only sells these nonbelievers copies of her books, but she also outsells the occult titles surrounding her inspirational ones.

When Linda isn't writing in the late eighteenth-century home that she and her late husband restored, she's busy speaking and/or playing music for writing workshops, faith seminars, libraries, and civic and church groups. She and her husband were professional musicians and singers in their country and old rock-and-roll band, Homespun. She also plays organ for her little country church in the wildwood. Presently, she's trying to work in some painting, wallpapering, and other house projects that are begging to be done. That is, when she's not Red-Hatting or, better yet, playing mom-mom to her grandchildren—her favorite role in life.

Visit Linda Windsor at her
Web site: www.LindaWindsor.com

OTHER BOOKS
BY LINDA WINDSOR

HISTORICAL FICTION
Fires of Gleannmara Trilogy
Maire

Riona

Deirdre

The Brides of Alba Trilogy
Healer

Thief

Rebel (Summer 2012)

CONTEMPORARY ROMANCE
Piper Cove Chronicles
Wedding Bell Blues

For Pete's Sake

Moonstruck Series
Paper Moon

Fiesta Moon

Blue Moon

Along Came Jones

It Had to Be You

Not Exactly Eden

Hi Honey, I'm Home

REBEL

BOOK THREE
The Brides of Alba
Linda Windsor

pROLOGUE

Carmelide
Leaf Fall
Late sixth century AD

Merlin was dead. The nightmare had begun for the Cymri—every Briton, Welshman, Scot, and Pict—be they Christian or still clinging to the old ways. Kella O'Toole bent over her desk in the queen's scriptorium, well aware that her countrymen's freedom to worship a god of choice in his or her manner was at stake—not to mention the threat of civil war. This small room adjoining Gwenhyfar's personal quarters was the only place where the official palace scribes would not know what Kella was about.

Her heart beat in her chest with each scratch of her quill as she hurried to finish the last page of the copy of one of the most precious books of all Albion, perhaps even the world. She'd hoped to work with the original Hebrew scripts, those recorded by the hand of Joseph of Arimathea or one of Christ's apostolic family, to practice her translation of the language. But Merlin Emrys and Queen

Gwenhyfar had seen them and their original translations already carefully packed and hidden away.

Kella's pen glided smoothly over the artificially aged vellum: *Arthur, Prince of Dalraida.* Only untold hours of practice as the queen's scribe and translator kept her hand from shaking. This copy had to be flawless. Kella had been working on it for the last year under Merlin Emrys' orders. She knew he'd been ill, yet the news of his death that morning still came as a shock. Emrys was bigger than life. It didn't seem real that the man of so many faces—abbot, advisor to the king, teacher, astrologer, and man of science—had gone to the Other Side.

Only a week ago, he'd retired to his cave with none but his devoted Lady Ninian, an abbess of the church in her own right, to take his last confessions and give him his last rites. Now that his last breath had expired, Ninian prepared his body to be sealed in the farthest reach of his cave for a year. Once the flesh fell away, leaving clean bones, the Grail priestess would return to transport them to Bardsley Island to rest in one of its holy caves with the bones of Alba's greatest holy men and kings. Gwenhyfar would transport Arthur's similarly one day.

A wave of nausea swept through Kella's stomach. Her pen froze. *Please, Lord, no. Not now.* She put the quill down and relied more on a sip of now-cold tea laced with mint and elderberry than prayer for relief. God was so distant, she often wondered if He was real. Not that she'd ever mention her doubts aloud. She took another drink of the tea and flexed her stiff fingers.

In the hearth in the opposite wall, a peat fire offset the damp of Leaf Fall in the chamber. This was no time for illness nor anything else to distract her from her duties. The heritage of Alba rested on her being able to finish this task before Cassian took total control of the church and its documents. The Davidic lineage passed on through the Milesian Irish royal families was well documented and kept in Erin, but Kella's project protected the foundation of the British church laid by Jesus' family and followers. Tradition had it that they'd come to Britain in the first century after being set adrift by the Sadducees in a boat with no oar, sails, or supplies on an unforgiving sea. Yet God waived the death sentence so that Joseph of Arimathea, his niece Mary—the mother of Jesus—and their company made it to the safety of Iberia, Gaul, and the Northern Isles to spread the Gospel from there throughout the Western world.

And here she was, a humble warrior's daughter with no such holy connection, at least within the last nine generations of her family, taking part in such a vital task. Kella would write for the queen till her fingers fell off.

Father, help me, Kella prayed, taking another swallow. *Even if I am unworthy, fallen in Your eyes, I'm trying to help Your cause.*

Nothing. Kella felt no relief from the threat of her stomach—only more frightened and alone than ever. Maybe she was the only one God didn't listen to.

Father, help us all.

Kella started from her introspection as Queen Gwenhyfar, garbed in hunter green robes with embroidered trim, entered the room. A band of beautifully worked gold crowned her long, braided raven hair, coming together at the center of her smooth brow in a interlocking curl of knots. Her sleek, dark beauty was a contrast to Kella's wild fair hair, porcelain complexion, and fuller build.

"I'm nearly done, milady. Only Arthur's late sons to add." She paused. "And King Modred."

Wryness twisted the skillfully painted heart-line of Gwenhyfar's lips. "Leave room for Urien of Rheged." At the surprised arch of Kella's brow, the queen added, "Cassian may yet have his way."

"Aye." The Roman bishop just might, but Kella didn't have to like it. The stern, richly robed priest had joined Arthur in Rome on the High King's return from a pilgrimage to the Holy Land, and nothing had been the same since. His presence dampened the gaiety of the court, as if it were a sin to enjoy life.

"Rome has found a new way to conquer, Kella," Gwenhyfar told her. "Christ didn't come to dictate, but Cassian has."

He'd even convinced the High King to renounce Modred as his successor in favor of Urien of Rheged. Considering Arthur's own queen and that the territory he fought most to protect was Pictish, choosing a Briton was not a wise move.

"Be sure Modred's name is written in first," Gwenhyfar warned her. "We want Cassian, should he get his hands on this, to believe he has the original. 'Twould be as good, as he would want to destroy any record of the British church having been established with authority equal to Rome's."

"Why is the king so blind to this man's purpose?" Kella exclaimed. Nausea rolled over her again. She fought the urge to put her hand on her stomach, instead embracing the tea with both hands.

Gwenhyfar watched her. "Are you not well?" She leaned over and wiped a smudge of ink from Kella's forehead. A hazard of a scribe's work.

Kella winced a smile. "Something I ate this morning does not agree with me. A piece of cold meat and bread on my way here."

"You must take better care of yourself. Take your meal at the board, not on your way to anywhere. No wonder your stomach protests."

The queen mustn't suspect. Kella didn't *want* to suspect the reason for her missed courses. Two, unless she commenced this week.

"I will tomorrow," Kella said. "Porridge, honey, and fresh cream." The very thought of her favorite breakfast made her shudder inwardly. "I promise to dine at the table as well."

Kella's shoulders dropped in relief as the queen walked over to the pages Kella had finished. They were all neatly rolled and stored in a wooden rack designed for that purpose, exactly where the originals had been. Gwenhyfar pulled one out, examining the worn and yellowed vellum. "Emrys' genius will be sorely missed. I can't tell these from the originals."

"All that mixing, smudging, smoking, and burning—it bewilders this feeble mind how he made them look so old without destroying them," Kella marveled. She'd once been to the Merlin's cave, although it was hardly the average hole in the side of a hill. It was many-chambered, and each one was a wonder.

Vials, pouches, jars, and strange burning contraptions filled one room, which was lined with books and scrolls. Another's roof was a funnel that opened to the sky, and mounted above the height of a man's head was a great glass disc said to bring the stars and planets down to earth for his examination. Since Kella's visit had been during the day, there was little to see but a fluff of cloud close enough that she thought she could touch it. The far, innermost chamber where the Merlin slept was little more than a tomb, sparsely furnished for comfort. It was there that his body now lay, his spirit already departed to be with his Savior.

Kella crossed herself, remembering Emrys' spontaneous bursts of laughter and, while his angry outbursts were just as unpredictable and thunderous, how he'd always been kind, even gallant, to her. But then he'd always been fond of the ladies, so 'twas said.

"Never say your mind is feeble, Kella," the queen chided, drawing Kella back to the window alcove where her desk was situated to make the most of the sunlight. "Few men can boast the mastery of five languages and a fair hand to match. My cousin Aeda would be so proud of you."

At the mention of the foster mother who'd raised Kella after her own mother died in childbirth, Kella smiled. "Aye, I hope she would."

Her foster brothers, Ronan, Caden, and Alyn, used to tease Kella mercilessly at Glenarden, where her father, Egan O'Toole, was champion. They'd called her Babel-lips because she talked endlessly and could pick up on any language or accent she overheard. While Kella had been schooled in Ireland, where her maternal aunt was an abbess, both her aunt and the queen agreed that the ease with which she learned new languages was as much the result of a gift as it was of study.

"You carry a Pentecostal fire in that brain of yours," Aunt Beda would tell her when no one else was about to witness the abbess's pride and affection for Kella.

But if that were so, why couldn't Kella feel God's presence, especially now when she needed it so much? And what would Aunt Beda think of her now? How many times had her aunt warned that a moment's folly could ruin a maiden's life forever? God would forgive the maid, but she and the child conceived would have to face the consequences.

"And I would have been lost without you," the queen continued, caught up in the church's concern, "especially since Cassian returned from Rome with Arthur."

The bishop had eyes everywhere—on the queen and Merlin Emrys in particular. Gwenhyfar had ceased to use the royal scribes for her communication, which led Cassian to scowl at Kella whenever they met by chance in the palace. Women had no place in the palace or the church, except as lowly servants or brood sows, as far as the Roman priest was concerned.

"What sway has the man over the king that you or Merlin Emrys do not?" Kella pressed. Emrys had long been Arthur's advisor, although the last year or so he'd kept to his cave.

"Better to ask what the Roman Church offers Arthur that the Celtic Church does not." Gwenhyfar's slanted eyes narrowed. At least they appeared slanted. Everything about the Pictish queen was exotic—from her accent to the perfumes she wore. According to those who had been in Arthur's service longer than Kella, Gwenhyfar was very different from Arthur's fair bride from an earlier marriage, the Guinevere who bore him two sons. Sadly, the constant conflict in Albion saw that neither survived the king or their deceased mother.

"I've never really understood the workings of the church," Kella admitted truthfully. Although she knew enough to be certain she would be condemned for her mistake—for allowing love to lead her down temptation's sweet path.

"Abbot Columba predicted when Arthur was a wet-eared youth that he would not survive to inherit his father Aedan of Dalraida's kingdom," Gwenhyfar explained. "And we all know the sway of Iona with God and kings."

Yes, Kella had heard of the curse. But now in his early forties, Arthur had changed, repented since his youthful indifference to the church.

"So now the king hopes to counter the curse of the British church in his early years with the blessing of Rome in his later ones," Kella thought aloud. She frowned. "You were … *are* a priestess of the Grail Church, even if it has been removed from Albion." With the increasing advance of the Saxons, the Angus of Strighlagh's son, a saintly warrior if ever there was one, had returned the Grail treasures to the Holy Land two years prior. "Is that how God works? Allowing one arm of His church to vex the other?"

Or maybe God had left with the relics. He didn't seem to be answering Albion's prayers for victory over the Saxons. They spread like a plague.

Gwenhyfar shook her head. "Nay, child. That is how *man* works." Her green gaze glazed over. The queen crossed herself and turned to peer out the slit of the window in the alcove. "How we must grieve the Heavenly Father."

Kella followed the queen's gaze, guilt cloying at her chest as she stared at the misty spray of the gray-green sea hurling itself against the rocks below the tower. When she dared not look at the tumult any longer, she spun away to take another sip of the tea.

Surely she had grieved God as well. And if she *was* with child, the consequences remained to be seen. Hers and those of her beloved, who served now with Arthur and Kella's father, Egan, in the hotbed of Gododdin against an uprising of Mithai Picts.

My father! Kella groaned in silence. Egan O'Toole would take off her lover's head if he suspected. No matter that her handsome Lorne had pledged his troth to her that night as she lay in his arms. He'd sworn his life was meaningless without her.

Oh, Lorne, hurry home to me! For all *our sakes.*